A Man from Bruckless

Eileen O'Donnell Sheehan Ginn

THE COVER

In 1906, Henry O'Donnell was employed as stationmaster for the Bruckless Station in County Donegal, Ireland. Along with his salary, the stationmaster was given use of a nearby railroad cottage. In 1907 Henry's son, John F. O'Donnell, was born in the cottage next to the Bruckless Station.

— William Turner, a rising 12th year student, painted this portrait of the Bruckless Station from an old photograph.

Copyright © 2010 Eileen O'Donnell Sheehan Ginn

All rights reserved. No part of this publication may be reproduced, stored in a retrieval system, or transmitted by any form or by any means, electronic, mechanical, photocopying, recording, or otherwise without written permission of the copyright holder.

Eileen O'Donnell Sheehan Ginn has asserted her moral right under the Copyright, Design and Patents Acts, 1988, to be identified as the author of this work.

Published by
[Eileen O'Donnell Ginn, 423 Carol Street, Charleston, SC]

ISBN: 1452844852
ISBN - 13: 9781452844855
LCCN: 2010906360

For my mother, Gwynne Large O'Donnell

Contents

List of Photographs	viii
Acknowledgments	x
PREFACE	xiii
PART I: JOHN F. O'DONNELL: THE PUBLIC MAN	xvii

Chapter One: SOUND OF THE SEA 1
  The Kennedy Family
  The O'Donnell Family

Chapter Two: FAR OVER THE FOAM 21

Chapter Three: GROWING AND BECOMING 37
  United Parcel Service
  Local 1-S Macy's Department Store Workers
  New York City Politics
  Law Partners
  O'Donnell & Harten
  O'Donnell & Schwartz

Chapter Four: THE TRANSPORT WORKERS UNION 67
  Craft VS Industrial Unions
  Employers Fight Back
  Transit Before TWU
  New Union
  TWU Takes On The Communists
  Sixth Biennial Convention

Chapter Five: TWU'S LARGE CITY LOCALS 89
  Philadelphia TWU Local 234
    1944
    1949
    Ten Months Later
    Two Years Later: 1952

Taft-Hartley Act
Houston TWU Local 260

Chapter Six: RIGHTS OF LABOR IN NEW YORK CITY   115
    City-Owned Lines and the Transit Workers
    Private Lines and the Transit Workers
    Pensions

Chapter Seven: SIGNIFICANT STRIKES IN NEW YORK CITY TRANSIT   143
    1966 Transit Strike
    1967 The Taylor Law
    New York City 1980 Transit Strike

Chapter Eight: COMMUNICATION WORKS UNION   165
    Local 1101

Chapter Nine: AMERICAN POSTAL WORKERS UNION   175
    The Great Postal Strike – 1970
    New Orleans Convention – 1972
    The Bulk Strike – 1974
    A New Frontier – 1980
    First Negotiations – 1981
    Interest Arbitration – 1984
    Interest Arbitration – 1991

Chapter Ten: FAREWELL   195

PART II: JOHN F. O'DONNELL: THE FAMILY MAN   207

Preface   209

Chapter One: SOME FAMILY STORIES   211

Chapter Two: HIS SIBLINGS   215

Chapter Three: NEW FAMILY IN AMERICA   219

Chapter Four: THE WAR YEARS   225

Chapter Five: CANDLEWOOD   227

Chapter Six: FAMILY HOMES   231

Chapter Seven: VACATIONS – OR WHAT NEXT CAN GO
    WRONG   235

Chapter Eight: THE NEED TO FISH   241

Chapter Nine: DAD AS A ROLE MODEL   245

Chapter Ten: THE GRANDCHILDREN REMEMBER   249

Chapter Eleven: THE LAST YEAR   257

List of Photographs

1. Henry and Ellen O'Donnell around 1906 — 64
2. Johnny O'Donnell around 1909 — 64
3. St. Eunan's School in County Donegal, Ireland — 64
4. Lily, Teresa, Harry, Paddy and Louis O'Donnell around 1928 — 64
5. Gwynne Large around 1933 — 65
6. John O'Donnell as a Fordham University Graduate in June 1933 — 65
7. John O'Donnell and Charlie Connolly at the "Irish Echo" in 1933. — 65
8. John and Gwynne O'Donnell around 1935. — 65
9. John O'Donnell's Naturalization Paper. — 66
10. John O'Donnell and Asher Schwartz in 1952 — 66
11. John O'Donnell around 1952. — 66
12. John O'Donnell at the family home in Bruckless, County Donegal, Ireland — 66
13. Omnibus Strike in July 1949. Pictured Gus Faber, Mike Quill, John O'Donnell — 140
14. John O'Donnell addresses L100 members as Matthew Guinan looks on around 1953 — 140
15. Mayor William O'Dwyer Luncheon 1954. Pictured John O'Donnell, Matthew Guinan, Patrick Mahedy, O'Dwyer and Michael Quill. — 140
16. John O'Donnell addresses members of L234 during Philadelphia Bus Strike in January 1953 — 140
17. John O'Donnell addresses L100 members at St. Nicholas Arena rally in June 1954. — 141
18. Arthur Goldberg confers with Matthew Guinan, Michael Quill and John O'Donnell during Cole Committee Hearings in 1957. — 141
19. John O'Donnell speaks with Pensioners in March 1962 about preparing to sue the Weinberg group for $25,000,000 to cover the pensions of those already retired and the 7,000 men who struck in March 1962 — 141
20. Michael Quill and John O'Donnell confer with Transit Authority Commissioner Joseph O'Grady in 1965 — 141
21. John O'Donnell in 1949 — 171

22.	John O'Donnell in 1952	171
23.	John O'Donnell in September 1955.	171
24.	Francis O'Connell, IEB Member and John O'Donnell confer In October 1965 during a break in the ICC Hearings in Washington DC relating to the protest of PRR-NYC merger.	171
25.	John O'Donnell confers with William Lindner and John Lawe during the 1980 strike.	172
26.	John O'Donnell in 1980.	172
27.	John O'Donnell receives an award from Josie McMillian, President of the New York Metro Area Postal Union. The award states: "To John O'Donnell, An extraordinary man of many achievements. Sincerely, quietly, modestly and with grace, he has demonstrated his loyalty and his deep interest in the welfare of the members of New York Metro Area Postal Union." At the presentation were (L to R) Gerald O'Reilly; Josie McMillian; O'Donnell; Moe Biller, President of the APWU.	172
28.	Father Harry, Gwynne and John O'Donnell at Notre Dame around 1950.	172
29.	Sisters Teresa O'Donnell McBreaty and Lily O'Donnell Henry in Katonah in the late 1980s.	262
30.	Louis O'Donnell and Maire McMullin O'Donnell.	262
31.	Brothers and Sisters: On top row Paddy, John, Louis. Seated are Teresa and Lily.	262
32.	Father and son: John Francis O'Donnell Sr. and Jr. fishing.	262
33.	Cathleen and Tricia O'Donnell with Santa around 1948.	263
34.	John O'Donnell with great-grandson John Francis O'Donnell Sheehan in the Dallas airport in 1991.	263
35.	John O'Donnell with great-grandson John Francis O'Donnell III in Katonah.	263
36.	John O'Donnell with Sheehan grandchildren: Rory, Eileen, O'Donnell, Sean Alison, Carol Schmidt Sheehan, Neil in the early 1980s.	263
37.	Gwynne and John O'Donnell celebrate their 50th wedding anniversary in 1985.	264
38.	My Father and I in *The Kiddle House* in December 1992.	264

39. Our home on Candlewood Isle on Candlewood Lake in
         Danbury Connecticut.   264
40. The family home on Worthington Road in Greenburg in
         Westchester County in New York   264
41. The family home in Katonah, New York   265
42. The Once O'Donnell Family Home in Bruckless.   265

Acknowledgments

Thanks first of all to my editor and sister-in-law, Mary Ann O'Donnell. Not just for editing my work, but for teaching me how to write a book. She supplied constant knowledge, encouragement and patient explanations concerning the intricacies of authoring.

Thanks to my mother, Gwynne O'Donnell for impressing on me that this was a project I should do myself and not keep looking for others to do it for me.

Thanks to friends and family members who read early drafts and the finished product and have offered constructive suggestions – Nancy Chiles, David McCann, Suzanne McCarthy, Frank Naughton, Hugh O'Rourke, John O'Donnell Jr., Julie Schutt, Neil Sheehan.

Thanks to the numerous people who allowed me to interview them – Darryl Anderson, Moe Biller, Joe Donoghue, Malcolm Goldstein, Seymour Goldstein, Sonny Hall, Scotty Henry, Theodore Kheel, Arthur Luby, Roberta Malmoli, Frank McCann, Richard Ravitch, David Rosen, Scoogie Ryers, Robert Snyder, and especially Asher Schwartz.

Thanks to the many people who helped me with the research - Gail Malgreen and Debra Bernhardt at Tamiment Library, Dr. Larry Kelber, Michael Marmo, Anna Quindlen, Dr. Joseph Tripp.

Thanks to Jim Gannon and Elizabeth Giegerich of the "TWU Express," who allowed me to use many photos from that newspaper.

Thanks to my sister, Tricia O'Donnell, for transferring all the tape interviews onto CDs.

Thanks to the friends and family members who have constantly encouraged me to keep at it for these twenty odd years - My children, My family both in the States and in Ireland, Monty Knight, Sandy Pell.

Thanks to my husband Jay Ginn for his patience and toleration of my time spent on the computer; also his encouragement to keep at it and get it finished.

Thanks to God for giving me my parents and the strength and wisdom to follow through.

PREFACE

In 1981, the prominent New York Times columnist Anna Quindlen wrote a column about my father, John F. O'Donnell, addressing his role in the labor movement in New York City. The article mentioned that it had been over forty years since Michael J. Quill, a founder of the Transport Workers Union, and John F. O'Donnell had first joined forces. As Quindlen saw it,

> together, [their] victories became more important and constant. The men won a five-day week, an eight-hour day. The labor leaders became accepted by their political counterparts; influential and well known. Mr. O'Donnell was never well known, but he was as influential as any man in New York City labor circles.[1]

I, like Quindlen, believe that my father's role in the New York City labor movement was quite a monumental one and has been almost completely overlooked, and my first goal in writing this account is to rectify this situation. I expect to offer a unique perspective on the history of the labor movement in the process of augmenting the historical record.

The unique perspective that I offer is a first-hand, primary account of history, since so much of this work is in my father's (and Mike Quill's and other labor leaders') own words. Because of my father's humorous and charismatic personality, what I am offering really imbues the history with life and vigor. My father did not take a textbook tone when relating the details of his career. My wish is that it should be noted in the history books that John Francis O'Donnell fought for the rights of the working man and that his accomplishments benefited many more than just the transit worker and the postal worker. The Transport Workers Union's actions and achievements also filtered down to benefit the City workers in New York. He fought with a tenacity and patience that makes me proud. During negotiations for labor contracts, O'Donnell was able to function well with both sides of the table with a foresight and patience that gave him the reputation of an excellent mediator.

I have another reason for writing this book. My parents educated my five children in addition to myself and three siblings. This is the only way I know to honor such foresight on the part of my parents. My grandchildren must learn about the solid family line in which they follow. I sincerely wish that these grandchildren of mine could have heard my father's laughter and seen his eyes light up with mischief when he told a story.

By exploring my father's roots, I had hoped to find the thread that followed through the family line in Ireland and continued in America, the attributes that gave the characteristics of strength and kindness to a wonderful human being. For this reason, the most reasonable place to start my quest was to question my father about life in Ireland. My father loved to tell tales about Ireland. In doing so, he favored anecdotes about the family but was more selective in his accounts about himself.

In using my father as a source of information on the labor movement, I had to have intelligent questions to ask him. Dr. Joseph F. Tripp, a history professor at The Citadel, in Charleston, South Carolina, came to my rescue. He was kind enough to furnish me with questions. These questions provided me with a solid start. From there I went to the labor library at New York University, the Tamiment Library. The archivist, Gail Malgreen, directed me to the Transport Workers Union files and the Michael J. Quill files. In these files I found many of my father's papers. While at Tamiment, I also met the author of The Labor Leader, Dr. Harry Kelber. He provided me with five questions to ask my father about the American Labor Party. Corresponding with several authors furnished me some wonderful information. Michael Marmo, author of More Profile than Courage, sent me the notes he took when he attended one of my father's New School speeches. In my copy of his book, Marmo wrote:

> Although thirty years has passed, I still vividly recall meeting your father, John F. O'Donnell. He was generous with his time and tried to help me in every way he could. It was a distinct pleasure to meet him.[2]

The bulk of my information, though, came from my father, who did sit down with me a few times but was freer talking on the telephone. Every Sunday from Charleston, I would phone him at his home in Katonah, New York, and he would answer all my questions. He never faulted my frequent mistakes—just corrected, gently corrected.

As a result of those phone conversations and a variety of other talks and newspaper articles, I am able to piece together fifty years of a part of New York City's labor scene.

This book then has a dual purpose: to capture as much of the man as possible—the fiery lawyer and union representative and the son, family man, and friend. Thus, the two parts of the book: the public John F. O'Donnell and family reminiscences of the private John F. O'Donnell.

ENDNOTES

[1] Anna Quindlen, "About New York: A Behind-the-Scenes Life in the Labor Movement," The New York Times, September 5, 1981, p. 23.
[2] Michael Marmo, More Profile than Courage (Albany: State University of New York Press, 1990).

Part I

John F. O'Donnell: The Public Man

Whenever the moon appeared from behind the racing clouds, the silent thatched cottages of the little fishing village of Ballysaggart assumed a ghost-like appearance. The cottages were scattered in two broken lines for about a quarter of a mile on both sides of the white limestone road, which leads from Donegal to Killybegs. The backyards of the cottages on the south side of the road ended at the brink of the low cliff, which, on stormy days, caused the wild Atlantic waves to throw their spray over the town. It was long after midnight and the boats were out on the fishing grounds. The women, the children, and the old men were asleep. Everything was silent except the sea. Fisherfolk are seldom aware of the sound of the sea.

John F. O'Donnell[1]

Chapter One

SOUND OF THE SEA

In Donegal, Ireland, in the softly falling rain, eighteen-year-old Johnny O'Donnell stood quietly at his parents' grave in the small cemetery in front of the Bruckless Church, the church where his parents had wed some twenty-five years earlier. The small Townland of Bruckless surrounded the Bruckless Church; thus, Johnny stood at the literal center of his youthful innocence. It was March 1926, and he was free on bail.

Hours earlier, he had appeared before a jury of his peers on the charge of treason and emerged with his first mistrial. Anticipating the retrial, he had returned to the place where he had first felt his world slipping away. He knew that if he were to climb the hill out of town, he would hear the waves beating against the cliffs and feel the strength of the sea, but at this moment he just needed to think.

Johnny thought back to his father's funeral two years earlier in 1924. Now, as on that past mournful November morning of the funeral, the curlews were whistling off shore. The sound was always a sure sign of approaching rain, and yet was so familiar that it usually brought him a measure of comfort. But the peace of the scene before him did little to calm his fears on this particular afternoon, nor did it in any way relieve his almost overwhelming sense of abandonment.

A sudden stroke had deprived Johnny and his seven younger siblings of their father, Henry O'Donnell, in 1924 when Henry was only forty-eight. The year before that had brought a summer of sadness, for that was when his mother, Ellen Kennedy O'Donnell, had died at the age of forty-three. With his parents gone and a terrifying trial still facing him, Johnny knew as he stood in the cemetery that his brothers and sisters needed him to be both strong and mature at this time of terrible stress, but he doubted his own ability to fulfill that need. His seven siblings—Charlie, Mary, Lily, Harry, Teresa, Paddy, and Louis—were split up among family, never again to spend time together under the same roof. Arrangements were made to send Charlie and Mary to America to live with relatives there. The other two girls, Lily and Teresa, were sent to the parochial house in Glenties to stay with their uncle, Charles Canon Kennedy,[2] a priest, and his housekeeper, Maggie Keyes. Harry, Paddy, and Louis remained at home under the supervision of various Kennedy relatives, until better accommodations could be arranged. They never did go, as they feared at one time, to an orphanage. A family council decided that Johnny should remain in Ireland, work for the railroad in a position similar to the one his father had held, and help support his siblings. He and his Aunt Min moved to Park House, a cottage, a few miles away from the family home in Bruckless.

Despite their difficulties after the death of their parents, Johnny and the other children persevered and flourished, in large part because of the care and influence of Ellen's family. Ellen Kennedy's brothers and sisters, several of whom took responsibility for one or more of the orphans, created a family legacy of industriousness, generosity, and success.

To understand the story of John F. O'Donnell's journey from child in Ireland to successful labor lawyer in New York, some background on both the Kennedy and the O'Donnell families is essential.

The Kennedy Family

The Kennedy family's strength and their ability to organize and raise Johnny and his siblings in such difficult times have always intrigued me. I had heard so often about the devastating effects of the Penal Laws in Ireland and of the Irish famine that plagued the country from 1845 through 1851 that I wondered how members of the Kennedy family had managed to become educated and to lease a farm at a time when poverty was so widespread. In the land records of Ireland, I was able to find the answers to some of these questions.

In the 1690s the Penal Laws, designed to repress the native Irish, were introduced.[3] The first laws proclaimed that no Catholic could have a gun, pistol, or sword. Over the next thirty years, other Penal laws followed. For example, Irish Catholics were forbidden to receive an education, engage in trade or commerce, or to purchase or lease land.[4] The system continued into the nineteenth century but slowly ended after the passage of the Catholic Emancipation Act in 1829.[5]

The great potato famine of 1845-51 caused the loss of approximately two and a half million Irish men, women, and children through starvation and disease, and from emigration to Britain and America.[6] The earliest records I could find relating to the Kennedys were land records dating back to 1857. From these I learned that as soon as the opportunity arose, Charles Kennedy, Johnny's maternal great grandfather, leased farm lands. When family members in Ireland were asked how the Kennedys managed to survive so well during such troubled times, some gave credit for the Kennedy's relative good fortune to the charitable nature of the local landlord; others said it was due to the strength of the women of the family. The women, they said, made a small but crucial profit selling eggs and butter, along with handmade lace and homespun fabrics.

According to Griffith's Valuation Lists of 1857, in the County of Donegal, Barony of Banagh, Parish of Inver, Townland of Kilmacreddan, Charles Kennedy Sr. leased just over thirty-one acres of rental property from Hugh W. Barton at a little over fourteen pounds.[7] Although thirty-one acres may sound like a large plot of land, such a farm might have had only a few acres of fertile land as a result of the primarily rocky soil of Donegal, a county in the northwest corner of Ireland, with strong scenic contrasts presenting an ever-changing spectacle of landscapes and seascapes against a backdrop of mountains and moors.

On February 17, 1867, Charles' second son, Francis (Johnny's maternal grandfather), married Mary McGeever, daughter of another farmer.[8] In December 1869, while they were living on the McGeever farm in Tawnygorm, Francis and Mary had a daughter they named Anne.[9] When Charles Kennedy, Sr. died around 1869, Francis inherited the farm lease in Kilmacreddan from his father[10] because his older brother, Charles Jr., was in America fighting in the American Civil War. When Charles Jr. returned to Ireland in 1870, he bought the lease to Kilmacreddan farm[11] from Francis with the money he had earned in America. This money then enabled Francis to lease land in the same county in the Township of Cashel. It was here in Cashel that Ellen Kennedy was born in 1879. Ellen's birth had been preceded by those of five other siblings: Charles (later Canon) in 1870, Bernard in 1872, Mary (Min) in 1873, Sarah in 1875, and Francis (Francy) in 1877.

Francis Kennedy's family clearly valued education.[12] Ellen's oldest brother, Charles, was the first formally educated male of the Kennedy family. After spending three years in the diocesan seminary in Letterkenny studying for the priesthood, Charles qualified to enter the class of philosophy in Maynooth. In the course of his career as a priest, Charles Canon Kennedy spent six years as a professor in St. Eunan's College in Letterkenny, the school that the young O'Donnell boys would later attend. Another of Ellen's brothers, Francy, also had a distinguished teaching career, as a 1959 Irish newspaper article, noted: "He [Francis Kennedy] was a very popular and efficient teacher, and is still regarded with deep affection by all his past pupils, who kindly refer to him now as 'the old master.'"[13] And Ellen herself, not to be outdone by the boys of the family, qualified as a teacher at a "Normal School"[14] in Dublin. One of her earliest assignments was at the Bruckless National School in County Donegal around 1900. It was here that she met and married Henry O'Donnell and set out to raise her eight children while remaining a teacher at the Bruckless school.

The O'Donnell Family

Unlike Ellen's family, the O'Donnell family line is very difficult to trace. Since they were not farmers, they did not necessarily lease land. The first of the O'Donnell family to appear in land records was Johnny's grandfather, Owen O'Donnell, who did not appear in any land records until he was already married and living in Bruckless on church property across the street from the church. Johnny referred to his grandfather, Owen, as one of the "men of no property."[15]

It was not until Owen O'Donnell married Mary Sweeny (also known as MacSwyne, McSwine, and Swine) in 1857 that his name appeared in any church records. The Registrar's District Records of the Parish of Killybegs indicate that Mary MacSwyne, the daughter of Charles MacSwyne of Binroe, a farmer, married John (Owen) O'Donnell, a shoemaker, on February 9, 1857, in the Church of St. Joseph and St. Conal (also known as the Bruckless Church).[16]

After the marriage, Owen and Mary Sweeny O'Donnell lived with her parents in Binroe. Birth records show that the couple's first three children were born in Binroe—Mary Ann in 1858, Margaret[17] in 1861, and Catherine (Cassie) in 1862[18]. After the birth of Cassie, land records show that Owen moved his family into the newly built Post Office building/house in Bruckless leased from the Bruckless Church.[19] The family then grew to include eight children with the births of Elizabeth in 1864, John in 1865, Patrick in 1869, Eleanor in 1871, and Henry in 1876. Thus, the Bruckless Church and the Post Office remained a pivotal point in the family of Henry O'Donnell.[20] His father, Owen, became Postmaster and his mother, Mary Sweeney O'Donnell, started a little general store that proved quite successful.[21]

Along with changes involving land leases and education, technological changes were also occurring in Ireland at the end of the nineteenth century. In the 1880s and 1890s, the British Government decided that one solution to the problem of poverty in Ireland was to build railways from the northeastern city of Londonderry to the more remote parts of the country. During this project, additional track was added to form the Killybegs and the Glenties railway lines in County Donegal so that farm products and animals along with coal and tourists could move between the area and the city of Londonderry.[22]

On August 18, 1893, when Henry O'Donnell, the youngest son of Mary and Owen O'Donnell, was seventeen years old, the Killybegs line opened. Henry had watched the laying of the Killybegs line in and through Bruckless, a land of gently rounded hills. He was drawn to a career with these railroads, and by August of 1906, just a month before his marriage to Ellen Kennedy, he was earning a monthly salary of 4 pounds, 6 shillings, 8 pence as the stationmaster for the Bruckless Station.[23] Along with this salary, the stationmaster was given use of a nearby railroad cottage, so Henry O'Donnell was now in a position to start his own family.

On September 6, 1906, Canon Kennedy performed the marriage ceremony for his sister Ellen Kennedy and Henry O'Donnell. The ceremony took place at the Bruckless Church of St. Joseph and St. Conal, the same church in which Henry's parents had been married fifty-one years earlier. Henry's father, Owen O'Donnell, had died four years before the wedding, but Mary Sweeny O'Donnell was still living in the Post Office with her daughters, Cassie, Lizzy, and Ellie, along with Cassie's husband, Roger Keenan.

On December 7, 1907, Ellen and Henry greeted their first born child, John Francis O'Donnell, my father. Two other children were born in this cottage: Charlie in 1909 and Mary in 1912. The O'Donnell family then left the railway cottage and moved to a larger house about a hundred yards away.[24] In the new house, which Henry himself had built on land adjacent to the school, five more children were born: Lily in 1913, Harry in 1915, Teresa in 1917, Patrick in 1918, and Louis in 1920.

Johnny, Charlie, and Mary, the three oldest O'Donnell children, were the only children of the family old enough to attend the Bruckless School during the time that their mother was the head teacher there.[25] At that time, the school had an average attendance of about forty-five pupils. Although I have not been able to acquire any records pertaining to Ellen's teaching career, her career was summarized in her death notice, which appeared in the local newspaper in 1923. In the article the local priest, Father Sheridan of Bruckless, stated:

> In their little community in Bruckless she would be sadly missed . . . The fathers and mothers of that district had good reason to bless Mrs. O'Donnell during her residence

among them there. They had equal reason to deplore her early and unexpected death. To their children she was not only a highly efficient teacher and instructor, she was also a mother and a guardian, and she could say with truth that not one of those little ones committed to her care, wherever their lot might afterwards be cast, had ever gone astray or wandered from the fold, so careful and efficient was the religious training which she imparted and which she placed higher than everything in the curriculum of her school. In the art of her instructions she maintained a very high standard of excellence.[26]

Johnny had only his mother as a teacher until he reached the sixth grade. The sixth grade was the top grade at the Bruckless School, so he spent a couple of years in that grade. When Johnny reached the age of fourteen, the age at which a boy could enroll at St. Eunan's College, he left home to board at that College. He distinguished himself by scoring first place on the College's Entrance Examination. For this achievement, he was awarded the McCormick Scholarship. Louis, the youngest O'Donnell, attended the Bruckless School long after his mother's death. He explained that the family "had no tuition—just scholarships. We had to get scholarships into St. Eunan's."[27]

Without parents to pass on land or income, the O'Donnell children had education as their only means of survival. Each did, in fact, achieve success through this means. With education and a persistent drive to succeed, the eight orphans transformed themselves into a lawyer (John), a nurse (Mary), a priest (Harry), a civil servant (Paddy), a veterinarian (Louis), and three teachers (Lily, Teresa, and Charlie).

Things changed a great deal after the death of Ellen. Henry continued as the Bruckless Stationmaster and cared for his eight children with the help of the O'Donnell and Kennedy families. But more misfortune was in store for the family. On September 17, 1924, fifteen months after the death of Ellen, a meeting of the County of Donegal Railway took place in Belfast that resulted in Henry losing his position as stationmaster in Bruckless Station. The following statement was recorded in the minutes of that meeting:

Bruckless Station. Reported that Bruckless Station had been placed under the supervision of the Dunkineely stationmaster effecting a saving of 140 pounds per annum. Noted.[28]

Eighteen years after Henry O'Donnell began as a stationmaster in Bruckless, the station became a "halt"[29] to save money, so Henry was transferred to the Killybegs station. Six weeks later, he died. While the cause may well have been a stroke, some say it was a broken heart, a heart broken by the loss of his beloved Ellen, which killed him. After the premature death of their parents, the family elders decided that Charlie and Mary were to be sent to relatives already relocated in America. The plan was for Johnny to remain in Ireland and work for the railroad in a position similar to the one his father had held, in order to help support his siblings.

Politics is a constant background to the story of John F. O'Donnell. County Donegal, while occupying the most northerly part of Ireland, is one of the twenty-six counties that form the Republic of Ireland but is almost entirely bordered by the six political units that are together known as Northern Ireland. In 1919, when Johnny was a very impressionable twelve-year-old, the Irish Republican Army (IRA) was created to fight against British rule in Ireland. The Irish War of Independence (the Black and Tan War of 1919-1921) followed. In the middle of the conflict, on December 23, 1920, the British Parliament created two governments in Ireland, one in Belfast (one hundred twelve miles due east of Donegal) for the six predominantly Protestant counties in the northeast, and another in Dublin (one hundred thirty-eight miles southeast of Donegal) for the twenty-six overwhelmingly Catholic counties in the south. After two years of fighting, the formal combat ended with a treaty between the Irish and the English. This treaty split the nation along the lines of the previously created governments. Writing of this treaty, historian Chris McNickle explains that

> Some Irish thought the arrangement was an enormous step forward and that in time the northern counties would reunite with the south. Others thought that if they did not insist on one united republic then and there, they would miss the chance for generations to come, if not forever.[30]

SOUND OF THE SEA

The terms of the treaty proved unacceptable to a substantial number of IRA members. The organization consequently split into two factions: one supporting the peace settlement, the other opposing it. The former group became the core of the official Irish Free State Army while the latter group became known as "the Irregulars." In the ensuing civil war (1922-23), the two groups engaged in a bitter conflict, a conflict ending with the surrender of the Irregulars to the Irish Free State Army.

As a teenager, Johnny was aware of the political situation in Donegal. He loved joining his father and the local men at their gatherings down at the old hall near the railroad cottage. The men would speak quietly about the war and their desire for a united Ireland. Although my father seldom spoke of these years, in one of his more reminiscent moments he described a barrack located in Killybegs. He recalled:

> The barrack was a two-storied slated building, the only one of its kind in the district. The people often wondered how the soldiers and police could sleep when the hailstones rattled on the slates. To see that the fishermen did not break the laws of England, as administered by the Irish Free State, fifty soldiers were stationed there at a time.[31]

In this same interview, my father told me about his cousin Louis Cunningham, who was interned for a while during the Irish Civil War of 1922-1923 but had escaped.[32] One night in October, after evening devotions, the men were gathered down at the old hall to play cards. Johnny's Aunt Lizzy had come down to the hall and told Johnny's father, Harry, that he should come right up to the Post Office. My father continued:

> I went right up with my father. I remember going in the front door and turning a left into the kitchen door. In behind the kitchen door—there was Louis, under the name of Henry Louis McGovern. He was very, very skinny from his jail time, with a beard. He was my cousin, my father's sister's son. Another brother, Charles, was a captain in the Free State Army, while Louis was a soldier of the IRA [the Irregulars, thus the brothers were on the two opposing sides]. Oh it was a terrible civil war.[33]

The political and civil strife was to engage the young John O'Donnell, and his attraction to the Irregulars (IRA) would lead to his appearance before a jury of his peers in 1926.[34] As he stood beside his parents' grave, Johnny relived the events that had ended in his arrest and trial. He was charged with violating the Treason Act, which provided the death penalty for being a member of an illegal organization conspiring against the safety of the state. The eighteen-year-old would face death if the twelve-man jury unanimously found him guilty. As the March rains fell outside the courthouse, the ten Catholic jury members each pronounced O'Donnell not guilty. The remaining two members, Protestants, judged him guilty. The court declared a mistrial and scheduled a retrial for later in the summer of 1926. It was March 1926, and Johnny O'Donnell was free on bail.

It had all begun in 1924. Five days after burying his father, he had left Saint Eunan's and moved in with his mother's sister, Min Kennedy, hiring on as a railroad clerk to help support his younger brothers and sisters.

Enjoying newfound freedom from the strict atmosphere and structure at St. Eunan's, Johnny mixed with some of the people who had split from the original Irish Republican Army. One member of this group of Irregulars, Timmy McCoy, had left Ireland rather quickly in 1925. Before his departure, however, he placed a Parabellum revolver—one with a history—into the unsuspecting Johnny's care. The revolver, records later showed, was one of the weapons seized after a raid on a Free State barracks in Mountcharles.[35] During that raid, at the height of the Civil War, the Irregulars killed two Free State policemen.

The raid took place on April 22, 1922, Fair Day in Mountcharles, the day the farmers brought in their cattle for sale. When there was a fair, it was important for the Free State Irish government to show some control, so they sent in two policemen on bicycles from the neighboring Donegal Town police barracks. In order for the bicycling policemen to maneuver up the steep slope into Mountcharles, the two had to get off their bicycles and walk. It was at one of these times that they were ambushed and shot dead. "One of them was a good friend of mine," said my father. "I knew him well." He continued:

This was when the Civil War was going on. The Black and Tans were with the police. They were sent in as an auxiliary force with the police. The police were not armed. The Black and Tans were recruited from the scum of England and sent over [to Ireland].

When there would be an ambush like this, they [the Black and Tans] retaliated. [This time] they shot a couple of men in Mountcharles—one of those shot was Jerry Britain and another was Brian, Brian—oh—the guy went to school with me and was the nephew of Seamus McManus, the Irish writer.

They [the Black and Tans] were very selective. They burned stores down and they knew the stores to burn. They knew those that were owned or operated by IRA people. Obviously, they had an informer.[36]

No one ever knew how Timmy McCoy came to possess the revolver, but he gave it to Johnny three years after the Mountcharles incident and Johnny kept the Parabellum in his desk drawer at the Dunkineely railroad station.

Later in 1925, on a November evening after work, Johnny joined his buddy Jack Meehan at Jimmy Gallagher's house. While they were there, Protestant Ernie Lawson came in. Ernie's family owned a pub, and as Protestants were "suspect" at a time when informers were greatly feared.

Ernie started to tease Jack Meehan about some girl. Meehan, always short-tempered, responded by asking Lawson where he had gotten the suit he was wearing. A similar suit had been displayed in Jerry Britain's clothing store before it had been burned down and the suit was the type of reward someone would receive for being an informer. Knowing what Meehan was insinuating, Ernie slammed Jack across the face and ran out of the house. Meehan, his temper flaring, also ran out of the house and up the street to the Meehan family's candy store. Johnny got on his bicycle and rode home. Later that same night, some shots were fired into Lawson's Pub.

Completely unaware of the previous night's shooting, Johnny rode his bicycle to his job at the Dunkineely station the next morning. Mary Burns, who worked the magazine stand at the station, knew that Johnny kept a Parabellum gun in his desk drawer. She told Johnny the story about the shooting at Lawson's, mentioning also that people were saying that he, as a pal of Jack Meehan, was in the shooting party, a charge that Johnny vehemently denied.[37] Mary was concerned that the authorities might be coming around to check on Johnny.

In the middle of the same day, before riding home for his midday meal, Johnny put the gun in his hip pocket. Park House, where he had been living with Aunt Min since March of 1925, was about a mile outside Donegal Town on the Ballyshannon Road. Intending to wrap up the gun and bury it before going into the house, Johnny dipped a cloth in some Vaseline, which would prevent the weapon from rusting underground. But Johnny could not resist the temptation to fire the gun before disposing of it. He went outside to the lean-to shack with a corrugated iron roof and fired the revolver. While the explosion itself was loud enough, it was not as loud as the sound made by the shell hitting the iron roof. Aunt Min came running out. "What was that horrible noise?" she asked. Johnny answered, "It was nothing."[38]

He quickly put the gun back in his pocket and went in for his dinner. During dinner Johnny read the newspaper as usual. From Park House Min could see across Donegal Bay to the train stops at Mountcharles, Dunkineely, and Inver. She could see the train coming at least twenty minutes before it arrived at the Dunkineely station. So when she told Johnny that the train was approaching, he ran out and jumped on his bicycle. He was halfway to the station before he realized that he still had the gun in his pocket. Before he had even made it to the train station, the Free State guards were at Park House questioning Min and searching for the gun.

On the next day, December 12, 1925, just five days after his eighteenth birthday, John Francis O'Donnell was arrested in Donegal and charged with unlawful possession of a revolver. Francis Gallagher, a solicitor employed by the Railway Clerk's Association of Great Britain and Ireland was hired to represent him.[39]

At his trial in March of 1926, Johnny explained to Judge Davitt how he had forgotten that the gun was in his pocket. When the Judge asked for the gun, Johnny handed it up to him. Judge Davitt held it in his hand as though weighing it. He said to O'Donnell, "You must have been used to carrying that." Johnny, realizing the implication, denied it. He felt, as he put it years later, "that this was a completely, completely wrong inference to draw."[40] The ten Catholics in the jury sided with Johnny, so a mistrial was called.

All these memories flooded the nineteen-year-old Johnny O'Donnell as he stood in the softly falling March rain next to his father's grave, knowing that the mistrial meant he would have to leave Ireland. Away to the southeast, above the church and the tower, a gray streak was rising into the heavens out of the sea. As he watched the scene, Johnny told himself that he might not be so lucky at the next trial. Yet he also thought of his role as the oldest of the eight orphans, and he knew that he had a responsibility to aid in the financial support of his brothers and sisters. His confusion and sadness were almost overwhelming.

Soon after his arrest, the family felt that Johnny would be safer staying with his mother's brother, Uncle Francy, in Ardaghy. As a man, the family reasoned, Francy might have more control over this restless teenager. Uncle Francy and his wife, Mary Ellen, had always been very good to Johnny. In the meantime, however, Johnny and his friend Jack Meehan were making plans to leave Ireland together on April 30, 1926. Meehan's brother-in-law, who lived in Glasgow, Scotland, assured the boys that he could get the two young men jobs there. From there, they would have the choice of going to Canada for 10 shillings or to New Zealand for free, under the British colonizing scheme.

The night before the boys were to leave Ireland for Glasgow, Johnny sat across the table from his uncle and wrote him a letter revealing his plans. In it, he told Uncle Francy that he had been very happy in Ardaghy and that his departure was not meant to be a reflection on his uncle's hospitality. Early the next morning, Johnny rode his bicycle to the Donegal station where he and Meehan were to meet. When Meehan did not appear, Johnny went over to the Meehan store. Mrs. Meehan met him at the door and was quick to tell Johnny, "We found out what Jack was going to do, and he's upstairs locked in his room. He is not going."[41]

Since Johnny had already written the farewell letter to Uncle Francy, he took the train to Derry alone. As planned, he then caught that night's boat from Derry to Glasgow. When he arrived in Glasgow early the next morning, May 1, 1926, he found the city in the throes of a strike. He discovered that there was not much chance of anyone getting a job on this, the first day of a British general strike in Glasgow.

Hoping that he would get a permanent position with the London and Northeastern Railway Company after the strike ended, Johnny started out with the company as a "Volunteer." The permanent job never materialized, but Johnny did earn a letter of appreciation dated May 14, 1926. A month later, Johnny received two shillings for an article he wrote for the Evening Citizen regarding an accident involving a school child. Finally, however, an empty stomach encouraged a drastic move. He decided to join the British Army and went to the Hope Street barracks to do just that. Since he was out on bail in Ireland, he reasoned that the worst thing that could happen to him was that he would be shipped back to Ireland. In the meantime, he figured, he could get something to eat and a place to sleep. As an under-aged teenager, however, he could not be sworn into the British Army without a letter from a guardian.

Johnny was given a place in the barracks to sleep, but it turned out that there was no food. Thus, he wrote a letter to Aunt Min asking for permission to go to New Zealand. Min spoke to her brother, Canon Kennedy. Soon a gentleman arrived and took Johnny back to Ireland. Fortunately for Johnny, the gentleman paid the way.[42] By the time Johnny returned to Donegal, however, the family had already sent his younger brother and sister, Charlie and Mary, to America. Once in America, the two children went their separate ways—Mary to an aunt in Detroit (Margaret O'Donnell Carpenter), and Charlie to an aunt in Brooklyn (Annie Kennedy McNelis).[43]

Johnny went on trial for the second time in July of 1926, this time with the added charge of bail jumping.[44] The jury's votes were evenly split, 6 to 6, and a mistrial was once again the result. A third trial was set for December of 1926. By that time, Johnny would be nineteen and no longer a minor, so the chances for a third mistrial would become slim indeed.

"Well, at this point, the prosecuting attorney, state solicitor they call them, looked upon the problem a little differently. He was a

SOUND OF THE SEA 15

relation, a cousin, somewhat distant," my father explained. So a deal was struck:

> John F. O'Donnell was found guilty of being in possession of firearms without a permit and sentenced to six months imprisonment with hard labour, this sentence to be suspended if the boy would enter into recognizances[45] to keep the peace for three years.[46]

A provision was added. John F. O'Donnell had to be out of the country by January 1, 1927.

The family decided that Johnny should be sent to the United States as soon as possible. Once there, he would join his younger brother Charlie in Brooklyn. Louis, the youngest of Johnny's brothers, told me that in the time between this decision and his departure, my father helped in the building of the new Bruckless School. In this way he earned some money towards his passage to American.[47]

In the end, it would be not money that proved Johnny's stumbling block, but time. Time was running out. The lines for visas were long, and a series of appointments had to be made with the American Consul, where the émigré would go to complete the required paper work, take an oral examination, and prove his good health. Johnny's final appointment was set for November 30, 1926. On December 6, the day before his nineteenth birthday, Johnny received his passport. On December 14, a Quota Immigration Visa was issued to him by the American Consul. He set sail for the United States on December 17.

The farewell was strained on that dark December morning as Johnny stood on the train platform for the last time. He was leaving behind his family, his home, his friends, and his pride. He knew that he had failed to help out when he was needed most and therefore felt that he had let his family down.

Uncle Francy introduced Johnny to Barney McGrawry while they were waiting on the platform for the train. Barney had already "been out" to America and he was trying to get back to his family in New York before Christmas. The platform was crowded with friends and relatives. Min stood to one side, tears running down her face, thinking about the pain of her loss as she watched yet another of her sister's children leave to cross the sea.

I will always remember my father's description of the moments as the train was pulling in: "The crowd parted. Paddy and Louis came in and said goodbye to me. Louis was only about five years old at the time and Paddy wasn't that much older."[48] Johnny wondered how his young brothers would remember him and whether he could make a life for himself in a new country after the questionable choices he had made in his own.

Since the transatlantic liner that Johnny and McGrawry would sail on would not come into Derry, passengers had to take a tender from Derry down to a village on the west of the Lough Foyle called Moville. It was usually a ten-minute trip on the tender, but on this night there was a bad storm, so it took a lot longer to get out to the ship. Then, when the tender got there, it tossed violently as the passengers were transferred to the ship. Johnny and McGrawry had to wait on the tender until the ship, *The Athenia*, anchored off Moville. Johnny's stomach was in as much upheaval as his life.

The Athenia was a small Cunard Line vessel that would later become the first vessel sunk by a torpedo in World War II. While the ship was not big, the food and the accommodations were fair. Each cabin had four bunks, two above and two below. Since it was Christmas time, there were only about forty or fifty passengers on the ship. Most of the passengers debarked at Halifax, on their way to Canada. This left only about twenty passengers destined for New York.

My father recalled the journey years later:

One of the fellows, I remember, had no overcoat. It was cold. I had an overcoat, but I also had a trench coat. I gave him the overcoat and kept the trench coat.

I remember that you had to have twenty-five pounds when you came to New York to be allowed to go through immigration. I only had fifteen pounds by that point. I borrowed ten pounds from Barney McGrawry until I got by the immigration inspectors. But McGrawry was waiting for me at the foot of the gangplank to get his ten pounds back.[49]

SOUND OF THE SEA 17

The *Athenia* docked at 45th Street in New York City on December 26, 1926. Because there were so few passengers on board, the ship was not required to go through Ellis Island.

On that dark and snowy evening, Johnny O'Donnell began a new life. He would no longer refer to himself as Johnny—that childhood name was in the past now. He was now John F. O'Donnell, and as such he had a lot to prove, both to himself and to his family back in Donegal. He tried to tell himself that this side of the Atlantic could not be so different from the other. If he just looked out on the Atlantic whenever he felt alone, he would remember the sound of the waves beating against the cliffs in Donegal and perhaps, for a moment, he would even hear the whistling of the curlews off shore. As he later wrote:

> Your manhood, dear Bruckless, deserts you of late,
> To the land of the stranger they now emigrate;
> For the want of employment they bid you adieu,
> But, Bruckless, their hearts will be always with you.
> For the strangers can't make your dear children a home,
> To compare with their old one far over the foam.[50]

ENDNOTES

[1] John O'Donnell, "His Homecoming," English 1.D. paper submitted to College of the City of New York, summer 1929. Copy in the papers of Eileen O'Donnell Sheehan, Charleston, South Carolina.

[2] A canon is a title given to priests who lived "within the precinct or close of a cathedral or collegiate church." (Oxford English Dictionary on-line s.v. "Canon.").

[3] See "Penal Laws." Encyclopædia Britannica 2007. Encyclopædia Britannica Online. 6 April 2007 <http://search.eb.com/eb/article-9059041>.

[4] "Penal Laws." Encyclopædia Britannica 2007. Encyclopædia Britannica Online. 6 April 2007 <http://search.eb.com/eb/article-9059041>.

[5] "Catholic Emancipation." Encyclopædia Britannica. 2007. Encyclopædia Britannica Online. 6 April 2007 <http://search.eb.com/eb/article-9021825 >.

[6] Cecil Woodham-Smith, The Great Hunger: Ireland 1845-1849. (1962). Qtd. in "The Great Irish Famine," New Jersey Commission on Holocaust Education. 6 April 2007 <http://www.nde.state.ne.us/ss/irish/irish_pf.html>.

[7] Great Britain. Office of the General Valuation of Ireland. General Valuation of Rateable Property in Ireland, 1847-1864. 170 vols. (Dublin: A. Thom, 1848-1861), Vol. 38

(1858) Donegal: Glenties Union: p. 75. Commonly known as Griffith's Valuation Lists or Valuation Books, this large set of volumes contains a detailed property and tenant survey of Irish counties conducted by Richard John Griffith between the 1840s and the late 1860s. Family History Library, Salt Lake City Utah.

[8] Ireland. General Register Office. Marriage Record, 1845-1870, with Indexes to Marriages, 1845-1921, in the General Registry Office of Ireland. 334 reels (Salt Lake City: Filmed by the Genealogical Society of Utah, 1953), microfilm #FHL 0101505. Family History Library, Salt Lake City Utah. Microfilm of original records in Custom House, Dublin.

[9] The daughter of Anne Kennedy McNelis, Bridget Tuffy, sponsored John and Charles O'Donnell in America.

[10] Great Britain. Office of the General Valuation of Ireland. General Valuation Revision Lists, Donegal Union 1858-1943. 12 reels (Salt Lake City: Filmed by the Genealogical Society of Utah, 1970), #FHL 0832511, p. 42. Family History Library, Salt Lake City Utah. Microfilm of original records at the Ireland Valuation Office, Dublin.

[11] Great Britain. Office of the General Valuation of Ireland. General Valuation Revision Lists, Donegal Union 1858-1943. 12 reels. (Salt Lake City: Filmed by the Genealogical Society of Utah, 1970), #FHL 0832511, p. 46. Family History Library, Salt Lake City Utah. Family History Library, Salt Lake City Utah.

[12] While the Penal Laws had restricted the education of the Irish in the seventeenth and most of the eighteenth century, these Laws ceased to be rigorously enforced around 1771. In 1782, an Act enabled Catholics to set up schools. "Penal Laws," The Catholic Encyclopedia (1911). 6 April 2007 <http://www.newadvent.org/cathen/11611c.htm#III>.

[13] [Article on Francis Kennedy], Derry People's Press, May 2, 1959. Copy in the papers of Eileen O'Donnell Sheehan, Charleston, South Carolina.

[14] Normal School is a school where people, usually high school graduates, are trained for teacher education offering a two-year course and a certificate.

[15] In the late 1790s, "the ordinary Catholic tenant had been forced off the land to be replaced with Presbyterian planters brought over from Scotland. This left a legacy of sectarian rivalry which helped the British to 'divide and rule.'" [Andrew Flood], "The 1798 Rebellion," Red and Black Revolution no. 4 (1998): 18-25. PDF version, Nov 2000. 6 April 2007 <http://struggle.ws/pdfs/RBR4.pdf>.

[16] Catholic Church. Parish of Killybegs (Donegal). Parochial Registers of Killybegs (Donegal), 1850-1914. 1 reel (Salt Lake City: Filmed by the Genealogical Society of Utah, 1984). FHL#1279234. Microfilm of original at Letterkenny, Co. Donegal. Family History Library, Salt Lake City Utah.

[17] Margaret O'Donnell Carpenter emigrated to America and served as a nurse in the Spanish-American War. She sponsored John O'Donnell's sister Mary in Detroit.

[18] Catholic Church. Parish of Killybegs (Donegal). Parochial Registers of Killybegs (Donegal), 1850-1914. 1 reel (Salt Lake City: Filmed by the Genealogical Society of Utah, 1984). FHL#1279234. Microfilm of original at Letterkenny, Co. Donegal. Family History Library, Salt Lake City Utah.

[19] Great Britain. Office of the General Valuation of Ireland. General Valuation Revision Lists, Donegal Union (Donegal), 1858-1943. 12 reels (Salt Lake City: Filmed by the Genealogical Society of Utah, 1970), #FHL0832509. Family History Library, Salt Lake City Utah.

[20] A visitor to the church today will find one of the Stations of the Cross dedicated "In Loving Memory of Our Deceased Parents John and Mary O'Donnell of Bruckless, R.I.P., and Presented by Their Children."

[21] Father Patrick Cunningham, Personal interview, St. Johns Point, Donegal, Ireland, April 2000. Around 1902, Mary's husband died, and she took over the Postmaster position. When Mary herself died in 1910, her daughter, Cassie O'Donnell Keenan, inherited the Postmaster job. Around the early 1920s, when Cassie's eyes started to fail, she turned the postmaster position over to her younger sister, Lizzy.

[22] Edward Patterson, The County Donegal Railways (London: Pan Books, 1962), p. 184.

[23] Copy of Henry O'Donnell's pay stub in the papers of John F. O'Donnell, Katonah, New York.

[24] Years later, Harry described the family home to me. He explained that it was built to accommodate the growing family. It was a two-story home, rather big compared to the houses around in those years. It's still standing there, after all these 80 or so years. Harry O'Donnell, Personal interview, April 15, 1992.

[25] In a 1999 conversation I had with Mary, she said, "I can remember walking to school with my mother and she telling me, because I was her daughter, I should behave." Mary O'Donnell Loranger, Personal interview, Grosse Point Farms, Michigan, November 1999.

[26] A copy of the article is among the papers of Eileen O'Donnell Sheehan, Charleston, South Carolina.

[27] Louis O'Donnell, Personal interview, Bruckless, Donegal, Ireland, April 2000.

[28] Copy of minutes in the papers of John F. O'Donnell, Katonah, New York.

[29] A halt is a railroad station without a stationmaster.

[30] Chris McNickle, "When New York Was Irish, and After," The New York Irish, ed. Ronald H. Bayor and Timothy J. Meagher (Baltimore: Johns Hopkins University Press, 1996), p. 351. In 1988 my father did not mince words when he offered me his opinion of the "in time" statement. "Look," he told me, "Don't tell me it's just a matter of time. Time, we've had time now, and you see what has happened; sixty years, almost seventy, more division than ever." John F. O'Donnell, Personal interview, June 15, 1988. Obviously his years in America had not eased his concerns about the tensions in Ireland.

[31] John F. O'Donnell, Personal interview, June 15, 1988. He added that these Irish Free State soldiers executed Rory O'Connor, Ian Bellows, and some of the best people they had. "Irishmen executed by their own people." I could hear the pain in his voice as he spoke.

[32] Louis's mother was Henry's older sister Mary Ann O'Donnell Cunningham.

[33] John F. O'Donnell, Personal interview, June 15, 1988. What happened to Louis Cunningham after he left my father's house, I was never able to learn.

[34] With a great deal of encouragement, my father did agree to tell me about his trials. I felt that knowing about this part of his life was essential to achieving my goal of unraveling the thread to his strong adult character. He placed certain restrictions on the interview process, however. While many of the interviews I did with my father took place in the comfort of his home, this was not to be the case when the time came for him to discuss his own political and legal past. We went out of the house, to the grocery store, for that part of the story.

[35] Irishmen who favored the treaty made with Great Britain were called Free Staters. The treaty made part of Ireland a free state at the expense of splitting Ireland into two countries.

[36] John F. O'Donnell, Personal interview, June 15, 1988.

[37] John F. O'Donnell, Personal interview, June 15, 1988.

[38] John F. O'Donnell, Personal interview, June 15, 1988.

[39] It has been hinted that there was more to John F. O'Donnell's involvement with the Irregulars. However, I have no means of checking out the stories. My father did tell me that the gun was not involved in any other activities.
[40] John F. O'Donnell, Personal interview, June 15, 1988.
[41] John F. O'Donnell, Personal interview, June 15, 1988.
[42] While my father told me this bit of information, no records have been found concerning the name of the gentleman or the source of the travel money.
[43] Sadly, Charlie and Mary would never meet again. Charles O'Donnell sadly died prematurely at the age of 35, leaving a wife and two children.
[44] This is all the information my father gave me about the time between his return to Ireland and the next trial.
[45] Recognizances to keep the peace involve posting a bond insuring that under penalty of losing the bond money, the person must keep the peace for three years.
[46] Francis Gallagher, LL.B., Solicitor, in a letter dated 26 November 1935 to the Committee on Character of Fitness, First Judicial Department of the Appellate Division of the Supreme Court of the State of New York, November 1935.
[47] The Bruckless School had burned down the year before the death of Ellen Kennedy O'Donnell.
[48] John F. O'Donnell, Personal interview, June 15, 1988.
[49] John F. O'Donnell, Personal interview, June 15, 1988. The tape recording of my father's voice relating this story was part of the sound track for a video my daughter Alison made for her grandfather's eighty-fifth birthday. The sound track would not have been complete without my father's singing "O'Donnell Abu" horribly off key. Also on the video were photos of various nostalgic landmarks in Donegal taken by my father on some of his return trips to Ireland. Much laughter and tears accompanied the showing of this video that evening, as has been the case every evening it has been shown afterwards, for his eighty-fifth birthday was the last my father would spend on this earth.
[50] John F. O'Donnell, Poem found among his papers in Katonah, New York.

On New Year's Eve, I came over by myself from Bay Ridge. I took the subway over to Times Square and I was in the crowd in Times Square that New Year's Eve 1926-27. That's something I'll never forget.

John F. O'Donnell[1]

Chapter Two

FAR OVER THE FOAM

Like any immigrant in a new country, John O'Donnell had adjustments to make and goals to set. To fulfill his vow to send money home to Ireland for his siblings, he would need to find a job.[2] O'Donnell also knew that he would have to finish his education in order to embark on a reputable career and regain his family's respect.

During the next eleven years, he would accomplish all of these goals. Needless to say, he would not do it alone. He relied on his religious upbringing, his family (both in New York City and in Ireland), and the Irish-American community. All this support would give him the strength, advice and political connections necessary to achieve his objectives. At the same time, in the back of O'Donnell's mind would remain the credo he had learned all too well in Donegal—that all work and no play makes for a very dull young gentleman.

His brother Charlie and his cousin Patrick John McNelis met O'Donnell at the 45th Street Dock in New York City on December 26, 1926. The young men appreciated the opportunity to celebrate a new beginning, and the fact that they had arrived in New York City in the midst of Prohibition did not pose a problem.[3] The taxi they took to Bay Ridge made a discreet stop on the trip. "The first house I put my foot in," O'Donnell told me, "was one that Patrick John had the taxi stop at. I forget the name . . . but I do remember we bought the liquor. God, terrible stuff."[4]

During those early months of 1927, John stayed at 722 58th Street in Brooklyn with Patrick John's sister, Bridget Tuffy. Bridget and Patrick John were the children of Anne O'Donnell McNelis, the first born of Owen and Mary Sweeny O'Donnell. In addition to her five grown working children, Bridget also kept two additional boarders in her house. As one of the boarders, O'Donnell paid $10 a week for his room and meals. One of Bridget's children, John Tuffy, secured O'Donnell a job with the help of his veteran buddies. So on 2 January 1927, six days after coming to America, O'Donnell began his first job in this country, working as a grocery clerk in a small A&P store in the Coney Island section of Brooklyn. He worked about seventy hours a week for a weekly wage of $12. He made a few extra dollars from five- and ten-cent tips for delivering groceries.[5] After a month, O'Donnell was able to secure a better paying job as an elevator operator at 22 East 40th Street in New York City, a job he remained at until the beginning of 1928.

Education had to be O'Donnell's second priority since his first concern was holding a job. Before he could finish his high school education, O'Donnell had to leave St. Eunan's to help support his orphaned brothers and sisters. Now he felt that the time had come to finish high school. Thus, he attended Harlem Evening High School from September until December 1927, while working days at his elevator operator job.

On January 12 of the next year, 1928, O'Donnell's brother Charlie telephoned about a vacancy in the school where Charlie was coaching. The New York Catholic Protectory at 1900 East Tremont Avenue in the Bronx, a residential school for delinquent boys, was willing to pay O'Donnell $50 a month as a teacher, and would provide him room and board at the school. O'Donnell quickly accepted the offer. The main qualification for the position required that O'Donnell contain 50 or 60 youths in a room for three hours without yelling for help.[6] This proved to be a more difficult task than O'Donnell had first anticipated. On one of my visits to Katonah, he showed me a small red diary he had kept for the beginning of 1928, his diary from his early days in the Protectorate. In this diary, my father recorded:

> Monday, January 16: Began work. Only fair. Boys hard to manage. Have 43 kids.
> Tuesday, January 17: Work only fair. Kept socking the kids.
> Wednesday, January 18: Beginning to like work. Kids quieter.
> Thursday, January 19: Beginning to have easy time.[7]

Knowing how the system worked meant that O'Donnell also knew the importance of play. He and Jim O'Rourke, another young Irishman working at the Protectory who was to become a life-long friend, spent a lot of time playing ball with the delinquent boys. If the boys did not behave, they were not allowed to play ball. These games allowed ample opportunity to vent a little built-up frustration. It was not unusual for teacher and student to get in a few licks.[8]

O'Donnell was now working and living in the Bronx, so he decided to finish his education at the closer Morris Evening High School. One of his teachers, a Latin teacher, thought O'Donnell's level of education quite superior to that of the average student at Morris, and so he encouraged O'Donnell to accelerate his educational process. With a letter of introduction from this teacher, O'Donnell set out to investigate the programs of study at CCNY, the City College of New York, and to determine the probability of his acceptance. When the advisor asked about his goals for the future, O'Donnell told him that he would like to study medicine. Unfortunately, however, a career in medicine would take money he did not have and would have required full-time attendance during the day. For these reasons O'Donnell figured there was nothing else for him to do but go in for teaching or the law. These thoughts were also recorded in his 1928 diary:

> Tuesday, January 24: Went to CCNY but have no law school. Feel blue. Will teach maybe. Trying to finish high school.
> Wednesday, January 25: Laid my plans. Going to graduate H.S. then to Fordham irrespective of number of years.

On February 16, 1928, O'Donnell received a letter from Horace L. Fields of the University of the State of New York. In the letter, Mr. Fields told O'Donnell that when he had submitted evidence of having met all the matriculation requirements of CCNY, and had satisfactorily completed at least one full year of college work, the State could issue him a law-student qualifying certificate. Mr. Fields emphasized, however, that the work had to be completed before October 15, 1929. After that date, the requirement would be increased to two years of college work.[9] Going to school part time while working at the Protectory made the 1929 goal impossible for O'Donnell to achieve. He attended CCNY from February of 1928 to June of 1930, alternating between part-time, full-time, day-, evening-, and summer-student status. He had accumulated the sixty-five credits necessary for his Law-Student Qualifying Certificate by June of 1930. He now had the two years of college work necessary to enter Fordham University School of Law. With that much of his goal accomplished, O'Donnell set off for Detroit to visit his sister Mary, whom he had not seen since their father had died five years earlier. He had not had a chance to bid Mary farewell when she left Ireland for America and felt that this would be his chance to make up for it.[10] This, however, was 1930, and the world was changing rapidly.

A year before O'Donnell started law school, on October 24, 1929, the Wall Street stock market crashed, precipitating the Great Depression, the worst economic downturn in the history of the United States. Since O'Donnell had the job at the Protectory and was going to school, the depression did not devastate him. When asked what he remembered of the hardships of the depression, he told me a story, but unlike many of his "stories," this one was not a joke. He recalled that he, his brother Charlie, and a friend had gone down to Gray's Drug Store in Times Square on December 7, 1929, planning to celebrate John's twenty-second birthday with half-price tickets for a Broadway show. All of a sudden, a well dressed man fell out of a window, landing on the sidewalk at the feet of the stunned young men. My father recalled the terrifying moment in this way:

> I was walking in front. Charlie and the other fellow were behind me. And suddenly—whoom right in front of me, right at my feet practically—this man was lying there. His head was too close to the ground. He caved his head in when he fell.[11]

My father assumed that the man who had fallen out the window had done so deliberately.[12] That scene left its mark deep in his memory.

On September 22, 1930, slightly less than four years after arriving in America, he attended his first law school lecture, at Fordham University School of Law, Evening Division, at the Woolworth Building in New York City. Looking back, he was obviously proud of his years there. During the day he still lived and worked at the Protectory in the Bronx.

In July of 1932, while still a full-time night student at Fordham, O'Donnell was able to obtain a part-time position paying twenty dollars a week as Assistant Editor of the *Irish Echo,* a weekly newspaper. The newspaper office was located in Manhattan at 152 East 121st Street. It was through his work at the *Irish Echo* that O'Donnell met many influential Irish American politicians, including the *Irish Echo's* founder, Charles F. Connolly. It was also during this time that O'Donnell's skills as a writer became apparent.[13]

Within the span of the next three years, while still working at his part-time jobs, John F. O'Donnell became an American citizen, completed his studies at Fordham, and passed the New York State Bar examination on a practice run. In June of 1933, when O'Donnell received his LL.B. from Fordham University, nearly thirteen million people were out of work, or about one in every four in the labor force.[14] This, of course, was not the best of times to set up a law practice. O'Donnell knew that he would have to rely on his Irish contacts to earn a living.

In July of 1933, O'Donnell left the Catholic Protectory and moved to 114 Remsen Street in Brooklyn. He shared the apartment with his brother Charlie and James J. Comerford. Years later, O'Donnell received an inscribed copy of Comerford's book *My Kilkenny IRA Days*.[15] Comerford, who had been a Justice of the Criminal Court Judge of the City of New York and long-time chairman of the New York City St. Patrick's Day parade, wrote:

> [You] and I have been friends since 1933, and will so remain. John, you taught me writing skills, in 1933-36, which I did not then have. Let me now tell you that these skills, given by you to me, supplied the needed tools I used to write this book.[16]

To become a practicing lawyer, O'Donnell still had two hurdles ahead of him. One hurdle, setting up a one-year clerkship, would be relatively easy to clear. Since O'Donnell had completed only two years of undergraduate work at CCNY, he needed to spend one year in clerkship before he would be eligible for admission to the Bar, even though he had passed the Bar exam. One of O'Donnell's law school professors paved the way for him to work with a negligence lawyer, James E. Smith at 280 Broadway. He served the clerkship with Smith from March of 1934 until July of 1935.[17]

The other hurdle, passing the Committee of Character and Fitness, would prove far more frustrating, as it involved O'Donnell's past history in Ireland. Today, potential lawyers must pass the Committee's review before they can take the bar exam, but for my father, this would be the last obstacle he would have to overcome before becoming an attorney. Both today and in 1934, applicants must fill out a multi-page questionnaire, listing every residence, every school, and every employer in their lifetime, among other information. The Committee of Character and Fitness would question and confirm the applicants' characters and intentions in pursuing a law career. Because of O'Donnell's police arrest record in Ireland, the Committee requested that O'Donnell have the fitness of his character attested to by the very people involved in his prosecution in Ireland. It took O'Donnell almost four years to gather the paperwork necessary to prove his fitness to be a lawyer. While he must have been incredibly frustrated by the overwhelming nature of this process, in the interviews I did with my father many years later, he said little about this period of turmoil.

While working at his clerkship with James Smith and writing and editing for the *Irish Echo*, O'Donnell found his evenings free for the first time since arriving in the States. During this time, then, he decided to request membership in the *Connolly Clan na Gael and IRA Club of New York*, a club with many influential branches.[18] It did not take O'Donnell long to learn that in New York City there were the "old" Irish and the "new" Irish. The *Clan na Gael and IRA Club* of which O'Donnell was to become a member had to be distinguished from the *Clan na Gael* organization that had already existed in New York City for many years.

Jerome J. Collins had founded the original *Clan na Gael* (The Family of the Gael) in 1887, intending it to become a powerful voice of Irish-American nationalism. Its objective to unite all Irish-Americans on behalf of their homeland, however, necessitated that it avoid any hint of radicalism that could alienate the influential clergy or middle class. Therefore, by the turn of the century, this older *Clan na Gael*'s aspirations and sentiments lay with the upper- and middle-class Irish,[19] going as far as favoring the 1921 treaty made with England that partitioned Ireland. O'Donnell, on the other hand, was part of a new group of exiles from Ireland who had arrived in New York City after the Civil War in Ireland. Many of these new arrivals had participated in the Irish Civil War, fighting with the Irregulars against the partition of Ireland and the treaty with England.

The old Irish and the new were distinguished by other differences, particularly socio-economic ones. A small "lace curtain" middle class had emerged among the city's earlier Irish immigrants.[20] These immigrants—professionals, small-scale entrepreneurs, and construction contractors—together with Tammany Hall[21] politicians and the bulk of the Roman Catholic clergy, eventually created a significant conservative force among New York City's Irish population.[22] The "new" Irish had yet to establish themselves either politically or economically. The two groups, "old" and "new," would clash many times over social and political issues in the late 1920s and early 1930s. The prejudices from Ireland had spread to New York City through the different groups of Irish immigrants.

Although O'Donnell was beginning a steady climb toward professional success, he still believed, as his father had before him, that a united Ireland was the source of its strength, and would be willing to put his success on the line to hold on to that belief. In a 1938 letter, O'Donnell wrote that he had been offered the nomination of President of the United Irish Counties.[23] He turned the offer down, however, explaining, "I have refused the nomination at the present time. With a number of other progressive Irishmen, we are working to wrest control of the United Irish Counties from the present Tammany-minded oldsters."[24] O'Donnell believed that any political group governing with little or no opposition is inclined towards despotism, and he was putting this principle into practice when he decided that he could not represent the United Irish Counties as its president.

O'Donnell's reputation while working as an assistant editor at the *Irish Echo* in 1933 was spreading among his fellow Irishmen during the height of the depression. It was during this period that Charlie Connolly, publisher of the *Irish Echo*, started an organization that he called Irish American Independent Political Units (IAIPU). In 1991, O'Donnell explained the reason the organization was founded:

> Charlie's claim, which was accurate at the time, was that many of the recent Irish immigrants were not getting proper recognition from the politicians, Old Irish, in Tammany Hall. The investigators from the Home Relief Agencies (Department of Social Welfare) were hostile to this new wave of immigrants—[and this had] racial intonations."[25]

O'Donnell's reference to "racial" came from the fact that under British rule in Ireland, the Irish were considered to be inferior, less than the superior Anglo-Saxons. O'Donnell felt that in America, the "old" Irish demonstrated their own prejudices against the "new" Irish, seeing the "new" Irish as immature and in need of guidance. This attitude did not sit well with my father and his colleagues; as the expression goes, "It got their Irish up."

Through his editorial position on the *Irish Echo*, O'Donnell had gained contacts in New York City, enabling him to be influential in the appointment of new investigators in the Home Relief Agencies. His position there also gave him the power to influence the predominantly Irish transit workers in their efforts to form a labor union. Most importantly, however, it allowed him to experience the power of the media and to discover how to use it.

Among some of O'Donnell's colleagues in the new *Clan Na Gael and IRA Clubs* were fellow exiles from Ireland: Gerald O'Reilly, Michael J. Quill, and Matthew Guinan. Gerald O'Reilly had spent two terms in prison in Ireland and had escaped shortly before he came to the United States in 1928. Michael (Mike) Quill was born in County Kerry, Ireland, and during the Irish Civil War, he fought as a volunteer in the Irregulars. When the struggle for a united Ireland was irrevocably lost, there was no longer any place for Mike in Ireland, and so he came to America in 1926. Matthew (Matty) Guinan, born in Geashill, County Offaly, immigrated to the United States in 1929 and became a trolley driver in the New York City transit system in 1933. When these 1920s Irish immigrants came to New York City, they transferred their allegiance from the IRA divisions in Ireland to IRA clubs here.

O'Reilly, Quill, and Guinan worked in the City's transit system and went on to become the backbone of the future Transport Workers Union. Later chapters will show that all these men would have a crucial influence on the career of John F. O'Donnell, and that he would have an equally strong impact on each of them.

The new *Clan Na Gael and IRA Clubs* held weekly meetings, each chapter in its own neighborhood. On Saturday nights, however, all the new clubs joined together to sponsor dances. The revenues from the dances enabled the new clubs to purchase a meeting and dance hall near Columbus Circle. The clubs also sponsored political meetings and get-togethers. At these meetings and dances, O'Donnell met many of the people who would influence his future.

While O'Donnell's career was growing in scope, his personal life was also growing in responsibilities. In the spring of 1933, at a *Clan na Gael* meeting, he met his future wife, Katherine Gwendolyn Large, known to all as Gwynne.[26]

In July of 1935, O'Donnell finished his clerkship with James E. Smith. Although the time had come to start building his own law practice, O'Donnell was still trying to clear his second hurdle, obtaining the paperwork necessary for passing the Character Board in order to be admitted to the New York State Bar. In May of 1935, the Appellate Division of the Supreme Court, First Judicial Department, Committee of Character and Fitness issued a questionnaire and statement form to O'Donnell. He had to fill it in, append letters from Ireland, and then submit it to the Committee for approval. In answer to question #16c on the form, which read, "State whether you have been charged with crime, or arrested," O'Donnell responded:

> Was arrested in Donegal, Co. Donegal, Ireland on December 12, 1925 and charged with unlawful possession of revolver. Pleaded guilty and on November 30, 1926 was given suspended sentence of six months. Full particulars in appended letters from prosecuting attorney, defense attorney, and District Justice who committed me for trial.[27]

In his letter, the prosecuting attorney, William T. MacMenamin, commented on the conditions in Ireland at the time of the offense. "[O'Donnell] grew up into boyhood during a period when conditions were very much disturbed in this country," wrote MacMenamin.[28] The defense attorney, Francis Gallagher, added the fact that "both his parents had died a short time previously and this boy was endeavouring to support a number of orphaned brothers and sisters."[29] Finally, District Justice Sean O'Shenrahan included information about O'Donnell's family in Ireland, saying:

> His father was amongst the most respectable, honourable and honoured men in this county; his mother's family was, and is, equally well thought of; his maternal uncle, the late Canon Kennedy, a distinguished ecclesiastic, was an intimate personal friend of mine.[30]

In conjunction with the letters submitted to the Character Committee were depositions by the *Irish Echo* publisher, Charles Connolly, and New York City Magistrate, William O'Dwyer. On October 18, 1937, four years after passing the bar exam and eleven years after arriving in America, John Francis O'Donnell became eligible to practice law. Hyman W. Garuso affixed the seal of the Appellate Division of the Supreme Court of the State of New York on the following declaration: "According to the record of this court he [O'Donnell] is in good standing as an attorney and counselor at law."[31]

While O'Donnell had been waiting for the response from the Committee on Character and Fitness, he had put his writing skills to good use. In April of 1935, O'Donnell wrote and addressed a commemoration of the Easter Rising. Although the 1916 Easter Rising was history and the Civil War in Ireland had ended in 1923, the new *Clan Na Gael and IRA Club* leaders felt duty bound to keep Ireland's history alive. It is important to include the key points of the address here because it shows the mindset of O'Donnell and his fellow Clan members in 1935.

> With the rumblings of war [World War I] growing ever louder, England began a campaign of appeasement toward Ireland. A so-called Home Rule Bill was introduced in the British Parliament. But even while the timid mouthpieces of liberalism proposed Home Rule for the Irish, the imperialist dictators of Britain backed Edward Carson in organizing his Ulster Volunteers [Ulster Irishmen]. [It was] a military organization designed to oppose forcibly, any loosening of the Imperialist grip. [The Ulster Volunteers] pledged to maintain the British system of exploitation of subdued peoples. And when the parliament of Britain made a hesitant move toward suppressing this force [Ulster Volunteers], the army of England mutinied against parliament—and the alleged democratic government of Britain yielded abjectly to the threat of the army. Carson [along with his Ulster Volunteers] was given a free hand.
>
> The existence of the Ulster Volunteers gave the Irish Republican Brotherhood their opportunity to organize an open military body [Irish Volunteers] ostensibly intended to support Home Rule. In fact, the Irish Volunteers were intended to supply the organized force for the hoped for insurrection.
>
> The war [World War I] broke. England was in difficulty. [James] Connolly worked with the revolutionary leaders in planning Ireland's fight. The Citizen Army was to take its place beside the Irish Volunteers in the fight for the Irish Republic—the Irish Worker's Republic. Redmond,[32] the conservative Irish leader, lost the confidence of the people when he agreed, in return for a promise of Home Rule after the war—that the men of the Irish Volunteers would join Britain's army and fight for the preservation of the

Empire. Britain prepared to force conscription of Ireland. The Irish revolutionary leaders fixed the date of the rising—Easter Sunday, 1916. . . . On the following day, Easter Saturday, a messenger arrived at the home of Eoin McNeill, the commander in chief of the Irish Volunteers.

[James] Connolly, [Padraig] Pearse, Tom Clarke, and most of the leaders of the insurrection were astounded when McNeill called off the rising. They knew they would never have another chance. Dublin Castle was already suspicious. Nationwide raids, arrests, imprisonments were imminent. And certain to follow would be the dreaded conscription when the young men of Ireland would be compelled to give their lives for the preservation of the evil and despotic Empire. James Connolly acted. He summoned the most trusted of the Irish leaders and at five o'clock on the morning of Easter Sunday we find Tom Clarke, Eamonn Ceannt, Sean MacDermott, Thomas MacDonagh and Joseph Mary Plunkett with Pearse and Connolly in Liberty Hall. Every man of them knew what the decision would be, but the destiny of a nation was at stake. . . . It was nine hours before the conference ended. The men went their separate ways and about their appointed tasks.

On the next day, Easter Monday, shortly before noon, a small body of marching men in green uniforms swung jauntily along O'Connell Street and into the General Post Office. The Dublin streets were thronged with the holiday crowds, but there was nothing unusual about uniformed Irish Volunteers on the march. But some of the holiday-makers paused when a green uniformed man appeared on the roof of the Post Office. There is amazement when this Volunteer lowers the flag of England, looses it from its halyards and tosses it to the street, and there are cheers when there rises aloft the new flag of Ireland, the tricolor, green, white and gold. And then Pearse, president of the new-born republic, emerges from the Post Office and at the topmost step begins to read, "In the name of God and of the dead generations from which she receives her old tradition of nationhood Ireland through us summons her children to her flag and strikes for her freedom."

The rising centered on the Post Office where the headquarters of the provisional government were established and where Connolly, Pearse, MacDermott and Clarke were in command. From Sunday until Wednesday there was an increasing suspense, waiting for the British attack. On Wednesday morning it came—not an open battle where the poorly armed Irishmen might have had some chance, where their courage and determination would have counted heavily. It was an attack that could not be replied to. A British warship sailed up the Liffey and trained her guns on the Irish strongholds. Liberty Hall was first gutted; then the beautiful buildings on O'Connell Street; and then the Post Office.

By Friday afternoon Dublin was in ruins. The Post Office was blazing, but the tricolor of Ireland still flew proudly from its flagstaff. The men inside who had hardly had a chance to fire a shot against the English foe were indeed hard-pressed."[33]

This speech reveals two important strings making up the fabric of my father's character: he valued the rights of his fellow man, and he researched and verified his facts when presenting information.[34]

O'Donnell's belief that a united Ireland was the source of its strength carried over into his work with unions—his belief that in union was power. An example of this attitude can be seen in a 1941 speech delivered in defense of Mike Quill when O'Donnell stated:

Mike Quill learned another lesson in that struggle—and that is that we must fight every effort that tends to split the ranks of the workers. For every time, the inspiration for the division comes from the enemies of the workers. He saw in Ireland how the wedge was driven between the workers— and he resolved never to let it happen again, be it in his power to prevent it.[35]

As a young man of twenty-eight, my father still had his youthful enthusiasm for his homeland, enkindled by the response to his writings at the *Irish Echo*. He had not been in this country long enough to change allegiances. He wanted to share this enthusiasm with his fellow Irishmen as well as with all the people of New York City. This desire led him, along with some fellow Irish-Americans—James E. Flynn, William O'Dwyer, James J. Comerford, Matthew J. Troy, Jack Feeney, and Roland Bradley—to start a radio show titled "When Ireland Speaks!" On air for the first time, O'Donnell announced:

> It has been my intention for some time past to produce an Irish radio program, interesting and amusing and at the same time instructive and always worthy of the country which is its inspiration. There is much in Ireland's treasury of literature, history and music, which it is not quite possible to present on the dance programs despite their otherwise general excellence. There is in fact so much in Ireland's treasury that it is an immense task even to make a choice of material for presentation. Therefore I have called upon the services of a few of those known to me to assist me.[36]

By the end of 1937, the thirty-year-old O'Donnell was beginning a new phase of his life as a New York City lawyer. As a member of *The Clan na Gael*, he became very interested in the discussions and problems of his fellow members—the transit workers. He accompanied Mike Quill to secret meetings and began to use his legal skills to help the working man.

ENDNOTES

[1] John F. O'Donnell, Personal interview held in O'Donnell's home, Katonah, New York, June 1988.
[2] Receipts show that O'Donnell did continue to send money home until he started law school.
[3] Prohibition laws forbade the sale of alcohol in the States from 1920-1933.
[4] John F. O'Donnell, Personal interview held in O'Donnell's home, Katonah, New York, June 1988.

[5] John F. O'Donnell, Letter to Miss Helen Dennison, January 15, 1976. Letter among the papers of Eileen O'Donnell Sheehan, Charleston, South Carolina.
[6] John F. O'Donnell, Letter to Miss Helen Dennison, January 15, 1976.
[7] John F. O'Donnell, Diary. The diary is with the O'Donnell papers in Katonah, New York.
[8] John F. O'Donnell, Diary.
[9] Copy of letter from Horace L. Fields to John F. O'Donnell, 16 February 1928, in O'Donnell papers, in Katonah, New York.
[10] Mary was attending nursing school when my father visited. Mary O'Donnell Loranger, Personal interview, November 1999.
[11] John F. O'Donnell, Telephone interview, March 17, 1991.
[12] John F. O'Donnell, Telephone interview, March 17, 1991.
[13] Unfortunately, although the *Irish Echo* is still being published, there are only a few issues of the newspaper dating back earlier than 1940, and none with any of my father's contributions. Thus, a closer examination of his early years in the newspaper business is impossible.
[14] John Kenneth Galbraith, *The Great Crash 1929* (Boston: Houghton Mifflin, 1988), p. 168.
[15] James J. Comerford, *My Kilkenny I.R.A. Days, 1916-22* (Leggettsrath, Kilkenny, Ireland: Dinan Publishing Co., 1978). After emigrating from Ireland in 1925, Comerford put himself through Columbia University while working nights as a subway change-maker beginning in 1934, at about the time he and my father were roommates. He later earned his law degree at Fordham University, as had my father. Comerford's obituary appeared in *The New York Times*, 25 March 1988.
[16] Copy among O'Donnell's effects in Katonah, New York.
[17] John F. O'Donnell, Papers submitted to the Appellate Division of the Supreme Court, May 29, 1937. In the O'Donnell papers, Katonah, New York.
[18] IRA stands for the Irish Republican Army.
[19] John R. McKivigan and Thomas J. Robertson, "The Irish American Worker in Transition, 1877-1914: New York City as a Test Case," *The New York Irish*, ed. Ronald H. Bayor and Timothy J. Meagher (Baltimore: Johns Hopkins University Press, 1996), pp. 302-303.
[20] "Lace curtain" is defined in the *American Heritage Dictionary* 4th ed. as "aspiring to or emulating the middle class."
[21] Named for Tammamend, a wise chief of the Delaware tribe, Tammany or Tammany Hall was the group that ran the New York City Democratic Party for over a hundred years through power and patronage. It lost most of its clout after failing to support Franklin Delano Roosevelt's campaign for the presidency. "Tammany Hall," *Encyclopædia Britannica*, 2006. Encyclopædia Britannica Online. 15 July 2006 <http://search.eb.com/eb/article-9071120>.
[22] John R. McKivigan and Thomas J. Robertson, "The Irish American Worker in Transition, 1877-1914: New York City as a Test Case."
[23] The United Irish Counties is the "[U]mbrella organization for affiliated Irish County associations in the New York area." New York Irish Center, 9 April 2007 <http://www.newyorkirishcenter.org/information.htm/>.
[24] John F. O'Donnell, Letter to Hon. B. Charney Vladeck, January 20, 1938. Copy among the papers of Eileen O'Donnell Sheehan, Charleston, South Carolina.
[25] John F. O'Donnell, Telephone interview, July 17, 1991.
[26] For further information on Gwynne O'Donnell, see Part 2.

27 John F. O'Donnell, Papers submitted to the Appellate Division of the Supreme Court, May 29, 1937.
28 William T. MacMenamin, B.A., Solicitor, Ballybofey, Co. Donegal, Letter to the Committee of Character and Fitness, First Judicial Department of the Appellate Division of the Supreme Court of the State Of New York, November 19, 1935. In O'Donnell papers, Katonah, New York.
29 Francis Gallagher, LL.B., Solicitor, Donegal, November 26, 1935. Copy among the papers of Eileen O'Donnell, Charleston, South Carolina.
30 Sean O'Shenrahan, Justice of the District Court, Irish Free State, December 7, 1935. Copy in the papers of Eileen O'Donnell Sheehan, Charleston, South Carolina.
31 Hyman W. Garuso, Appellate Division of the Supreme Court of the State of New York, First Judicial Department, October 18, 1937. Copy in the papers of Eileen O'Donnell Sheehan, Charleston, South Carolina.
32 John Redmond, leader of the Irish Nationalist Party.
33 O'Donnell's notes are located in his personal papers in Katonah, New York.
34 While my father knew the story of the Easter Week Rebellion, when telling the story, he had to have the specifics. In his papers at the family home in Katonah, I found ten handwritten pages of notes (titled Research on Easter Week Rebellion 1916) along with a bibliography. He had researched the details at the New York Public Library on April 5, 1935, before giving his address. This was my father's way. This zeal was apparent in his approach later in union negotiations where he was known for his many exhibits and charts.
35 John F. O'Donnell, Speech on behalf of Mike Quill, before the Bronx Committee of the American Labor Party, October 1939. Original in the Tamiment Library, New York University. Copy in the papers of Eileen O'Donnell Sheehan, Charleston, South Carolina.
36 Script from radio broadcast in 1935. Copy in the papers of Eileen O'Donnell Sheehan, Charleston, South Carolina.

*As for my reputation and standing among my own
people—I can assure you that it is of the first rank.
I have already served several times as President of my own
county organization. I have held office in numerous Irish
and Irish-American fraternal and social organizations.
I have been offered the nomination of President of the
United Irish Counties [a position later accepted].*

John F. O'Donnell[1]

Chapter Three
GROWING AND BECOMING

John Francis O'Donnell was now ready to leave the shelter of his network of Irish immigrants. In Ireland, he had witnessed the destructive struggles between religious, political, and economic factions, and he quickly learned the importance of a unified cause. He had seen Protestants and Catholics fight and die for the same country, for the same homeland freedoms. He came to understand, after his years in America, that different religious and ethnic backgrounds actually strengthened the backbone of a country. With this conviction, he opened his law practice and offered his service to anyone who sought his help.

United Parcel Service

John O'Donnell did not have the option of studying labor law at Fordham Law School since labor law did not even exist as a subfield in law. It was to come into being with the turbulent years of the depression and with government's efforts to spur the economy.

When President Roosevelt took office during the depression in 1933, he feverishly created program after program to give relief, create jobs, and stimulate economic recovery in the United States. One such program, the National Industrial Recovery Act (NIRA), which was enacted in June 1933, included a section guaranteeing the rights of employees to organize and bargain collectively. To ensure orderly and fair competition in business, the act also authorized the President to set up a National Recovery Administration (NRA). Its purpose was to draft a set of codes for each of the nation's more than 500 industries. The NRA director Hugh Johnson tried to gain corporate endorsement of the reemployment agreements. According to a 1933 article in *The New York Times*:

> As each agreement is signed pledging the carrying out of the President's proposal, the signer, whether firm or individual, will be authorized to display at his place of business the "Blue Eagle" insignia of the NRA. Violation of the agreement, according to General Johnson, would mean, "that that blue hawk comes down."[2]

However, in 1935, when the U.S. Supreme Court nullified the codes as an unconstitutional delegation of legislative power to the executive, the NRA was abandoned and along with it, the "blue eagle" or company-unions. Congress immediately enacted the National Labor Relations Act (NLRA), also known as the Wagner Act. This act protected workers' rights to unionization and guaranteed "un-supervised employees the right to self-organize, choose their own representatives, and bargain collectively or choose not to do any of these things."[3] Labor law was born. This law became the principal labor-relations law between employers and workers in all private businesses except railroads and airlines. The National Labor Relations Act attempted to protect the rights of both labor and management and sought to settle disputes between them.[4]

One of the companies affected first by the National Industrial Recovery Act of 1933 and then by the Wagner Act was the United Parcel Service (UPS). The company was started by two teenagers, James Casey and Claude Ryan, as the American Messenger

GROWING AND BECOMING

Company in Seattle in 1907, with deliveries by bicycle.[5] In 1919, the company began using the name United Parcel Service (UPS), and in 1930, the company expanded to the East Coast, to New York City.[6] Shortly after the passage of the National Industrial Recovery Act in 1933, UPS formed a company union for its employees, a Blue Eagle union. At the time, management was giving the company union additional financial support as well as paying one man on a full-time basis to handle any employee grievances. Then in 1935, when the Supreme Court ruled that it was an unfair labor practice for management to pay the union's expenses and unconstitutional for management to pay someone to be employed full-time on union business, "the blue eagle union at the United Parcel Service was suddenly cut adrift. Ted Johnson, who was Vice President of UPS, told the employees that they were on their own."[7]

The employees at UPS were thrown into chaos, and two of the UPS employees decided to ask help from a friend, John O'Donnell. While O'Donnell was working at the *Irish Echo* and still pursuing his admission to the bar, the two UPS drivers, Bill Courtenay and Jimmy Hayes, came to see him. Courtenay explained that the men at UPS were going through some turmoil and needed advice. The problems had to do with the new labor law, the Wagner Act. O'Donnell's career as a labor lawyer began that day. As O'Donnell recalls:

> I went down to a bookstore beside the Woolworth Building and bought a copy of the Wagner Act. I studied it so I could know what the hell I was talking about. That's how I got into labor law.[8]

Although O'Donnell still had not been admitted to the bar to practice law, he helped the employees of UPS form an independent union—the Delivery and Allied Workers Independent Union, with headquarters at 55 West 42nd Street in New York City. William J. Courtney became the union president; John Brophy, the first vice-president; William F. Duane, second vice-president; and James F. Hayes, secretary-treasurer. Two years later, O'Donnell, by that time a practicing lawyer, wrote a constitution and bylaws for the independent union.[9]

Clearly remembering the benefits of unified strength from his earlier years in Ireland, O'Donnell went to see Tommy Lyons, head of the New York Council of Teamsters, on November 18, 1937. He and Tommy Lyons agreed to an arrangement wherein the United Parcel Service employees would receive a charter as Merchandise Delivery Drivers and Employees, Local 804, which was affiliated with the International Brotherhood of Teamsters. In a December 8, 1937 letter addressed to O'Donnell at the *Irish Echo*, Dr. John P. Boland, Chairman of the New York State Labor Relations Board affirmed, "Accept once more my congratulations on your clever and thoroughly approved handling of the United Parcel matter."[10] Once the employees joined the Teamsters, O'Donnell stepped out of the picture. He would again have dealings with this new union when he represented Local 1-S, Macy's Department Store Workers.

Local 1-S — Macy's Department Store Workers

O'Donnell's reputation as a lawyer familiar with the problems of labor was growing. His association with Mike Quill opened doors for him and reinforced his status as a lawyer who would cheerfully give clients the benefit of his time and knowledge. Sam Kovenetsky turned to John O'Donnell for help in his early days of organizing in the department store union.

Kovenetsky, a Rumanian immigrant, had been a stockroom worker at New York City's Macy's Herald Square Department Store since 1929. He began his union-organizing activities in the Macy store by smuggling in leaflets and publications in 1933, when a union for Macy workers was still only a dream. Organizing would change a great deal in two years, however, with the passage of the NLRA in 1935. As my father explained it to me:

> In the early 1930s [before the NLRA], department store employees came under the **State** Labor Relations Act. In Kovenetsky's case, the State Labor Relations Board certified the units organized. That could never happen today under the **National** Labor Relations Board. Today you have to have a unit, a cohesive unit—all under the same management. You can't just snip off a piece here and a piece there—but under the State law at that time, you could.[11]

In a 1991 telephone interview, Kovenetsky told me that he had learned of my father through Mike Quill and a general labor orga-

GROWING AND BECOMING 41

nizer for the Congress of Industrial Organizations (CIO), Tom Darcy. Kovenetsky explained,

> When I needed some legal advice or help, John was ready, willing, and very capable in helping. So I depended on him. Then when we first got our union organized, in 1939 I think, we asked him to become our counsel on a retainer, which at that time was $50 a month.[12]

Two thousand workers of the warehouse, delivery, and manufacturing divisions were organized into Local 1-S of the Department Store Organizing Committee, CIO, and in their new agreement of April 1939, achieved closed-shop status.[13] A June 9 press release, "R. H. MACY SIGNS UNION CONTRACT FOR STORE EMPLOYEES," stated:

> After four weeks of negotiations the R. H. Macy Co. has signed a closed shop union contract covering approximately eight hundred of its non-selling employees in its headquarters at 34th Street, with the Department Store Organizing Committee, CIO, John F. O'Donnell, Attorney for the Union announced today. In addition to the closed shop, the contract provides for wage increases of from 5 to 15 per cent, overtime at time and one half, seniority, mediation of discharge, the check-off, and a continuation of the present vacation plan by which employees get from one to three weeks annual vacation according to years of service.
>
> The company was represented in negotiations by Jack I. Straus, vice-president; John E. O'Gara, General Manager; and E. B. Lawton, director of personnel. The union was represented by Samuel Wolchok, of the DSOC, John F. O'Donnell, Attorney for the committee, T. Darcy, General Organizer for the Committee, and Miss Rhoda Goodman, Robert McLean, Leslie T. Francis, Irving Eisenberg, Tom McCoer, Sol Gottlieb, Sam Kovenetsky, Phil Hoffenstein [for the Union].[14]

In addition to negotiating with Local 1-S, the Macy organization had to negotiate with other unions representing some of its employees. Macy executives soon tired of this procedure. According to O'Donnell:

> Jack Straus, one of the Strauses, was the head of Macy and he had a labor relations' specialist advising him—Anna Rosenberg. She was in the Roosevelt cabinet afterwards. Rosenberg was a wealthy lady here in New York and had a lot of ties with unions and with some employers. The Macy management then, through Anna Rosenberg, worked out a deal with Sidney Hillman [Vice President of the CIO] recognizing the Retail, Wholesale and Departments Store Union (RWDSU) for all of Macy employees.[15]

Harmony between the RWDSU and the CIO lasted for about seven years until the Macy delivery service was sold. After eighty-eight years of maintaining its own delivery service, Macy New York announced on June 26, 1946 that it would begin deliveries through the United Parcel Service. *The New York Times* announced that "Macy 500 Red Star trucks that brought 65,000 packages a day to customers will become part of the United Parcel truck fleet."[16] Thirteen days later, the package sorters struck at Macy "in the first step of a strike that officials of the Retail, Wholesale and Department Store Union [RWDSU], CIO, predicted would prevent the department store, largest in the world, from opening today [July 11, 1946]."[17]

A jurisdictional battle took shape between the CIO union (RWDSU) and the International Brotherhood of Teamsters, AFL (Local 804), "both of whom claim the right to represent 900 drivers, handlers and helpers who had been employed in the now defunct Macy delivery departments."[18] As Sam Kovenetsky observed:

> In 1946 we had a strike when the delivery system was sold to United Parcel. . . . I pulled a strike to safeguard the interest of the workers in the Macy delivery system. . . . We went out on strike for two and a half weeks.[19]

O'Donnell also recalled the strike:

> We had a strike in Macy—not all of them struck by any means—the delivery men went out and Sam's [Kovenetsky] group went out also. Sam Wolchok was head of the International Union [RWDSU]. He was helpless. He went to see Sidney Hillman [Vice President of the CIO]. Hillman told him that the strikers were decent people and

GROWING AND BECOMING 43

"You'd better settle this strike." Wolchok said, "I can't settle it." Hillman said, "All right. Then I'll send in Mike Quill." So they [CIO] sent in Quill as a mediator. That upset Wolchok no end.[20]

I had represented Local 804, which was the United Parcel Service. They did not deliver Macy merchandise when I worked for them. At the same time, I represented Sam Kovenetsky who came from the store. [When] Mike came in as mediator, I went over with him to the delivery warehouse over in Long Island—that's where the big warehouse was and that's where the drivers were located. And it was raining—oh it was miserable. There were a handful of pickets there, standing in the doorways out of the rain. Mike got up on the rear of the car and made a speech to them.

Then we came back to Macy—to the store and we were taken up to the thirteenth floor. The store was closed because of the strike. We went up to the thirteenth floor where the head offices were. They [Macy] had all their top people there. Jack Straus was there, Anna Rosenberg was there, John O'Gara, the operating head of Macy, was there. They were all very worried. But there was one man there, sitting at the end of the table—Beardsley Ruml.

Beardsley Ruml had been with the Roosevelt administration. He had introduced the "pay as you go" method of tax collecting. Previously, at the end of the year, everybody had to get up his or her taxes. Ruml was a well-known economist. At this time now, Beardsley Ruml was a member of the Board of Directors at Macy. He was also with them at the meeting on the thirteenth floor. He was in great shape—laughing. He thought it was wonderful that these people who get such low wages had the courage to walk out on strike. He said, "They must be a wonderful people." Meantime O'Gara and Straus were dying at the same time.

That was that night. We finally settled for a very small increase, but at least we got a settlement and ended the strike.[21]

After the strike, Sam Wolchok, President of the International RWDSU, demanded that Kovenetsky get rid of John O'Donnell as Local 1-S general counsel. As Kovenetsky tells the story:

> Wolchok said he [O'Donnell] was not good for the union . . . that John O'Donnell was a Communist. So I said to him, "If we get rid of John, you're getting rid of us."
>
> I had a meeting with John and told him what was going on. John's attitude was, "Well look Sam, we've got to organize. We can't afford to have any arguments. Why don't you just leave it alone? If you need my help, I'll help you. You don't have to have me on a retainer." You know he gave up $50 a month. So we agreed that he would step away.
>
> Then the international union made some suggestions that I get other counsel. The irony of it was that they gave me a guy that wanted a dollar per month per member, which at that time would have been something like a little over $2000 a month and we couldn't afford to keep our electricity on all day. Then another group [of lawyers] came along. When Sam Wolchok told me to get rid of John O'Donnell because he was a Communist, the other group that came along—they actually were Communists.[22]

As personal attorney and advisor to Michael Quill since their days together in *The Clan Na Gael*, O'Donnell was never without a challenge. The "Communist" label, becoming more prevalent at this time, the late 1940s and 1950s, had spread from Quill to O'Donnell, but he never saw it as anything more than a meaningless label.

Since the early 1930s, O'Donnell, in addition to his other work, became very involved with the Transport Workers Union (TWU), which will be discussed in a later chapter. By now, in the 1950s, Mike Quill and the TWU occupied more of my father's time. However, old friends were never forgotten. For a few years, Kovenetsky and O'Donnell each went his own way in the labor field. Kovenetsky describes his relationship with O'Donnell at that time and in the years after:

We [O'Donnell and Kovenetsky] kept in contact. It was in 1948 we [Local 1-S] pulled out of the international union. We went independent. Phil Murray, who was the head of the CIO, asked me why I was leaving the CIO. I told him I was not leaving the CIO, that I was leaving the international union [RWDSU]. I couldn't stay there with Sam Wolchok, who demanded that I sign a noncommunist pledge. . . . I refused to be dictated to by anybody. So I just—our union just pulled out. We went independent. We took on an attorney who was at that time with the National Labor Relations Board. He was a young fellow. He was competent but he lived by the book, which John [O'Donnell] never did. John would say that we do what is good for the union and what is good for the people and the book is going to have to be rewritten for us. That's why I love him. . . . When I worked with him as my advisor, as a negotiator, he'd say, "Look, Sam, I think you've got a very, very important point there, and if you feel it's that important; let's go and fight for it. Don't let's deviate. Keep going even if it means a strike. We've got to go and get what we want." He gave me a hell of a lot of confidence in my struggle to get certain things. So his advice was not one that said, "Look, it's not that important. Let's wait for another time." He was not a procrastinator.[23]

O'Donnell returned to Local 1-S again a few years later. Around 1952, Kovenetsky phoned O'Donnell to find out if he was available. According to Sam, O'Donnell said, "Sure. If you want us, we'll be there." O'Donnell was still the attorney representing Local 1-S at the time of the 1991 interview.[24]

New York City Politics

The main sum of my father's education in and experience with labor law and labor unions was accomplished through New York City politics. New York City began the year 1938 under a new charter. In 1936, the voters had accepted a new charter with provisions that a new City Council replace the Board of Aldermen. After the required year's delay, elections were held in 1937.[25] According to my father, Ruben Lazarus wrote the administrative code which replaced the old aldermanic code in New York City. Lazarus's intelligence so impressed my father that he made sure that I understood the significance. O'Donnell remarked:

> Ruben Lazarus had been a Page in the Senate up in Albany. Al Smith, Governor of New York State, got to know Ruben Lazarus very well and appreciated him. Ruben Lazarus was the only one that was ever admitted to the Bar in New York State who had never gone to law school. Al Smith saw to it. Lazarus was a very brilliant lawyer. He was head counsel to the Charter Revision Commission in New York. When the aldermanic code was eliminated, the City Council took seats.[26]

Elected on the American Labor Party (ALP) ticket to that first City Council was O'Donnell's friend, Michael J. Quill, as well as B. Charney Vladeck. Baruch Charney Vladeck was an immigrant from Minsk, Russia. A noted writer, lecturer, and general manager of *The Jewish Daily Forward*, he was first elected as a member of the Board of Aldermen in New York City in 1917. According to *The New York Times*:

> He [Vladeck] was one of the first members of the Socialist party to be elected to that body and was reelected despite a coalition effort to defeat him in 1919. He was defeated for a third term in 1921. He was not active again in politics until the formation of the American Labor Party. He was one of that party's earliest sponsors, and was high in its councils from the start.[27]

In January 1938, John O'Donnell has written a letter to Vladeck, with reference to O'Donnell's application for a position as assistant District Attorney in Thomas E. Dewey's office. When Vladeck took his seat on the new City Council, he responded to O'Donnell's request by asking him to become his own legislative assistant. By December of that year, according to an article in the *Irish Echo*, O'Donnell was appointed "as secretary to the Labor Party in the

GROWING AND BECOMING

New York City Council."[28] The same article notes that "in the short period that he has been practicing law he has gained wide prominence and is now counsel to the Federation of Irish Musicians, Local 804 of the Teamsters Union, [and] the South Bronx Civic Association."[29]

The American Labor Party was founded in New York in 1936, when Franklin D. Roosevelt, already on the Democratic line, wanted another line on the New York State ballot for President. When running for President, candidates knew that more lines meant more votes that could be taken from the opponent. A deal was worked out between James J. Farley, Roosevelt's campaign manager, and Sidney Hillman and David Dubinsky, heads of the powerful and well-organized unions in the clothing workers' field. As a 1937 *New York Times* article noted:

> The party [the American Labor Party], from the beginning has been run by neither idealists nor radicals. The leaders of it, Mr. Hillman, Mr. Dubinsky, Luigi Antonini and Alex Rose won reputations in the labor field for practicality years ago. . . . Communist influence in it to date has been negligible.[30]

At the time of its inception, the creators of the Labor Party meant it to promote liberal and socialistic programs, though Dubinsky, more conservative than the other Labor Party's co-founders, felt that the programs should not be too liberal. Since they could not get anywhere in a party of their own, the Communists did eventually flock to the Labor Party.[31]

The American Labor Party was a strong New York City party in the 1937 elections, and Mayor Fiorello LaGuardia was reelected as the City's mayor on that ticket in that year's election. LaGuardia had lost his earlier campaign to be mayor when he ran as a Republican in 1929; in 1933, he had run on the Fusion ticket and won.

As the new City Council took seats, O'Donnell was present as the legislative assistant for Vladeck. Later O'Donnell remembered:

> I was employed by Charney Vladeck, who was the leader of the Labor Party group. He was originally destined for majority leader but because Mike Quill went to Ireland at

> the wrong time,[32] Vladeck wound up as the minority leader. Still we had the large room at City Hall, the majority leader's room, where we had settled.[33]

Later he added: "My connection with the American Labor Party grew out of my association with the Transport Workers Union.... I began to write a weekly column [1933] in the *Irish Echo* on "Labor."[34]

Late in 1938, O'Donnell ran in his first public election as a member of the American Labor Party. With the endorsements of Mayor Fiorello LaGuardia and Michael J. Quill, he ran for the Assembly in the 6th District in the Bronx. Although O'Donnell received over 20,000 votes as American Labor Party candidate, he lost the election to the Democratic Party incumbent, Peter A. Quinn. Still, the knowledge that he had earned the endorsements of the Mayor of New York City and of the Transport Workers Union must have added strength to O'Donnell's choice of direction.

The American Labor Party suffered later under Communist infiltration. As my father explained it to me:

> Dubinsky quit the party because the Communists gloried in the Labor Party. A lot of the people who voted for them [Labor Party candidates] were not Labor Party minded. They were really Democrats at heart and they went back to the Democratic Party when they got a chance. I think that basically it is a two-party system. You see there was a former Labor Party out in Minnesota long before there was a Labor Party in New York. There are still segments of it around there yet. But by and large, on a national basis, you are either a Democrat or a Republican. Locally, labor can be important. For instance, labor is important in New York. Now why isn't it important nationally? Well, it's one thing to be important in a [single] state, but unless you're important in a lot of states you don't mean much nationally. [The Labor Party] is important in big cities, where there is big industry, where you have fairly strong organized labor. Now you go down to a big city in the South, you can forget it. Start a Labor Party in Charleston and how many votes do you think you would get?[35]

GROWING AND BECOMING 49

By 1939, right-wingers dominated the Bronx branch of the American Labor Party. David Dubinsky and the International Ladies Garment Workers Union represented the extreme right wing. "In their way of thinking," said O'Donnell, "if you were an ardent supporter of Hitler, you wouldn't be half as bad as if you were an ardent supporter of the Russians and the Communists. Michael Quill was too leftist for Dubinsky. There is no question—Mike was close to the Communist party."[36] The Communists had helped Quill get his union on its feet. However, it has never been proved that Quill was a card-carrying member of the Communist Party. Then, and in the years to follow, accusations of Communist affiliation leveled against Labor Party members were simply unfounded, a guilt by association.

The Labor Party in the Bronx had a strong contingent of right-wingers but the Communists were also quite strong. The split became quite apparent when Quill began his run for a new term on the City Council. In this context, the American Labor Party Third Assembly District Bronx County sent out a resolution to its Party members in October of 1939:

> WHEREAS the world is torn asunder by a war which threatens the destruction of civilization itself, and
>
> WHEREAS the aggressor in this conflagration has recently consummated an agreement with Joseph Stalin, dictator of the Soviet Union, and
>
> WHEREAS this treaty has brought world-wide denunciation upon Joseph Stalin, the Soviet Union and the Communist Parties of the world, and
>
> WHEREAS in the United States feeling against the Communist Party has been running particularly high, and
>
> WHEREAS City Councilman, Michael J. Quill, now running for re-election, has been charged in an article in the *Saturday Evening Post* with being a member of the Communist Party, and

WHEREAS such charges, if generally believed, will have a disastrous effect upon the vote cast by the workers of New York for the American Labor Party in the forthcoming election, therefore:

BE IT RESOLVED: that the 3rd AD Club of the American Labor Party, Bronx County, at a regular meeting requests that Councilman Michael J. Quill, in a public statement, make it known that he is not now and never was a member of the Communist Party or under their influence, and that he in common with the rest of organized labor abhors the very idea of entering into contractual agreement with Adolf Hitler, and

BE IT FURTHER RESOLVED: that copies of this resolution be sent to the County and State offices of the American Labor Party as well as to Councilman Michael J. Quill, and

BE IT FURTHER RESOLVED that Councilman Michael J. Quill be and hereby is now invited to appear before and speak at a regular membership meeting of the 3rd AD Club of the American Labor Party, Bronx County, on Thursday, October 12th, 1939, so that an opportunity may be afforded him to address such meeting.[37]

At Quill's request, John O'Donnell wrote and delivered the nominating speech before the Bronx County Committee of the American Labor Party at that meeting. Parts of the speech follow:

In taking the floor here tonight I feel a deep sense of responsibility and therefore I am going to dispense with the usual formalities and inform you now at the beginning, rather than at the end, that it is my purpose to put in nomination the name of one of America's greatest labor leaders, a man beloved by the people, our own Councilman from the Bronx, Michael J. Quill. . . .

Mike Quill has enemies. No man who has accomplished so much for the working people could fail to have made enemies—powerful enemies—enemies who are always

GROWING AND BECOMING 51

ready to strike back. The transit, utility and banking trusts hate and fear Mike Quill. He and his union have cost them many millions of dollars. Even when he beat them, even as they unwillingly came to terms with their employees, he knew that they were already scheming to bring about his downfall and the destruction of the union. But Mike knew too that he had nothing to fear from any source as long as he held his union solidly together. That the companies realized too. And so Michael Quill and his fellow workers waited for the attack. Many attacks came—insidious, surreptitious, indirect. But the union held firm. Then the companies appraised the result. It was a period of reconnaissance; and the utility trust decided that the union could be weakened only by racial or religious conflict. England had vanquished the Irish only when she was able to divide them. And she divided them on a religious issue. Maybe with a little change—to suit the changed background—it would work here, too. The bosses decided that they would drive between the workers the wedges of race and religion. Suddenly it became rumored about Michael Quill—that he was a Communist. The strategy was diabolically simple. The Transport Workers are mainly Catholic. Repeat the charge of Communist often enough and it would begin to stick. That would be the first crack in the union....[38]

Mike Quill has taken his stand. He says to you, 'I am not a Communist.... I never have been and am not now a member of the Communist party. I believe wholeheartedly in the democratic process and have dedicated myself both in the labor organization which I represent and in public life to its preservation and extension. I reject dictatorships of all forms and under whatever name.'

That's Mike Quill. That's what he stands for.[39]

When O'Donnell concluded his speech, the vast majority of the 400-member Committee gave him a standing ovation. An immediate vote would have ensured a Quill victory. Two hard-line Communists, however, could not resist the opportunity to get on the bandwagon. So, encouraged by the anti-Quill chairman, Judge

Matthew M. Levy, they made remarks that antagonized so many of the Committee members that by the time it got to a vote, what had looked like an easy victory for Quill had turned into a defeat. Two years later, the Amalgamated Clothing Workers reversed itself, supported Quill, and the union's assistance helped him to regain his seat for two further terms.

When Quill lost the election in 1939, my father was dropped from the Council staff. The change in situation caused him rethink the path that he wanted to follow. He explained to me:

> Now when I was dropped, Mike sent for me and said, "Look. John Santos is going to call you. He is going to offer you two jobs. You can have the pick of them." One was as the Associate Counsel for the National Association for the Protection of the Foreign Born. They are in Washington DC. The second job was as an attorney, handling workmen compensation cases for the Transport Workers Union (TWU) in New York City's Local 100. While the first job—the Washington job—was full time with better pay, the job with TWU paid $40 a week and was only for eight weeks. I told Quill that I was sticking with Local 100. My decision was made. Mike told me, "You made the right choice. You wouldn't be long in Washington before you would have to join the Party."[40]

By about 1940, the American Labor Party's influence began to wane as disputes broke out between right and left wing factions. David Dubinsky and other New Deal liberals withdrew from the ALP and went on to found the Liberal party in New York State in 1944. However, O'Donnell chose not to give up on the American Labor Party, and he became Treasurer of the "Progressive Committee to Rebuild the American Labor Party." In 1944, John F. O'Donnell ran on Row "C" of the ALP ticket for Justice of the Municipal Court. Michael J. Quill ran for City Council, while William F. O'Dwyer, who had sponsored O'Donnell for admission to the Bar of the State of New York, ran for mayor. All three ran on the ALP ticket.[41]

Both O'Donnell and Quill lost their elections, while O'Dwyer won the office of Mayor of New York City. At that time, O'Donnell

GROWING AND BECOMING 53

was general counsel to Local 804, Teamsters; to Local 3 (Div N.) Electrical Workers Union; and to Local 56 Firemen and Oilers Union—all AFL affiliates. He was also general counsel to the Brotherhood of Consolidated Edison Employees, Independent, and special counsel to the Transport Workers Union, CIO. If, in fact, O'Donnell had become a judge, his future accomplishments in labor would never have been realized. He never again ran for office and he never again strayed from the labor movement.

The newly elected mayor, William F. O'Dwyer, was born in Bohola, County Mayo, in 1890 and came to the United States in 1910. While working as a New York City policeman, O'Dwyer attended law school at night at Fordham University, graduated in 1923 and by this time was deeply entrenched in the politics of New York City. John F. O'Donnell, Michael J. Quill, and William F. O'Dwyer would have many meetings, both friendly and contentious, in the years to come, during negotiations between the TWU and the City of New York.

Law Partners

A benefit promised to the members of the Transport Workers Union (TWU) in New York City Local 100 in 1940 was free legal advice. O'Donnell provided Local 100 members this free service, three nights a week, for twelve weeks. After the twelve weeks were up, O'Donnell continued to work at the union hall without compensation. Primary among O'Donnell's responsibilities was the handling of the workmen's compensation cases.

One of O'Donnell's more interesting compensation cases involved a union member called "Joe H." According to O'Donnell:

> Around 1942, Joe was a conductor for Fifth Avenue Coach Company on a double decker bus. As a conductor he made $40 a week. His bus-run traveled up Fifth Avenue to 59th Street and then across the 59th Street Bridge to Northern Boulevard. Northern Boulevard ran under the El train [elevated train]. The El train was held overhead by support posts. The buses traveled down the Boulevard between the posts. When it was time for a bus to stop, the bus driver pulled the bus over to the curb on the far side of the post.

On this particular day, Joe's bus was going along Northern Boulevard underneath the El. Concurrently a Bond Bread truck was parked at the curb so that the driver could make a bread delivery. When the bread delivery was finished, the Bond Bread truck driver pulled out onto the Boulevard in front of Joe's bus. The bus driver swerved trying to avoid hitting the bread truck. In so doing, the bus ran into the El pillar and the driver was killed. Some of the passengers had serious injuries and Joe—the conductor—hurt his back.

All in all, Joe was pretty badly banged up and had to spend time in the hospital. Mr. Tierney, who handled workmen's compensation for the Fifth Avenue Coach Company, came to see Joe at the hospital. Tierney assured Joe that he would receive the maximum amount of money allowed under workmen's compensation. He would receive $25 a week. Tierney added that the Company's President, John E. McCarthy, said that Fifth Avenue Coach Company would personally see to it that Joe was well cared for.[42]

Some of Joe's buddies felt that he was, in fact, not at all "well cared for" by the Company. Although Joe was not a very ardent union man, his buddies assured him that he was entitled to advice from the Union's compensation lawyer. So finally, Joe did go to the union hall to seek advice from John O'Donnell.

After listening to Joe, O'Donnell explained what his rights were under the Workmen's Compensation Law. Since Joe was already receiving the maximum workmen's compensation, there was nothing O'Donnell could do for him in that respect. However, the issue of the Bond Bread Company was not resolved. Joe could sue the Bond Bread Company. O'Donnell added, "It was very nice of Mr. Tierney and Mr. McCarthy to be concerned, but if I were you Joe, I'd protect myself."[43] Joe left the union hall after he had told O'Donnell that he would think it over. It was two years before Joe returned for additional advice.

When he returned to the union hall, Joe complained to O'Donnell that the Company had "done him dirty." The Fifth Avenue Coach Company had cut his compensation to $15 a week.

GROWING AND BECOMING 55

This happened after the trial in which the widow of the bus driver sued Fifth Avenue Coach Company in her claim for the loss of her husband. During these proceedings, Joe was called as a witness. O'Donnell described his imagined impression of the scene with Joe in the courtroom:

> Joe, the dapper man with a cane, went up on the stand and broke down in tears, talking about his friend the bus driver. Joe wasn't acting; he was not that kind of a guy. The jury had all kinds of sympathy. They awarded the widow $60,000, payable by the Fifth Avenue Coach Company. In the early 1940s that was a tremendous amount of money.[44]

Joe seriously hurt the Fifth Avenue Coach Company with his testimony, so John E. McCarthy no longer felt any obligation to care for Joe. Thus his compensation was cut.

Joe was finally ready to sue the Bond Bread Company, remembering that O'Donnell had told him that this was an option. O'Donnell explained:

> Joe, I did tell you that you could sue. But two years have passed and your right to sue Bond Bread Company is gone. Your right to sue has passed to the Fifth Avenue Coach Company. Now they have to give you permission to sue. If the accident was the fault of the Bond Bread Company, after two years, Fifth Avenue Coach has the right to sue Bond Bread. Fifth Avenue Coach has the right to get back the money that they paid you these past two years in compensation. Between you and me, Joe, I know damned well what happened. McCarthy and the Bond Bread Company made a deal. They have settled the claims of the people who were riding the bus. They settled them all up between themselves. You're not going to get permission [to sue].[45]

O'Donnell proposed that Joe get a second opinion. He told Joe that he would mail him his files and suggested that Joe take them to any lawyer he preferred. However, O'Donnell pleaded, "Please don't pay the lawyer any money. If you have a legitimate lawsuit here, there is a lot of money involved. The lawyer can take your case on a percentage basis."[46]

Joe did go to see another lawyer, Carl K. Harten. Harten called O'Donnell and they talked it over, agreeing that Joe had no claim. In the meantime, O'Donnell did the best he could do for Joe. He fought for workmen's compensation and got Joe back his maximum compensation of $25 a week, at least for a while.

In due time, Mr. Tierney of the Fifth Avenue Coach Company gave Joe a good job in the swing room at 110th Street at the edge of Harlem. A swing room is where one crew gets off a bus and another waiting crew takes over. Joe's job was to sit in the swing room and keep an eye on things. The job was only for the afternoons. Joe lived in Queens, so in the morning he would take the bus to 59th Street and then cross over and take the uptown bus to 110th Street.

About six months later, John O'Donnell got a phone call from the Metropolitan Hospital on Long Island. Joe was in the hospital again. When O'Donnell went to visit Joe, there was a new tale of woe. As Joe was on his way to work, he crossed Fifth Avenue to catch the bus to 110th Street. Unfortunately, as he crossed, another Fifth Avenue bus had come along and hit him. Besides being banged up, Joe was upset because he remembered that O'Donnell had told him he could not sue the Fifth Avenue Coach Company.

"On the contrary," O'Donnell assured Joe, "when you were walking across Fifth Avenue, that wasn't in the course of your employment. You were just a pedestrian like everybody else. Of course you can sue Fifth Avenue Coach Company."

O'Donnell started the action. Fifth Avenue Coach claimed that most of Joe's injuries were the result of his prior application. O'Donnell was quick to point out that all the medical reports of the Fifth Avenue Coach Company's doctor claimed that Joe was completely recovered from the accident that had occurred when he was a conductor on the double-decker bus. The case was wrapped up at that point: "So Carl and I never went to trial. We got an excellent settlement for Joe. Joe recovered rapidly after that. That's how Carl Harten and I became partners."[47]

O'Donnell & Harten

After O'Donnell became an attorney, in October 1937, he set up a practice at 152 East 121st Street in New York City. In 1938, the address listed in his papers changed to Suite #517 at 280 Broadway. It was not until October 1944 that the firm name and address changed to O'Donnell & Harten at 291 Broadway. In 1991, my father explained why he and Harten had become partners:

> Carl saw the potential in my job with Local 100. Handling workmen's compensation cases was an entrée to what are called third-party actions. Handling workmen's compensation, you get whatever fee the referee allows and it's usually very small. In a tough case, you might get $20. A third party action would be an independent lawsuit where I would have a percentage retainer.
>
> Carl was the son-in-law of Abraham N. Levy. Abe Levy was a very well known trial lawyer in those days in New York. There have always been half a dozen or so top negligence trial lawyers in New York. Abe was one of them. So, immediately after Carl and I became partners, Abe turned over to me the trials in Queens County. He just didn't do so well over there. An Irishman would do better.[48]

Queens County had a large concentration of Catholics both in the general population and in the legal and political circles. And at the time it was believed that an Irish lawyer would have been more likely than his Jewish counterpart to receive a favorable jury ruling in such an environment.

By the mid 1940s, in addition to his work as an advisor to Michael Quill, O'Donnell was becoming more and more involved in the new field of labor law. Harten, on the other hand, was not interested in the labor law branch of the practice. Eventually, each lawyer went his own way.

O'Donnell & Schwartz

John O'Donnell and Asher Schwartz met and became good friends while they both worked for the New York City Council. Schwartz stayed with the New York City Council slightly longer than O'Donnell did. City Councilman Robert K. Straus and Councilwoman Genevieve B. Earle, for whom Schwartz worked, were reelected while Quill, with whom O'Donnell was associated, was not. According to Schwartz, the job with the City Council ended for him when he went to Washington to join the Department of Justice. His time with the Justice Department was interrupted by three years in the Army. He was back at the Justice Department in 1946. Schwartz explained how the partnership was formed:

> After I came back from the army, John and I met, just socially. We discussed the law practice that John had developed during the period after he left the City Council. He was representing various unions: a division of Local 3, Local 56, and the Firemen and Oilers Union. He suggested the possibility of my leaving the Department and joining him in a new firm in New York. . . . We had several meetings, sometimes in New York, sometimes in Bethesda, where I was living at the time. I decided that the partnership was a good idea. So we agreed.[49] As I recall it, we let Carl Harten know about it and indicated that he could be a part of it if he wished. Harten declined the offer.[50]

The firm of O'Donnell & Schwartz was formed in 1948. Their office was located at 51 Broadway. Schwartz explained how the firm associated itself with the TWU:

> One evening we were both about to go home. We read in the evening paper that the Transport Workers Union had fired Harry Sacher [TWU's general counsel].[51] So we kind of looked at each other and we didn't go home. We went over to the Union Hall. When we got there, we spoke to the powers, like Mike [Quill] and Matty Guinan and a few others. We volunteered our services. We said, "If you would like to have interim counsel while you replace Harry Sacher, we're available." They agreed with that because John had a very good relationship with Mike Quill—a personal relationship. I had also met Mike so he knew me. We then became interim counsels to Local 100, TWU.[52]

The O'Donnell & Schwartz partnership took shape without any complicated paperwork. Agreements were made by discussion and a handshake. David Rosen, in retrospect many years later, provided the best assessment of what the partnership was like:

GROWING AND BECOMING 59

> You know the relationship between them was really inspiring for anybody who is interested in practicing law. They never had a formal partnership agreement until numbers of other people got involved in it. I always thought to myself that if you really want to have a real partnership, that's the way you want to do it.... I always used to enjoy seeing what a good relationship they had. They were very different kinds of lawyers. I don't mean just in terms of who the clients were that they mainly advised but they had a different perspective on things. They complemented one another. I think Asher was much more of a traditional legal thinker and John could always turn things over and look at things from an odd perspective. He could look at a situation and say maybe there is a way out—another way to look at this.[53]

In an earlier opportunity that I had to talk with David Rosen, he recounted a story that illustrated my father's way of turning things over and catching the other perspective as well as his way with words. It concerns going to court with not much to say. According to Rosen:

> It was in the Quill era, and it had to do with the Pennsylvania Railroad. I asked your father what it was like—"you must have gone into court a whole lot of times having absolutely nothing to say...." O'Donnell replied, "I'll tell you about one of those times"—he [O'Donnell] said he went in there [to court]—made his usual argument that was designed to have a lot of words in it. This was down in Philadelphia and the judge, against his [O'Donnell's] expectations, said, "You've really given me something to think about." The judge told both lawyers, "Come back in tomorrow morning after I've thought about it." O'Donnell quickly called Quill and told him, "I may have beaten the injunction." Quill said, "You beat that injunction and you're fired."[54]

If the injunction had been brought against the union, it would have prevented a strike that the union leadership did not want to call in the first place. If the injunction was defeated, the unwanted strike would have taken place.

This story about the injunction brings to my mind a response to a question I had asked my father. I was curious about how he, as a labor lawyer, balanced the requirements of the law with the desires of the union membership. At the time I questioned him, my father's experiences included his role as General Counsel to the American Postal Worker's Union [APWU], so he incorporated the attitudes and comments by the APWU's president, Moe Biller. As with other union leaders, Moe relied on my father for advice. My father explained:

> When Moe has a problem and turns, for instance, to me for help, he'll invariably say, "I'm not talking to you as a lawyer. I'm talking to you," in Moe's own language, "as a million years of experience." When labor leaders like Quill or Moe Biller have a particular problem, they may need action. They may need to do something, because of the parties of the situation, because of the reputation of the union as a fighting organization.
>
> There are many times a union leader has to fight. When a union leader asks for counsel, . . . some lawyers would research the problem, know all the risks there are, and why it would be much better not to do anything. But that's not what the labor leader wants. He says, "Look I've got to do something and this is what I think is best to do and I'm going to do it." And you're in with him on it. You know what he's going to do, you know the risks involved, and you prepare and are ready to defend against those risks. In a vigorous, aggressive labor union, the leadership is always running risks.
>
> Something else that relates to that—in the old craft unions, the local unions didn't have lawyers. The international unions may have had a lawyer but not for collective bargaining. There was no collective bargaining in those days. When the industrial unions were created, . . . many of the lawyers who went to work for the unions were at previous service with the National Labor Relations

GROWING AND BECOMING

Board or some labor relations board. But in those days we [lawyers] were a part of the policy-making body of the union. Lawyers were in the CIO. The General Counsel of the union was always very close to the National President. He might not be a member of the executive board, but he attended most of the executive board meetings, as I do today in the Postal Workers and as I do today in the Transport Workers.

Even though I do [attend most meetings], my position in both [TWU and APWU] has been—I shouldn't use the word "downgraded" but it's not the same as it had been—because there are many in both unions now who resent lawyers, who feel, "What the hell, we know this business and we know how things should be done, and we're the ones that are elected by the membership, not them."

If you have good rapport and if you do your job properly, you [the labor lawyer] still have a strong voice at the top policy-making level. But in many unions, the policy-making function of the lawyer has been eliminated. He is a lawyer. He is a guy that's paid to work out their pension-plan problems and that sort of thing.[55]

ENDNOTES

[1] O'Donnell's statement in a letter to Councilman B. Charney Vladeck, January 20, 1938. The original is among the papers of Eileen O'Donnell Sheehan, Charleston, SC.
[2] "Support Pledged for Blanket Code," *The New York Times*, July 22, 1933, p. 5.
[3] Brian Bain, "The NLRB: The Wagner Act of 1935," University of St. Francis, 2002. March 26, 2006. <http://www.stfrancis.edu/ba/ghkickul/stuwebs/btopics/works/wagner.htm>.
[4] *Brief History of the American Labor Movement*, 5th ed. (Washington, D.C.: U.S. Department of Labor, Bureau of Labor Statistics, 1976), p. 23.
[5] Paul Lukas and Maggie Overfelt, "UPS: United Parcel Service," *FSB: Fortune Small Business*, April 2003, p. 24.
[6] United Parcel Service, "Company History: Timeline, 1930-1980." 1994-2006. March 26, 2006. <http://www.ups.com/content/corp/about/history/1980.html>.
[7] John F. O'Donnell, Telephone interview, July 17, 1991. In 1992, my father once again came in contact with Ted Johnson, the former UPS vice president. After all those years,

the fact that Johnson would still remember my father made him proud. His pride was evident when he shared the experience with me, saying:
> Let me tell you an interesting story. Gwynne gets this magazine about stock, and there was an article in it this week about a fellow that had about seventy million dollars. He was giving thirty-six million dollars to some charities. I read it and there was something that struck me as unusual about it. The man had started life with the United Parcel Service in the 1920s. Some of this money he had left had to go to the children of United Parcel employees. The name of the man was Theodore R. Johnson, Del Ray Beach, Florida. So I got on the telephone, called Del Ray Beach, asked them if they had a telephone number for Theodore R. Johnson. They gave me the telephone number. I called that number. Ted Johnson came on. He had been a Vice President, labor relations. I recognized his voice right away. He's 90. We talked about Courtney and Hayes and things. I am writing to him.

John F. O'Donnell, Telephone interview, February 4, 1992
[8] John F. O'Donnell, Telephone interview, July 17, 1991.
[9] Letters and papers found in the UPS files, Tamiment Library, New York University. Courtesy of the Tamiment Library, New York University.
[10] Letters and papers found in the UPS files, Tamiment Library, New York University. Courtesy of the Tamiment Library, New York University.
[11] John F. O'Donnell, Telephone interview, August 4, 1991.
12 Sam Kovenetsky, Telephone interview, August 11, 1991.
[13] The term "closed shop" is used to signify an establishment employing only members of a labor union. Bartleby 9 April 2006 <www.bartleby.com/65/cl/closedsh.html>.
[14] The press release sent from O'Donnell's office at 230 Broadway, New York City; copy in O'Donnell's papers at Tamiment Library, New York University. Courtesy of the Tamiment Library, New York University.
[15] John F. O'Donnell, Telephone interview, December 1, 1991.
[16] "Macy Uses United Parcel," *The New York Times*, June 27, 1946, p. 36.
[17] "Strike Threatens to Close Macy's," *The New York Times*, July 11, 1946, p. 13.
[18] Lawrence Resner, "2 Hurt as Violence Marks Macy Strike," *The New York Times*, July 13, 1946, p. 3.
[19] Sam Kovenetsky, Telephone interview, August 11, 1991.
[20] John F. O'Donnell, Telephone interview, December 1, 1991.
[21] John F. O'Donnell, Telephone interview, August 4, 1991.
[22] Sam Kovenetsky, Telephone interview, August 11, 1991.
[23] Sam Kovenetsky, Telephone interview, August 11, 1991.
[24] Sam Kovenetsky, Telephone interview, August 11, 1991.
[25] August Heckscher, with Phyllis Robinson, *When LaGuardia Was Mayor: New York's Legendary Years* (New York: Norton, 1978), p. 183.
[26] John F. O'Donnell, Telephone interview, July 17, 1991.
[27] "B.C. Vladeck Dies: City Councilman," *The New York Times*, October 31, 1938, p. 1.
[28] Copy of a clipping from the *Irish Echo*, December 7, 1938, found in John F. O'Donnell's papers in Katonah, NY.
[29] Copy of a clipping from the the *Irish Echo*, December 7, 1938.
[30] "Labor Party Is Key," *The New York Times*, November 3, 1937, p. 1.
[31] John F. O'Donnell, Telephone interview, February 10, 1991.
[32] Mike Quill sailed for Ireland to marry Molly O'Neill in December 1937. He was not present when the majority leader was elected so his vote was not counted.
[33] John F. O'Donnell, Telephone interview, July 18, 1990.

34 John F. O'Donnell, Personal interview, December 28, 1989.
35 John F. O'Donnell, Telephone interview, February 10, 1991.
36 John F. O'Donnell, Telephone interview, July 18, 1990.
37 Resolution found in the papers of Michael J. Quill, Tamiment Library, New York University. Courtesy of the Tamiment Library, New York University.
38 The Catholic Church leaders were very vocal in their denunciation of the Communists and encouraged their members to do the same.
39 John F. O'Donnell, Speech found in the papers of Michael J. Quill, Wagner Labor Archives, Tamiment Library, New York University. Courtesy of the Tamiment Library, New York University.
40 John F. O'Donnell, Telephone interview, August 25, 1991. I never followed up on this statement to discover why my father said going to Washington would mean joining the Communist Party.
41 For this election, I can remember that my brother, Sean, and I passed out campaign literature for my father in our apartment complex in Parkchester.
42 John F. O'Donnell, Telephone interview, August 25, 1991.
43 John F. O'Donnell, Telephone interview, August 25, 1991.
44 John F. O'Donnell, Telephone interview, August 25, 1991.
45 John F. O'Donnell, Telephone interview, August 25, 1991.
46 John F. O'Donnell, Telephone interview, August 25, 1991.
47 No paperwork has been found for this partnership.
48 John F. O'Donnell, Telephone interview, August 25, 1991.
49 Again, no paperwork has been found for the original O'Donnell & Schwartz partnership.
50 Asher Schwartz, Personal interview, Schwartz's office, 501 Fifth Avenue, New York, New York, July 11, 1991.
51 Harry Sacher, a Communist, was fired during the Communist purge of TWU.
52 Asher Schwartz, Personal interview, July 11, 1991.
53 David B. Rosen, Personal interview, December 23, 2003. In 1991, during most of my written communication with my father, his office letterhead confirmed the growth over the years. It named the firm as O'Donnell, Schwartz, Glanstein & Rosen. In addition, the associates were Malcom A. Goldstein, Carl Rachlin, Manlio Di Preta, and Virginia Pettinelli.
54 David B. Rosen, Personal interview, March 25, 2002.
55 John F. O'Donnell, Telephone interview, July 19, 1990.

Henry and Ellen O'Donnell
Around 1906

Johnny O'Donnell around 1909

St. Eunan's School in County
Donegal, Ireland

Lily, Teresa, Harry, Paddy and
Louis Around 1928

GROWING AND BECOMING 65

Gwynne Large around 1933

John O'Donnell as a Fordham University Law School Graduate in June 1933

John O'Donnell and Charlie Connolly At the "Irish Echo" in 1933

John and Gwynne O'Donnell Around 1935

A MAN FROM BRUCKLESS

John O'Donnell's Naturalization Paper

John O'Donnell and Asher Schwartz
In 1952

John O'Donnell around 1952

John O'Donnell at the family
Home in Bruckless, County Donegal
Ireland around 1990

I want to present to you at this time, one who has been working with the Transport Workers Union for many years, one who was in our first fight in the TWU in 1934, and who never made too much noise, but who worked quietly, and who is now our General Counsel—John O'Donnell

Michael J. Quill [1]

Chapter Four
THE TRANSPORT WORKERS UNION

From the time O'Donnell started in labor law, to this very day, there have been jurisdictional battles between unions. Some of the dissension comes right down to basic differences in philosophy, as craft unions and industrial unions embody many philosophical differences. It was important for O'Donnell to understand these differences and respect them in his role as legal advisor during negotiations.

Craft Vs Industrial Unions

In 1888, the American Federation of Labor (AFL) began organizing street railway workers into federal craft unions-workers grouped together according to their trade. In 1893, the AFL issued a charter to the Amalgamated Association of Street and Electric Railway Employees of America.[2] As the union membership grew, an internal struggle developed in the AFL over the question of whether unions should be organized to include all workers in an industry or whether the unions should be organized strictly on a craft or occupational basis. For instance, membership in the Amalgamated Transit Union reflected the different types of jobs in the transit industry. It was divided up into crafts: motormen, conductors, guards, brakemen, janitors, porters, laborers, etc. Each craft was in its own group, and unfortunately, the groups eventually became antagonistic and competitive with one another.[3] In examining the transit industry in general and Amalgamated in particular, James J. McGinley commented, "Actually, Amalgamated lost out by missing a natural tendency to exclusively industrial unionism within its field of local transportation."[4]

This issue of craft versus industrial unionism would become much more complicated over time, and ultimately would bring about modifications of the methods used in collective bargaining. For instance, as my father explained to me, in the old AFL craft unions as well as in the craft unions today, the local unions usually do the bargaining. "Very often," my father said, "the locals are more powerful than their international union. For instance, the Teamsters' International organization is powerful, but some of the Teamsters' locals, in their own areas, are just as powerful."[5]

The Congress of Industrial Organizations (CIO) approached collective bargaining the industrial way. A CIO union was an industry-wide union; thus it did not categorize unions by crafts. In New York City, for example, the Transport Workers Union (TWU), as an industrial union, represented all of the employees of the Fifth Avenue bus company, not just one group or craft. Distinguishing between the TWU and the Amalgamated, O'Donnell added:

> The Amalgamated followed the old AFL way of bargaining. This meant that the International Union maintained the strike fund, but it didn't do any bargaining for the local. In New York City, it was the business of the local to bargain. If the negotiations broke down, the international union didn't send them any help. In more recent times, some help was provided. For example, if the local wanted an economist or something similar, the international would help. However,

THE TRANSPORT WORKERS UNION

this was not true in the old days. The locals were very independent. If the local called a strike, its members wouldn't get strike benefits unless the international approved, because the international was very jealous of its strike fund.[6]

Employers Fight Back

As unions got stronger, the employers used various means to resist employees' demands. They used every political and economic weapon at their disposal, including the courts and the politicians who wrote and passed stringent anti-labor laws. As unions were forming in the late 1800s, management, including management in the transit industry, hired Pinkerton agents to infiltrate these unions.[7] At one time, some of the men working on the transit jobs were more Pinkerton agent than they were transit worker. Companies also took steps to prevent the unionization of their workers by establishing company unions, raising wages, and forcing workers to sign individual non-union contracts.

Forcing a strike was one of the techniques employed by the infiltrating Pinkertons. For instance, when a group of transit workers was struggling to get a union going, a Pinkerton agent planted by the employer would urge the group to strike. When the workers did strike, they were usually poorly prepared; in addition to that, management would then know who the union organizers were and fire them.[8]

In time, employers met the occasional strikes, strike threats, sit downs, and similar union activity with injunction proceedings that required a defense by the union's general counsel. To this end, the legal department of every union has had to assume far greater burdens because of the extent to which the law, the courts, and governmental agencies have intruded into the affairs of labor unions.[9]

Transit Before TWU

Prior to 1934, with the exception of the craft-oriented Amalgamated, the entire transit industry in New York City was either non-union or was under company-union domination. In 1916, the Interborough Rapid Transit Company (IRT) set up a company union officially known as the Brotherhood of IRT Company Employees. O'Donnell referred to the Brotherhood in a speech honoring the late Gerald O'Reilly, one of TWU's founders, at the Robert F. Wagner Archives in New York City in January of 1991. O'Donnell recalled that this was the first union membership that O'Reilly (as well as all transit workers in the late 1920s) maintained:

> Before the TWU was born, Gerald, in order to get a job and hold a job, had to join the Brotherhood—the old Paddy Connolly Brotherhood. To get a job in transit at that time, there were a few places, mainly liquor stores, gin mills, around that had contact with Connolly. You went there and you got a reference to Paddy Connolly. You got a card from Paddy Connolly and then you got the job. If you lost that card, you lost the job. When the TWU was getting going, Paddy Connolly held a meeting up in a hall where the Polo Grounds used to be. In the course of the meeting Mike [Quill] made some remark and PJ [Paddy Connolly] pointed to him and said, "Look, that man is a red." Mike jumped up and said, "I'd rather be a red than a rat."[10]

Paddy Connolly's Brotherhood was a company union, and company interests were its main focus. Because the workers' interests were so clearly secondary, Quill felt that Connolly was a "rat."

Every Brotherhood member had to sign a "yellow-dog" contract—a contract stating that the individual could not join a bona fide union. In 1932, Congress passed the Norris-LaGuardia Act, which outlawed "yellow-dog" contracts. At the time, the average transit work week was 12 hours a day, 7 days a week, with no vacation, no paid holidays, and no sick leave. A pension plan was also forced on the workers. Although it was presented as "voluntary," most employees had to contribute. Circumstances such as these forced a handful of workers, in 1933, to meet in secret and lay the foundations for the Transport Workers Union among IRT employees.

A New Union

At the time of the secret meetings, those few transit workers who had gathered decided to form the new union along industrial lines rather than follow the craft-union model. In so doing, they ensured that all workers in a specific transit company would be in one union. That was the initial step. Secrecy was essential.

THE TRANSPORT WORKERS UNION 71

Secrecy among Irish immigrants was by then an ingrained trait, and the majority of the IRT employees in 1933 were, in fact, Irish. The concept of secrecy was used by James Stephens, an Irishman who in the mid 1800s had become involved with radical and revolutionary secret societies in Paris. During that time, he became conscious of a new approach to the problems of Ireland. Stephens was determined that informers should not break his organization, the United Irish Brotherhood, so he gradually set up an elaborate system of security. This secret society consisted of closed "circles" in which only one member of each circle was supposed to know only one member of any other circle.[11] This was the same device Michael J. Quill and Gerald O'Reilly used in 1934 when organizing in closed circles. All this was necessitated by the presence of Pinkerton agents.

O'Donnell explained the background of the formation of the Transport Workers Union (TWU) in his 1991 speech in New York City:

> Gerald [O'Reilly] and I met about fifty-seven years ago, in 1934. We were both members of THE JAMES CONNOLLY CLAN NA GAEL AND IRA CLUB of New York. I worked for the *IRISH ECHO* at that time and Gerald was a conductor in the subway, in the IRT. Gerald came over to the *IRISH ECHO* every week with a story for me to run in the paper. The stories were meant to be helpful in the organizing.[12]
>
> The young fellows of the IRA clubs had their headquarters in the Tara Ballrooms on West 66th Street. After a meeting they would go across the street to a little coffee shop. And it was there, in 1933 that the talk of a union was born. That's where the union was formed because the Pinkerton couldn't get in.
>
> The Communist Party played a very important role in the founding of the Transport Workers Union, but it was ***not*** the original group. It did not help ***start*** the union. The small group that decided to form a union needed money. They went to the Ancient Order of Hibernians (AOH). Quill and O'Reilly stressed to organization members that they had to work seven days a week and didn't get time off

even to go to Mass. The group of workers wanted money and help to start a union. AOH's response was, "Sorry we can't get involved. We can't get involved in politics."

The group then went to the Friendly Sons of St. Patrick. The Friendly Sons pointed out to them that one of the top men in the IRT management was a member of the Friendly Sons organization. The Friendly Sons couldn't help them.

Now there was one member of that small group [of transit workers] who was also a member of the Communist Party, and his name was Tom O'Shea. Tom O'Shea suggested to the group that they go to the Communist Party and ask for help. Michael Quill, Gerald O'Reilly, Michael Cloone, and a couple of others were members of that small delegation. They went to Party headquarters at 80 East 13th Street in Manhattan. They met with Earl Browder, Israel Amter, Rose Worters and other Communist Party leaders. Israel Amter gave them a dressing down as to the difficulty, the impossibility of organizing transit workers in New York. They were not reliable. You could not depend on them. They were not union kind of people. He cited the illustrations of what had happened before in the previous strikes that were broken by the infiltration of beakies.[13] Mike and Gerald assured the Party leaders that, "There are no beakies going to get into our group, because we don't have any beakies in the IRA."

Despite the difficult time they had with Amter at that meeting, the Communist Party did promise them support of two kinds: one was financial support, and the other was to send them some experienced men to help them organize. They sent them John Santo, Maurice Forge, and Bubbles Lee [Leo Rosenthal].

The dues at that time in the union were ten cents a week. There weren't that many in the union, so it couldn't pay very much. The Communist Party subsidized the union in its earlier days. It paid the rent at 153 West 64th Street. Without the Communist Party, the union as we know it would never have gotten started.[14]

THE TRANSPORT WORKERS UNION   73

The date of the founding of the Transport Workers Union (TWU) was fixed at April 12, 1934, when Santo and Hogan first met with the Clan group in Stewart's Cafeteria at Columbus Circle. Shortly after that initial meeting, a lawyer, Harry Sacher, was assigned to handle the new union's legal problems, and John Santo and Austin Hogan (also known as Austin DeLoughrey) were assigned as organizers. Each Clan member was assigned the task of organizing in his own shop, depot, or barn. In the early formative months, each new recruit met only with his particular organizer and only the organizers met together, usually with Santo, Hogan, and Forge in attendance.[15]

At an August 1935 meeting of the Delegates' Council, the organizers decided that Quill, then a subway change-maker on the IRT, and Douglas MacMahon, a BMT mechanic, should resign from their transit jobs to work full time for the Union. Quill recalled this time at a convention seventeen years later:

> At the meeting in the Odd Fellows Hall on the 10th of August, 1935, . . . a small group of us known as Delegates Council [made a decision]. Then and there it was decided that I should write a letter to the Interborough Company of New York saying, "Greetings, we have news for you; we are building an independent union and I have been chosen by the Delegates Council to take a leave of absence and work full time." And I did. I was never answered so fast by the Interborough Company. They said, "Go and don't come back."[16]

Douglas MacMahon was one of the few in the inner circle who had no Clan connections, even though he was of Irish descent. All others began their associations and built their trust in each other at Clan meetings. The officers were each paid $18 a week, which again was made possible by a subsidy from the Communist Party. On January 26, 1936, in Room "C" at 153 West 64th Street, Michael Quill was elected President of the Transport Workers Union, Douglas MacMahon became Vice-President, and John Santo won the Secretary-Treasurer position.

Since the TWU wanted to form along industrial lines, it had problems almost immediately in the AFL. In the AFL, the industrial or craft organization issue arose in earnest at the 1935 AFL convention. A few weeks after the convention, a "Committee for Industrial Organization" was formed. John L. Lewis, president of the United Mine Workers Union, was chairman of the committee. Its stated purpose was to promote the organizations of workers in mass-production and unorganized industries and to encourage their affiliation with the AFL.[17] The "Committee for Industrial Organization" changed its name in 1938 to Congress of Industrial Organizations (CIO).

Late in 1937, it was reported that the AFL was considering an action of expulsion of all unions associated with the CIO:

> At the meeting it was said that Michael Quill, president of the Transport Workers Union, told the AFL committee that his union had grown from 1,000 to 90,000 in the last three years, that it had not received any assistance from the AFL, which had asked it to divide itself up among twenty craft unions. Mr. Quill ended by asking the AFL committee whether the federation would issue an industrial charter to his union.
>
> According to Mr. Quill, he and several associates went to Detroit several years ago and called on W. D. Mahon, president of AFL Street Car Men's Union. Mahon refused to give them a charter because the Street Car Union had spent several million dollars in attempting to organize the transport workers of New York City and had failed.
>
> Later, said Mr. Quill, the Machinist Union of the AFL, which was engaged in a jurisdictional dispute with the Street Car Union, welcomed the new organization, according to it the right of retaining all members of various crafts. Then, he said, the Street Car Union laid claim to some of the union's men, while other craft unions made similar demands.
>
> The AFL, Mr. Quill added, sought to have the new union turn its craft members over to existing unions, but it refused to do so and obtained a charter in the CIO.[18]

Finally on June 2, 1937, William Green, president of the AFL, instructed the New York Central Trades and Labor Council to drop

THE TRANSPORT WORKERS UNION 75

all locals affiliated with the CIO. The TWU was suspended from the AFL.

At the same time, to add more strength to the transit industry, an attempt was made to unite TWU and the Amalgamated Transit Union. Unfortunately, basic philosophical differences were difficult to overcome. As O'Donnell explained:

> The Amalgamated Transit Union had a couple of million dollars in strike funds and the TWU had nothing in a strike fund. The Amalgamated owned a building in Washington and the TWU then owned a building nowhere. So it was very hard to merge the two organizations. This was especially true since the TWU was the larger and the more aggressive. It was difficult because philosophically they were different.
>
> In the earlier days in the Amalgamated, the locals did all the bargaining and they had a great deal of independence. With the TWU, the international union not only helped, but actually did most of the bargaining.... The TWU had international representatives assigned around the country where they had larger locals. The international representatives really did most of the bargaining, if not all of it. The contract would [then] have to be submitted for ratification to members of the locals. It is that very close relationship that had its roots in the communist influence in the early days of TWU. Because they were interested in the finances, that interest permeated the operation in the TWU.[19]

Crowning the activities of three and a half years, the First National Convention of the Transport Workers Union of America (now calling itself an International union) took place on October 4, 1937. It started with a grand parade and a public opening in Madison Square Garden, where John L. Lewis; Sidney Hillman; Pennsylvania's Lieutenant-Governor Thomas Kennedy; Heywood Broun; and Michael J. Quill were the keynote speakers.[20] As *The New York Times* reported:

> The Transport Workers Union, formerly an affiliate of the American Federation of Labor, joined the CIO ranks last

May. Since that time it has made rapid progress on the City's rapid transit, streetcar and bus lines and in the taxi-cab field.[21]

Immediately after the convention, Mike Quill and a small group of leaders attempted to organize in the Philadelphia Transit system. The TWU was on the move. New York City's Local 100 remained, however, the backbone of the International union and continued to make great strides forward.

TWU Takes On The Communists

"During TWU's first thirteen years [1933-1946], while Earl Browder was General Secretary of the [Communist] party, Mike and his fellow TWU leaders maintained a close relationship with the Party," according to Gerald O'Reilly, one of the founders of TWU.[22] In a 1991 telephone interview, my father explained to me:

> In 1947, Mike [Quill] was still going along with the party as long as the party went along with him. Mike had always stuck to the five-cent fare. He had taken the strong populace line, "the nickel fare or no fare at all". Earl Browder, who was a good friend of Mike's and knew Mike's problems, reasoned with him. "Now look Mike, the union is more important than anything else is. You can't save the union and save the nickel fare at the same time. You've got to drop this battle to save the fare. You're going to lose your union if you can't produce this time." So finally Mike agreed with Browder and dropped his plank about saving the nickel fare.
>
> Now he's [Quill's] looking for a wage increase for his own people. At this same time, there was trouble in the Party and Browder was removed. William Foster became the Secretary of the Party. He was a hard-nosed guy, and he went to Mike and said, "You've got to stick to the nickel fare. That's more important than anything is." Mike said, "Look you so and so, you're also telling me I've got to support Wallace.[23]" (They were also pushing for the Wallace candidacy.) Mike said, "You're going to ruin me in the

THE TRANSPORT WORKERS UNION 77

union. I won't have anybody with me, so the hell with you. I won't support Wallace and I'll forget about the nickel fare." They were the two issues at that time that Mike broke with the Party on.[24]

Quill continued to press for higher wages for his TWU members. As labor historian Joshua Freeman notes:
On April 6 [1948] the TWU struck the East Side and Comprehensive Omnibus Company. . . . The real motive for striking this small Manhattan bus company was probably to lay the basis for a renewed push for a city-wide fare increase by creating a crisis atmosphere without paralyzing the city. Reportedly, Hogan [Austin Hogan, a known Communist] had opposed calling the strike, while Quill had been its main proponent.[25]

With this strike, the battle lines were drawn. For the first time in public, Quill and the Party—in the person of Austin Hogan—were on opposite sides of the fence. The Communist Party was very much against a fare increase of any amount.

About a week later, the three largest private transit companies (New York City Omnibus Corporation, Fifth Avenue Coach Company, and Third Avenue Transit Corporation), all announced that they would not meet the TWU's wage demands unless they were allowed to increase their fares. To avoid a general transit strike, Quill asked New York City Mayor William O'Dwyer to raise the transit fare.[26] It is important here to understand that there were two different entities involved in the New York City transit system: the City-owned lines and the privately owned lines. The New York City Mayor could raise the fares on the City-owned lines only. However, if the City raised the fares, then the private lines would be able to justify raising their fares as well.

On April 16, 1948, the New York City Mayor, William O'Dwyer, met with the TWU leadership and executives from the private lines. O'Donnell gave a behind-the-scenes view:
In early '48, we were in negotiations with the Transit Authority. I say "we," the union was. The union was

demanding twenty-five cents an hour raise. Mike and I went down to see O'Dwyer about the demand. In the cab going down Mike said to me, "Look, if we can get *fifteen cents* out of Bill, we'll beat the bastards [referring to the communists on the Executive Board of TWU]." That was about all he said about what we were going to look for.

So, down we go to see Bill [Mayor O'Dwyer]. Finally Bill said, "Well, Mike, look. How much will it take for you to beat the bastards?" Those were O'Dwyer's words. And without batting an eye Mike said, "*Twenty-four* cents, Bill." "Mike, will twenty-four cents do it?" Mike said, "Look, you give me twenty-four cents and I'll beat them." Bill answered, "You've got it. Now you can go upstairs."

That same day we were meeting with the private lines people upstairs. The TWU contract [with the city-owned lines as opposed to the private lines] didn't run out until the end of the year, but the private-lines contracts ran out at the end of July, I think it was. This was towards the middle of August I'd say. So Bill said, "You go upstairs and tell them you got twenty-four cents from me." Mike said, "Bill, look, why don't you come up and tell them?" And Bill said, "Ok, ok, I'll go up."

So Bill went up and I can still see him sitting in the desk in the front of the Board of Estimate room. All the private-line owners were there, [John E.] McCarthy was there from Fifth Avenue, [Thomas F.] Fennell, [Esq.], and [John M.] MacDonald with Third Avenue. . . . Bill came up and told them, "Look, the Transit Authority is going to give a twenty-four-cent [wage] increase. Now I suggest that you people think that over." They [the owners] were all looking for a fare increase too, you see, to finance it [the wage increase].

Bill said, "I'll take care of you people. I'll be fair with you." There was silence for a while and finally one great big guy, William J. McCormick, Mr. Big, who owned McCormick Sand & Gravel, he was quite an operator in New York. He was a great big man. He stood up in the

THE TRANSPORT WORKERS UNION 79

rear of the Hall. "Bill", he said, "if you're giving them twenty-four cents, I'm giving them twenty-four cents."[27]

It was soon after this meeting with O'Dwyer that *The New York Times* reported:

> Michael J. Quill, international president of the Transport Workers Union, CIO, resigned from the American Labor Party of which he was one of the founders. In his resignation letter, Quill denounced "the screwballs and crackpots, who," he wrote, "will continue to carry on as if the Communist Party and the American Labor Party were the same house with two doors."[28]

The internal fight between right- and left-wing factions for control of the TWU reached the public showdown stage late in the summer of 1948. Michael Quill controlled Local 100 in New York City, the largest local in the TWU. The left-wing faction, however, controlled the executive board of the International. Quill predicted total victory for his anti-Communist forces at the International union's biennial convention starting in Chicago on December 6. "We will have to make changes in the constitution," Quill said, "and elect board membership based on their membership strength, one for each 2000 or 3000 dues-paying members, and not as now on committee nominations."[29] The committees were the source of the Communists' voting strength. By moving the voting power to the dues-paying members, there was a better chance of out-voting the Communists for the future election of board members.

At the convention itself, one of the proposed speakers was Harry Sacher, the union's general counsel. Sacher, however, had been dismissed in September by Quill-sympathizers from his $6000-a-year job as attorney for the TWU's Local 100. For this reason, Sacher did not show up at all in Chicago. "John F. O'Donnell, who succeeded Mr. Sacher, is now acting as Mr. Quill's legal adviser here [in Chicago]."[30] O'Donnell's post as General Counsel for Local 100 would become the stepping stone for his future position as General Counsel for the International TWU.

Sixth Biennial Convention

O'Donnell recalled the events leading up to the 1948 Convention in Chicago:

> In the earlier days of TWU, before 1948, after Local 100 got on its feet and got going as a union—it was Local 100 that financed the International's organization in the airlines. Particularly, we organized the maintenance employees and the flight attendants of Pan American. That was very, very important to the Communist Party because the flight attendants on Pan American were a communication method.
>
> Local 100 used its money very effectively, not just in Local 100, but in organizing generally in TWU. Then we fell on bad times. After unification [of the transit systems in New York City under public control in 1941], Mayor LaGuardia sent a letter out to every employee of the transit system. He didn't say, "You don't have to join a union," but he practically said that. He said, "You are now civil servants." He has a reputation of being pro-labor, but that was a dirty trick that he did to TWU. Immediately a lot of our people dropped out [of the union] thinking, "What do we need a union for, we're in the civil service." Then it soon became apparent that the civil service didn't mean that much to them.
>
> In any event, come 1948, technically Local 100 owed the International a lot of money. It was behind in its per capita. The per capita is the percentage of dues that the local pays the International. In theory we owed the International money, although the International really (although it wasn't a matter of owing) owed us their shirt. The Commies were smart.... They were going to keep the International.
>
> They first of all planned the convention for Chicago. That meant that we would have to take the Local 100 delegation to Chicago. That would be very expensive. If we didn't take our full quota of delegates, we wouldn't have much of a voice in the convention. If we were going to have any chance at the convention, we would have to get them all out there, and to get them all out there meant

THE TRANSPORT WORKERS UNION   81

money. So, where were we going to get the money? I was with Mike when we met with Phil Murray and Arthur Goldberg. Phil was then the head of the CIO and Arthur Goldberg had just replaced Lee Pressman [as CIO General Counsel].[31] In any event, Mike and I met with Arthur and Phil and explained our situation. Phil wanted to know how much it would cost us, and Mike said he'd need to have $150,000. We had to be protected against the Communists' tricks. If they thought that we were short of money, that our fellows were short of money, or we just had enough to get them out there for two or three days—they would drag that convention on and on and on—hoping that a lot of our fellows would get hungry and go home. Mike said we had to have $150,000 and Phil Murray right there and then gave Mike a check for $75,000. Then he said, "Mike, when you go back to New York, see Sidney." Sidney was Sidney Hillman, the head of the Amalgamated Clothing Workers who had been close to Roosevelt.[32]

So we came back to New York and I was referred to the bank—The Amalgamated Bank. I went to the bank and the bank said, "Sure we'll lend you $75,000. What security do you have?" We had nothing, no security.

We told O'Dwyer our problem. O'Dwyer gave us the checkoff,[33] and we mortgaged the checkoff as security for the loan. That's how we got the checkoff. Now there was a serious question as to whether it was legal or not; but there was nothing wrong with it. No man *had* to sign—it was just any man who wanted to sign. It was a voluntary checkoff. If you wanted the money taken out of your pay, you could sign the checkoff card. So the drive then was to get the checkoff card signed. And then, incidentally, we made them irrevocable for one year.[34]

Now Local 100 had enough money to bring its full quota of voting Local 100 delegates to Chicago. Their voices would be heard.
On December 3, the Communist-controlled International Executive Board approved the convention agenda and called for the elections of new officers on the day before the end of the

convention. Quill urged the delegates, some of whom were in the middle-of-the-road group in the union, to move the election up to Tuesday, December 7, 1948, the second day of the Sixth Biennial Convention in Chicago. By a 20-5 vote, Local 100 lost the first battle of the convention; the agenda was adopted for elections late in the convention, but Quill had not yet given up the fight. He was still International President of the Transport Workers Union.

On Monday afternoon of the first day of the convention, December 6, one of the first orders of business was the report of the Chairman of the Committee on Rules, Robert Franklin:

> Mr. Chairman and Delegates, our committee met and adopted the following rules unanimously. These rules that will govern the rest of the Convention have been put together with the guidance of the proceedings of the Convention recently held in Portland, the national CIO convention.... Rule 11. Order of business for the remainder of today's session: ... 6:30 PM Election of International Officers and Executive Board members.[35]

With this report, the Communist-controlled Executive Board's hope for dragging out the convention beyond the financial capability of the delegates was killed. With the same reasoning in mind, the previously approved convention agenda and further demands for a roll-call vote were ignored by Quill. The delegates voted to stand by the recommendation for an election at Monday night's session. Four of the men most closely associated with Quill in the building of the union—Austin Hogan, executive vice president, John Santo, international director of organization, Douglas L. MacMahon, secretary-treasurer, and Gerald O'Reilly, union organizer—lost their jobs in the election. My father spoke very highly of both MacMahon and O'Reilly:

> Douglas was ousted at the convention in Chicago in 1948. He opened a little candy store out in Bay Ridge, Brooklyn, for a couple of years. Mike always had a great deal of respect for MacMahon. MacMahon was a very able guy. MacMahon [was the only one who] stood up at the convention and said, "I'm a Communist." Well in any event, after a

THE TRANSPORT WORKERS UNION

couple of years, Mike snuck him back into TWU. He didn't give him an elected job; he gave him some kind of appointive job. I forget what it was. Then he ran for International Secretary Treasurer and was elected. The membership really had a great deal of respect for MacMahon.[36]

In speaking of Gerald O'Reilly, my father said:
Gerald never had very much money, although he donated a lot of it to causes in Ireland. . . . I wrote his will and I know that he left a thousand dollars to the Connolly Club; and he left a thousand dollars to the IRISH DEMOCRAT . . . because Gerald was a devoted man. The causes that he had at heart he really stuck solidly by. He never forgot where he came from; never forgot his union. He was as fine a man as I ever knew.[37]

O'Reilly likewise was returned to the TWU by a back door.[38] Also at the convention, the union membership voted out five of the international union's six vice presidents, and eleven of its seventeen executive board members.[39] The Transport Workers Union had purged its leadership of the Communist influence, but the battle was still not completely won. The Communists would continue to use their influence in the smaller locals of TWU and would manage to cause friction for some years to come.

On Thursday morning, the fourth day of the convention, Theodore W. Kheel, head of Division of Labor Relations in New York City,[40] read a message to the convention from New York City Mayor William O'Dwyer:

This is a great day for the Transport Workers Union. It is, moreover, a turning point in transit history for the people of New York City. And it is also a triumph of national scope and importance for all of the people of this country.

The reason is that the answer to Communism is contained in the historic and dramatic fight of the rank and file of the Transport Workers Union—your fight—led by Mike Quill to restore control of this great union to the rank and file.[41]

Over fifty years later, in March of 1999, Joseph Donoghue, a retired International Vice President of the TWU, recalled this particular convention:

> I went to work . . . as a bus driver in Surface Transit in 1935. Then we organized the union in Surface Transit. The union was certified in June 1936 and I was active in the union from then on.
>
> The union had a certain amount of its leadership in the Communist Party when I first joined in. That created a problem as far as I was concerned. I didn't want to disrupt or make any trouble for the union because I'd rather be with the Communists than with the management of the Company. . . . We had the president of the Local—Austin Hogan [a communist]. His real name was DeLoughrey. He came from New York Omnibus. He was a gifted man, a gifted speaker and an intelligent man—a hell of a decent man to know. Individual problems in your group, he'd break his back to help you out.
>
> There was a convention being called in Chicago. . . . . It was a kind of bitter convention to be at. . . . . As a matter of fact, I personally went in to talk to Austin Hogan to see if I could prevail on him to turn against the Communist Party. He would not, on account of his friendship with the people he was exposed to. I could understand that—anymore than I could turn on friends of mine. He was removed.
>
> It's no longer called the International Transport Workers—now it's called the Transport Workers Union of America. Originally their idea was they [the Communist Party] wanted to form an International Union. You know what that meant—it meant International with Germany and Russia. It stopped being called the International after the 1948 convention.[42]
>
> Mike and your father were as close as two human beings can be in a free world. Your father was a big asset to the Transport Workers Union in my lifetime. I think he was one of the blessings to the Transport Workers Union.[43]

THE TRANSPORT WORKERS UNION 85

While there is no denying that Mike Quill's greatest assets were his talent as an orator and his ability to play with the press, my father's greatest assets were his knowledge of both the law and human nature and his dedication to each and every worker. He made it his business to know every local, and he worked as hard for a twenty-three-member local as he would for a 1000-member local. Scoogie Ryers, Executive Assistant to the first five of the TWU's International Presidents, had high regard for my father. In a personal interview, she described what it was like to work with him:

> Your father was an all-rounder. He was like the father of the union. He could walk into a room and immediately he was one of the boys. From the beginning to the end of a contract, your father was there. Nothing was done without consulting him. He analyzed the whole. . . . He knew what every penny would buy for this and that. . . . He would call the lawyer from the other side; he had that kind of a relationship with them. We never had bad relationships with the people we dealt with. Your father would break the ice.[44]

ENDNOTES

[1] Michael J. Quill, Transcript of Thursday Afternoon Session, December 9, 1948, *Report of Proceedings: Sixth Biennial Convention*, Chicago, IL, December 6-10, 1948 [New York: Transport Worker's Union, 1949], p. 168.

[2] It has since changed its name to the Amalgamated Transit Union (also known as Amalgamated), and is in existence to this very day.

[3] John F. O'Donnell, Personal interview, July 17, 1991.

[4] James J. McGinley, *Labor Relations in the New York Rapid Transit Systems 1904-1944* (New York: King's Crown Press, 1949), p. 259. Industrial unionism meant that the union was industry-wide, not just concerned with a particular craft.

[5] John F. O'Donnell, Personal interview, July 17, 1991.

[6] John F. O'Donnell, Personal interview, July 17, 1991.

[7] Allan Pinkerton began a detective agency in 1850 and achieved both fame and notoriety as he and his men pursued bank robbers and later served as strike-breakers and union infiltrators. See Stephen H. Norwood, *Strikebreaking & Intimidation: Mercenaries and Masculinity in Twentieth-Century America* (Chapel Hill: University of North Carolina Press, 2002) (NetLibrary) and Robert P. Weiss, "Private Detective Agencies and Labour Discipline in the United States, 1855-1946," *The Historical Journal* 29.1. (March 1986): 87-107 (JSTOR).

[8] John F. O'Donnell, Telephone interview, March 10, 1991.

[9] John F. O'Donnell, *Report of the President*, 18th Constitutional Convention, October 1989, p.89.
[10] John F. O'Donnell, Mimeographed copy of speech, "Pillar of Labor for Gerald O'Reilly," given at Robert F. Wagner Labor Archive, January 16, 1991. Copy in the Tamiment Library, New York University. Courtesy of the Tamiment Library, New York University.
[11] Robert Kee, *Ireland: A History* (London: Abacus, 1995), pp. 104-106.
[12] These newspaper articles have not been found, to date.
[13] The "Beakies" were a plain-clothes security force that patrolled the transit properties as company spies. They got their name from their boss, H. L. Beakie.
[14] John F. O'Donnell, Mimeographed copy of speech, "Pillar of Labor for Gerald O'Reilly."
[15] Gerald O'Reilly, *The Birth and Growth of the Transport Workers Union*. N.p.: n.p., 1988, p. 3. Copy in the Tamiment Library, New York University. Courtesy of the Tamiment Library, New York University.
[16] Michael J. Quill, Transcript of Thursday Evening Session, December 11, 1952. *Report of Proceedings, Eighth Biennial Convention*, Philadelphia, PA, December 9-13, 1952 [New York: Transport Worker's Union, 1953], p. 170.
[17] *Brief History of the American Labor Movement*, 5th ed., Bulletin 1000, (Washington, D.C.: U.S. Bureau of Labor Statistics, 1976), p. 24.
[18] Louis Stark, "Labor Groups Firm on Terms of Peace," *The New York Times*, October 29, 1937, p. 6.
[19] John F. O'Donnell, Personal interview, July 17, 1991.
[20] Sidney Hillman founded the Amalgamated Clothing Workers of America and served as its president until 1946. A strong proponent of industrial unionism, he broke from the AFL to join John L. Lewis in organizing the CIO. *AFL-CIO* 7 April 2007 <http://www.aflcio.org/aboutus/history/history/hillman.cfm>. Heywood Broun was the president of the Newspaper Guild of America.
[21] "Lewis Will Speak in Garden Tonight," *The New York Times*, October 4, 1937, p. 6.
[22] Gerald O'Reilly, *The Birth and Growth of the Transport Workers Union*, p. 8.
[23] Secretary of Agriculture Henry A. Wallace was running for the presidency of the United States against Harry Truman in 1948.
[24] John F. O'Donnell, Telephone interview, April 14, 1991.
[25] Joshua B. Freeman, *In Transit: The Transport Workers Union in New York City, 1933-1966* (New York: Oxford University Press, 1989), p. 302.
[26] Freeman, p. 303.
[27] John F. O'Donnell, Telephone interview, August 25, 1991.
[28] "Quill Quits ALP; One of Founders," *The New York Times*, April 21, 1948, p. 22.
[29] Alexander Feinberg, "TWU Executive Board Urges Removal of 2 Leftist Chiefs," *The New York Times*, September 5, 1948, p.1.
[30] A. H. Raskin, "Illinois CIO Chiefs Shun TWU Session," *The New York Times*, December 4, 1948, p. 28.
[31] Arthur Goldberg was later to go on to become U.S. Secretary of Labor under President John F. Kennedy, Supreme Court Justice, and Ambassador to the United Nations. See more at the AFL CIO website, <http://www.aflcio.org/aboutus/history/history/goldberg.cfm>. Despite his refusal on principle in 1947 to sign an anti-Communist affidavit required of union leaders by the Taft-Hartley Act, Murray was known for his anti-Communist stance <http://www.aflcio.org/aboutus/history/history/murray.cfm>.

32 The famous phrase, "Clear it with Sidney," was allegedly coined by Franklin Delano Roosevelt referring to Sidney Hillman concerning the choice of Harry Truman as vice-presidential candidate on the 1944 Democratic ticket.
33 Checkoff gave the employer the authorization to deduct union dues from an employee's pay.
34 John F. O'Donnell, Telephone interview, April 21, 1991.
35 Transcript of Monday Afternoon Session, December 6, 1948. *Report of Proceedings, Sixth Biennial Convention*, Chicago, IL, [New York: Transport Worker's Union, 1953], p. 16.
36 John F. O'Donnell, Telephone interview, August 11, 1991.
37 John F. O'Donnell, Mimeographed copy of speech, "Pillar of Labor for Gerald O'Reilly." The Connolly Club, now the Connolly Association, was founded in London in 1938 "to work for the complete freedom of the Irish people" and to promote Irish culture. <http://www.irishdemocrat.co.uk/about/ca-history/> 7 April 2007. The *Irish Democrat* is its newspaper.
38 Gerald O'Reilly became a Local 100 delegate.
39 A. H. Raskin, "Quill Re-Elected as TWU Ousts Left From 14-year Rule," *The New York Times*, December 7, 1948, p. 1.
40 Ted Kheel was known as a voice of reason in both labor and management circles. In 1949, he also became an impartial mediator for public transit in New York City, a position in which he was involved in over thirty thousand decisions by 1982. He sought to" protect management rights and at the same time demand fairness to workers in these disputes." For more information, see the website of the Kheel Center for Labor Management Documentation and Archives at Cornell University <http://www.ilr.cornell.edu/library/kheel/about/history/theodorekheel.html>, 7 April 2007.
41 Transcript of Thursday Morning Session, December 9, 1948, *Report of Proceedings, Sixth Biennial Convention*, Chicago, IL, p. 131.
42 While the title of the TWU no longer includes the word "International," that word is used to this day to refer to the parent union.
43 Joseph Donoghue, Telephone interview, March 1, 1999.
44 Scoogie Ryers, Personal interview, January 19, 1999.

Among his [John F. O'Donnell's] early victories was getting $1.1 million in back pay for workers on the old Third Avenue Railway in 1950 and helping win a five-day, 40-hour work week in the 28-day strike of eight bus lines in 1953.[1]

Chapter Five

TWU'S LARGE CITY LOCALS

The 1940s and 1950s were crucial years for O'Donnell and for the unions. There were major tensions regarding race relations and the remnants of Communist membership. I believe that no matter what the issue, my father consistently attempted to do what was morally and ethically right, making decisions that were not always popular with the union members.

Philadelphia TWU Local 234

It was especially important at this time for O'Donnell to be familiar with the needs of the many locals of TWU. Such familiarity required his constant travel. This seemed to be particularly true in the late 1940s. Only two months after taking over the office of General Counsel for the Transport Workers Union, O'Donnell was challenged with a "walk-off" by the Philadelphia Transportation Company (PTC) employees, Local 234. The workers walked off their jobs at midnight on February 10, 1949. To deal with this situation, O'Donnell had to make sure that he was very familiar with the political background of this second largest local in the TWU. Our own understanding of this background would be incomplete without an explanation of the activities of Local 234 earlier in the decade.

1944

In Philadelphia in 1944, the Transport Workers Union (TWU) won the National Labor Relations Board election to represent the transit workers. Although O'Donnell was not yet General Counsel to the TWU, he had been Quill's advisor. Almost immediately there was a work stoppage. As O'Donnell recalled:

> We won the election in Philadelphia. We had some—although there were very few—Communists in Philadelphia then; the few there were, were active in the union and were in positions of power in the union. They were our friends for a while. World War II was going on. The split hadn't taken place yet in TWU, and Harry Sacher was the attorney. In its advance literature, TWU said: "In TWU there's no discrimination." That was one of the promises we made—but it wasn't made very loudly. Not too many of the white people, I guess, heard it. There were no mechanics that were black and certainly no drivers.[2]

The first thing that the Philadelphia Transit Company (PTC) did as soon as TWU won the election in 1944 was to promote or hire some black motorman. Up to that point, the motormen were all white, and so to protest the hiring of non-whites, the white motormen immediately struck. According to O'Donnell, "This strike was a revolt of the employees, anti-black you know. They were the motormen in the subways in Philadelphia. The strike affected some of the bus lines too, so Mike was called into Philadelphia right away."[3]

On August 1, 1944, the day the strike began, Douglas L. MacMahon, Secretary-Treasurer of the International TWU, issued the following statement:

> The Transport Workers Union knows that the vast majority of the 10,000 PTC employees are patriotic Americans

who believe in law and order and who want no part of such moves against their Government.

We appeal to them to stay on the job of transporting the millions of war workers and soldiers in the vital Philadelphia-Camden-Chester naval and military supply area.

The security of the nation calls for unity, discipline and uninterrupted work on the home front while our soldiers and sailors are fighting the most decisive battles of the war. We are confident that the good sense and devotion to America on the part of the PTC worker will prevail.[4]

On August 3 of that same year, President Franklin D. Roosevelt issued an Executive Order authorizing and directing the Secretary of War to take possession and assume control of transportation in Philadelphia. Two National Guard units were shipped immediately to Philadelphia because the trolley operation in Philadelphia was vital to the war effort. Quill met with Major General Philip Hayes in the Union League Club. According to O'Donnell, Quill explained to the General, "Look, you've got to break this strike and I'll give you all the help I can because this is a strike against blacks."[5] Quill explained to the General that it was necessary to put guardsmen on the buses to the Navy yard because he was determined to break the strike. This was not a union strike. This was a strike against the union; this was a strike against the government. General Hayes did order two guards to be placed on every bus to protect the drivers who were driving. Unfortunately, this order caused more problems than had originally existed. My father explained it to me this way:

> There was one problem. One of the National Guard regiments was from Alabama. When they got down to the Navy Yard [Philadelphia], the guards put all the blacks that were being transported from the Navy Yard in the rear of the bus. Now there was real hell to pay. The news hadn't gotten around very far yet, but immediately there was a big ruckus. Mike was called back to Philadelphia and met again with General Hayes. Quill told him, "Look, you've got to stop this. This is terrible. This is a frightful thing."

So the General ordered the soldiers to cut it out and make no discrimination at all, in any way whatever.[6]

On August 9, after the stoppage had ended, Arthur S. Meyer, Chairman of the New York State Board of Mediation, addressed a letter to Mike Quill:

> For the past fortnight all other news, including even the war news, has been eclipsed by the news from Philadelphia. What a blow you have struck against hypocrisy and faint-hearted compromise! You have forced the discrimination issue into the open and actually compelled obedience to the law as a substitute for lip service and evasion. As an important by-product, you have perhaps recaptured the Negro vote for the President [Roosevelt] after some of his fellow Democrats had done their best to lose it.[7]

Settling the strike did not, of course, settle the issue at the heart of the walk-out. While O'Donnell and Quill had exposed the malignancy, discrimination would remain an overwhelming issue for many years to come. O'Donnell always found that he was working with a Local whose support was fragile. And yet, there was a relatively quiet period for the union for the next few years. By 1949, however, tensions were heating up again, and were about to boil over.

1949

At midnight, on February 10, 1949, the Philadelphia Transportation Company (PTC) employees again walked off their jobs. At this time, O'Donnell was the TWU General Counsel, and was therefore directly involved in the negotiations. The Union was demanding a twenty-five-cent hourly pay increase while PTC was offering two cents. Ten days later, late at night, an agreement to end the strike was reached in a stormy session after a seven-hour conference of PTC and union officials in Mayor Bernard Samuel's office. An eight-cent-an-hour raise and ten "fringe" benefits were in the agreement. Although the Philadelphia Transportation Company had sought a contract of two years' duration, the contract was for one year.[8]

TWU'S LARGE CITY LOCALS

Even though the negotiations team agreed to a settlement, the union membership had to approve the contract. That would not prove to be easy. An out-of-state newspaper provided a good picture of the confusion surrounding the vote in the following description of the union rallies:

Local TWU President Andrew Kaelin announced that negotiators for the company and union had agreed on the eight-cent offer. He put it up to the membership.

Some cheered. Some booed. Many made speeches.

Kaelin called for a vote. Those in favor were to stand up. Most of the unionists remained seated. Kaelin announced the strike was over.

Opposition leaders stormed to the stage, fought for the microphone, screamed, "To hell with it."

Then Kaelin announced no decision. He summoned the workers to another mass rally.

That one started at 2 p.m. An hour earlier, the union's executive board rejected the agreement and directed the rank and file to continue on strike.

Kaelin urged acceptance. Vice President Robert High argued against it.

Then International President Michael J. Quill took over and exhorted the workers to accept the agreement.

"I don't like this contract," Quill barked, "But sometimes you have to take half a loaf or less to make an advance."

"Go back to work. Go back today. Maintain union solidarity. Don't split the union down the middle. That's what the company wants."

He called for a vote. All but 25 men stampeded to their feet and screamed acceptance.

"The strike is over," Kaelin declared.

For PTC workers, it was the third strike in six years.

High said the union "lost the strike."

"No," Quill shouted. "You now make one cent less than New York bus drivers. It took them 15 years to get $1.44. It took you four to get $1.43."

Then he fired a parting shot that drew wild cheers: "I'll be back next year."[9]

My father informed me that from that day on Quill was never welcomed by the Local 234 union leadership. There was a difference of philosophy between him and the leadership after the Communists left. My father explained:

> The new leadership were at heart, Mike thought, Christian frontiers. They were friends of Mike's now, but they weren't friends of Mike's in the old days. Mike knew them to be very hostile before the '48 convention. Mike was still a Communist at heart in a lot of ways. There was only one man in Philadelphia in the leadership that Mike got along with, and that was Andy Kaelin.[10]

Ten Months Later

Since the February 1949 contract that was finally agreed on had a duration of only one year, it was soon time to negotiate the next contract. The Negotiating Committee of Local 234 succeeded in convincing the management of the PTC to open the existing contract two months before its expiration date of February 10, 1950. Negotiations therefore began in December of 1949. By January 10, 1950, little progress had been made, so O'Donnell sent the following press release to the editor of the *Evening Bulletin*:

> The contract between the Philadelphia Transportation Company and the Transport Workers Union expires at midnight on February 10 [1950]. Representatives of the union and of the management have had eighteen conferences during the past six weeks on the union proposals. The newspapers have correctly reported that no progress toward a settlement has been made. It should be apparent now that continuance of the present conference method is fruitless. These same methods last year led up to a ten day strike. The strike was some six days old before the Board of Directors met with the union and then two conferences, with no more than five hours of vigorous discussion, brought an agreement.

> Surely it is not necessary to point out that strike is the most expensive and least satisfactory method of settling a labor dispute. It is costly to the employees, to the employers, and to the city. Animosities are created and aggravated which are detrimental to labor-management relations. And agreements worked out under pressure and tensions of a strike are rarely satisfactory. . . .
>
> The plea of inability to pay means that the management wants the employees to accept a lower wage and poorer working conditions than they are otherwise entitled to. It means that the families of Philadelphia's transit workers are to have a lower standard of living so that Philadelphia's transit system may continue to operate. That is subsidy; subsidy for which there is no moral or economic justification.[11]

My father really enjoyed telling me the story about the final conference before the contract settlement was announced to the union members. He was stressing how important it was to know your membership when making quick decisions regarding a union contract. He said that Quill really shone when it came to making quick decisive judgments.

> We were down to the tail end, and Charlie Ebert, the President of the company, was in there with his group: Hamm Connors, the lawyer, and William J. McReynolds, the Vice president for labor relations. Mike [was there with] his delegation from the Local (the Executive Board), and I was there. As a matter of fact, we knew there was a settlement, because a lot of negotiation is not necessarily done across the bargaining table.
>
> But we had one hitch, and that was the length of the contract. Charlie wanted a six-month extension. Ordinarily it was a two-year contract [ending December 1952], and Charlie Ebert wanted two years and six months [ending June 1952]. He was very adamant.
>
> Mike said, "Ah, we can't give you that Charlie. You know we can't break the mold. That's the way it's always

done—two years." But finally Mike says, "Charlie, I'll tell you what I'll do here. I'll split the difference."

You see Mike was in a position—he hadn't talked to the other members of the executive board. He didn't really have the authority to do that because the contract had to be ratified by the membership. But Mike knew what he was doing. He knew what he could sell and what he couldn't sell. And he knew that, for the money they were getting, they would take two years and three months [ending March 1952]. As long as he got money now, what happened two years from now was not critical—and money now, without striking.

Charlie jumped up, leaned across the table, "Mike, we have a deal," and shook hands. As usual, Mike said at that point, "Alright now Charlie, you know, I'd like to have a word with my board here." We were in the Transportation Company's boardroom in Philadelphia. In those days we weren't afraid of it being bugged. "Oh," Charlie said, "sure."

The board meeting had gone on for about five minutes or so when suddenly Charlie Ebert comes running in. "Michael, Michael, I've made a terrible mistake. Oh Michael, I can't go for two years and three months. That would mean the contract would be expiring in March 1952 [Spring break]. I can't go for that."

"Ah now," Michael says, "You know Charlie, we have a deal. Now you know that." Mike was in his usual way, and Charlie was all upset because his own board, his own people were telling him, "What the hell did you do that for? This guy Quill trapped you into something."

Mike just makes the suggestion off the cuff as an act of suggestions. Ebert said, "I'll tell you what I'll do, I'll take two years four months rather than two years and three months."

Mike wouldn't give it to him. But he said, "I'll tell you Charlie, I'll give you a thirty-day cooling off period." "Good." Another shake of hands. "Fine. That's it."

> Now when Hamm Connors draws up the contract, he writes the thirty-day cooling off period into the contract—but with the provision, that in the event there is no settlement [by March 1952], that it would be continued without strike for thirty days—cooling off period.[12]

Two Years Later: 1952

The story of that contract did not end there. Two years went by and O'Donnell was in Philadelphia to negotiate again. My father continued the story in the same interview:

> Management was being very stubborn. Charlie Ebert usually wasn't in the negotiation nor was Mike himself—until the very last day or so. Mike came in.... Ebert wasn't in because—what the hell he thought—he had plenty of time. He had another thirty days. Michael says, "Oh, no. We strike on the last day of the contract." "You can't," says Ebert, "The contract says there's to be a thirty-day cooling off period." "Ah," says Michael, "yes, but that was conditioned on your bargaining in good faith. You haven't bargained in good faith."
>
> Hamm Connors goes to court to get an order to "show cause." The way you get an injunction is—you first get an order to show cause. This is when you have the pressure of time. It is returnable in a day's notice, maybe less—to show cause why—showing that greater harm will be done, you know, the balance of equities, irreparable damage. So Hamm Connors gets the order to show cause why an injunction shouldn't be issued. It's set down for a hearing before Judge Kun, a big tall man with grayish hair, very Germanic-looking, crew cut; a man of about 65 who had a terrible reputation as a strict judge.
>
> I had no witnesses in Philadelphia because I knew I was dead. I knew I was going to get an injunction against me. [Many times] I never had to bother preparing a case because I was dead before I started. Mike would be photographed ripping up a piece of paper, and I had to be in the next day before the judge.

I go down to Philadelphia to represent Mike and TWU. Since I am not admitted to practice in Pennsylvania, I had to get a lawyer who practices in Pennsylvania to introduce me to the court. It's a formality. I asked Hamm Connors (Hamm and I knew each other well) to introduce me to the judge. On what you call "the return day," before the court opens, the tipstaff[13] came down to Hamm Connors and said, "Judge Kun would like to see you and Mr. O'Donnell in chambers." This is not an unusual thing.

Hamm (a big tall man from one of the big old Philadelphia law firms—conservative firm) and I went in. Hamm introduced me to the judge. We shook hands and had a very pleasant conversation for a while. We talked about the problems of transit: passengers declining, costs going up, employees restless, broken and rundown, ah, just talked generally. After about ten or fifteen minutes the Judge said, "Well look, I'd better go to work. You'll be called first."

Hamm and I go back out to the courtroom to the front part—the lawyers' tables. The tipstaff announces "Now hear yea, hear yea," whatever the hell it is they say and in comes Judge Kun. After he takes his seat, Hamm Connors stands up. Since he is the one that was looking for the relief, he speaks first. He is for the plaintiff.

Hamm started off, "Your honor, this is an application for an injunction. I appear for the Philadelphia Transportation Company. We have a contract." "Mr. Connors," the Judge interrupts, "just a minute please." And then he pointed to me. "What did you say your name was?" Now you know we had just been talking in his chambers. I stood up. "Your honor, O'Donnell, the name is O'Donnell." "You represent the Union?" I said, "Yes, your honor." "You represent Mr. Quill, Mr. O'Donnell, is that right?" In this case because Quill is also the defendant, I said, "Yes, your honor."

Judge Kun shuffled some papers on his desk and he pulls out this big picture from the *Philadelphia Inquirer* showing

> Mike tearing up the show cause order. I don't think he tore up the show cause order, but when he was asked a question by the reporters, "What are you going to do about the order?" Mike answered, "This is what I'm going to do. See!"—something like that, and tears up a piece of paper.
>
> There the picture is. So the Judge takes it out and holds it up and he says to me, "Is that Mr. Quill?" I said, "Yes, I think it is, yes your honor. I'm sure it is." "Do you see what he is tearing up?" "I'm not sure what he's tearing up, your honor." "Were you there, Mr. O'Donnell? As a matter of fact, Mr. O'Donnell, look over here. Isn't that your face in the background?" I said, "I think it is, your honor." "Well, I'm now holding Mr. Quill in anticipatory contempt." That is something I had never heard of in the law—anticipatory contempt. In other words he is anticipating. Ah, well.[14]

Nothing was simple in Philadelphia, which was becoming quite obvious to me as my father continued to relate his account of the proceedings. For another perspective on this court scene, then, I decided to take a look at the convention literature.

Lou Dwyer, a shop worker who was International Representative of Local 234, Philadelphia, described his version of the injunction court scene to the Eighth Biennial Convention of the TWU/CIO in December of 1952.

> We were not in court with Judge Kun, in Philadelphia, very long today, before he made it very clear to all of us, that not only would he hand down the injunction, but he would deliberately curtail our right to present our case. The first point he made to our attorney was that he was not in New York and that here we have a different type of law....
>
> I think that of the probable hour or hour and a half that we were in court, our attorneys were not allowed to talk uninterrupted for more than one minute at any time. And any time they tried to make a point, they were interrupted, and that is the way the case went on, until it got to a point where the attorney said, "No more defense" and the Judge said, "Injunction granted."

> We went out in the hall, and the reporters had a mimeographed copy of the injunction, complete and ready, by the time we got out the door.[15]

For TWU, even after the injunction was granted, the worst was yet to come. O'Donnell continues:

> We were enjoined from striking until the 15th of January 1953. That's when the real problems started. We settled it on a Saturday—at a late hour, not too late—probably around 3 P.M. Barney Samuels represented the mayor [Joseph F. Clark Sr.] and Greenfield represented PTC. He [Greenfield] also represented the people of Philadelphia—in his words. Greenfield was a member of the Board of Directors of PTC also. Charlie Ebert was probably the President [of PTC] and Bill McReynolds was the Labor Relations Vice President.
>
> We came out of the inner room in City Hall. Mike and I came out and we were talking with Barney [Barney Samuels, the mayor's representative]. Barney's sitting on a desk, looking up Broad Street. I can still see him swinging his leg there and telling Mike how happy he was that they were settling. Barney said, "Everyone will be working tomorrow." "No," Michael said, "we won't meet until tomorrow. We'll have everybody back at work on Monday." "Ah," Barney said, "No, I want everyone back tomorrow so that the stores will be ready to open on Monday. They'll know, they'll have their preparation...." Mike said, "No. We can't meet before tomorrow at noontime or afternoon." Samuels said, "Oh no, you'll meet tonight. I called a meeting," and he pointed to *The Bulletin* building. The building had the sign going around it: "TWU meets tonight in Town Hall on new contract settlement. Settling strike."
>
> Mike said, "Good God, Barney, what have you done? The only people that will know about it are the drunks. It'll be on the radio, you see. The only ones that will be listening to the radio will be the fellows in the saloons." Barney said, "Look, you can handle it, Mike." Michael said, "You called the meeting; you handle it." Barney said, "Michael, it's your job."

So we went to the meeting, but we hadn't had a chance to get to the executive board of the local before the meeting. The executive board was hostile at that point because they were annoyed that they hadn't been consulted. When we got to the meeting hall, they sat on one side of the platform by themselves, and Mike, Andy [Kaelin], and I sat at a desk in the middle. That's where the microphone was. Everything was on the radio at that time. They had a radio station in Philadelphia that carried all the local news. I remember the announcer—I can hear him. We get there, and there are—not many—maybe 300 people there. Bob High was there, and Sally Werner was there. Sally was in the front of the balcony; Bob High was down on the floor.

So there is shouting, and you know—there's some commotion there. Finally Andy says to Mike, "What do we do?" Mike said, "Get the meeting going." Andy says, "Who'll sing 'The Star Spangled Banner'?" Mike says, "Andy, you sing it." So Andy called the meeting to order, and he started in a voice that's exactly like mine—no sense of sound at all. He sang "The Star Spangled Banner." Then, when he did that, he called the meeting to order, and he read off the terms of the settlement. People were shouting, "No, no, no, no, no." Then Andy said, "Well, I'll take a motion to adopt. Who moves to adopt?" So the motion is made. And seconded. "Anybody for discussion?" Bob High, as I remember it, started off the discussion, denouncing the contract. Then Sally Werner did. And then one or two others.

Then Mike said, "It's time for a vote, Andy. It's time for a vote." So Andy said, "All right. You've all had a chance to express yourself." Nobody spoke in favor of it [the contract]. "All those in favor of the new contract say aye." There was, "No, no, no, no." "All those opposed say nay." "No, no, no, no." Mike says, "Andy, tell them it's carried."

Andy said, "The motion is carried." And we were carried, into the scenery at the back of the stage—into the arms of about 50 cops. Barney knew enough to do that, to have them in the back of the stage and to protect us.[16]

Sometimes, even understanding the sentiments of the union membership is not enough to prevent trouble. However, the membership at large still had not expressed an opinion. Only the membership present at the meeting refused to vote in favor of the proposed contract. Without an agreement, however, Local 234 was not able to work for four days—a wildcat strike. It took four days to receive and count the secret ballots on a contract that included a 23-cents-an-hour increase in basic rates. After the final count, the contract had been approved by about a 3 to 1 margin. Using this very same wildcat strike as an example, O'Donnell illustrated the inadequacies of the Taft-Hartley Act when he appeared before a House Committee on Labor.

Taft-Hartley Act

Labor law had taken a new turn with the Taft-Harley Act. In June 1947, this bill passed Congress only to be vetoed by President Harry S. Truman. Congress then overrode the President's veto and the Act became law.[17] As my father was to recall many years later:

> The Taft-Hartley Act was an anti-labor act. It was sponsored by Senator Taft and Congressman Hartley, both Republicans. What they did was amend the National Labor Relations Act. The Taft-Hartley Act put a lot of restrictions on unions. It has been modified, but it is still an Act that you have to be very careful of. For instance, it governs union elections, and the finances of unions. You'd better be open and above board.[18]

Several years after it became law, in 1953, John O'Donnell appeared before a House Committee on Labor to present the CIO's position on part of the Taft-Hartley Law—the inadequacies of the current union security provisions. With the union security provision, an employee had to be a member of the union.[19] Since O'Donnell used the Philadelphia wildcat strike as an example of weaknesses in the Taft-Hartley law, I have included some of his presentation here:

> Basically we believe that the present law is founded on premises which are morally, economically, logically, and practically unsound. It cannot, therefore, give to our country the solid foundation needed on which to build an

effective, workable, productive, and fair labor-management relationship.

But we are practical people and we accept the unfortunate fact that the majority of the Congress is not yet convinced of the inherent weakness of the thing it has built—not yet prepared to embark on what I believe to be the inevitable—the razing of this creaking, faulty pile and its replacement by an enduring structure on a worthy foundation of sympathy, understanding, knowledge and foresight.

Consequently, at this time, and for the immediate protection of our way of life, the CIO goes along with you in planning some makeshift repairs and alterations. . . .

In January of this year the economy of the City of Philadelphia was seriously disorganized by a four-day strike which shut down all local transit in this nation's third largest city. Business in Philadelphia lost millions of dollars; the workers who were unable to get to their jobs suffered a tragic loss of earnings; the ten thousand employees of the transit lines alone lost half a million dollars in wages; factory production, much of it vital war material, was seriously curtailed; work in the Navy Yard there was substantially disrupted—all because of a needless, foolish strike.[20]

He made very clear why the strike was needless and foolish, all the result of what he called an "unfortunate incident":

An unfortunate incident then took place. One of the management's top representatives, on leaving City Hall, assured the newspaper men that there would be no strike. Now, our union is a truly democratic organization. Our membership makes all-important decisions. They and they alone ultimately determine whether a proposed contract is acceptable. Yet on their way to the meeting, where they were to hear the terms of the proposed agreement and to decide whether or not to accept, they read in huge newspaper headlines that the decision had already been made—and by a spokesman for management at that.

Naturally, they were incensed and aroused—but an explanation of the newspaper story and an exposition of the terms of the settlement backed by the recommendation of the union leadership would surely prevent any untoward incident. The meeting was broadcast in its entirety and directly from the meeting hall over one of Philadelphia's larger radio stations so that the members who could not attend would know what transpired and so that the general public would also learn how a good union functions—and incidentally whether they would have transportation the next day.

In most every union, as in most every other democratic organization, there is an irresponsible fringe. We do not choose our members. We do not have a closed shop. The Philadelphia Transportation Co. hires at its pleasure. We accept as members whom they employ. In the employ of the Philadelphia Transportation Company there are the usual small wayward groups. Some are typical demagogues, loud and irresponsible. Some are disappointed and resentful union office-seekers or company job seekers. There are the chronic malcontents who are allergic to peace—troublemakers and crackpots—they are everywhere.

Neither Philadelphia nor trade unions have a monopoly of them. They have an extraordinary capacity for causing trouble. No power on earth—or perhaps even in Heaven—could weld them together for a constructive purpose. But let there arrive an occasion for mischief, and some strange amalgam gives them an incredible cohesion.[21]

O'Donnell then went on to talk about the evolution of the strike:

In the two hours or so between the appearance of the newspaper headlines and the start of the meeting, the malcontents had organized. When we got to the meeting hall they were prepared. There were not more than six to ten ringleaders in command of a hundred troublemakers. They formed a cordon between the officers on the stage and the two or three thousand members in the seats. They carried the newspaper headlines as banners. The grabbed the microphones, screamed and shouted, and prevented any explanation of the false story—any exposition of the proposed agreement. . . . Our proposed agreement was never

> explained. Instead, when the contract expired at midnight all Philadelphia transit was on strike.
>
> Next day the union officers and I went on radio and television. We explained what we had negotiated. The union published a detailed analysis of the agreement and arranged for a secret ballot vote on the proposed contract to be conducted by the American Arbitration Association. The vote was overwhelmingly for acceptance. But it took four days to arrange—four days of senseless, useless strike. Why?[22]

He then connected the unfortunate and unnecessary strike in Philadelphia to the Taft-Hartley Act, an act that organized labor was asking Congress to amend:

> The provisions of the Taft-Hartley law, which I am discussing, deny to a union any effective means of disciplining its recalcitrant troublemaking members. That was not the first occasion on which we had trouble with those very few employees of the Philadelphia Transportation Company who seek to disrupt and destroy democratic union procedures. They have learned that the union has been emasculated by your bad law and that Taft-Hartley provides an excellent weapon for malcontents, discontents, the lunatic fringe, and others with more sinister purposes.
>
> And gentlemen, the situation will get worse unless you restore to the union the necessary power to maintain the peace, to discipline those who would turn union procedures into anarchic chaos, who refuse to meet their obligations to their fellow-employees, to their union and to their employers. . . What could the union do under your existing law, with this handful of willful people who disrupted the life and economy of Philadelphia for four days? We could have had charges preferred against them. There is no doubt of their guilt. Then what punishment? Expulsion is surely a reasonable penalty for such conduct. But all the expulsion would mean would be relief from the obligation to pay their union dues. They could not be deprived of any of the substantial benefits the union had won for the employees of the Philadelphia Transportation Co.

> Your law demands that they enjoy every benefit running from the employer to their decent, self-respecting, law-abiding, responsible fellow employees. They would be excused, however, from paying any part of the cost of obtaining and preserving those benefits. Why, we couldn't effectively impose a fine on them! We couldn't have them suspended for even a day or an hour from their employment![23]

Finally, he asked that Congress consider the anti-union bias of the Taft-Hartley Act and amend it to allow for unions and management to negotiate the discharge from the company of any employee expelled from the union:

> Isn't it obvious, gentlemen, that the authors of this law were blinded to the realities of everyday problems of labor management relations by their unreasoning hostility to unions?
>
> You cannot justify this Taft-Hartley provision by pointing to some past abuse of the closed shop or the union shop. As long as we are a free people there will be abuses of every right we cherish. Let us find some corrective for the abuses. . . .
>
> I recognize, gentlemen, that there are still some people in this country who regard unionism as an evil which they hope soon to exterminate. To them Taft-Hartley is founded on beautiful idealism. But I am not presumptuous, I hope, gentlemen, in assuming that all of you are in agreement with me on accepting as a dynamic influence for good, and essential constructive element in our way of life. We want to preserve good trade unionism. . . .
>
> I urge you, gentlemen, to so amend the law as to validate any labor agreement provision which requires the discharge by the employer of any employee duly expelled from membership by the union. Such expulsion, of course, would have to be in accord with the procedures in the union's constitution.[24]

Try as I may, I have been unable to discover if my father's presentation resulted in any changes to the Taft-Hartley Act.

TWU'S LARGE CITY LOCALS 107

Around this same time frame, trouble was brewing in Houston, Texas. Again race became an issue.

Houston TWU Local 260

Almost two years after the 1948 convention in Chicago, O'Donnell, as the Union's General Counsel, was sent to Houston, Texas to help with the negotiations of Local 260, a new union affiliated with the TWU. O'Donnell explained the background of the situation that faced him when he arrived in Houston in November 1950:

> Earlier, in 1947-8, the TWU lost an election [to unionize] down there. The situation in Houston at that time was that transit had three seniority lists: bus drivers, mechanics, and maintenance—bus drivers all white, mechanics all white, maintenance all black—mainly porters and that sort of thing.
>
> The organizing had been done by the Oil Workers Union for us. That was the old CIO organizing committee. They had organized it, turned it over to TWU and we had plenty of card signatures [accepting TWU]. But at the last minute Charlie Smolikoff, an "expert" who came out of the Communist Party, went down to Houston to check the card signatures to make sure we were in good shape. When he checked, he found out that we had almost no cards from maintenance, only one or two. He said, "What the hell is this?" [The reply was] "Don't worry about maintenance, they'll vote for us. They're all black."[25]

Smolikoff, disturbed by the discovery of three seniority lists, put out a leaflet right away to the maintenance people stating that in TWU there would be no discrimination. Word spread quickly, and the white workers were not happy. The company, opposed to the organizing, fueled the fires. As a result, the employees voted against the union in the first go-round. The next year the union rectified that, and won. In September of 1949, Local 260 received its charter as a member of the TWU.

In September of 1950, two months before O'Donnell was sent in, John (Jack) J. Ryan, International Representative of TWU, began contract negotiations with the Houston Transit Company. The chief stumbling block had to do with fare problems in Houston. In 1991, at the Tamiment Labor Library at New York University, I found the following correspondence between Michael Quill and Jack Ryan. In the letter, Quill explained TWU's position to Ryan. I have included the letter because it encapsulates the philosophical outlook of Quill, one shared by O'Donnell, when dealing with the privately owned transit companies:

> With private companies . . . we have taken the position that the fare is not our business. We have threatened strikes; held demonstrations; shouted bloody murder on the questions of wages, hours, working conditions and a contract. All this noise, of course, helped the companies indirectly to get an increased fare. . . .
>
> Now I think your line in Houston should be to try to sell the city administration on strict parking regulations in the midtown area, but I would do that off the record, since this is not our business. . . . Carry on all kinds of demonstrations to bring the plight of the workers to the public, and make a public demand for a Fact-Finding Board—a board that will find facts—as regards management, as regards the city and state in relation to the transit company.
>
> The state is getting taxes on oil, gas, and license plates. The city is raking in a handsome franchise tax. The company is financed, I believe, by some Wall Street firm. . . . When these facts are brought before the public, you can say that the company, city and state should carry the burden, but that our members no longer can be saddled with the problem of subsidizing the cost of transit operation in Houston.
>
> This is a correct trade union line in dealing with private management.[26]

Unfortunately, all negotiations failed, and on November 11, 1950, the Houston transit workers went out on strike. Ryan, as an International representative of TWU, appeared before a fact-finding Committee headed by the President of Rice University, Dr. W. V. Houston, and explained that he did not feel competent to present the union's case. He added that Quill had been scheduled to be

TWU'S LARGE CITY LOCALS 109

there on the Thursday night before the strike took place, but was stricken with a heart attack on his way out to LaGuardia Airport. Quill turned the case over to John O'Donnell. Ryan explained to the fact-finding Committee that he had contacted O'Donnell "and he assured me that he is taking a plane out of New York today and will be here at 10 o'clock tonight."[27]

After considerable discussion, the fact-finders agreed to recess the hearing until John O'Donnell came from New York. The union had until the next afternoon, November 12, 1950, to get its case together. O'Donnell remembered:

> I got in at midnight. Jack Ryan and Clay Stone [the President of Local 260] met me at the airport and told me that the fact-finding committee had been appointed and that they were going to meet at twelve noon Sunday. The officers worked with me all night. We were ready to go ahead noon Sunday. We worked all Sunday night. Then we went on Monday and Tuesday. And by Tuesday that southern transit company that is managed by Stone & Webster from New York was in a desperate position of having to have recourse, a stupid recourse, to local prejudices. They had a southern fact-finding board headed by the President of Rice [University], a very distinguished physicist,[28] and yet they were stupid, as many transit group managements seem to be, and the only argument they had left Tuesday night: the high-priced legal talent stood up and stated he was just a country boy. He couldn't cope with the slick lawyers from New York.[29]

It is difficult for me to imagine my father, an immigrant, as a "slick" New York lawyer. Yet this was not the first time I had come across this viewpoint.

After each side presented its case, O'Donnell for TWU Local 260 and William R. Brown for Houston Transit Company, time was allowed for rebuttal. John O'Donnell ended his rebuttal with the following arguments:

> Labor is not a commodity for sale.
> Why should a bus driver or a mechanic have less dignity than a tire? . . . You see, when you say that labor is not a

commodity for sale, we intend that to mean that labor has more dignity than a commodity, but when these people use the argument of inability to pay—they pay for their commodities that they buy at the going rate, but they don't want to give to labor even that dignity. Labor to them is not a commodity. It is less. . . .

As long as they pay the going rate for the buses, gentlemen, as long as they pay the going rate for the rubber and the gasoline and the oil and for everything else that they buy and as long as they pay the going rate to Stone and Webster, there is no reason why they should not pay the going rate to their employees, as we can establish from the exhibits we have put in evidence. . . . The proper basis of comparison is comparable cities across the United States.

Our international president always has had a stock answer when they claim they are losing money. He will always tell them: "Look; we have worked out an arrangement with the bankers. We have agreed we won't go into the banking business as long as they keep out of the union business." That is our situation here. We are not finance experts. We don't know how this transit facility should be financed. That is a problem that is certainly outside the union's scope. If that is not a managerial prerogative, I don't know what is. . . .

In the good old days the companies never offered or never wanted to sit down with the union or its members to figure out what they should do with their excess profits. It is only in hard times that they want the union and its members to sit down and share their poverty. Never the profits.[30]

Even though the men were on strike for twenty days, the union got a very satisfactory decision from the fact-finders. But still the issue of race prevailed. As O'Donnell explained:

About four or five years later, the company was not in good shape. They were looking for a fare increase. The Mayor was unwilling to give it to them until they got better buses—and they wouldn't get better buses until they got their fare increase.

TWU'S LARGE CITY LOCALS   111

A fellow from Kansas [I never found his name] came down and he made a proposition to the City of Houston. He said he would buy a whole new fleet of buses if he got a fare increase. So they made a deal with him. They gave him a fare increase effective a certain date. He agreed to bring in the new buses. And he did.

Well, you ask, how was he going to pay for them? Very easy. They won't need any maintenance practically, for the first year or so. In place of having one out of every three men working in the shop, he had only one out of every five men working in the shop. That's where he was going to save the money, and that he paid into the buses.

But, what about our fellows in maintenance that are being laid off? There was really no division between the blacks and whites on the job. They were friendly, very friendly. You'd never know there was any difference—they wouldn't visit each other's homes or that sort of thing. That was a little different.

The officers of the TWU now saw the opportunity to break up the seniority divisions. They explained to the Local 260 membership that "These maintenance fellows are going to be laid off. Where the hell are they going to get a job? Why don't you let them drive buses? You know—this is a special situation." The majority of the bus drivers voted "OK". So that was how we got the black bus drivers. And when that happened, M. D. Hendricks, (we always called him Preacher Hendricks) said to me, "Look", he said, "I'm all for this, but remember. You know what I'm telling you. This is going to be a 'nigger' job. You won't get any white men taking this job now." And that was true. In no time at all, it turned out to be practically all black—all the drivers are black. Maybe six of the old timers were white. The mechanics are mainly white. The drivers are nearly all black—90%-95%—because a white man wouldn't take that job down there.[31]

A decade before the Civil Rights Movement affected the move of African Americans from the back of the bus, this daring move in

Houston put a large number of African American drivers up front. This is a good example of my father's understanding of the way discrimination worked and his ability to find a way for the Black employees to upgrade their jobs and visibility.

During these first twenty years after the passage of the Wagner Act, my father worked in labor law to help unions establish their charters and lay the groundwork for present and future contracts. The next twenty to thirty years would challenge O'Donnell's patience, humor, and legal knowledge as he built on the foundation of his earlier accomplishments, striving to achieve even more for the sake of the union worker.

ENDNOTES

[1] Bruce Lambert, "John F. O'Donnell, 85, A Lawyer and Advocate for Union Workers," [Obituary], *The New York Times*, January 29, 1993, p. A17.
[2] John F. O'Donnell, Personal interview, July 17, 1991.
[3] John F. O'Donnell, Personal interview, July 17, 1991.
[4] Douglas L. MacMahon, TWU papers, Tamiment Library, New York University. Courtesy of the Tamiment Library, New York University.
[5] John F. O'Donnell, Personal interview, July 17, 1991.
[6] John F. O'Donnell, Personal interview, July 17, 1991.
[7] Arthur S. Meyer, TWU papers, Tamiment Library, New York University. Courtesy of the Tamiment Library, New York University.
[8] "Philadelphia Pact Reached in Strike," *The New York Times*, February 20, 1949, pp. 1, 47; William G. Wiert, "Transit Men Back in Philadelphia," *The New York Times*, 21 February 1949, pp. 25, 40.
[9] "8-Cents Boost Ends Tieup in Philadelphia," [Rochester, NY] *Times-Union*, February 21, 1949.
[10] John F. O'Donnell, Personal interview, July 17, 1991.
[11] John F. O'Donnell, Letter to the Editor, *The Evening Bulletin*, Philadelphia, Pennsylvania, January 10, 1950. Copy in the papers of Eileen O'Donnell Sheehan, Charleston, South Carolina.
[12] John F. O'Donnell, Personal interview, July 15, 1991.
[13] A tipstaff is a bailiff who bears a staff.
[14] John F. O'Donnell, Personal interview, July 15, 1991.
[15] Louis Dwyer, Transcript of Friday Afternoon Session, December 12, 1952, *Report of Proceedings, Eighth Biennial Convention*, Philadelphia, PA, December 9-13, 1952 [New York: Transport Worker's Union, 1953], p. 303.
[16] John F. O'Donnell, Telephone interview, December 8, 1991.
[17] "The Labor Bill Becomes Law." *The New York Times*, June 24, 1947, p. 22
[18] John F. O'Donnell, Telephone interview, March 3, 1991.
[19] 'Union-security' is a requirement that the employees be members of the union. There are various forms of union security. The old form was a closed shop but those

TWU'S LARGE CITY LOCALS 113

days are gone. In a closed shop, one had to be a member of a union to get a job. A union shop is where one had to join the union after getting the job. An agency shop is where one did not have to join the union but did have to pay the equivalent of dues because the union has to represent the employee anyhow.

[20] John F. O'Donnell, Address before the House Committee on Labor, April, 1953. Typescript in possession of Eileen O'Donnell Sheehan, Charleston, South Carolina.
[21] John F. O'Donnell, Address before the House Committee on Labor, April, 1953.
[22] John F. O'Donnell, Address before the House Committee on Labor, April, 1953.
[23] John F. O'Donnell, Address before the House Committee on Labor, April, 1953.
[24] John F. O'Donnell, Address before the House Committee on Labor, April, 1953.
[25] John F. O'Donnell, Telephone interview, May 19, 1991.
[26] Michael J. Quill, Correspondence with Jack Ryan, Local 260, TWU-CIO, Houston, Texas, September 28, 1950. Courtesy of the Tamiment Library, New York University.
[27] John J. Ryan, Hearing before a Fact-Finding Committee in the City of Houston, Texas, p. 5. Copy in the Tamiment Library, New York University. Courtesy of the Tamiment Library, New York University.
[28] Dr. W. V. Houston was the Chairman of the Fact-Finding Committee.
[29] John F. O'Donnell, Transcript of Friday Afternoon Session, December 8, 1950, *Report of Proceedings, 7th Biennial Convention,* December 6-10, 1950 [New York: Transport Worker's Union, 1951], pp. 149-150.
[30] John F. O'Donnell, Hearing before a Fact-Finding Committee in the City of Houston, Texas, pp. 523-529. Copy in the Tamiment Library, New York University. Courtesy of the Tamiment Library, New York University.
[31] John F. O'Donnell, Personal interview, July 12, 1990.

O'Donnell was not only the one who set up TWU's pension plan, he was the pension plan. They have one of the best pensions in the country. It is a fact [that] it was the forerunner, with the direction of your father, for the fire department and the police department. . . . You could retire after John O'Donnell struggled with the management.

Joseph Donoghue[1]

Chapter Six

RIGHTS OF LABOR IN NEW YORK CITY

While the fight for racial equity never faded completely, the prominent issue of worker's rights dominated O'Donnell's involvement in contract negotiations in the late 1950s and throughout the 1960s. Usually overshadowing these negotiations were management's ability and willingness to pay. To complicate matters, O'Donnell had to work with different management groups. For example, railroad and airline labor-management relations involved different laws; therefore, O'Donnell would have to use different strategies. In the transit industry, particularly in New York City, there were city transit workers and private-line transit workers, with different laws applying to each group. With the city workers, the concept of sovereignty had to be understood.

City—Owned Lines And The Transit Workers

My father carefully explained this concept of sovereignty to me more than once:

> This gets into a kind of an ethical question. Why shouldn't a union of city workers have the right to strike? Why shouldn't the transit workers, the sanitation workers, or the teachers—why shouldn't they strike? There was no law against it until the Condon-Wadlin Law—because the theory was that you cannot strike against the sovereign. You can't strike against the king. This goes back to the old common law. Now what happened was that initially there was no problem. A soldier couldn't strike. Everybody realized that. A policeman couldn't strike because he was striking against the sovereign; he was striking against law and order. And initially, cities and states simply maintained law and order. Other than that, they had no business. But then cities and states began to go into business. For instance, you had the question of picking up garbage. Now is that a sovereign function? Is that the function of the king, as it were? We said, "No." Our transit system had been privately operated. But once it became publicly operated, then the cloak of sovereignty was spread to cover it.[2]

On June 11, 1940, the New York City Board of Transportation took control of the Interborough Rapid Transit (IRT) and Brooklyn Manhattan Transit (BMT) lines. The workers on these lines now worked for the City of New York rather than for a private company. For the next ten years, Local 100, representing the employees of these city-owned transit lines, fought for a signed collective bargaining agreement with the Board of Transportation. Finally, on February 26, 1946, Mayor William O'Dwyer appointed an Advisory Committee consisting of Arthur S. Meyer, Chairman; Theodore W. Kheel; Edward P. Mulrooney; Anna M. Rosenberg, and Samuel I. Rosenman. They were "charged with the responsibility of studying the working conditions, wages and labor relations between the workers and the Board of Transportation of the City of New York."[3] The Committee recommended that the Board of Transportation fix wages, hours, and working conditions of its employees through

RIGHTS OF LABOR IN NEW YORK CITY 117

the process of collective negotiation. Four years later, on January 9, 1950, a New York City Transit Fact-Finding Board, chaired by David L. Cole, and including Theodore W. Kheel, Thomas A. Morgan, and Edward P. Mulrooney, announced:

> Various employees and labor organizations representing employees of the New York City Transit system have requested the Board of Transportation for (1) a reduction in working hours, (2) an increase in wages, and (3) changes in other working conditions. . . .[4]

During his tenure as TWU's general counsel, Harry Sacher did not believe that the city-run Board of Transportation could legally sign a contract with a union. O'Donnell always disagreed with Sacher on this point. After the Chicago convention, O'Donnell pursued his belief. He presented the TWU's case to the fact-finding committee. In February of 1950, *The New York Times* reported:

> In spelling out the case for the city's transit workers, Mr. O'Donnell stressed demands for a flat 21-cents-an-hour across the board increase for all employees, a reduction of the work week from the present forty-eight hours to forty hours with no reduction in pay, the setting up of new grievance machinery, and the abolishing of what he called a "beakie" or company spy system.
>
> Mr. O'Donnell urged the fact-finding board to embody its recommendations in a written memorandum of agreement to be made with the union as representing the great majority of the city's transit workers, holding that such a contract was legal so long as the agreement itself did not violate the law. He asked that the recommendations be made retroactive to July 1, 1949, the beginning of the last fiscal year.
>
> Waving aside the Board of Transportation's anticipated defense, the city's inability to meet increased wage demands, Mr. O'Donnell appealed to the fact-finding body as public representatives to see to it that the public lived up to its responsibilities toward its transit workers.
>
> In support of the union's case for a forty-hour week Mr. O'Donnell cited the report to President Truman by the emergency board created in October 1948, under the

Railway Labor Act. The report said that "forty basic work hours per week with time and a half for overtime is the prevailing practice in American industry.⁵

Almost six months later, an editorial in *The New York Times* described the success of this first step in the union's fight for a collective bargaining contract for its public transit employees.

> The memorandum of understanding signed, sealed and delivered late yesterday [July 27, 1950] afternoon at City Hall between the Board of Transportation and union labor on the transit lines is the most constructive step in a long time for improving transit labor relations. We heartily congratulate Mayor O'Dwyer, the board and the Transport Workers Union. The memorandum puts into effect for two years the pledges, guarantees and mediation machinery recommended recently by the Mayor's Transit Fact-Finding Board and offers the prospect—if all hands honor their responsibilities as well as their promises—of two years without strikes or slowdowns.⁶

As he had when winning other victories for the workers, O'Donnell remained silent in the background when these congratulations were issued. What thread of his character pulled him into the background? Maybe he had had his share of notoriety during his troubles in Ireland.

While the Fact-Finding Board did not recommend the 40-hour week at this time, it did state that:

> The Board shall retain without delay competent industrial engineers to study and report on a program for achieving a 5-day, 40-hour work week for all employees now having a scheduled work week in excess of 40 hours.⁷

A year later, on June 27, 1951, the Memorandum of Understanding was amended as follows:

> Transition to a 5-day, 40-hour week shall be accomplished in two steps as follows:
>
> Step 1: All employees, by January 1, 1952, shall be placed on a 44-hour week on the basis of the straight time earnings they would receive for a 48-hour week, but

the 44-hour week shall begin on October 1, 1951, for all employees whom the Board believes it is feasible to place on such a basis at that time. . . .

Step 2: All employees shall be placed on a 5-day, 40-hour week by July 1, 1952, and their hourly rates of pay shall then be such as will give them for 40 hours what they would have received, exclusive of any overtime premium, for 48 hours' work on the basis of present wage scales.[8]

While the Memorandum of Understanding was a big step forward, it was not a collective-bargaining contract. O'Donnell was still a long way from reaching this goal. When the Memorandum of Understanding expired on June 30, 1954, the 40-hour work week was in place, but Local 100, with the firm leadership and guidance of John O'Donnell, was determined to gain a binding labor agreement. The agreement must include collective bargaining for Local 100's public employees. At a 1957 Convention of the TWU, O'Donnell described to the audience the ins and outs of the seventeen-year struggle. He stated:

A legal precedent of great significance to public transit employees throughout the country was established earlier this year [1957] when the Appellate Division of the Supreme Court of the State of New York unanimously upheld the collective bargaining contract entered into July 1, 1954, between the New York City Transit Authority and Local 100 of this union [TWU].

Ever since the City of New York acquired ownership of the IRT and BMT transit lines in 1940, our union has been engaged in a relentless struggle to win the same basic labor rights and guarantees for public transit employees as are enjoyed by workers in private industry. Through the years, the Board of Transportation of the City of New York stubbornly refused to sign a labor contract with TWU, concealing their anti-labor motives behind the pretext that it was "illegal" for a public agency to sign a collective bargaining agreement with a union of its employees. Shortly before its demise, the old Board did sign what it called a "Memorandum of Understanding" [27 June 1950].

When the Transit Authority replaced the Board of Transportation in 1953, it too, disclaimed the power to sign a binding labor agreement.[9] But finally, in 1954, after the Mayor's Fact Finding Committee had recommended collective bargaining with the majority union as determined in a representation election, the Transit Authority signed a labor contract with TWU providing for collective bargaining over wages, hours and working conditions and granting exclusive recognition for the processing of grievances.

Shortly thereafter, the Civil Service Forum,[10] a splinter group with a "paper" membership, brought an action in the New York Supreme Court to set aside the labor contract as unconstitutional, illegal and void. The court granted TWU's request to intervene as a full-fledged party in the legal proceeding.

Significantly, the Civil Service Forum was joined by the Brotherhood of Locomotive Engineers in seeking to nullify the labor contract between the Transit Authority and TWU. The fact that the Brotherhood enjoys the benefits of exclusive collective bargaining contracts on many railroads did not deter it from sending attorneys into the New York Court to argue that it was "illegal" for the Transit Authority to sign a labor contract with TWU.

After a lengthy presentation of the issues, Justice Cone, in Kings County Supreme Court, in a strong opinion upheld the TWU's collective bargaining agreement in all respects. In obstructionist desperation, the Civil Service Forum, the Brotherhood and other splinter groups appealed to the Appellate Division.

In a precedent-making decision, the five judges of the Appellate Division handed down a unanimous 18-page opinion upholding the collective bargaining agreement and the exclusive representative status of TWU as the majority. Thus, for the first time, an Appellate Court in the State of New York has upheld:

1. The power of a public agency to enter into a collective bargaining contract binding for a fixed period of time.

RIGHTS OF LABOR IN NEW YORK CITY

    2. The right of a public agency to grant *exclusive* recognition to a majority union.

    3. The power of a public agency to conduct a representation election of its employees for the purpose of determining the majority union.

    4. The right to provide in the collective bargaining agreement for impartial arbitration to make binding decisions concerning grievances which cannot be settled between the parties through the grievance machinery set forth in the contract.[11]

While the fight for the rights of the city workers was unfolding, O'Donnell also had to deal with the pressing matters involving private-line transit workers.

Private Lines And The Transit Workers

Sovereignty was not an issue with the private-line transit workers. What these workers had to worry about, however, was the solvency of the private company that employed them. Such was the case with the employees of the private line, Third Avenue Transit System. In 1949, the Third Avenue was involved in bankruptcy procedures.

Late in 1949, an arbitration hearing began for the working conditions of the employees of this private bankrupt line. O'Donnell was called in to present the case of the Third Avenue employees before Mayor O'Dwyer's appointed arbitrator, Professor Emanuel Stein of New York University. However, any decision had to meet with the approval of Federal Judge Samuel H. Kaufman, who was supervising Third Avenue's bankruptcy. In February, 1950, *The New York Times* reported the arbitrator's decision:

> Under the terms of the award the employees will get a wage increase of 6 cents an hour as of July 1, 1949; three-week annual vacations for those with ten years' service, and the distribution of retroactive pay on a $20-a month basis.[12]

The next contract with the Third Avenue Transit Corporation ended on December 31, 1952. On this same date, the contracts with eight other private bus lines also expired. The other eight lines included the New York City Omnibus Corporation; the Fifth Avenue Coach Company; the Triboro Coach Corporation; Jamaica Buses, Inc.; the Steinway Omnibus Corporation; the Queens-Nassau Transit Corporation; the Queensborough Bridge Railway Company; and the Avenue B and East Broadway Transit Company.

At the midnight hour, when 1952 was turning into 1953, eight thousand of these private line employees in New York City walked off their jobs. A. H. Raskin, a columnist for the *New York Times,* referred to the four-week strike that followed as the "biggest bus strike in the city's history."[13]

The TWU leadership were under a lot of pressure to come up with a proposal that would satisfy the union workers, the private-line owners, and City Hall. It took four weeks for O'Donnell and the union leadership to come up with a formula that would be acceptable to all concerned. The proposal included the recommendation for a three-man arbitration board headed by Walter A. Lynch, former Democratic-Liberal Representative for The Bronx and unsuccessful candidate for governor of New York State against Thomas Dewey. The arbitration board was to study the union's demand for a forty-hour week with no cut in pre-strike take-home pay. The proposal did not satisfy any of the parties involved. The first step was to deal with the workers who gathered on January 28, 1953 at the St. Nicholas Arena for an explanation of the arbitration plan. A. H. Raskin of *The New York Times* described the ruckus:

> Mr. Quill had been hooted down in an attempt to explain the arbitration plan at a rally attended by more than 6,000 of the strikers at St. Nicholas Arena. The session got so unruly that the union leaders had to cut it short, turn off the microphones and the lights and beat a hasty retreat while 500 insurgents held a rump session, at which they denounced Mr. Quill for his handling of the strike.
>
> Mr. Quill took to television three hours later to get his message across to the union rank-and-file. . . . Even among the rebels at yesterday's meeting, there was a strong undercurrent of belief that the wisest course was to accept arbitration and return to work in a body.[14]

RIGHTS OF LABOR IN NEW YORK CITY 123

This was not the first time that O'Donnell and Quill had had to leave a rally by the back door, and it would not be the last. Striking workers are very set in their view of the present and often have a difficult time envisioning future issues. More than once, a second presentation of the same proposal, in less contentious surroundings, accomplished what O'Donnell, Quill, and the union leadership wanted in the first place. In the next day's *New York Times*, Raskin wrote:

> The break in the four-week strike that had kept the buses off the streets since New Year's Eve came after union members on all eight struck companies had voted 4313 to 994 to accept a union-approved formula for arbitrating the strike issues.[15]

Once O'Donnell and Quill had the union squared away, they then had to deal with the private company's owners. Only one of the nine struck companies, the bankrupt Third Avenue Transit Corporation, accepted the union's formula. The officials for the eight other companies said they had no objection to the naming of Mr. Lynch as head of the arbitration panel, but that they wanted protection for their companies similar to the protection that the union was willing to extend to the Third Avenue Company. In the January 28 *New York Times*, A. H. Raskin explained:

> The big hitch in the negotiations with the other bus operators was the union's unwillingness to give them the same "out" that it gave to Third Avenue.
>
> The union's agreement with the Third Avenue management made the arbitration award subject to approval by the Federal Court, which is supervising the company's reorganization in bankruptcy.... Union officials said the protective language in the Third Avenue accord was mandatory under the bankruptcy laws.
>
> The [other] companies contended that this left it up to the three-man arbitration panel to decide what would happen if the city failed to allow the operators enough tax forgiveness to pay for the forty-hour week, whereas the Third Avenue had a blanket assurance that it would not have to

pay the union members one penny more than the company got from the city or state in extra revenue.

> The union said it was prepared to extend the Third Avenue terms to any other company that wanted to file a petition in bankruptcy but made clear that it had no intention of giving such safeguards to solvent enterprises.[16]

Eventually all the companies agreed to the arbitration formula and to the designation of Mr. Lynch as chief arbitrator. This occurred at 2 A.M. on January 27, 1953, but seven of the companies had changed their minds by 10 A.M. when the conferees got together at the Park Sheraton Hotel. According to Raskin,

> John F. O'Donnell, general counsel for the Quill group, joined with Mr. Quill in charging that the upset had been caused by the "interference" of some of the Mayor's [Impellitteri's] advisers. Mr. O'Donnell asserted that the aim of "the people from City Hall" was to keep the strike going long enough to force the debt-ridden Third Avenue line into liquidation.
>
> "The enforced liquidation of the Third Avenue by the union is the real objective of the city administration," the union attorney charged.[17]

Finally, at 3 A.M. on January 29, with the help of Theodore Kheel, impartial advisor in the transit industry, all parties signed back-to-work-agreements. Now O'Donnell had to present TWU's side to the arbitration panel.

The arbitration hearings ran from February 26 to June 17, 1953 before a panel that included former Democratic Congressman Walter A. Lynch as chairman, along with John F. Curtin, Philadelphia transit engineer, as industry representative, and Michael Mann, regional director of the Congress of Industrial Organizations, as the union representative. At the time that I interviewed my father about this strike, he was deeply involved in another one, so he gave me clippings to review for the facts. According to one of the *Times* articles:

> John F. O'Donnell, counsel for the Quill union, told an arbitration panel considering the union's demand for a

forty-hour week with no cut in pre-strike take-home pay, that a municipal subsidy for the bus companies represented the only way to keep some of the lines out of bankruptcy.

Mr. O'Donnell contended that the city had no right to expect the bus workers to "subsidize" a 10-cent fare by confining themselves to the wages that could be paid within the limits of city and state tax relief.

The union counsel said it was up to the city to subsidize the private bus lines in the same way that it subsidized the city-operated bus lines in Brooklyn, Queens and Staten Island.[18]

In the middle of the arbitration proceedings, the Board of Estimate placed in escrow part of the franchise taxes paid by the private bus companies to the City. This was in line with a recommendation by the Transit Commission that no franchise taxes be forgiven until the companies had proved they were running as efficiently as possible. This decision created a renewed fear that the City was backing away from what had been considered assurances by the Board of Estimate that there would be substantial tax forgiveness to pay the bill for the forty-hour week. Stanley Levey of *The New York Times* explains O'Donnell's reaction:

> The union counsel called the transit commission's action a "vicious effort to intimidate" the arbitrators and warned that if any weight was given "to the unsupported and unfounded conclusions" of the commission, the TWU would withdraw from the proceeding.[19]

The findings of the arbitration panel headed by Walter Lynch finally came in November of 1953.

> The arbitrators recommended that their award form the basis for new two-year contracts between the Transport Workers Union, which represents the employees, and eight of the companies to replace the contracts that expired last Dec. 31. A three-year contract for the Third Avenue line was recommended.
>
> In their opinion, the arbitrators observed that the Board of Estimate, which controls the fares on the private

lines, must grant the lines a fare rise and relief from franchise taxes to pay the cost of the forty-hour week, or some of the companies might face bankruptcy.[20]

Sixteen months after the city-owned transit worker won a forty-hour workweek, the private-line worker won the forty-hour work week. Eventually some of the private lines had to be sold, either to other companies or to the City itself.

In union circles, my father was now well known and generally well respected, but he had stepped on toes along the way to achieve this status. At this point, someone apparently thought it was time for him to be brought down a peg or two. On New Year's Day, 1955, *The New York Times* reported:

> John F. O'Donnell, counsel for the CIO Transport Workers Union, pleaded not guilty yesterday [December 31] in Federal Court less than an hour after he was indicted on charges of failing to file income tax returns in 1951 and 1952.
>
> O'Donnell, who lives at 69 Desmond Ave., Bronxville, was released on his own recognizance for trial Jan. 14. The 47-year-old attorney faces penalties of two years in jail and fines up to $20,000 if convicted.
>
> His law partner, Asher B. Schwartz, told the court that O'Donnell was anxious to settle the case, claiming he owed only $6,000 because he recently paid $6,000.[21]

While my father did file a tax return for each of the years in question, they were partnership returns. It took until September of that year to clear the case. At that time, *The New York Times* reported:

> John F. O'Donnell, counsel to the Transport Workers Union, CIO, yesterday received a ten-month suspended jail sentence, was placed on probation for two years and was fined $6000 for failing to file income tax returns for 1951 and 1952.[22]

Child at heart that I was at the time, I was crushed to think that my father could do anything wrong. Although in my dramatic way, I thought this was the beginning of the end, I never saw my father lose a step in his forward fight for the union worker. It must, however, have brought back memories of his days before a judge in his youth. He never said.

Returning to the more humorous side of my father's work, we can focus on a 1961 *New York Post* article by Murray Kempton regarding automation on the subways. Mike Quill was appearing before Theodore Kheel, impartial arbiter of the transit industry. The contract ran out on New Year's Day:

> "Let automation begin at the top instead of the bottom," Mike Quill screeched on. "Let's put a little black box in place of the chairman." There was dutiful laughter. TA Chairman Patterson [Charles Patterson] bridled as dutifully: "I think this sort of thing is entirely out of order."
>
> Mike Quill ceased to trouble. Kheel [the impartial chairman] quietly restored the aura of judicial dignity to the proceedings and Transport Workers Union counsel John O'Donnell began presenting the case against automation. Kheel's compliments to the presentation were particularly heartful and thus indicative of his intention to find to the contrary; and O'Donnell's case was masterfully done, and full of revelations to those of us who have to ride the subway. I did not know before, as an instance, that it is a penal offense for a conductor to allow me to be garroted by a door.
>
> O'Donnell made so grand a case against the machine that for a moment it was possible to dream that it might be heard. . . . [23]

The automated shuttle, a train without motormen or conductors, was tested from early 1959 until the idea was scrapped in 1964.

The union growth of the 1950s gave way to the turbulence of the 1960s. One of the more serious causes of this turbulence occurred when a private line bus company was sold to another company. What happened to the pensions?

Pensions

In a letter addressed to Matthew Guinan, as President of Local 100[24] in April of 1954, O'Donnell depicted TWU's policy regarding the transit worker's pension:

A MAN FROM BRUCKLESS

The people who have been serviced by the facilities of Avenue B & East Broadway have no obligation to the corporate owner. The riders never knew whether it was a corporation or an individual who owned the lines, and they never cared. It was the men who drove the buses and the men who kept the buses in shape who really served the people of the East Side. They are the men who, through the long, lean years, worked incredibly long hours with miserable equipment to do a job for the riding public.

Now that the corporate owners are in difficulties, the City proposes turning over or selling the operation to some other corporation or operator. The City administration and the Board of Estimate have a right to pass upon the responsibility of the corporate owners, but they have absolutely no right to interfere in any way with the men who have served the public so well for so many years.

We don't care what the name of the corporation is, as written on the buses. We don't care what color they paint the buses, but we are irrevocably concerned with the welfare of the men who drive the buses. There is no principle more basic in the TWU than the determination of the Union to protect the men who operate transit in New York City.

Corporations have come and gone; New York City Omnibus and Third Avenue have gone through their receiverships and their reorganizations; new corporate names appear and buses are painted different colors; but down through the years, day in and day out, the same employees do the same job. This Union is determined to maintain its record of protecting the employees against this corporate maneuver. We don't care whether New York City Omnibus, or Fifth Avenue Coach, or Third Avenue Transit, or Queens-Nassau Transit Lines, or Jamaica Buses, or the New York City Transit Authority, operates surface transit in the territory now covered by Avenue B, but the full strength of the Union is behind the struggle to make certain that the men involved are not hurt.

When the City took over the IRT and the BMT, they took the employees and preserved their pension rights; when the Yonkers Railway took over the operations up there from Third Avenue, it took the men and it preserved their pension rights; when New York City Omnibus took over New York Railways, it took over the employees and, much as they tried to evade it, the pension rights of those men for their prior years of service are fully protected. That is an established principle in New York transit—established by TWU—the principle on which we will absolutely not yield one iota.[25]

One of the strike-provoking actions of Fifth Avenue Coach & Surface Transit in early 1962 was that company's arbitrary discontinuance of pension payments to their 1200 pensioners.

To grasp some of the difficulties facing Fifth Avenue Coach, it is necessary to return to the early 1950s. In 1953, a group known as the Weinberg group, Harry Weinberg, Roy M. Cohn, and Lawrence I. Weisman,[26] began buying Fifth Avenue stock.[27] It soon became obvious that this group intended to take over Fifth Avenue.

At contract negotiations in November, 1961, Fifth Avenue Chairman Howard S. Cullman, with the knowledge of a possible proxy fight early in 1962, demanded a fare increase from the City in his attempt to safeguard his company. Mayor Robert Wagner offered $4.5 million, as subsidy for Fifth Avenue, but Cullman wanted a five-cent fare increase, or a guaranteed profit of 7%. O'Donnell, representing TWU, stated that if Fifth Avenue accepted the Mayor's offer for the subsidy and at the same time agreed to the 28-cent package offered in contract negotiations by TWU, it would still have a $2.5 million profit for the year 1962, compared with a loss of $600,000 in the year 1961.[28] Fifth Avenue, however, would not budge in its demand for a fare increase; the company was eager to use a threatened Local 100 strike as a weapon against the Mayor. The Company succeeded in its wish for a strike. Thus, 7,000 members of TWU struck at midnight on New Year's Eve of 1961. After a four-day strike, the company and TWU agreed to a one-year contract.

As expected, Harry Weinberg wanted a position for himself, plus a five-man representation on the board of Fifth Avenue Coach. Not wanting the financially ailing company to become involved in a costly proxy fight, Howard S. Cullman[29] and the Board of Fifth Avenue Coach Lines decided to yield five places[30] on the fifteen-man board to the dissidents.[31] Weinberg now had the power he wanted. According to a *TWU Express* newspaper article in 1962:

> Weinberg smashed the transit union in Honolulu . . . [and] he smashed the union in Scranton, PA and in Dallas, TX. . . . Then Messrs. Weinberg, Weisman and Cohn had their first experience with TWU in the City of New York. Once this gang got control of the largest private bus system in the world, the Fifth Avenue Coach Lines, employing some 6500 members, men and women as drivers, maintenance workers and office personnel, they handed TWU an ultimatum which called for the immediate firing of 1500 regular workers and the abolition of pensions for 1200 retired men who had worked as many as 41 years in New York transit. They called for the elimination of night bus service and of Saturday and Sunday bus service-the only means of transportation for 1,500,000 people. This was the Scranton-Honolulu-Dallas formula.
>
> At a televised public hearing Mr. Weinberg handed us [the TWU] a twelve-page document embodying his arrogant policy. He called the pensioners "used up fellows" as if he were talking about the worn out motor or axle of an old bus. The officers and members of TWU, meeting in the spirit of "an injury to one is an injury to all," informed Weinberg, Weisman and Cohn that as soon as the first man or woman was fired, TWU would strike their properties. The three "gentlemen" would then have the opportunity to run the transit lines themselves. They thought we were bluffing and at 4:30 P.M. on March 1st they laid off 29 men. Some were not members of TWU because they belonged to the supervisory force, but at exactly 4:30 P.M. we struck the Fifth Avenue Coach Lines and all its subsidiaries.[32]

RIGHTS OF LABOR IN NEW YORK CITY 131

O'Donnell pointed out later in 1962 that the Weinberg forces had deliberately created the strike situation:

> Harry Weinberg is the man who deliberately fomented the strike, the man who created a situation where TWU had no alternative but to lead a strike against those companies in March.
>
> One of the questions you are going to have to answer in this matter is whether or not a company has the right to go out of business and walk off with assets of $100 million or more without meeting its obligations, leaving its employees holding the bag. It is just as simple as that from our point of view.
>
> It is the law of the highest court of this state that those who are retired are entitled to their pensions for a lifetime; no ifs, ands, or buts.[33]

On March 8, 1962, eight days into the strike, the Board of Estimate voted unanimously to strip the strikebound Fifth Avenue Coach Lines of thirty-eight Manhattan franchises.[34] Fifth Avenue Coach, in return, argued that the condemnation action against it was unconstitutional. The strike continued. To clarify the power of the city to take over the struck company, Mayor Wagner proposed legislation, in the form of three bills, in Albany. The first bill would empower the city to condemn any of the Fifth Avenue Coach lines' properties, including the company's franchises. The second bill would strip the Board of Estimate of the power to raise the basic fare.[35] The third and last acquisition bill would create a subsidiary corporation of the Transit Authority that would be called the Manhattan and Bronx Surface Transit Operating Authority (MABSTOA). The bill authorized the City and the Transit Authority to enter into an agreement under which the non-civil-service subsidiary corporation would operate the bus lines. Fares would be set by contract between the City and the new corporation. Agreement on the bill was reached between Leo A. Larkin, City Corporation Counsel, and Robert MacCrate, counsel to Governor Rockefeller.[36] The New York State Legislature officially formed MABSTOA on March 19, 1962.

The City took possession of eighty-five percent of Fifth Avenue's facilities on March 21, after State Supreme Court Justice Peter A. Quinn approved condemnation papers and the Appellate Division turned down a company plea for a stay.[37] On March 29, the buses were running on all but four of the company's routes.

Earlier, on March 9, Fifth Avenue Coach Lines had filed a $37,305,000 damage suit against the TWU and its president, Michael J. Quill. The suit in Federal Court charged that the union had breached its contracts. The company asked $17,330,000 damages for Fifth Avenue and $19,975,000 for Surface, as well as interest and costs. Roy M. Cohn, a director and general counsel for the company, filed the action.[38] The damage suit was voided as a result of a Supreme Court decision, which declared that Federal Courts have no jurisdiction in labor disputes. O'Donnell said he would move for dismissal of the damage suit.[39]

Towards the end of March in 1962, *The New York Post* reported:

Fifth Av. Coach Lines was making a last-gasp bid in court today to stave off a total take-over by the city.

Two successful condemnation actions by City Hall have left the firm, once the largest bus company in the world, with only about 5 percent of its facilities.

Roy M. Cohn, general counsel to the bus company, vowed the lines would go ahead with plans to provide service on the 10 routes granted to the company.[40]

The following day, however, the *Post* reported that
Vice President Lawrence Weisman had announced that some buses would roll at 3 P.M. yesterday [March 27th] but the appointed hour came and went without the movement of a vehicle.[41]

After the buses were back in business, the long battle began in the courts. When the public authority took over the bus operations, the involved companies then tried to insist that the takeover relieved them of their pension obligations altogether. Three years later, in 1965, the conflict was not yet fully resolved.

O'Donnell reported to the membership in the 1965 Convention Bulletin:

> Their [Fifth Avenue Coach Lines, Inc. and Surface Transit, Inc.] attempt to have the courts prevent TWU from bringing to arbitration this blatant contract violation was ultimately unsuccessful and the subsequent award of the Impartial Chairman [Ted Kheel] resulted in a pension liability of close to $10,000,000 against the two defaulting companies.
>
> Legal proceedings to enforce the award and collateral lawsuits are still being processed [1965] by our General Counsel [O'Donnell] in the courts. In the meantime, by virtue of a TWU collective bargaining agreement, the operating Authority is advancing monthly to each pensioner his regular pension payment. These advances are contingent upon TWU's attorneys prosecuting the pension claims against the Companies.[42]

Eventually, early in 1964, the Weinberg group (Harry Weinberg, Roy M. Cohn, and Lawrence I. Weisman) sold the company to a new group, the Muscat group (Victor Muscat, Robert L. Huffines, Kenneth P. Steinrich and Edward Krock). The new group also did not abide by any pension obligation:

> Control of Fifth Avenue Coach Lines, Inc. yesterday [29 January 1964] was purchased for about $3 million by the BSF Company, a diversified investment company headed by Victor Muscat.
>
> The sellers were Lawrence I. Weisman, who resigned as chairman, president and a director of Fifth Avenue Coach, and the Dallas Transit Company controlled by Harry Weinberg, who formerly headed Fifth Avenue Coach.
>
> Mr. Muscat was elected chairman and Kenneth P. Steinreich, a director of Fifth Avenue Coach since 1954, was elected President. Mr. Steinreich formerly was President of Jacob Ruppert Brewery.
>
> Edward Krock, a close associate of Mr. Muscat and another holdover director, was named chairman of the

finance committee. Robert L. Huffines, president of BSF, was elected a director of Fifth Avenue Coach and chairman of its executive committee.[43]

In a letter addressed to Hon. Leo A. Larkin, Corporation Counsel for the City of New York, dated November 13, 1964, O'Donnell explained:

> As attorney for the Transport Workers Union and for the pensioners of Fifth Avenue Coach Lines, Inc. and Surface Transit, Inc., I recently told you of our position with respect to advance partial payments by the City to these companies in the pending condemnation proceeding. In accordance with your request, I am restating that position in writing on the facts as I believe them to be.
>
> The interests of the pensioners whom we represent, the interest of the City and probably even of the stockholders, may be seriously impaired by any advance payments to the companies under their present managements.
>
> I am aware that the refusal of the City to make advance payments may mean receivership for either or both corporations in the early future, but of what benefit is it to the City, to the pensioners or to the stockholders, to help maintain a management which, in my opinion, is squandering the assets of the corporations.
>
> I am sure you know and can readily verify the fact that annual salaries of $50,000 plus highly questionable expenses are being paid to Messrs. Muscat, Huffines, Steinrich and Krock, and that somewhat lesser but equally unjustified salaries are being paid to certain other members of the Board of Directors. By comparison, the Weinberg group were pikers. According to the proxy statement on March 12, 1963, the only officer who received compensation in excess of $30,000 was Lawrence I. Weisman, whose salary as Executive Vice President plus Director's fees totaled $43,000. In the prior year, when the companies were operating, the Chairman of the Board, Mr. Cullman, was paid $15,000. Obviously, Mr. Muscat considers his services as much more valuable than Mr. Cullman's services.

In contrast to this lavishly generous treatment of themselves, the Muscat group—like the Weinberg group—refuse to pay a dime to the pensioners. . . .

Whatever the extent of the pensioners' present equity may be, I see no justification whatever for any advance to these companies unless that equity is absolutely protected. To put it another way, why make any advance to this management to enable it to retain control, if such control will mean only further depletion of the free assets of the corporations? The past conduct of this management inclines me to believe that a receivership might well be preferable in the interest both of the City and of the pensioners. For there is the fundamental fact that must be kept in mind: the City is going to have to make good in full the pension deficit. Every dollar that this management pays out in exorbitant salaries and for other questionable purposes will probably mean a dollar less for pensioners and a dollar that the City will have to pay. The City has already paid out $3,000,000 to pensioners.

As I have already advised you, I have a good reason to believe that these companies do not accept as binding obligations their pension liabilities as fixed in the Kheel award, even though the award has been confirmed. For that reason alone, I suggest that it is extremely prejudicial to the City's interests and to the pensioners' interests for your office to give any serious consideration to making advance payments to these companies until they first explicitly and unequivocally accept the pension liabilities as fixed in the arbitration proceeding and as determined for the non-union pensioners in Scoville v. Surface, Inc. (Quinn, J., NYLJ 7/15/63). After such acceptance, you would then have the serious responsibility of securely minimizing the City's contingent pension liability.

I assume that you would under no circumstances consider an advance unless MABSTOA be reimbursed the $3,000,000 it has advanced to the pensioners. About half of that amount has been advanced toward the obligations of Surface. Advance or no advance, Surface faces probable bankruptcy or a related proceeding in the near future. In such an eventuality, might MABSTOA have to pay back $1,500,000 to the trustee, to be made available for all creditors? Fifth Avenue is also, of course, in shaky circumstances and the entire reimbursement might be in danger. There are other similar problems in this matter, which I have no doubt you will consider before arriving at a decision.

We have had some chastening experiences in dealing with these companies over the past two years. I wish you better luck.[44]

In 1965, in one of the largest arbitration awards made under a labor contract at that time, 800 former employees of the Fifth Avenue Coach Lines received more than $9 million. Each pensioner was identified by name and given the amount of monthly pension he would be paid. As *The New York Times* stated:

John F. O'Donnell, lawyer for the union, said the individual awards indicated that more than $2.4 million in pension payments was owed up to last Jan. 31 [1965]. In addition, he said the individual awards showed the companies were responsible for monthly pension payments of about $100,000.

Actually, he said, the Manhattan and Bronx Surface Transit Operating Authority, which has been operating the bus lines since 1962, advanced the money so that the pensioners could be paid. He said, however, that the awards were of the "utmost significance" to the pensioners and the union, which has been seeking to enforce the individual claims.

Last August, Supreme Court Justice William C. Hecht Jr., after a trial lasting more than a year, set $30,232,494 as the sum the city should pay for Fifth Avenue Coach and Surface Transit. He said the companies must pay claims of $19.5 million, including $9.4 million in pension obligations.

In Mr. Kheel's [Theodore W. Kheel, impartial arbitrator] first decision in the pension dispute in December 1962, he ruled that Fifth Avenue Coach and Surface Transit

RIGHTS OF LABOR IN NEW YORK CITY

were responsible for pension payments to more than 800 retired employees, but he did not specify the individuals or the amounts due them.

The award was subsequently reviewed and affirmed by the State Supreme Court, but last June Justice Sidney A. Fine entered an order referring back to Mr. Kheel the questions of the identity and monthly pension amounts of the individuals covered and the period of eligibility.[45]

In a 1991 telephone interview, I asked Theodore W. Kheel what, in his opinion, made John O'Donnell a good labor lawyer. He responded:

> He does something that many lawyers don't do; and that is to advise his clients on policy as well as on the law and he assists them in reaching conclusions. His skills in that respect enable him to be what I'd call the *complete labor lawyer*. That's someone who knows the law, knows the right procedures to follow; but also knows what the main goal is; and addresses himself to the question of how to achieve it in a way that's in the best interests of his client. So that's my answer to why your father is such a good labor lawyer. It's his integrity; it's his ability and his practicality.[46]

ENDNOTES

[1] Joseph Donoghue, International Vice President of TWU, Telephone Interview, March 1, 1999.

[2] John F. O'Donnell, Telephone interview, April 21, 1991.

[3] "Report of the Mayor's Advisory Transit Committee to Honorable William O'Dwyer, Mayor of the City of New York," September 9, 1946, p. 1

[4] "Report of the New York City Transit Fact-Finding Board to Honorable William O'Dwyer, Mayor of the City of New York," May 31, 1950, p. 1.

[5] "TWU Completes Fact-Board Plea," *The New York Times*, February 8, 1950, p. 16.

[6] "A Pledge of Transit Peace" [Editorial], *The New York Times*, June 28, 1950, p. 28.

[7] "Memorandum of Understanding between Board of Transportation and Various Labor Organizations Representing Its Employees," June 27, 1950, p. 5.

[8] "Amendment to Memorandum of Understanding between Board of Transportation and Various Labor Organizations Representing Its Employees," June 27, 1951, pp. 1-2.

[9] The New York State Legislature created the New York City Transit Authority (NYCTA) as a separate public corporation to manage and operate all city-owned bus, trolley and subway routes on June 15, 1953.

[10] The Civil Service Forum is listed at the Tamiment Library of New York University as a public employees union. <http://www.nyu.edu/library/bobst/research/tam/new/collections.html.>

[11] John F. O'Donnell, *The President's Report*, 10th Biennial Convention, October 21-25, 1957, pp. 81-83.

[12] James P McCaffrey, "$1,100,000 Back Pay Won by 3rd Ave. Men; Line Asks 10c Fare," *The New York Times*, February 8, 1950, p. 1.

[13] A. H. Raskin, "4-Week Bus Strike Is Ended; Third Ave. Service Resumed; Other Lines to Roll Today," *New York Times*, January 29, 1953, p. 1.

[14] A. H. Raskin, "Bus Men to Ballot on Formula Today," *The New York Times*, January 28, 1953, pp. 1, 21.

[15] A. H. Raskin, "4-Week Bus Strike Is Ended."

[16] A. H. Raskin, "4-Week Bus Strike Is Ended."

[17] A. H. Raskin, "4-Week Bus Strike Is Ended." Vincent R. Impellitteri became the acting mayor of New York City on September 2, 1950 when William O'Dwyer resigned before completing his term of office. He was elected in his own right in November 1950 and served until Robert A. Wagner, Jr., who defeated him in November 1953, took office on New Year's Eve, 1953.

[18] A. H. Raskin, "Bus Economy Plan Advanced for City," *The New York Times*, March 6, 1953, p. 19.

[19] Stanley Levey, "City Units Accused by Bus Arbitrator," *The New York Times*, April 29, 1953, p. 18.

[20] Leonard Ingalls, "Bus Award Reduce Hours, Raises Pay on Private Lines," *The New York Times*, November 19, 1953, p. 23.

[21] "TWU Counsel Denies Income Tax Cheating," *The New York Times*, January 1, 1955, p. 26.

[22] "TWU Aide Sentenced, Counsel Gets 10-Month Term Suspended, Fine in Tax Case," *The New York Times*, September 24, 1955, p. 16.

[23] Murray Kempton, "The Big Wheel," *The New York Post*, December 14, 1961, p. 57.

[24] Matthew Guinan became President of Local 100 when Michael J. Quill moved up to become President of the International Transport Workers Union.

[25] John F. O'Donnell, Letter to Matthew Guinan, April 7, 1954. Original in the Tamiment Library, Robert W. Wagner Archive, New York University.

[26] Weinbert was at that time the Chairman of Dallas Transit and Weisman, a lawyer, was Vice Chairman. Roy Cohn, who was previously associated with Senator Joseph McCarthy, was a partner in the law firm of Saxe, Bacon, and O'Shea, and served as legal representative for the Dal-Tran, a subsidiary of Dallas Transit, which had bought up Fifth Avenue stock. See Alfred R. Zipser, "5th Avenue Coach Management Assailed by Critics of Policies," *The New York Times*, May 9, 1961, p. 53.

[27] Russell Porter, "'Bonanza' Is Seen in Bus Take-Over," *The New York Times*, March 4, 1962, p. 48.

[28] *TWU Express*, February 1962.

[29] Howard S. Cullman was chairman of Fifth Avenue Coach Surface Transit and Westchester Street Transportation Company in November 1961.

[30] The selected five were Harold Leventhal, described by the company as a lecturer on public utilities at Yale University; Leon Tate, President of Mr. Weinberg's Dallas Transit Company; Edward de Harne, head of Mr. Weinberg's Honolulu Rapid Transit

RIGHTS OF LABOR IN NEW YORK CITY 139

Company; William Weinberg, brother of Harry Weinberg; and Robert Goldman, a partner in a Baltimore law firm.

[31] Alexander R. Hammer, "Pact Due in Fight at 5th Ave. Coach," *The New York Times*, February 15, 1962, p. 39.

[32] "A Tale of Two Cities; Dublin-New York," *TWU Express*, September 1962.

[33] John F. O'Donnell, "TWU Fights for Oldsters' Pensions," *TWU Express*, December 1962, p. 2.

[34] Stanley Levey, "Estimate Board Denies Permits to 5th Ave. Line," *The New York Times*, March 9, 1962, p. 1.

[35] Ralph Katz, "Governor Plans Own Legislation on Bus Take-Over," *The New York Times*, March 11, 1962, p. 1.

[36] Douglas Dales, "Senate Puts Off Action on Buses," *The New York Times*, March 16, 1962, p. 1.

[37] Alan Levin, "First Buses Set to Roll on Saturday," *The New York Post*, March 22, 1962, p. 5.

[38] Ralph Katz, "5th Ave. Bus Line Sues Quill Union for $37,305,000," *The New York Times*, March 10, 1962, p. 1.

[39] "Court Decision Voids $37m Suit against TWU," *TWU Express*, July 1962.

[40] Bernard Lefkowitz, "Non-Union Bus Drivers," *The New York Post*, March 26, 1962, p. 4.

[41] "Beset 5th Av. Lines Again Turn to Court," *The New York Post*, March 28, 1962, p. 5.

[42] John F. O'Donnell, *The President's Report*, Twelfth Biennial Convention, October 11-15, 1965, p. 152.

[43] Alexander R. Hammer, "Control of Fifth Avenue Coach Sold to B.S.F. for $3 Million," *The New York Times*, January 30, 1964, p. 37.

[44] John F. O'Donnell, Letter to Leo A. Larkin, 13 November 13, 1964. Original in the Tamiment Library. Copy in the papers of Eileen O'Donnell Sheehan, Charleston, South Carolina.

[45] "$9 Million Listed For Bus Pensions," *The New York Times*, May 10, 1965, p. 28.

[46] Theodore W. Kheel, Telephone interview, August 4, 1991.

Omnibus Strike in July 1949. Pictured Gus Faber, Mike Quill, John O'Donnell

John O'Donnell addresses L100 members as Matthew Guinan looks on around 1953

Mayor William O'Dwyer Luncheon 1954. Pictured John O'Donnell, Matthew Guinan, Patrick Mahedy, O'Dwyer and Michael Quill

John O'Donnell addresses members of L234 during Philadelphia Bus Strike in January 1953

RIGHTS OF LABOR IN NEW YORK CITY 141

John O'Donnell at L100
Rally in June 1954

Arthur Goldberg confers with Matthew
Guinan, Michael Quill and John
O'Donnell during Cole Committee
Hearings in 1957

Michael Quill and John O'Donnell
confer with Transit Authority
Commissioner Joseph O'Grady in
1965

John O'Donnell speaks with Pensioners
in March 1962 about preparing to sue
the Weinberg group for $25,000,000
to cover the pensions of those already
retired and the 7,000 men who struck
in March 1962

> *John F. O'Donnell, a white-haired grandfatherly man, is not widely known as a public figure. Yet if power is what power does, he is a man of power.*
>
> William Serrin[1]

Chapter Seven

SIGNIFICANT STRIKES IN NEW YORK CITY TRANSIT

Striking was one method of calling to the attention of the public the needs of the transit worker. Two significant strikes shaped the transit workers' intended position in New York City labor.

1966 TRANSIT STRIKE

On January 1, 1966, a transit strike began in New York City that was historic in that it was an example of multilateral collective bargaining. This type of bargaining occurs when "government decision makers weigh the political 'clout' of each of the interest groups seeking to influence the bargaining process and then make a decision to maximize their political well being."[2]

It would be counterproductive to mention all the politicians and media personalities who expressed an opinion and attempted to exert influence during this confrontation. The main characters, however, and their organization affiliation were

1) THE TRANSIT AUTHORITY: The three members of the Transit Authority were Republican John J. Gilhooley, selected by Governor Rockefeller, and Democrats Joseph E. O'Grady and Daniel J. Scannell, selected by Mayor Robert Wagner. The agency is supposed to charge a fare that would produce sufficient income to give them enough operating revenue to meet all their obligations. Years later, my father reminded me that the Authority was not a city body. The Authority was a state body. However, it affected the city mainly.[3]

2) THE TWU NEGOTIATORS: These were Michael J. Quill, International President; Matthew Guinan , International Executive Vice President; Frank Sheehan, International Vice President; Daniel Gilmartin, President of Local 100; Ellis Van Riper, Financial Secretary of Local 100; Mark Kavanagh, Recording Secretary of Local 100; Douglas MacMahon, International Vice President; Jim Horst, International Vice President. John F. O'Donnell, represented the International TWU as General Council, and Louis Waldman represented the Motormen's Benevolent Association as General Council.

3) THE ATU (Amalgamated Transit Union): They were represented in negotiations by John Rowland, Executive Board Member; William Mangus, President Local 726; and Frank Klees, President Local 1056.

4) THE MEDIATORS: Those selected by Mayor-elect John V. Lindsay to mediate were Nathan P. Feinsinger, Sylvester Garrett, and Theodore W. Kheel.[4]

5) THE MAJOR POLITICIANS: In late 1965, they were Nelson Rockefeller, the New York State Governor; Robert Wagner, the outgoing New York City Mayor; and John V. Lindsay, the New York City Mayor-elect.

SIGNIFICANT STRIKES

This strike was also momentous in that for the first time a union of public employees achieved these four successes: first, they struck despite hostile laws and court injunctions; second, they completely immobilized a major city; third, they forced a public employer to engage in genuine collective bargaining; and finally, they obtained a signed union agreement with vast and far-reaching benefits for the striking employees.[5]

The events leading up to the strike began to unfold with the appearance of what would become a much talked about lead editorial in *The New York Times* on November 6, 1965. The editor writer stated:

> The banshee of the subway system has come forward with his usual grab bag of unrealizable demands for post-Christmas delivery to his union members on the city-owned transit lines.
>
> Since Mr. Quill's two-year contract with the Transit Authority expires at 5 A.M. on New Year's Day, five hours after John V. Lindsay takes over as Mayor, the terms of the new agreement—and the certainty that there will be no strike—are matters of urgent concern to Mr. Lindsay.[6]

The collective bargaining process itself began in late October of 1965 between the Transit Authority and the negotiating team of the Transport Workers Union and the Amalgamated Transit Union (ATU). Two years later, O'Donnell explained the thought process behind the bargaining:

> No bargaining results, for the most part, in a resolution until people feel that they have come to the end of the line. In the buy-sell process you reach an agreement when you find that you are buying at the best price you can buy it for, or selling at the best price you can get. The same thing is true in labor management affairs, and in the absence of this kind of pressure, it becomes extremely difficult to reach a conclusion, and the bargaining continues without an end.[7]

The editorials in *The New York Times* continued to fan the fire:

> Chairman Joseph E. O'Grady of the Transit Authority reports that, even after using up all its bookkeeping balances, the municipal subway and bus system will be $43 million in the red by June 30 [1966].
>
> The plain need is for designation of an advisory arbitration panel by Mayor Wagner and Mayor-elect Lindsay to appraise all the relevant factors and squeeze the hot air out of the stratospheric demands submitted by Michael J. Quill.[8]

The collective bargaining ended in a stalemate and the strike began at 5:00 A.M. on New Year's morning. For defying court orders against the strike, Quill and some union leaders proudly went to jail.

Author Michael Marmo attended a speech made by my father four months after the 1966 strike ended.[9] Marmo's notes provide the following record of O'Donnell's words on that day:

> The 1966 strike did not have to happen. It did happen because no one on the management side made any real effort to negotiate an agreement until the 9th day of the strike. Why that failure to negotiate? It is a mean story rooted in the resolve of *The New York Times* (in concert with some politico-labor geniuses from the Lindsay establishment) to write the script and determine the outcome of the transit labor dispute. They knew how to tame Quill! All they needed was an obedient servant in City Hall.
>
> It began with the lead editorial in the Times of November 6, 1965, which first adverted to the Mayor-elect's campaign promise to maintain the fifteen cent fare and to the impending expiration of the transit labor agreements on New Year's Day. . . .
>
> But then—in an incredible *non sequitur*—the same editorial admonished the Mayor-elect to "leave the negotiations under the sole control of the Transit Authority without interference from City Hall." This was a strange instruction indeed; that in matters of urgent concern to

him, Mr. Lindsay should assert no voice, exercise no control, but entrust them entirely to three strangers to his administration. . . .

It was truly unfortunate, for himself and for the city which elected him, that Mayor Lindsay chose to follow the *Times* script; to reject the opportunity to learn and to lead. Thereby he made the strike inevitable.

Transit workers needed, deserved and were determined to secure substantial improvements in their wages and working conditions. Mr. Lindsay should have known that and would have had timely knowledge of it had he come to the bargaining table when invited.

The Transit Authority revenues from the fifteen cent fare permitted no improvements in the labor agreements. It was a deficit operation. Chairman O'Grady had never offered a cent in any negotiations unless he knew exactly where the offsetting revenue or other income was coming from. In November and December 1965, he had neither the money nor the promise of it. Mr. Lindsay knew that. Mr. Lindsay made a campaign pledge to preserve the fifteen cent fare, and he remembered that. Was he so naïve as to think that the members of the Authority, two of them Democrats, all of them from the world of politics, would undertake the responsibility of raising the fare to protect him from the impact of a strike and relieve him of a campaign obligation?

I submit that the law, which gives these three gentlemen exclusive control over the fare, is a bad law. I submit that the rate of fare on New York's subways and buses is so vital a factor in the economic life of our city that it is properly the exclusive concern and responsibility of the elected city administration.

In any event, as December dragged on, the one man whose presence could give meaning to the meetings of the Authority and the Union representatives with the mediators, the one man with the ultimate power and responsibility, continued to obey the *Times'* direction and stayed away. . . .

The *Times* cabal did not rest on the editorials alone to hold Mr. Lindsay in line. They visited with the Mayor-elect to impose their personal pressures. Mr. A. H. Raskin, in a signed column on Monday, December 27, 1965 (appearing in the customary Krock-Reston spot) tells of one such meeting and directly quotes what an unidentified "prominent labor leader"[10] in the group told the Mayor. He pleaded, according to Raskin, the cause of the tens of thousands of workers who made only $1.25 an hour and must ride the subway to work.

Now, TWU is aware of the hurting effect of a high fare on low paid workers, but it is absolutely opposed to the exaction of a subsidy out of the hides of transit employees. The labor leader who would make poverty more palatable by extending it is a fraud. I think it is contemptible to try to make a pathetic dollar and a quarter an hour stand up longer or look better by sabotaging the efforts of other workers to achieve decent levels of living.

Then at the eleventh hour, unable any longer to choke back the fearful suspicion that the line between hero and villain in the *Times* script was becoming distressingly slim, the Mayor-elect rushed to the Americana Hotel; hopelessly unaware of the dimensions of the problem facing him, completely confused between the purported wage statistics of the *Times* and the arguments of the Union. He had no idea of what the Union might accept in settlement. Such knowledge is acquired only by an experienced, persevering effort. It does not come to you in 5 minutes, or in 5 days, at a strange bargaining table. And not only was he in the dark as to the possible cost of a settlement, he was without the remotest idea as to how it might be financed.

On that New Year's Eve, Mr. Lindsay was a lost and lonely figure. All he could do then was urge the Union to continue working without a contract while he was familiarizing himself with the issues and the facts. An impossible request from the one who had for two months summarily rejected the Union's invitation to come to the bargaining table and learn at first hand the basics of transit economics.

The *Times* screamed editorial horror at Quill's refusal to provide a quiet period for the Mayor to catch up with his homework; but dropouts usually incur some subsequent inconveniences. Nor did it faze the *Times* a bit that its own script was built on the premise that Lindsay would have nothing to do with the negotiations. After first counseling its noble warrior to stay clear of the battle, it now demanded a truce so that he could don his armor undisturbed. . . .

The grand strategies had collapsed. The following day, Bob Price[11] asked for a meeting with Quill in the Bellevue prison ward.[12] Quill told him flatly that the strike would have to be settled with MacMahon and Horst across the bargaining table.[13]

On the night of Sunday January 9, Mayor Lindsay made a serious effort to end the strike. He offered major concessions. Some of them were in areas which Chairman O'Grady had refused to consider on the ground that the ultimate cost was incalculable and the effect on other city employees unsettling. On wages, the Mayor agreed to go up to four dollars an hour or better—an increase of over fifty-four cents an hour, for motormen and mechanics, with proportionate increases along the line.

It could only have been his inexperience (because I am sure he was acting in good faith) that prompted him to divide in impossible steps the 15% necessary to hit on the top the four dollar rate. [Lindsay proposed]: 2% on January 1, 1966; 2% on January 1, 1967; 2% on April 1, 1967 and 9% on July 1, 1967. This was so patently a device to have the transit workers subsidize the fifteen cent fare for another year that it was not only unacceptable but also provocative. Of course, from that point on the Union knew it had at least the four dollars.

The Mayor added a mathematically impossible limitation. The cost of his offer, he said, would include the value of similar improvements for the clerical and other employees of the Authority outside the TWU union and would also include the price of a similar settlement for the 6,000 employees of MABSTOA. The total cost for all, he told us, would have to be no more than $45,000,000. Someone had flubbed his arithmetic. The offer for the union employees alone already exceeded that figure.

When the Union rejected his proposal and Dr. Feinsinger [one of the mediators] suggested a recess until the next day, the Mayor made one last stab at ending the strike. He asked Doug MacMahon to recognize his offer as evidence of his good faith, to have the men return to work in the morning and then to continue the negotiations on his promise that the ultimate settlement would be retroactive. "Let's get the wheels rolling," he urged. Mr. MacMahon's response was brief and to the point. "If I were to accept that proposition, Mr. Mayor, the only thing that would roll tomorrow morning would be Doug MacMahon's head!" The meeting broke up and we went back to the Americana and gave the surprised representatives of the TA the details of the Mayor's offer.

Two days later, the mediators, Dr. Feinsinger, Theodore W. Kheel, and Sylvester Garrett submitted to the Mayor and the parties their recommendations for a settlement. Their recommendations were so close to TWU's last position that MacMahon and Horst considered the continuance of the strike to be unjustified. They consulted with Mr. Quill in Bellevue and with the other jailed leaders: Guinan, Gilmartin, Van Riper, Sheehan, and Kavanagh. The decision of the officers was unanimous; to recommend acceptance to the Local Executive Board, and if approved by that Board—to the membership. The Board approved, the membership ratified.

The New York Times, which usually had no trouble coming up with precise figures, weaseled and said that the settlement was, "estimated at from 52 million to 70 million dollars." The actual price, calculated as the TA has historically figured the cost of settlements, was 71 million dollars.[14]

Theodore W. Kheel was in accord with O'Donnell's description of the cause of the strike. In his book, *Administering the Taylor Law*, author Ronald Donovan referred to an interview he conducted with Mr. Kheel on September 25, 1985:
> Kheel attributed the length of the [1966 transit] strike, if not the strike itself, to the part played by the editors of *The New York Times*. According to Kheel, Lindsay was a captive of the newspaper. He claims that union bargaining proposals made one day would immediately be addressed the next day on the editorial page without having been reported in the news columns of the paper.[15]

One of the sad results of the strike was the loss of Michael J. Quill. Two hours after Quill went to jail, he suffered a heart attack and was hospitalized in serious condition. Although his condition improved somewhat during his stay in jail, Michael Quill was never the same again. His executive assistant, Scoogie Ryers, remembers the last day of Quill's life:
> When he [Mike Quill] came out of the hospital he said to me, "Bring me any letters from my sisters." . . . Mike was happy. He said that he was going to Ireland in May because May is when the cuckoo came out. He spoke to his sister Mary. He must have spoken to everybody in his family that day. . . . He spoke to your dad, naturally. And then he shaved and he told me he was going to take a rest. . . . Later, [when I went in to check on Mike] his lips were blue. . . . And he had died.[16]

My father also remembers that day well:
> I was the last one to talk to Mike. We talked about the lawsuits against the union. The plaintiffs were suing the union for damages and there were many of them. I'll give you an illustration. You had an outfit that owned the stands in the subway. . . . Now those places were shut down. Joe O'Grady

shut them down during the strike. The people couldn't do business, so they sued the union. Do you follow? But they lost. It went to the appellate division, as I remember it, and it wasn't a well thought out lawsuit at that time. Just because somebody hurts you doesn't mean you have a lawsuit.

We were just starting with these problems when I talked to Mike. I was just reporting to him; maybe how many there were. There were a bunch of them, maybe forty or fifty by that time. And then what we did, we consolidated them. We moved to bring them all on together. The court ordered them consolidated. It was the same issue in every case, except the damages were different.

She [Scoogie] knew he [Mike] was talking to me. And then later on she heard the phone ring and went in and Mike was dead. He had a heart attack.[17]

Michael J. Quill died on January 28, 1966. When I asked my father about his relationship with Mike Quill, he replied:

You see, I respected Mike, I learned from him. I knew what Mike was doing. He had charisma and that was part of it. He played to the galleries, of course he did. You have to play to the galleries. To be a union leader, you have to play to your membership. You have to get them enthused. You have to get them worked up every so often, and Mike was a master at that. And you don't need a lawyer explaining to you in advance what you should or shouldn't do.[18]

For the next twenty-seven years, John F. O'Donnell worked with the succeeding five union presidents. He always kept the same sense of purpose as General Counsel for the Transport Workers Union.

1967 The Taylor Law

At the time of the strike, in 1966, the Condon-Wadlin Law, which forbids strikes by public employees, was still in effect. According to author Ronald Donovan, "Negative in thrust and severe in its

penalties, the Condon-Wadlin Act proved difficult to implement."[19] My father explained the consequences of this same law to me:
> First of all, you would lose your job if you went out on strike. If you were reemployed—**if**—, you would be on probationary status (you could be fired without a hearing, in other words) for the next two years, as I remember it; **and** you could not get any increase in your pay.
>
> Rockefeller promised us [the TWU] a new law. First of all, he absolved us from violating the Condon-Wadlin Law. I was there. I met him in his town house on 52nd Street and we had a very pleasant session, a couple of times. He didn't promise us anything specific. That first session was a Sunday. Before we knew it, he had a new bill introduced the next morning. That was not the Taylor Law, but a bill absolving us from the strike and the appointment of a committee, the Taylor Committee. They [the committee] studied the problems of collective bargaining and public employment and came up with the Taylor Law.[20]

The Taylor Committee and the legislation that resulted from the Committee's work took their name from George W. Taylor, a professor of labor relations at the University of Pennsylvania, who was the chairman of the committee. The other members of the committee were David L. Cole, director of the Federal Mediation and Conciliation Service; John T. Dunlop, professor of industrial relations at Harvard; E. Wight Bakke, director of the labor and management center at Yale; and Frederick H. Harbison, professor of industrial relations at Princeton.[21] New York Governor Rockefeller appointed Taylor to come up with something better than the Condon-Wadlin Act. My father explained:
> The Taylor Act was the finest thing that ever happened for public employees. The Taylor Law recognized the right of public employees to bargain collectively. It recognized the right to have unions and [the law] set up a procedure for workers to elect unions. We didn't like it at TWU because we had everything it gave the other people. We had it all. We had collective bargaining. We got it the hard way; but

we had it. We had contracts. The other public employees didn't have contracts.

It was very well received by public employees, in general. In other words, public employee unions now are large and pretty powerful. They couldn't organize before the Taylor Law. They could, but they had to use clout the way TWU did. The Taylor Law gave them the right to bargain collectively. You see the hospital union and you see the other employee unions now that are large and powerful. They wouldn't have grown at all without the Taylor Law. Now as far as TWU is concerned, we had collective bargaining because by the dint of our strength we got it.[22]

The Taylor Law went into effect on September 1, 1967, almost two years after the transit strike. To prevent unions from striking, the law provided that injunctions could be obtained from the State Supreme Court. If a union disobeyed such an injunction, for each day of the strike the court was empowered to fine the employee organization an amount equal to one week's dues collections from its members or $10,000, whichever was less. This shifted the penalties from the individual employees to the employee organization. Now, it was also possible for a striking union to lose the privilege of a dues check-off for up to eighteen months.[23] According to author Michael Goldfield:

In the recent period New York City has been both the pacesetter and the most militant arena for the organizing of hospital workers, teachers, and municipal workers in general. New York area postal and telephone workers have been among the most aggressive in the country, both at different times rejecting national leadership and, during the 1970s, striking for more far-reaching concessions from their employers.[24]

The New York City transit workers remained content for a few years. By the late 1970s, the membership of the TWU had changed. The Irish-Americans were no longer the dominant force, and respect for the union leadership had eroded. Most of the members of the 1970s had not had to fight for the basic workers' rights and did not really understand what it meant. This was the situation at the beginning of 1980.

New York City 1980 Transit Strike

In 1991, I asked my father to list his three most memorable successes in negotiations. One of the successes that he mentioned was the settlement of the 1980 transit strike. He recalled that this strike was a particularly rough one. At the time, Michael Oreskes, Labor Editor of the *Daily News*, wrote that my father's "wealth of knowledge will be a crucial counter weight for the relative inexperience of the TWU's top officers, Lindner [International union president] and Lawe [Local 100 president]."[25]

Because it was a publicly owned mass-transit system, state public authorities operated the strike-affected systems. Public employees' right to strike had been outlawed in the Taylor Law. The one redeeming feature in the situation was that local mass transit had become more and more dependent on federal grants, both for capital expenditures and operating subsidies. Under existing law, an essential requisite for any grant is a certification by the Secretary of Labor that the wages, collective bargaining rights, and jobs of the affected employees are protected.[26]

Five years before the 1980 strike, the New York City administrator introduced austerity measures. There was a budget crisis in the City, and pay increases were delayed. The City was having a serious brush with bankruptcy. Still, three years after that, under the leadership of a new mayor, Edward Koch, the City Council voted itself a 40% pay raise, effective in July of 1979. Koch did, however, turn down a 33 1/3% pay raise for himself. In the budget that year, Koch allowed 4% for municipal unions' pay raises. In his 1978 negotiations with the TWU, Koch demanded fifty-six givebacks. Not only did he not get any givebacks, the TWU settled for 8% over the next two years. Mayor Koch was incensed and was now on the war path in dealing with the TWU.

In 1979, John Lawe won the presidency of the City's TWU Local 100 by only 43% of the vote. As part of his platform, Lawe promised the 31,000 bus and subway workers a 33% increase in wages over the next two years in the upcoming contract. Still, twenty-one members of the forty-five-member executive board were opposed to Lawe and would fight him throughout his term in office.

The 1980 TWU contract ran out on April 1. Negotiations for a new contract started at 10:00 a.m. on February 4, 1980 at the Sheraton Centre Hotel. At that time, representing the TWU and Local 100 were TWU's International President, William G. Lindner; Local 100's president, John E. Lawe; the full negotiation team for Local 100; and General Counsel, John F. O'Donnell. Among the representatives for the Metropolitan Transit Authority (MTA) were the chairman and local real-estate developer, Richard Ravitch; MTA vice-chairman Daniel T. Scannell; MTA Senior Executive Officer; and General Manager Steve Kaufman. At this first meeting, Lawe submitted the general demands and departmental demands for the TWU. On February 11, Steve Kaufman opened for the MTA. He suggested that he did not consider wages as the whole story nor did he expect the union to give in on all its demands, but he did expect bargaining. Due to the lowering of the standard of living all over the world, people had to make sacrifices, Kaufman contended.[27]

As negotiations progressed, on March 7 Michael Oreskes, the labor editor of the *Daily News*, printed a warning by O'Donnell. This was, O'Donnell claimed, "precisely the same script as we went through in 1965."[28] O'Donnell claimed that the cries of poverty from the MTA, the refusal of state and federal officials to provide new sources of revenue, and Gov. Carey's insistence that the 50-cent fare must be held, all added up to the same scenario as there had been before the 1966 strike.[29]

By March 17, the talks had moved to the forty-seventh floor of the Sheraton Centre Hotel. Koch even showed up. He was quick to mention that he lived in the City so he knew something of the City's financial problems. The next time O'Donnell met with Koch was at a group breakfast on Saturday, March 29.[30]

From March 17 on, meetings were continuous, right up until the contract deadline of March 31. For two days, March 17 and 18,

SIGNIFICANT STRIKES 157

the TWU presented its case to a mediation panel. Walter Gellhorn, a Columbia University law professor, was named chief mediator. Another member was Edward Kresky, an investment banker from Brooklyn. On March 24 and 25, the TA presented its case to the mediation panel. Despite these last minute attempts to avoid the strike, on 27 March, the union members in a noisy demonstration at City Hall made clear their determination to strike.[31]

A few years before this, in reward for his decades of service to the TWU, O'Donnell had been awarded a pension by the union, but with a strike looming, his pension was in danger. Several days before the TWU contract with the MTA expired, O'Donnell sent a letter to the union's national president, William Lindner, announcing his retirement on March 31, the strike deadline, and taking his pension. Inevitably, O'Donnell's "retirement" was far from placid. He spent the next eleven days and nights attempting to find a solution to end one of the most difficult strikes in the city's history.

The morning of March 31 Lawe, along with O'Donnell and Ravitch, arrived at a precarious agreement of raises for 7%-7% over the two years of the contract and a 3% COLA, cost of living increase. At 11:30 P.M., the mediation panel, the MTA people, and the TWU people met for one last-ditch effort to resolve the differences. In an interview with Richard Ravitch, I learned the story of what went on behind the scenes.

> I don't know if you ever heard this story.... The night of March 31st we [Daniel Scannell, John Lawe, John O'Donnell, Richard Ravitch] got together, this small group, and we came to an agreement. We shook hands. I mean, we had been at it intensively for a week and the question was, "How do we sell it?" "How does John [Lawe] sell it?" So John O'Donnell, who had a rather wry sense of humor and didn't waste words, said, "Are you [Richard Ravitch] prepared to make John Lawe look good?" I said, "Absolutely." I said, "All I want to do is get a deal." We couldn't afford a strike at this point. I'm satisfied with the deal we made. So we worked out the following scheme: that at about 10 that night, I was to be invited by John Lawe and John O'Donnell in to meet with the Executive

Committee. I was to say, "Here is my final offer," and relate something which was not the deal we had negotiated. John Lawe was to say, "That's totally unacceptable," and throw me out of the room. Then he was to turn to his Executive Committee and say, "Let's not go out on strike without having the last offer on the table." That I remember was O'Donnell's point, "We can't go out on strike without having an offer on the table. So let's make a final offer to Ravitch that the so-and-so will never accept." They were to call me back into the room. (This was the plan that we worked out about 3:00 in the morning of the 1st.) I was going to hang my head low and I was going to accept it. John Lawe was going to be a hero and there would be no strike.... Finally at 9:30 [P.M.] I went over to the hotel and sure enough at about a quarter to ten, I got the call from John O'Donnell. "Come on over." I walked in, I made the proposal that we agreed I was to make, and John Lawe said, "It's unacceptable. Get out of here." Then what happened, because John O'Donnell told me the story about 1 in the morning, what happened then is Lawe's Executive Committee, a lot of them had been drinking a lot. When he said, "Let's make a final offer to Ravitch that he will never accept," they said, "The hell with him," and they wouldn't approve the offer. That's why the strike began at midnight. He could not get his Executive Committee to approve the counter proposal—which I would have accepted.[32]

In an April 13th newspaper article, Michael Oreskes told the public that O'Donnell outlined the 7%-7% proposed package to the Local Executive Board (LEB). While Lawe did not push too hard for the proposal, the LEB hooted it down. Dissident transit workers rallying in corridors and chanting in the halls threw the whole meeting into turmoil. The dissident members of the LEB even hooted down the tentative 8%-8% proposition offered by the mediation panel.[33]

SIGNIFICANT STRIKES 159

John Lawe announced a strike on April 1, at 2:05 A.M. in the Princess Ballroom pressroom. In a later interview with *The New York Times* writer William Serrin, O'Donnell said that the union's problem in the talks was that it had to negotiate an agreement that could be sold to the restive workers. And that agreement must come, he said, before the State Legislature provided money for the transportation system.

> Suppose the Legislature should guess that the settlement will be 20 percent. If the union knows what that appropriation is—well, the union is going to hold out for more. That is human nature.[34]

In the same interview, O'Donnell remarked on his receiving a round of joyous applause from the union men. This reception occurred when the men observed him questioning an economist. He chuckled that he had been playing to the house. "You've got to answer these people," he said of the union rank and file. "Otherwise the boys will think you've let them down."[35]

In one of my interviews with my father, he claimed that that strike caused the greatest hardship for the poor and the Black communities. A lot of the women in Harlem worked during the day as housekeepers, and in various jobs necessitating travel on a bus or in the subway. They did not have the taxi fare to get to work. Also, there were serious threats that some of the out-of-work residents in the same area would apply for the transit jobs of the strikers. This might have been one of the only ways an unemployed person could get a job, and many were certainly going to take advantage of the opportunity. This added a lot of pressure to an already difficult situation.

Ravitch and O'Donnell spent long periods discussing the causes of the strike. The two agreed that it could not have been avoided. Ravitch also "talked about 'the bond' that develops between the negotiators—'all looking for a way out.'"[36] As *Times* reporter Michael Serrin summed it up: "Publicly, the negotiators repeatedly said they wished to end the strike," but privately, it was a different story. According to Serrin, shortly after the strike had begun, Scannell, the MTA vice chairman, and O'Donnell privately agreed that the strike would have to last 12 to 13 days, and John Lawe was quoted as saying "The strike as far as we were concerned was a must. We had to get it out of our system."[37]

On the tenth day of the strike, April 10, Ravitch, Lewis B. Kaden (a Columbia law professor assisting Mr. Ravitch), and Scannell met at 9 AM for breakfast with Lawe and O'Donnell in O'Donnell's Sheraton Centre room. Lawe needed a package that he could sell to the union's executive board. That night, in continuous talks between Ravitch, Lawe, and O'Donnell, the union men dropped their demands to nine percent and eight percent plus a cost of living agreement. At about 10 P.M., both sides agreed.[38]

Forty-four members of the Local Executive Board (the forty-fifth was off at weekend National Guard duty) discussed the proposal, and a secret ballot was taken. The union secretary announced the vote: 22 to 22. In the event that the board had rejected the pact, according to Kaden, O'Donnell had considered asking Justice Monteleone to order the proposal submitted to the membership. As it happened, Lawe directed that the proposal be sent to the membership and ordered the workers back to their jobs.[39]

The 31,000-member TWU returned 22,362 mail ballots to the American Arbitration Association. The count was 16,718 votes in favor of the pact and 5,477 against. About 200 ballots were not counted for various reasons.[40]

Under the provisions of the Taylor Law against strikes by public employees, the strikers were penalized two days' pay for every day they were out on strike, which completely canceled out the raises in the first year of the contract.[41]

My nephew Sean O'Donnell was part of the early negotiations with his grandfather. As he recalls:

> The final days of the 1980 negotiations between the NYC Transit Authority and TWU Local 100 fell during spring break of my sophomore year in high school, so I put on my best suit and spent several days sitting in on the meetings, presentations, and negotiations. I was amazed at how carefully choreographed the whole dance was: in private, there was laughter and earnest conversations among the folks from both sides—Dick Ravitch, John Lawe, [and

others], but of course in public, they appeared very much adversaries. I remember one elevator ride with the negotiators from both sides trading jokes. As the elevator doors started to slide open, someone said quietly "lights, cameras, action!" The newspaper and TV cameras started in and suddenly everyone was in character—solemn and serious and weary.

I was amazed that Grandpa could lay out how the negotiations would go, not *might* go or *could* go, but would go. Each offer and each counter offer, every step of the process laid out in advance, and unfolding as he described, headed towards what everyone agreed would be the final contract. If everyone knew what the settlement would be, why did the negotiations have to go through all these steps, and why were we risking a strike that no one wanted? The answer he gave me was a very detailed lesson on all of the issues that don't show up "on the table": That Governor Carey campaigned on a promise to keep the fares at 50 cents. Mayor Ed Koch needed to look tough as he faced New York's myriad problems at the time. Dick Ravitch was trying to save a system that was nearly bankrupt and sinking fast. The "old guard" union leadership was struggling to maintain control, with the up and coming union leaders working hard to look tough and capable, and lastly, that many of the rank and file, having never been through a strike, were itching to try one. Each of the many sides had a constituency to please and to control, and Ravitch and Grandpa were all too aware of the havoc that would result if those constituencies, primarily the public or the rank and file, lost faith in the process.[42]

Again quoting noted *The New York Times* writer William Serrin during the 1980 strike:
> Since affiliating with the bus and subway workers' union as a nonelective official in 1948, he [O'Donnell] has been in the words of an associate, "a wise old fox." As a negotiator, Mr. O'Donnell knows numbers…And he looks behind the obvious for solutions.[43]

ENDNOTES

[1] William Serrin, "Grandfatherly Power behind Transport Workers' Bargaining," *The New York Times*, April 1, 1980, p. B8.
[2] Michael Marmo, *More Profile than Courage: The New York City Transit Strike of 1966* (Albany: State University of New York Press, 1990), p. 1.
[3] John F. O'Donnell, Telephone interview, April 21, 1991.
[4] The mediators were appointed after January 1, 1966 when John V. Lindsay was mayor.
[5] John F. O'Donnell, *Report of the President*, 13th Constitutional Convention, Transport Workers Union of America, AFL-CIO, September 8-12, 1969, Bal Harbor, Florida, p. 160.
[6] "End of the Line in Transit," *The New York Times*, November 6, 1965, p. 28.
[7] John F. O'Donnell, Columbia University Seminar on Labor, April 19, 1967, p. 21, found in O'Donnell's papers in Katonah, New York.
[8] "Facts in Transit," *The New York Times*, December 8, 1965, p. 46.
[9] John F. O'Donnell, "1966 New York Transit Strike," at Labor Management Luncheon, New School for Social Research, May 4, 1966. I am most grateful to Michael Marmo for sharing with me his extensive notes of O'Donnell's speech.
[10] The labor leaders referred to were David Dubinsky, President of the International Ladies Garment Workers Union, and Alex Rose, President of the United Hatters, Cap and Millinery Workers Union.
[11] In 1966, Robert Price was Deputy Mayor of New York City under Mayor Lindsay.
[12] Michael J. Quill had suffered a heart attack soon after arriving at the jail and had been moved to the prison ward at Bellevue.
[13] William Serrin, recalling the 1966 strike on the eve of the 1980 strike, wrote about this hospital meeting: "Mr. Quill lay in an oxygen tent and, when asked by Mr. Price what it would take to settle the strike, Mr. Quill raised five fingers three times, meaning 15 percent—the exact settlement figure, it turned out." "Lindsay Led Talks in '66, But Koch Remains Aloof," *The New York Times* 2 April 1980, B3.
[14] A copy of Michael Marmo's notes are in the possession of Eileen O'Donnell Sheehan, Charleston, South Carolina.
[15] Ronald Donovan, *Administering the Taylor Law: Public Employee Relations in New York* (Ithaca: ILR Press, School of Industrial and Labor Relations, Cornell University, 1990), p. 22.
[16] Scoogie Ryers, Personal interview January 19, 1999.
[17] John F. O'Donnell, Telephone interview, May 26, 1991.
[18] John F. O'Donnell, Telephone interview, May 26, 1991.
[19] Ronald Donovan, *Administering the Taylor Law*, p. 6.
[20] John F. O'Donnell, Telephone interview, April 21, 1991.
[21] Ronald Donovan, *Administering the Taylor Law*, p. 25.
[22] John F. O'Donnell, Telephone interview, February 24, 1991.
[23] Marmo, p. 270.
[24] Michael Goldfield, *The Decline of Organized Labor in the United States* (Chicago: University of Chicago Press, 1987), pp. 230-231.
[25] Michael Oreskes, *[New York] Sunday News Magazine*, March 16, 1980, p. 23.
[26] "Report of the President," 16th Constitutional Convention Transport Workers Union of America, Legal Section, September 28, 1981, p. 165.
[27] John F. O'Donnell, Personal notes. Copy in the possession of Eileen O'Donnell Sheehan, Charleston, South Carolina.

[28] Clipping of newspaper article in the papers of Eileen O'Donnell Sheehan, Charleston, South Carolina.
[29] Michael Oreskes, "TWU: MTA Is April Foolish," *[New York] Daily News*, March 7, 1980.
[30] John F. O'Donnell, Personal notes. Copy in the possession of Eileen O'Donnell Sheehan, Charleston, South Carolina.
[31] Damon Stetson, "Transit Workers Shout Approval of Tuesday Strike," *The New York Times* 28 March 1980, A1.
[32] Richard Ravitch, Personal interview, New York City, February 3, 2006.
[33] Michael Oreskes, "The Inside Story of Transit Strike," *[New York] Daily News*, April 13, 1980, p. 3.
[34] William Serrin, "Grandfatherly Power behind Transport Workers' Bargaining."
[35] William Serrin, "Grandfatherly Power behind Transport Workers' Bargaining."
[36] Michael Oreskes, "The Inside Story of Transit Strike," p. 3.
[37] William Serrin, "The 1980 New York City Transit Negotiations: Public Battles and Private Deals," *The New York Times*, May 7, 1980, p A1.
[38] William Serrin, "The 1980 New York City Transit Negotiations."
[39] William Serrin, "The 1980 New York City Transit Negotiations."
[40] Richard Edmonds, "Transit Workers OK New Contract," *[New York] Daily News*, May 13, 1980, p. 1.
[41] Jerry Bornstein, *Unions in Transition* (New York: Messner, 1981), p. 34.
[42] Written statement from John F. (Sean) O'Donnell III in the papers of Eileen O'Donnell Sheehan, Charleston, South Carolina.
[43] William Serrin, "Grandfatherly Power behind Transport Workers' Bargaining," *The New York Times*, April 1, 1980, p. B8.

[John O'Donnell] told me—he said, "You're going to be in a lot of trouble but we are going to beat them in appeals. You wait and see." And I put my trust in him.

Howard Banker[1]

Chapter Eight

THE COMMUNICATION WORKERS UNION: LOCAL 1101

The second of my father's three proudest accomplishments in the field of labor evolved over a period of two years. The main participants in the crisis were an international union, the Communications Workers of America, AFL-CIO (CWA), and one of its locals, Local 1101. Howard Banker was the President of Local 1101, and my father was both his personal and union lawyer. In 1971, CWA was the recognized collective-bargaining agent of a unit consisting of about 33,000 employees of the Plant Department of the New York Telephone Company throughout the State of New York. Included in this international union were installers, repairmen, maintenance and construction personnel, and some others.

The International had assigned Local 1101 jurisdiction over the 15,000 Plant Department employees in Manhattan, the Bronx, and Brooklyn. The Local had a very limited status under the collective-bargaining agreement between the Telephone Company and the International Union. For instance, it had no authority to invoke the arbitration procedure. On January 11, 1971, fifteen hundred repairmen and installers struck the New York Telephone Company but were ordered by a Federal judge to return to work or pay heavy and progressively more severe fines for violating a court order.[2] The violated order, issued months earlier, should not have been invoked at all, according to O'Donnell. In a brief, O'Donnell described the situation as he viewed it:

> On January 11, 16, and 20, 1971, the appellants Local 1101 and Banker—without a hearing—were summarily adjudged in civil contempt, and fined $1,112,500 and $99,250 respectively, for alleged violation of a temporary restraining order entered seven months earlier in an action involving a labor dispute long since settled.[3]

This "long since settled" dispute had occurred in May of 1970. At that time, the New York Telephone Company temporarily transferred thirteen switchmen from the offices where they usually worked in Brooklyn to other offices in the same borough. The Company and Local 1101 disagreed as to which thirteen should be transferred. The Local contended that the collective-bargaining agreement required that the transfers be made in inverse order of seniority. The Company insisted on selecting those whom it considered most qualified, without respect to seniority. When the Company made the transfers on its own terms, Local 1101 responded by urging its members to refuse overtime assignments. So, on Friday, June 12, 1970, the Company, without invoking arbitration, instituted an action in the Southern District Court against a work stoppage in the form of an overtime boycott.[4]

In an interview, my father explained that Local 1101 did not have a lawyer at the time of the work stoppage in 1970. He went on to say that the locals in the New York Telephone Company were not like most locals. They actually did very little collective bargaining; they were merely administrative arms of the international union.

THE COMMUNICATION WORKERS UNION

This made the international union the collective bargaining agent of the employees, not the local. At this point in time, the local union leadership and the international union leadership were not getting along. The lawyers involved in the 1970 hearings were the lawyers for the International. These representatives of the International went into court and conceded that the Telephone Company was entitled to an injunction against the Local. Not only did the lawyers agree to the temporary restraining order that the company asked for, but they also agreed to a temporary injunction. Because under the Norris-LaGuardia Act a judge cannot issue a restraining order without a hearing in the Federal Court, the temporary restraining order was only good for something like five days, and it could not be extended for more than ten days.[5] This was the basis of O'Donnell's argument.

The mandatory overtime work, which the temporary restraining order was intended to protect over the weekend of June 13-14, was duly performed. Thus the dispute was settled. And later on, in August, the thirteen switchmen were returned to the offices from which they had been transferred. Consequently, neither the action nor the motion for a preliminary injunction was ever prosecuted. The whole thing had become moot. The proceeding was dead.[6]

The strike in question, in 1971, began with the plant employees of the New York Telephone Company in Manhattan, the Bronx, and Brooklyn walking off the job in a dispute over the importation of workers from other companies. These workers were then assigned to work alongside the regular Company employees. The imported workers, however, were offered more advantageous terms of employment than the regular employees had been. The Telephone Company did not go into Federal Court to get an injunction against the strike; instead, they moved to have Howard Banker and the union declared guilty of contempt for violating the existing injunction. Before going into court, O'Donnell asked Banker if he had any money. "The Telephone Company," O'Donnell said to Banker, "is going to grab whatever you've got." Banker said that he had some bonds. "Look, that's my fee, OK?" questioned O'Donnell. Banker agreed and brought O'Donnell the bonds, allegedly as the down payment on O'Donnell's fee for defending Banker. "Of course, I gave them back to him afterwards," my father told me.[7]

In court, O'Donnell told his Fordham classmate, Judge John M. Cannella, that the New York Telephone Company was not entitled to this contempt charge because the injunction was no good. Judge Cannella disagreed and initially fined Banker $250 and the union $7500; the fine was to double each day the workers stayed off the job. O'Donnell assured Banker and the workers, "Listen, the judge is wrong; but you know now this is my judgment. You're taking my word for it. I might be held wrong later on but I don't think I'm wrong. I'm positive I'm right. That injunction is no good."[8] So Banker and the strikers told O'Donnell that they would trust him, and they did not return to work.

In a personal interview with Tamiment Archivist, Gail Malmgreen, Howard Banker explained that he was unprepared for the responsibilities and knowledge involved in being a union president. He thought this was true of most of the international and local union presidents in CWA. "Consequently that's why I think the Company won most of what they did."[9]

When Banker first went into court with O'Donnell, the New York Telephone Company took the Local leadership to task, which Banker expected. What he did not expect were the actions of the CWA'S International vice president, Morton Barr. In an interview with Gail Malmgreen, Banker stated:

> Morty [Barr] was sitting right next to me. I turned around and said, "What is going on?" And Morty broke into tears and said, "I'm doing my job. I got a family, kids," and so on down the line, "and I don't want to go to jail." I said, "Neither do I and I also got a family." Well anyway, the International really did a job on me. John O'Donnell got up and he did a job for me. He's quite a character.[10]

The strike spread to many areas upstate and threatened to involve the parent American Telephone & Telegraph Company and its manufacturing subsidiary, Western Electric. The strike spread after an overflow crowd at the auditorium of Manhattan Center, on 34th Street, voted to continue the walkout, in spite of the court order and continuing fines, because the New York Telephone Company refused to send home the 1,000 craftsmen borrowed from out-of-town districts.[11] Eventually 48,500 workers in the State were on

THE COMMUNICATION WORKERS UNION

strike. The money from fines, none of which had been paid yet, was eventually to go to the Telephone Company for damages.[12]

At 8:00 A.M. on January 24, the striking telephone locals in the state agreed to return to work after the presidents of the CWA and the New York Telephone Company worked out an agreement to end the fourteen-day walkout. The issues that divided the company and the locals were to be submitted to arbitration, and an arbitration award was to be made by 5 P.M. on Friday, January 29.[13] The three-man arbitration board headed by Mitchell M. Shipman, a New York lawyer, included the union representative, John Rank, President of CWA Local 1106 in Queens, and the Telephone Company representative, Charles C. Cushing, retired Assistant Vice President for Personnel.[14]

The award of the arbitration board called for equalizing opportunities for overtime pay and work between local workers and the out-of-towners. It also limited the incoming workers' numbers and length of stay. Howard Banker was quoted in *The New York Times* as saying; "I feel we got more than we were looking for in the beginning."[15]

With the end of the strike, the focus of those involved turned to the accumulating fines. My father explained his next move:

> Then I moved in the Court of Appeals. Sure enough, after about six or seven days—the fines by this time are way up—the Court of Appeals reversed and found that the injunctions really were no good. So that was that.[16]

According to the United States Court of Appeals for the Second Circuit:

> We hold that these judgments of civil contempt are appealable. We also hold that defendants were not in contempt of the restraining order of June 12, 1970, as extended by consent. Accordingly, we reverse.[17]

In his years in labor law, my father had gained the knowledge and reputation for working with unions and their leaders involved in illegal strikes. It was not that he condoned these strikes. That was not his call. His job was to advise the union leaders on where to go next once the illegal strike was called.

A MAN FROM BRUCKLESS

After about thirty-five years in the field, my father, now approaching sixty-five years of age, was about to open a second law firm and take on a very large union.

ENDNOTES

[1] Personal interview between Howard Banker and Gail Malmgreen, Tamiment Library, New York University, September 15, 1994. Courtesy of the Tamiment Library, New York University.
[2] Emanuel Perlmutter, "Judge Orders End to Phone Strike," *The New York Times*, January 12, 1971, p. 28.
[3] John F. O'Donnell, "Brief for Defendants-Appellants Local 1101 and Howard Banker," March 10, 1971, p. 5. Copy of Brief in papers of Eileen O'Donnell Sheehan.
[4] John F. O'Donnell, "Brief for Defendants-Appellants Local 1101 and Howard Banker," p. 7.
[5] John F. O'Donnell, Telephone interview, January 6, 1992.
[6] John F. O'Donnell, "Brief for Defendants-Appellants Local 1101 and Howard Banker," p. 10.
[7] John F. O'Donnell, Telephone interview, January 6, 1992.
[8] John F. O'Donnell, Telephone interview, January 6, 1992.
[9] Personal interview between Howard Banker and Gail Malmgreen, Tamiment Library, New York University, September 15, 1994.
[10] Personal interview between Howard Banker and Gail Malmgreen, Tamiment Library, New York University, September 15, 1994.
[11] Will Lissner, "Phone Union Votes to Continue Strike; Upstate Offices Hit," *The New York Times*, January 15, 1971, p. 1.
[12] "Union Aides Back Telephone Strike," *The New York Times*, January 18, 1971, p. 19.
[13] Paul L. Montgomery, "Phone Workers to Return Today," *The New York Times*, January 25, 1971, p. 17.
[14] "Panel to Decide Telephone Issue," *The New York Times*, January 26, 1971, p. 37.
[15] "Company Upheld in Phone Dispute," *The New York Times*, February 1, 1971, p. 28.
[16] John F. O'Donnell, Telephone interview, January 6, 1992.
[17] United States Court of Appeals, For the Second Circuit, Nos. 856, 857, 858—September Term, 1970, Argued April 2, 1971, Decided June 22, 1971, Docket Nos. 71-1140, 71-1141, 71-1142, p. 3783. Copy in the papers of Eileen O'Donnell Sheehan.

THE COMMUNICATION WORKERS UNION 171

John O'Donnell in 1949

John O'Donnell in 1952

John O'Donnell in September 1955

Francis O'Connell, IEB Member and John O'Donnell confer in October 1965 during a break in the ICC Hearings in Washington DC relating to the protest of PRR_NYC merger

John O'Donnell confers with William Lindner and John Lawe during the 1980 strike

John O'Donnell in 1980

John O'Donnell receives an award from Josie McMillian, President of the New York Metro Area Postal Union. The award states: "to John O'Donnell, An extraordinary man of many achievements. Sincerely, quietly, modestly and with grace, he has demonstrated his loyalty and his deep interest in the welfare of the members of New York Metro Area Postal Union." At the presentation were (L to R) Gerald O'Reilly; Josie McMillian; O'Donnell; Moe Biller, President of the APWU.

Father Harry, Gwynne and John O'Donnell at Notre Dame around 1950

Now in 1970, . . . there was a postal strike. It got a lot of public attention. Moe Biller came to see me and asked if I would represent the Postal Workers. I said [that] I was a mediator, but I knew a very good lawyer who would be ideal for him—and that was John O'Donnell. The Postal Workers hired him.

Theodore W. Kheel[1]

Chapter Nine

AMERICAN POSTAL WORKERS UNION

The third of my father's proudest accomplishments in the field of labor dealt with the 1991 interest arbitration involving the American Postal Workers Union.[2] For the twenty-one years preceding the arbitration, O'Donnell had worked closely with Moe Biller and the union.

The Great Postal Strike—1970

On March 18, 1970, at the Statler Hilton Hotel in New York City, about 3,000 clerks and mail handlers, members of the Manhattan-Bronx Postal Union (MBPU), demanded that their leadership join them in an immediate sympathy strike in support of the striking Branch 36 of the National Association of Letter Carriers (NALC) union. Earlier that day, at 12:05 A.M., the Letter Carriers had placed a picket line at Grand Central Station, which the MBPU's clerks and mail handlers had refused to cross. These two New York City union locals were the largest union locals in the world. While the MBPU was an industrial-type union made up of clerks, mail handlers, maintenance workers, and motor-vehicle employees, Branch 36 of the NACL was a craft organization.[3] Days later, on Saturday, March 21, at the Manhattan Center, a vote for a strike was passed by the members of the MBPU, the Manhattan-Bronx Postal Union. Since 1959, Moe Biller had been president of the MBPU, which was an affiliate of the National Postal Union (NPU). Biller, now faced with an illegal strike, was in need of advice and counsel from a lawyer familiar with illegal strikes such as this one. John F. O'Donnell filled the requirement, accepted the challenge, and was on the scene by March 22, 1970. Twenty-seven years later, Moe Biller autographed a poster for me:

> To Eileen Sheehan, Daughter of my General Counsel and dear friend [O'Donnell] who helped me thru the eye of the storm in the great postal strike of 1970. He also guided me through many troubled waters. I learned so much from him and will always cherish the great memories of our joint activities from 1970 until he left us.[4]

To understand the unrest that lead up to the strike, we would have to go back years earlier. In 1962, President John F. Kennedy had signed Executive Order 10988, which for the first time officially recognized the legitimate role of federal employee unions in the workplace but did not offer them the right to strike.

Soon after the signing of the order, representative elections took place across the country in which seventy-seven percent of the eligible postal employees participated. The result was that seven unions were certified as the exclusive bargaining agents for each of the postal crafts. The National Postal Union, with which Biller's MBPU was associated, was not certified as one of the seven nationally recognized craft unions. This meant that the MBPU, with the largest number of members of any postal local, could not negotiate with management concerning working conditions, promotional standards, grievance procedures, or safety and other matters. The seven craft unions would do it for them. However, a major flaw for all postal workers was that none of the recognized unions could negotiate over wages and fringe benefits, nor was there anything in writing that could compel the Post Office management to reach an agreement with the unions. In any dispute, management would still have the last word.

The 1970 strike was the result of many years of bad feelings among postal employees, who believed that their grievances had been neglected for too long. A major point of contention was that their salaries had fallen far below salaries in private industry. The strike spread quickly across the country, finally involving more than 200,000 workers. After promises, threats, and the intervention of President Richard Nixon, the strike ended in New York City on the afternoon of March 25. After some delayed negotiations, on August 12, 1970, President Nixon signed Public Law 91-375. The law, known as the Postal Reorganization Act of 1970, established an independent governmental agency named "The United States Postal Service." Now, for the first time ever, postal unions had the right to negotiate on all matters concerning wages, fringe benefits, and cost-of-living adjustments. Private industry's salaries and benefits were to be used for comparison. The right to strike, however, was still conspicuously absent.[5]

After the passage of the Postal Reorganization Act, Biller promised the members of his MBPU that he would go to Washington with attorneys Eugene Victor and John O'Donnell to determine the validity of the agreement being negotiated between Secretary of Labor George Shultz and the seven recognized craft unions. Biller and O'Donnell both knew that an agreement was being worked on to settle the complaints of postal workers, and they wanted to be included in the Washington talks. They arrived in Washington in late evening and went straight to the Moreschi Building, where the negotiations were being conducted. Guards told them that only those with a certain grade pass were allowed to go upstairs. Biller sent a message up to Assistant Secretary of Labor, William Usery, asking to be heard. The answer, "not now," came back by way of the elevator. The elevator doors remained opened, however, so O'Donnell said to the others, "Come on, let's go." They got in the elevator and up they went. When they arrived on the right floor, they encountered the press and Biller raised a sufficient ruckus that they disrupted the meeting.[6] According to Biller:

> They might have thrown us out physically if not for Usery. Or, they might have got people to escort us out. But, Usery mollified us and told us he would get us a meeting with Schultz in the morning.[7]

The next day, Secretary of Labor George Schultz met with Biller's group.

The Biller-Schultz meeting provided the basis for the merger of several non-represented unions.[8] After three months of negotiations, Francis S. Filbey, President of the United Federation of Postal Clerks, one of the nationally recognized unions, worked out a merger with Biller. The American Postal Workers Union (APWU) was born as a result of "the storm that rocked the country in March of 1970."[9] Now with the passage of the Postal Reorganization Act, the APWU had the right to bargain collectively. The APWU consisted of the following merged unions: the entire National Postal Workers Union (which included Biller's MBPU); the United Federation of Postal Clerks; and the three craft unions, the Motor Vehicle Operators, the Maintenance Employees, and the Special Delivery Messengers.

New Orleans Convention—1972

Two years later, in August 1972, the newly formed APWU gathered in New Orleans for its first biennial convention. The new officers were elected by referendum on this occasion. The President's position was won by Francis S. Filbey, former President of the United Federation of Postal Clerks, while David Silvergleid, former President of the National Postal Union, became General Executive Vice President. Also elected were six union officers (five of whom were former members of a craft union) and the forty-eight-person Executive Board (thirty-five of whom were former members of a craft union). As Mangum and Walsh noted, "It was not altogether certain that the craft and industrial factions would be able to get along with each other. ... It would not be until 1980 that a slate of the NPU candidates defeated craft candidates for the top positions in the APWU."[10]

AMERICAN POSTAL WORKERS UNION

Biller, as head of the New York MBPU local, was kept to one side—the proper place for a local. Although the MBPU local was very strong, at that time it was not strong enough to take over control of the APWU. The newly appointed lawyer for the APWU made sure that as MBPU's general counsel, John O'Donnell, was not allowed on the floor with Biller. Since he was relegated to the gallery, O'Donnell was forced to communicate by signs with Biller. Biller had his job cut out for him to gain more bargaining power in the APWU, but during the convention, O'Donnell conceived of a way to do just that.[11]

To fully understand what happened at the 1972 convention, we need to look at an event that preceded it. In the month before the 1972 convention, "the AFL-CIO Executive Council had voted to launch a nationwide boycott of Farah Manufacturing Company products until a satisfactory settlement of a strike against the Texas-based clothing company was reached."[12] On the first day that O'Donnell was in New Orleans, there was a large full-page advertisement in the local newspaper for Farah slacks. Two local stores, Maison Blanche and Holmes Godchaux, were selling the pants made by members of the Amalgamated Clothing and Textile Workers Union who were now on strike. O'Donnell approached Biller and showed him the newspaper ad and suggested that they picket the two department stores. Biller agreed that it was a good idea.

Biller went to APWU President Francis Filbey and asked him to appeal to the convention membership for support for a picket line. Filbey reminded Biller that a permit from the New Orleans police department would be required. O'Donnell remembered:

> Moe came to me and told me about it [the need for a permit]. I said, "Forget the police permit and go ahead and picket." I knew damn well [that] I could never get a permit in New Orleans.[13]

Biller thought it would be wise to secure the support of Jacob Potofsky, President of the Amalgamated Clothing and Textile Workers, the union striking Farah. So Biller decided that a telegram of support from Potofsky to APWU president, Filbey, would be needed in order to picket. O'Donnell responded, "If you need a telegram from Potofsky, I'll get it for you." When the telegram from Potofsky arrived the next morning, Filbey authorized the picketing. Biller later told me:

> I did go to your dad and ask, "John, how did you reach Potofsky so fast?" He said, "I was Jacob Potofsky." Filbey went to his grave never knowing about the telegram and John F. O'Donnell.[14]

When there is to be a picket line, there have to be signs to carry. O'Donnell phoned the Amalgamated Clothing Workers, which happened to have an organizer in New Orleans, a representative. He was able to give O'Donnell oaktag and some marking pens. My son Neil, eleven years old at the time, was a guest of his grandfather's on this particular trip to New Orleans. He remembered years later:

> Something was going to go on, but I wasn't sure exactly what. Grandpa and I brought back a bunch of oaktag placards and made protest signs in our hotel room. It must have been more than 30 or 40. We worked fast. I think I drew lines and Grandpa basically lettered them all.... [W]hen it came time to actually hit the streets, Grandpa disappeared. Oh, he could not be seen doing that. That was *verboten*, I remember that.[15]

In his description of the event, O'Donnell added:

> The night before, Neil drew the lines on the oaktag and I wrote in what the signs would say. We got up about fifty signs that night. We were up until midnight. We distributed them the next day, and Neil was there in the front carrying his own sign. Moe led the picket line. He took it over because none of the rest of them liked that kind of thing. It wasn't what postal workers did. They were a dignified group of people—except in New York.[16]

Neil did indeed carry a picket sign. It said, "I told my mother I would not wear Farah slacks." He later remembered that:

> Within the organization, it was apparently made known that Moe was to be credited for it [the picketing]. You know,

you think about what it accomplished. On the surface it showed that the Postal Workers' Union was definitely pro-labor and relatively militant. And within the organization, it established him [Biller] as a player; or gave him some creditability that he must not have had in the first place—that I have only learned since.[17]

O'Donnell's ability to think quickly on his feet while maintaining his composure was quite apparent. These talents would be even more visible during his court appearances four years later in the 1974 Bulk Strike. In an interview with Moe Biller years later, I was told that my father's presentation was the chief factor affecting the judge's decision.[18]

The Bulk Strike - 1974

Late in 1973, the Postal Service relocated the New York Bulk and Foreign Mail facility from the old Brooklyn Army Terminal to Jersey City, New Jersey.[19] Soon after opening the facility, the Postal Service decided to change the employee work schedules in order to cope better with peak mail-flow times. This decision caused a dispute between the United States Postal Service and the Metro Area Postal Union. The problem arose when management arbitrarily changed the starting time of the scheduled 7:00 A.M. work shift to 10:15 A.M. and 3:15 P.M. work shift to 7:00 P.M. Since many of the bulk employees were women, traveling home from a shift that ended at 3:15 A.M. was almost impossible, considering the remote location of the facility.[20]

Biller told his MBPU members to disregard the new schedules and report for work in accordance with their original schedules. When the workers arrived at work at 7:00 A.M. on January 12, 1974, the facility was locked, and so began what some called a strike and others called a lockout, depending on which side of the dispute they were on.

Negotiations were going nowhere. Therefore, on February 1, both sides in the labor dispute were ordered to report on the status of their negotiations to Judge Lawrence A. Whipple, Chief Federal Judge in New Jersey of the United States District Court. According to Walsh and Mangum:

> John O'Donnell, arguing the case for the union before Judge Lawrence Whipple, asserted that a plaintiff seeking an injunction in a court of equity has to come to court with "clean hands," a prerequisite that the Postal Service could not satisfy. They had misrepresented to workers the types of schedules to which they would be assigned and therefore were not entitled to any relief from the court.[21]

The Judge gave the parties a week to negotiate and resolve the schedule problem.

> A week later, the Postal Service was represented by its top trial counsel from Washington whose arrogance did not find favor with Judge Whipple. By contrast, O'Donnell presented a picture of injured innocence. Whipple ordered to parties to arbitrate. . . .[22]

Eventually, a settlement was reached without going to arbitration. After a four-day lockout, the agreement specified that no one who worked at the Bulk as of January 1, 1974 could be involuntarily assigned to a late tour: "[N]ew Bulk workers could be assigned to the new tours, but the original workers could work the late shifts only if they volunteered to do so."[23]

A New Frontier - 1980

While O'Donnell was working in New York, Biller had his eye on Washington. After his wife's death in the late 70s, Biller decided to run for an executive office in the APWU. At the time, Biller had two characteristics that could get in the way of his plans. First, he was a New Yorker, and national unions, in general, do not trust New Yorkers. And second, he was a Jewish New Yorker.[24] In spite of his outsider status, Biller ran for the office of president in 1980 and won. This victory required that he move to Washington, D.C. He got a small apartment around the corner from an Irish pub called The Dubliner. Biller frequently ate at The Dubliner and enjoyed the atmosphere and Irish music. During the war, Biller had spent a few years in Ireland. It was not long before O'Donnell was enjoying the atmosphere of The Dubliner along with Biller. Eventually they began having dinner together whenever O'Donnell was in Washington. O'Donnell always enjoyed the staff at The Dubliner, comprised primarily of new arrivals in America from Ireland. Amid the memories of home, the Irish jokes, the Jewish jokes, and the good food, Biller urged O'Donnell to come to Washington and help him reorganize things.[25]

O'Donnell saw the challenge in working with the APWU. He once described the United States Postal Service, for whom the APWU members worked, as "the largest single non-military employer in the free world."[26] So in 1980, O'Donnell & Schwartz started a second law firm in Washington, D.C. Asher Schwartz dealt with the hiring process in Washington while O'Donnell held the fort in New York. The first new member of the law firm was Darryl Anderson. Anderson later told me that one of the things that he thought remarkable about my father's career was that at the age of seventy-three, he agreed to take on the general counsel ship of a huge union. The new office that they opened in Washington was practically double the size of existing O'Donnell and Schwartz practice.[27]

When Asher Schwartz let it be known that the firm was looking for lawyers, Darryl Anderson was at the same time looking into changing to private practice. Anderson, who came from a position of counselor with the Senate Labor Committee, realized it was time to go when the Democrats were replaced by Republicans in Reagan's win in 1980. Through his position with the Labor Committee, Anderson was acquainted with Tom Donoghue, who at that time was secretary-treasurer of the AFL-CIO. When he asked Donoghue what he thought of the law firm of O'Donnell & Schwartz, Anderson was told by Donoghue that if he had a chance to work with John O'Donnell that he should go, because he was terrific.[28]

In 1992 the corporation of O'Donnell, Schwartz & Anderson, P.C. was officially set up. At that time, the shareholders in this corporation were Darryl J. Anderson, Susan L. Catler, Martin R. Ganzglass, Anton G. Hajjar, Arthur M. Luby, Penny A. Pilzer, and Asher W. Schwartz. O'Donnell was not at that time a member of the D.C. bar. As it happened, he never had a chance to remedy this situation.

When Anton Hajjar was hired, one of Anderson's favorite stories about O'Donnell emerged. The first time O'Donnell had met Anton Hajjar was around 1982. O'Donnell came down to Washington to meet with all the new partners at a dinner. As Anderson tells the story:

> Anton Hajjar was born in Brooklyn and raised Catholic but his background is Arab. Anton and John are sitting next to each other at the Prime Rib and we're having a jolly time, you know. . . . Anton turns to John and says, "John, I just want you to know that I think it is a real credit to your firm that you hired me. Most of the firm is Jewish—the president of your biggest client is Jewish—and the fact that you would hire an Arab really speaks well of you and the firm." John looked at him and he said, "You're an Arab?" Classic—total deadpan, like it was really news to him.[29]

First Negotiations - 1981

The first contract renewal that Biller encountered as president of the APWU with O'Donnell as its general counsel involved the difficult negotiations in 1981. At the time, Vincent Sombrotto was also a fledgling as president of the National Association of Letter Carriers (NALC). Since it was their first time as negotiating union presidents, Biller and Sombrotto decided to join forces as the Joint Bargaining Committee (JBC) of the APWU and NALC, thus jointly representing 80 percent of all postal employees in their clash with the U.S. Postal Service and its leader, Postmaster General William F. Bolger.[30] Negotiations went down to the wire and then some. There was a possibility of a strike and therefore a great deal of tension. In later years, Moe Biller told me how he relieved some of the tension:

> I remember things looked really bleak. We were supposed to go back to the negotiations on the Monday. John [O'Donnell] just wanted me to be very relaxed before we went into all of that. He invited me to the home up in Katonah on the Sunday before. I spent a lengthy day there. We really had a good time—what a wonderful human being.[31]

AMERICAN POSTAL WORKERS UNION 183

During the negotiations, there was a major miscommunication. The Postal Service negotiator proposed raises of $750-600-600 for a three-year contract. Biller and Sombrotto seemed pleased with the offer but said that they would have to caucus. It was decided that the leaders would keep the information to themselves until everything was set. Unfortunately, somehow it was leaked to the press. O'Donnell insisted that the unions get the proposal in writing. When this happened, the misunderstanding became apparent. There was no increase in basic wages, just a lump-sum increase. This meant that the wages would start at the same fiscal amount for the next negotiations in three years' time. In a later interview, Darryl Anderson remarked to me that this misunderstanding almost caused a postal strike. Fortunately, the strike was avoided. "Moe and Vince were furious. Of course John's calming influence was very helpful in times like that."[32]

Another problem that arose during the same negotiations had to do with the postal workers' retirement pay. The Postal Service had proposed a radically different way of dealing with the retirement pay. But O'Donnell was concerned with the pay of the people who were going to retire within the next few years. This concern led to a very important program called the annuity protection program, which was a hallmark of those negotiations. Anderson told me:

> It was John who had the insight to say that something had to be done to protect the benefits of the people who were going to retire within the next few years. If John hadn't reacted quickly, at the time he did, there might have been an agreement without that and people would have lost their rights. That's just one example of John's knowledge and intelligence.[33]

The union settled for a contract that provided for three annual salary increases of $300. Although they settled to avoid a strike, the union's position was that the sacrifices in the 1981 agreement were utterly unwarranted. Things would be different, however, in the 1984 agreement.

Interest Arbitration - 1984

The 1984 negotiations did not proceed with any degree of success. Darryl Anderson gave one description of the situation.

> We [APWU and NALC] had been preparing for arbitration because we were in joint bargaining. Our star witness was this high power economist [Joel Popkin]. John was working with him to prepare our arbitration case for the joint bargaining—for both sides.
>
> That evening Moe and Vince, who personified the two unions APWU & NALC, were in disagreement about how to deal with the overtime issue—very important to both unions. They said they had a falling out about how the negotiations had gone, what the agreement was, and then how to resolve that disagreement. The Letter Carriers, in what was a fine bit of treachery, ultimately agreed that they would go separately from us.
> The Postal Service [USPS] saw it to their advantage to try to divide the two unions and agreed that they would do this.[34]

Moe Biller added to this story:

> We had a call on a Friday afternoon from the Counsel of the Postal Service. Sitting in my office was your Dad, Darryl Anderson and two or three of the other top officers. They [USPS] attempted to get us to bend or to yield (that will be more expressive I guess). Then the threat came that they [USPS] were going to pull out on us and just going to sit down and arbitrate with the Letter Carriers and we weren't going to be involved.
>
> So on a Sunday, the Counsel for the Postal Service called him [your father] up and said, "You know John, we are going to arbitration tomorrow with the Letter Carriers and we're going to need those exhibits." He said, "I don't care where you're going," he says, "I'm on my way home. You told us we were are not going to be doing a damn thing about this."[35]

Darryl Anderson takes the story from there.

> It was sort of classic O'Donnell. In a crisis he was always one to smile, sort of grin around his cigar, and he said, well we've got the exhibits. It was true. They were kind of stalemated. They couldn't go ahead. It was sort of a classic O'Donnell moment because he was positioned in a way that made it impossible for them to shaft his client. They really wanted to do [that] and he wouldn't let them do it.
>
> As a result they had to find another way. At the opening day of what then became a joint arbitration, but with the two unions at each other's throats, Vince Sombrotto announced his intention to make a statement at the beginning of the arbitration. John said, "Whatever you do, don't let Moe be in the room because he's liable to get involved with him." So we made Moe stay in his hotel room while Vince was talking. It's a good thing because Vince accused the APWU of trying to cut a separate deal with the Postal Service—turning the truth around 180 degrees. I think if Moe had been in the room, Moe would have blown his top, so John's advice is as always—sage. Then both came in later after Vince had made his statement and we just went on. It was rather a bizarre proceeding, at least at the outset, because of the conflict between the two unions. But, as with most of these conflicts between the two unions—it's like—with enemies like that—you won't need any friends. Ultimately we had them working together. It worked out but it was very difficult.[36]

All the parties involved failed to reach an agreement. Since the unions do not have the right to strike, they proceeded instead to interest arbitration, a type of arbitration that permits an arbitrator, or a panel of arbitrators, to establish the terms of the collective-bargaining agreement. In handing down the decision, Clark Kerr,[37] panel chairman and an experienced labor arbitrator and mediator, warned:

> Arbitration of interests, as this arbitration is, sometimes may be necessary. It is never desirable. Arbitration of

interests, if it becomes the practice rather than the occasional exception, can become lethal in the long run. It is far better for the parties and American society, that the parties themselves write their own contracts.[38]

The interest arbitration proceedings convened on Tuesday, December 11, 1984. The panel of arbitrators included the following members: Dr. Clark Kerr, Chairman; Bruce Simon (chosen by the NALC); Theodore Kheel (chosen by the APWU); Peter Nash and Joseph Mahon (chosen by the United State Postal Service, the USPS). George J. Tichy, Richard H. Harding, and D. Richard Froelke appeared on behalf of the United States Postal Service; Keith Secular and Vince Sombrotto represented the NALC; John F. O'Donnell and Darryl J. Anderson represented the APWU.[39]

For this arbitration, the APWU and the NALC again joined forces and formed the Joint Bargaining Committee (JBC). As lead counsel, John O'Donnell made the initial presentation on behalf of over five hundred thousand employees of the United States Postal Service (USPS). O'Donnell had to tackle an issue that was dividing the APWU and NALC at the time: whether the JBC would submit a particular dispute to the interest arbitrators for resolution. He addressed this subject in his opening. Keith Secular, the attorney for the Letter Carriers, objected to O'Donnell's addressing the issue as he did. Thus the conflict between the two unions began right at the beginning of the arbitration.[40]

When asked where he would like to speak from, O'Donnell answered: "I'd like to speak from where I am, I think—because I don't want to turn my back on my friends in the back. It's the only place I have friends, I think."[41] After some laughter, the hearing began. The previous contract had expired on July 20, 1984, leaving a five-month span without a contract. O'Donnell contended:

> For a labor practice of up to fifty years, it's been my destiny to have represented unions and employees and industries that were almost invariably facing financial termination . . . all of them at one time privately owned when I knew them first, but the private owners were forced out and could no longer exist.[42]

Dealing across the table with people who did not have anything to give made it very difficult. In the 1984 negotiations, however, O'Donnell felt that he was finally representing the employees of an industry that was flourishing. That opinion was based on a speech made by William Bolger, who was appointed the sixty-fifth Postmaster General in 1978, to the National Association of Postmasters on August 29, in 1984. Bolger stated:

> We are just one month away from the close of the fiscal year, and it is already clear that 1984 will be a record year.[43]

A barrage of economists followed with data, charts, and presentations by Michael Wachter for the USPS and Joel Popkin for the JBC. Although both men used the same data, they drew different conclusions from the data. O'Donnell contended that the JBC's position was that the sacrifices in the 1981 agreement were unwarranted. They were the result of misleading statistics and the failure of the Postal Service to disclose that it was about to increase the postal rate to the point where it would get very much out of the red and well into the surplus side.

The main issue of the arbitration involved comparable worth, in other words, a comparison of the postal workers' hours and pay with the hours and pay of the white-collar general-schedule employees. In his presentation in the 1984 negotiations, O'Donnell returned to the words of one of Bolger's predecessors, Postmaster General Winton M. Blount, and cited Blount's overview of the postal service at the time of the Postal Reorganization in 1970:

> The nexus of existing benefits would constitute a bargaining floor for future improvements of the wages, hours and working conditions of rank and file postal employees—and would be determined at the bargaining table under statutory provisions guaranteeing that postal employees cannot fall behind their counterparts in private industry—and guaranteeing that negotiating impasses would be resolved in a kindly, fair and equitable manner.[44]

In his award, the chairman of the arbitration panel, Clark Kerr, remarked that the arbitration was unusual in that it directly involved "half-a-million people—the largest number ever covered by an arbitration in the history of the United States."[45] He emphasized moderate restraint, or a slowing of wage increases. He went on to say that it "may also be necessary in future years to approximate the guideline of comparability as established by Congress."[46] The award included a 2.7% annual increase in wages for "incumbent" employees and major improvements in working conditions, especially a reduction in mandatory overtime.[47] The contract was established for three years, July 1984-July 1987. Then in 1987, an agreement was reached but the expiration date was changed to November 1990, so that it would be a three-and-a-half-year contract. This was the result of a negotiated agreement.[48]

Interest Arbitration - 1991

November of 1990 came and went without an agreement. The APWU and the NALC disagreed among themselves about what should be included in the interest arbitration. The main issue for the APWU concerned the postal service's right to contract out certain work normally done by the clerks, who were members of the APWU. The letter carriers wanted that issue addressed in a "rights arbitration," not in the interest arbitration. If it had been included in the interest arbitration, the arbitrator could have put the terms in the contract itself. As it was, the APWU did indeed take it to a "rights" arbitration.[49]

The interest arbitration did not begin until March 5, 1991. The arbitration panel consisted of APWU panel member Theodore W. Kheel; NALC panel member Bruce Simon; USPS panel members Joseph Mahon and Peter Nash; and neutral arbitrator and panel chairman Richard Mittenthal.

Mittenthal made a poor judgment call almost immediately[50], when he attempted to arrange a private meeting between the two union presidents of the JBC, the USPS team, and all their lawyers. At the meeting, Mittenthal hoped he would be able to settle the differences between Biller and Sombrotto. However, as Darryl Anderson recalls:

As a result Moe and Vince had an incredible shouting match in front of the assembled group, which was the only time they had ever truly lost their tempers with each other in the presence of the postal service.[51]

Even with such trying moments, or especially because of them, my father considered the third of the high points in his career to be the role he played as lead presenter for the largest unit ever covered in an arbitration in this country. He had this opportunity both in 1984 and in 1991. When told that the panel hoped he would be brief in his presentation, O'Donnell said that he could not cut his remarks shorter, but he would try to talk a little faster. From there, O'Donnell immediately went on the offensive and attacked the deal between the USPS and the leaders of the Mail Handlers Union. The USPS was quoting the results of this arbitration in their presentation. "So that there be no question about it . . . I am now demanding that if they're going to refer to that so-called arbitration, that they produce the transcript of the record made before that arbitrator."[52]

Continuing with his presentation, O'Donnell ridiculed the inconsistencies in the USPS case. On page 2 of their brief, the USPS said that
> [I]n the last few years the Postal Service has seen increased resentment over price increases and poor service resulting not only in calls for privatization, but supporting the development of alternative delivery systems and new technologies which permit customers to bypass the mail stream entirely.[53]

Yet at the same time, as O'Donnell observed, Postmaster General Anthony M. Frank had published a report not too long before the 1991 arbitration. In this report, which became Exhibit 46 in the hearing, O'Donnell claimed that Frank said something entirely different. Frank cites the April 1990 statistics of the semi-annual national tracking study, which O'Donnell quoted from p. 23 of Frank's report:
> 83 percent of the general public reported overall satisfaction with the Postal Service. The 83 percent favorability

rating is the second highest rating the Postal Service has received since the semi-annual studies began in 1973.[54]

In addition, the Postal Service sought to erode full-time employment by using part-timers. Since Postmaster Frank was insisting that "more part-time workers are needed because post offices are busier at certain times, like the noon hour, and many Americans want part-time work,"[55] O'Donnell countered by cautioning the panel about the use of part-timers to cut costs:

> Surely, a competent man ought to be able, in the larger offices, to arrange and schedule its work force to do the best job possible but the easy thing is for the top man [to say]. "No, I'm not going to bother scheduling. Listen, I'll hire a part-timer." That's what they're doing. There's a lot of ineptitude in management, and they're taking it out, now, on the unions by asking for more part-timers, more flexis, more part-timers.[56]

He continued to attack the insistence that part-timers were needed to the extent claimed by the Postal Service:

> There you have the answer. The easy way is to take part-timers. Why bother adjusting the schedule? They're spending millions and millions of dollars for equipment, and they propose to have the equipment stand idle during the hours when the part-timers are not there. . . . [T]hey're spending billions for automated equipment that's going to stand there idle, rather than make a little effort, a little ingenuity, and schedule the employees to a full-time day's work.
>
> Sure, they'll talk about supermarkets and pickle factories. Well, the Postal Service is neither a pickle factory, nor a supermarket.[57]

O'Donnell went on to state that the JBC was not bargaining down: "We had a floor, and we want to bargain up from that."[58]

The award of the arbitrators made gave the unions a pay raise of 5.8% over the four years covered by the contract. This was less than they demanded, but more than was originally offered. Management, however, would be allowed more flexibility. Although my father and Moe continued to work together, this was the last time John F. O'Donnell negotiated a contract on behalf of the APWU.

In 1993, right after my father's death, Biller paid tribute to his friend and closest adviser.

> John O'Donnell was many things to me—friend, lawyer, counselor, a steady hand during times of stress. But more than that, he was a gutsy fighter in the struggle for human rights and labor rights.[59]

ENDNOTES

1. Theodore W. Kheel, Telephone interview, August 4, 1991.
2. For the other achievements my father noted in our conversation of February 18, 1991 as successes he was proud of, the 1980 New York City transit strike and the prolonged struggle for the Communication Workers of America in the early 1970s, see chapters 7 and 8.
3. John Walsh and Garth Mangum, *Labor Struggle in the Post Office* (Armonk, NY: M. E. Sharpe, 1992), p. 16.
4. The poster is a copy of a painting by Thomas Germano entitled "The Great Postal Strike, 1970," in the possession of Eileen O'Donnell Sheehan, Charleston, South Carolina.
5. Walsh and Mangum, p. 16.
6. Walsh and Mangum, pp. 35-36.
7. Walsh and Mangum, p. 36.
8. Walsh and Mangum, p. 37
9. Walsh and Mangum, p. 39.
10. P. 97.
11. John F. O'Donnell, Telephone interview, March 24, 1991.
12. Walsh and Mangum, p. 103.
13. John F. O'Donnell, Telephone interview, March 24, 1991.
14. Moe Biller, Telephone interview, September 5, 1993. Much the same story appears in Walsh and Mangum, pp. 103-105, since they interviewed both Moe Biller and my father in 1990, shortly before I interviewed them.
15. Neil Sheehan, Telephone interview, March 24, 1991.
16. John F. O'Donnell, Telephone interview, March 24, 1991.
17. Neil Sheehan, Telephone interview, March 24, 1991.
18. Moe Biller, Telephone interview, April 7, 1997.
19. Walsh and Mangum, p. 115.
20. "Jersey Mail Facility Disrupted in Dispute Over New Hours," *The New York Times*, January 22, 1974, p. 1. Walsh and Mangum (p. 115) give different starting times, citing

that the new schedules assigned "the majority of employees to work between 4 p.m. and midnight,"

21. Walsh and Mangum, p. 115.
22. Walsh and Mangum, p. 116.
23. Walsh and Mangum, p. 116.
24. John F. O'Donnell, Personal interview, July 7, 1988.
25. John F. O'Donnell, Personal interview, July 7, 1988.
26. Transcript of 1984 Postal Arbitration, December 11, 1984, p. 32. Copy in the papers of Eileen O'Donnell Sheehan.
27. Darryl Anderson, Personal interview, April 8, 1997.
28. Darryl Anderson, Personal interview, April 8, 1997.
29. Darryl Anderson, Personal interview, April 8, 1997. Art Luby, a former partner in the Washington office, recalled the same story as one of his favorites in a telephone interview, February 23, 2006.
30. Walsh and Mangum, p. 171.
31. Moe Biller, Telephone interview, September 5, 1993.
32. Darryl Anderson, Personal interview, April 8, 1997.
33. Darryl Anderson, Personal interview, April 8, 1997.
34. Darryl Anderson, Personal interview, April 8, 1997.
35. Moe Biller, Telephone interview, September 5, 1993.
36. Darryl Anderson, Personal interview, April 8, 1997.
37. Clark Kerr was a former President of the University of California system.
38. Walsh and Mangum, p. 198.
39. Transcript of 1984 Arbitration Proceedings, pp. 1-2. Copy in the papers of Eileen O'Donnell Sheehan.
40. Darryl Anderson, Personal interview, April 8, 1997.
41. Transcript of 1984 Postal Arbitration, p. 31. Copy in the papers of Eileen O'Donnell Sheehan.
42. Transcript of 1984 Postal Arbitration, p. 36. Copy in the papers of Eileen O'Donnell Sheehan.
43. Transcript of 1984 Postal Arbitration, p. 36. Copy in the papers of Eileen O'Donnell Sheehan.
44. Transcript of 1984 Arbitration Proceedings, pp. 66-67. Copy in the papers of Eileen O'Donnell Sheehan.
45. Walsh and Mangum, pp. 197-198.
46. Walsh and Mangum, p. 197.
47. Walsh and Mangum, pp. 197-198.
48. Walsh and Mangum, p. 200.
49. Darryl Anderson, Personal interview, April 8, 1997.
50. Darryl Anderson, Personal interview, April 8, 1997.
51. Darryl Anderson, Personal interview, April 8, 1997.
52. Transcript of 1984 Arbitration Proceedings, p. 8. Copy in the papers of Eileen O'Donnell Sheehan. See also Walsh and Mangum, p. 225.
53. Transcript of 1984 Arbitration Proceedings, p. 17. Copy in the papers of Eileen O'Donnell Sheehan.
54. Transcript of 1991 Arbitration Proceedings, p. 18. Copy in the papers of Eileen O'Donnell Sheehan.
55. "Postal Workers' Contract Talks Break Down," *The New York Times*, November 22, 1990, p. B14.

56. Transcript of 1991 Arbitration Proceedings, p. 27. Copy in the papers of Eileen O'Donnell Sheehan.
57. Transcript of 1991 Arbitration Proceedings, pp. 29-30. Copy in the papers of Eileen O'Donnell Sheehan.
58. Transcript of 1991 Arbitration Proceedings, p. 35. Copy in the papers of Eileen O'Donnell Sheehan.
59. Moe Biller, *The American Postal Worker*, February 1993, p. 5.

Any union which relies on the bargaining table to accomplish its goals and achieve a better way of life for its members is doomed to disappointment and frustration, because union bargaining strength has been eroded and seriously diminished by shackling legislation, hostile judges and administrative agencies dominated by employer-minded appointees.

John F. O'Donnell[1]

Chapter Ten

FAREWELL

In this last chapter of my examination of my father's life and career, I will focus on three subjects. First, I will take a close look at his last report to a Transport Workers' Union Convention (which he wrote in 1989). Second I will share thoughts of his fellow lawyers and union workers. Finally, I will share some personal reflections on his last days battling the cancer that finally overtook him in January of 1993. The Transport Workers' Union's (TWU) report illustrated O'Donnell's enduring commitment to the labor movement as well as his passion for ensuring its future, while my recollection of my father's difficult and painful days serves as a reminder of the essence of his character and personality. In both cases, John O'Donnell remained true to himself to the very end.

In my father's last report, he decided to concentrate on those developments in the field of labor law that have had the most damaging impact on the labor movement. He wished to, as he put it, "provide the Convention with background information for its serious consideration in determining TWU's future programs and policies."[2] One of his major points concerned the Wagner Act, which was the major labor law when he became the General Counsel of TWU in 1948. That law, he explained, had since then become, "emasculated by amendments which distorted its essential purpose."[3]

In the late 1940s, not many union contracts provided for grievance arbitration. Today grievance arbitration is a widespread procedure that occupies a considerable amount of the labor lawyer's time. Forty years ago, three attorneys were more than adequate to serve the TWU, but by 1989, each of his two offices, in Washington and New York, had six partners and two associate attorneys all specializing in labor law. This great burden placed on the legal department in more recent years was not, as one might initially suspect, a result of the growth of union membership, but rather, a reflection of the extent, "to which the law, the courts and governmental agencies have intruded into affairs of labor unions."[4] In essence, unions today have to defend their very existence.

In New York City transit, the signature of the union officers on recent agreements was hardly dry when management turned loose a bevy of lawyers "whose principal mission seemed to be to recapture as much as possible of the benefits won for the employees in the negotiations."[5] In 1985, the Transit Authority (TA) officials built up a supervisory and administrative force out of all proportion to the number of hourly personnel. As O'Donnell wryly observed: "In the upper reaches of the TA Labor Relations Department there are: a Vice President, a Deputy Vice-President, an Assistant Vice President, and a Director of Labor Disputes and Arbitrations, all of them lawyers and all of them without an iota of relevant experience in labor relations."[6]

The Legal Department of the TWU is, as my father observed, "aware of the extent to which the Reagan administration has undermined and weakened organized labor and negated many of the rights of minorities and working people generally."[7] This is not a union-oriented judgment. Neutral observers are in agreement.

FAREWELL

My father also noted that Federal Judges hold lifetime positions and there is little that labor can do about them for many years. For this reason,

> [t]here is only one available road for labor to follow if it is to prevent further erosion of its strength and, hopefully, to regain the lost ground. That road is through the Congress. The only available strategy is more effective political action.[8]

O'Donnell did not just write this report and then sit back and relax. He was always ready when help or advice was needed. Three years after he wrote the report, in 1992, my father was diagnosed with cancer. He had radiation treatment, which helped in the short term but could not prevent the metastasis. However, true to form, O'Donnell was still working and driving himself to the hospital for his radiation treatments.

David Rosen, a law partner whom my father held in high esteem, told me:

> Your father was especially adept at knowing how to work with union leaders—which is a whole area of law that nobody teaches in any law school. Everyone has to know how to deal with their clients but these are clients where the personnel, on one hand, . . . is a steady group that goes on from year to year; [and] on the other hand, some get old and go and new ones come in. At this union he was certainly one of the sources of continuity from the beginning practically.[9]

When asked if my father suddenly came back to life these ten years later, would he be out of touch with the union today, David answered

> I don't think he would be lost at all. I think he would recognize the problems, I think he would be very interested in the direction they had taken. He was certainly aware—the New Directions group began at Local 100 in the mid 80s. . . . He would have recognized that situation right away. . . . He'd recognize the problems and have his usual

extra-perspective that would help in dealing with the problems. I'm a firm believer that the more good minds that look at a problem, from different directions, the better a chance for a really difficult problem for finding some way to deal with it. The thing with your father—because he was there from the beginning of the union, he could speak as a union person—which I can't. I mean I am a union person but I don't have the same credibility that you get from having been there at the creation of the union——having been in it for all that time. I have to speak much more as a lawyer, I think.[10]

On a lighter side, another law partner, Darryl Anderson told me in a 1997 interview in Washington DC:

John loved to tell jokes. He always had the newest jokes. Whenever he came to town, we could depend on him to sit down with Moe Biller and we'd all share jokes. That was actually a revelation to me when I came to work here in 1981 because telling jokes, . . . ethnic jokes, was really not in fashion, and Moe and John were the old school. And actually, now that I think about it, I think perhaps that's not quite true. But certainly they loved telling Jewish jokes and they loved telling Irish jokes, primarily. It was jarring to me because I wasn't used to hearing ethnic humor. You didn't hear this stuff anymore, at least with people my age and among lawyers, and so forth. But I got used to it, and I soon learned that it was done with absolute good will and never in a context where it could offend anyone—and always with humor. It was actually a delightful part of the way John was. Everyone around him reveled in it.

One of John's jokes was about the guy who was wearing a green suit who came and sat at the bar and he didn't say anything. The bartender said, "What will you have?" The guy said, "Thank you very much – I'll have a Hennessy." The bartender gave him the whiskey and he drank it.

FAREWELL   199

The bartender said, "That will be $4.50." The guy said, "Wait a minute." The bartender said, "You drank it now you have to pay for it." The guy said, "No, you offered it to me." The bartender said, "You bum. Get out of here. Never come into this bar again." A couple of weeks later the bartender looks up and the man in the green suit was sitting there again. The bartender said, "Hey you, I remember you. Didn't I throw you out of here a few weeks ago for not paying for your drink?" The guy said, "No, I have never been in here in my life." The bartender said, "Well then you must have a double." "Well, thank you very much," said the man in the green suit, "make it a Hennessy."[11]

A side of my father that I did not see too often, thank heavens, was described by Darryl in his interview:

On one occasion, I only remember one occasion over all the years that I worked with him, John lost his temper with me and I didn't enjoy the occasion at all, I must tell you. The Washington partners wanted a bigger share of the pie, in contrast to the New York partners. We talked among ourselves and decided what we thought was the right thing to do. I think I told John by phone. [When he came to Washington] I think John only had a brief meeting [with the Washington partners] and then we all went out to dinner. During dinner, John turned to me with some anger and said that he thought I was being unreasonable and unfair. I don't remember his words now but I remember I was quite stunned by his criticism. I had never seen that look in his eyes directed at me before. It was most uncomfortable, I mean to tell you.

We talked about it. I don't want to go into the details but we went ahead and did what was fair given the fees we were getting from various clients. I never talked about it with him after he got mad other than at that dinner table. We worked it out—right within a few minutes. It was history. It never interfered with our relationship. It didn't last. It blew over in ten minutes. But I remember being very impressed. It was no fun being the subject of John O'Donnell's wrath. It's not something I enjoyed, and I'm sure whoever else had to cross swords with him had a very different view of him than I did—which was a very congenial fellow. In fact I often said in those days as soon as I got to know John, one of my ambitions in life was to practice law with John O'Donnell as long as I could because it was a great joy.[12]

With each lawyer, I was intent on finding that special trait of my father's that I could imitate, a trait that enabled John O'Donnell to gain respect in difficult situations. Ted Kheel told me in 1991 that my father was a good lawyer because

First of all he knew the law. That helps. Second, he understood the labor movement. A labor lawyer has to understand the labor movement. There is a lot of politicking within the movement. Thirdly, John is very practical minded and he's also a dedicated person. He believes in the trade union movement but he is very practical. He doesn't tilt with windmills.[13]

Another point of view was offered by Arthur Luby of the Washington law firm. While he was no longer with that law firm, he recalled:

The good thing about working with [John] was that there was nothing new under the sun. You could be jumpy about something . . . or concerned about something . . . or believing you were one step away from disaster . . . and John had always lived through it before, and he could convince you, correctly, that you would find your way through it . . . and that there was always a way of avoiding disaster. And, there always was.

I remember, in 1984, we were in interest arbitration, . . . which is a form of arbitration in which the arbitrator dictate the terms of the agreement . . . and he had been through that many times with the New York Transit Authority. That was one of my first experiences with it. We were getting ready to put on the first day. It seemed like it was a very high stakes game, we were nervous. The Postal Service had the Reagan administration behind them. They were pursuing their regressive objectives, very aggressively. John and I were walking over, and he could see that I was kind of sweating on it, and he told me: "You know, today's an interesting anniversary." I asked him what he meant. He said, "Well, sixty years ago today I saw the coast of Nova Scotia after I had been deported from Ireland." That was sort of his way of telling me . . . "look, more important things have happened in my life and more important things are going to happen in yours." He was right and that was the right attitude to come into any kind of pressure proceeding.

I think that John had a real talent for being able to develop relations with managements in which you could find solutions. He was capable of putting on a good piece of litigation and standing up to management . . . but he was the kind of person that was not looking for confrontation. He was looking to find solutions and the people who worked with him understood that and because of that they would offer him solutions and he would bring those home to his clients. And that method of proceeding, which really in a lot of ways is a lost art, was certainly his primary contribution to both in the Postal Service and in dealing with the Transit Authority. There were a lot of disasters that were avoided because of him.[14]

Malcolm Goldstein opened my eyes to the reasons for the frustrations I detected in my father in later years when I started interviewing him for this book.

> I think over the years the leaders became less inclined to listen to [your father when he suggested] that they co-opt the best of the dissident talent. If somebody came along

and really was gifted and went into the opposition, it was customary in the early years to find a place for them—to make a place for them within the hierarchy—to find a way to creatively challenge their talents and to take the sting out of the opposition. One guy . . . [was] apparently a very thoughtful and scholarly guy, and eventually they took him out by making him the safety director. And this guy put his enormous energies into safety issues. He became a very dedicated and loyal worker for the union, and I assume achieved a great deal of good as the safety director. But at the same time, he laid aside his political opposition.

The mistake that the union made more and more after your father and John Lawe were not around to guide the way was that they left the talented young vocal opponents stay out there and fester. Eventually they came to critical mass. Enough of them realized that if they got together behind one guy, they could overthrow the old guard. That's what happened in 2000. But that is virtually ten years after your father was off the scene.

Your father never harbored false illusions—never got caught up in any of the rhetoric. He understood what it took. Mind you, he always said you can't ignore the troublemakers and the loud ones and the vocal ones. If everybody did their job right, there would be no need for a union and we'd be out of a job. So there is a place for them. But he certainly never deluded himself that the things that the hotheads advocated were actually good policy or made a strong organization. He was very attuned to the realities.

He was very careful never, never to flaunt his role—never. He always played low key; he was never a publicity hound. When he spoke, he spoke with the authority of Mike Quill, Matty Guinan or John Lawe—and people listened and they knew they were getting the benefit of both John Lawe's authority, Matty Guinan's authority and John

O'Donnell's wisdom. But he was very careful never to be at the center of the picture.

He was a wonderful teacher by example. The thing I loved most about your father, as a lawyer, was—it wasn't deviousness—it was almost transparency. Because what he'd do, he would sit across the table from you. He'd smile at you. He'd behave in the most genial manner. He would tell you exactly what he was going to do to you if you didn't go along with what he needed or wanted and then he'd do it—and all done in the most pleasant terms and never any malice and never any bitterness—never any partisanship. He knew what he had to do. He would tell you what he was going to do—give you plenty of time to decide whether you wanted to risk having done to you what he was planning to do, and then if you didn't agree—he'd do it. His great facility was that he could always take a problem and sort of rotate it—you know rotate it 90 degrees—and come at it from a different angle. Asher was the book guy. If you needed a legal solution to something, you went to Asher, and Asher would know chapter and verse what law applied and what the precedents were. Your father always looked at it from a different perspective. He would know where the sensitivities were, what the pressure points were, what the political nuances were, and he was always prepared to exploit those—to go after those and to take the problem from being a surely dry legal issue to something that really had substance and mattered.[15]

Finally, on a lighter note, a union leader, Scotty Henry, told of my father's golfing talents:

I was a general chairman for the Bronx bus division. I used to be up at the King Street Garage. . . . I remember one time when we went, I think it was, to Las Vegas. There was your father and John Lawe. They asked me, "Do you want to go and play golf?" I said, "Sure, I got my clubs with me."

So I went and got the clubs and we played golf. Your father and John Lawe were absolutely hopeless. I would hit a ball, we had carts you know, and I used to have to sit in the cart because your father would hit the ball and it would go 50 feet—and I've hit one over 100 yards. So I just had to sit there while they'd keep pecking at it. I remember when we got to one of the holes and I said, "John, it's obvious to me that you don't understand this game." "What do you mean?" he says. "It seems to me that you think that the more times you hit that ball from the tee until you get it in the hole, that makes the winner." [I had to tell him:] "It's not the way it works. You are supposed to get less strokes."[16]

In mid-January 1993, John O'Donnell entered the hospital for the last time, but he continued to conduct business from his hospital bed by phone and with visitors from the union and from the firm. The day before he died, he was giving legal counsel over the phone and sharing stories with friends, family, and fellow patients.

His obituary in The New York Times noted that he "was at the center of many intense transit negotiations, including the 11-day strike in 1980. Among his early victories was getting $1.1 million in back pay for workers on the old Third Avenue Railway in 1950 and helping win a five-day, 40-hour week in a 28-day strike of eight bus lines."[17] Summing up the man and his impact, the Times added: "Mr. O'Donnell was known among labor insiders for his gargantuan cigars, Irish brogue, meticulous preparation and articulate presentation."[18]

Ted Kheel, the labor mediator who would eulogize him at his funeral on a cold, clear February morning a few days later, was quoted in the obituary: "Some people specialize in problems, but he was always looking for solutions."[19]

John F. O'Donnell was indeed a man who faced problems—but he was also a man who sought solutions, and found them.

FAREWELL

ENDNOTES

1. John F. O'Donnell, "Legal Department," *Report of the President, Transport Workers of America*, 18th Constitutional Convention, Miami, FL, October 2-6 1989 (New York: TWU, 1989), p. 88.
2. O'Donnell, p. 88.
3. O'Donnell, p. 88.
4. O'Donnell, p. 89.
5. O'Donnell, p. 93.
6. O'Donnell, p. 93.
7. O'Donnell, p. 95.
8. O'Donnell, p. 95.
9. David Rosen, Personal interview, December 23, 2003.
10. David Rosen, Personal interview, December 23, 2003.
11. Darryl Anderson, Personal interview, April 8, 1997.
12. Darryl Anderson, Personal interview, April 8, 1997.
13. Theodore W. Kheel, Telephone interview, August 4, 1991.
14. Arthur Luby, Telephone interview, February 23, 2006.
15. Malcolm Goldstein, Personal interview, January 28, 2006.
16. Scotty Henry, Personal interview, March 25, 2002.
17. Bruce Lambert, "John F. O'Donnell, 85, a Lawyer and Advocate for Union Workers," *The New York Times* 29 January 1993, p. A17.
18. Lambert.
19. Lambert.

Part II

John F. O'Donnell: The Private Man

PREFACE

As planned, this second part of the book will address the private life of my father. From family vignettes of son, brother, father, and grandfather—even as great grandfather—a man with mischievous eyes and a beguiling voice—a man of great wisdom—will become apparent.

As Johnny O'Donnell's daughter, I hope that by taking a biographical journey through his life, I will discover the magical thread to unravel the mystery of my father's personality, for he was a powerful presence and a positive influence on so many people, and yet he lived his life in a remarkably quiet and unassuming manner. This work has been in preparation for many years, and much of what is in the first part came from my father's many conversations with me both in person and by phone. I have also pooled the memories of my brother and two sisters, and of his grandchildren.

In our many conversations about Ireland, my father never really opened up about his early life, about his family, or about his feelings regarding the role he played as the oldest O'Donnell offspring. Much of what I was able to recover has come from other sources.

Chapter One

SOME FAMILY STORIES

Describing my father physically is difficult. Growing up, I always thought he was very tall; that is until I surpassed him in height, so I must admit that he was in fact, small in stature—about 5'8". As I picture him now, the ears that stood out from the side of his head and that wonderful half smile are the first characteristics that come to mind. He had hazel eyes and a head full of gray hair he wore in a crew cut. In his earlier years his hair was coal-black with a large white spot towards the top, and he was referred to as a "dark Irishman." One of his most endearing qualities was the fact that he was absolutely tone deaf but still loved to sing. I can see him now, after I'd goaded him into his flat and tuneless rendition of "O'Donnell Abu," smiling and laughing as I winced with each note.

John O'Donnell's sense of humor was certainly one of his most defining characteristics, and I suspect that it was a trait handed down to him from his mother. Looking through papers my father kept at home, I found a letter his mother had written to him in 1921 when he was at St. Eunan's. Ellen wrote:

> Willie Burns' boy left in 4 bags flour this evening - and after night Jeannie baked in the old stove - and as you know one leg turns in all directions and if not straightened would topple over. Jeannie didn't know this. The stove was right beside the flour. I went up to bed with Louis and Min was up with Paddy when I heard the shouts. I couldn't leave Louis or he'd have a fit. So I had to gather from sounds what was wrong. Jeannie was opening the oven when over went the stove or partly over. She called Charlie to straighten it. So excitable to the last, Charlie dropped it and out fell the oil and the flour and all began to burn. Charlie ran and took a full bucket of water from the scullery and dashed it over the whole thing. Min then arrived on the scene and blamed Charlie for throwing water on paraffin oil—that it was salt should have been put on it. You should have seen that piece. Charlie was at boiling point—so was Min as she was rushing to save the flour. Only one bag got damaged and we kept it ourselves as it didn't look so bad, but we get an odd mouthful in the bread. I hope you didn't taste it in the pancakes and buns. I could die laughing after all was over thinking of how you used to make fun of Charlie about the stove burning up.[1]

Unfortunately, that is the only correspondence I found from my Grandmother. Considering the small number of papers my father was able to save from his youth, it suggests to me how important that memory from home was to him and how significant to him was his mother's ability to find humor where others might have seen only hardship.

I was able to interview Father Patrick Cunningham, one of the parish priests from the Bruckless Church in his retirement residence at St. John's Point, Donegal. In the interview, Father Cunningham enjoyed telling me a famous local story about my

SOME FAMILY STORIES

great-grandmother, Mary Sweeny O'Donnell. Mary, according to this legend, started a little general store on the church property in Bruckless soon after her marriage. This shop was the only one within a two-mile radius of the Bruckless Church. The fact that Mary's store appeared to be doing quite well had attracted the attention of fellow entrepreneur and neighbor John Morrow. Morrow decided to find out just how well Mary was doing; after all, he wondered, just how well could a woman run a store? According to Father Cunningham, Mr. Morrow went into Mary's store with a £20 note (a considerable sum at the time) and bought some little thing. Apparently he hoped to determine her success by sizing up her ability to make change for such a large denomination. He apologized to Mary for having nothing smaller in the way of currency, but she just smiled and made the change with care. Morrow then decided that it was obvious that the area around the church needed a local store, so he decided to supply the goods necessary in his own store. Unfortunately, he misjudged his competition and his store failed. The neighbors, it seemed, were already comfortable with Mary's business.[2]

In time, Mary O'Donnell's general store in Bruckless became the local Post Office as well as the family residence. Her husband Owen became the Postmaster. But Morrow did not give up hope easily. He then started a pub/restaurant that is still there today, known as Murrins. The Post Office, on the other hand, closed around 1947. Years later, when I was in Ireland in 1998, I found the post office completely gone, replaced by a church parking lot.

According to Seamus MacShane of Dunkineely, Cassie (Catherine O'Donnell Keenan) had inherited her mother's business aptitude as well. In a conversation I had with him in his pub in Dunkineely, Mr. MacShane told me a story about Cassie that brought to mind Father Cunningham's tale about Mary and her business sense. Around the end of the 1800s, there was a professional photographer touring the Bruckless area and taking pictures of local landmarks. When the photographer had run out of money, but still had the plates, he contacted Cassie. With her financial backing, the photographer developed the plates and together they sold the photos at the Post Office for about halfpence each. This was a very successful enterprise and those pictures, rare as they are, are worth a lot of money today, according to Seamus.[3] He made sure to show me one of these photographs, a picture of the Bruckless Church taken before it burned down (with all the church records) in 1912.

Chapter Two

HIS SIBLINGS

One of the rare times my father spoke about the troubles, he recounted a time shortly before his mother's death when some British soldiers arrived at the Bruckless house late at night and took his father away with them. His mother was upset since she knew the results of such "visits." About an hour later, she heard a single shot. To her, it was the end. A few hours later, his father returned unhurt, but my father always felt that that incident began the sudden decline leading to the death of his mother.[4] Otherwise, he said very little.

I thought that I might find some of the threads I hoped for in the tales of my father's siblings. I had some measure of success when I spoke to his younger brother Harry, who related some stories about the difficult years after his parents passed away. Harry recalled that when he was only nine, he had overheard a conversation between the adult family members convened to discuss the future of the eight O'Donnell orphans. "I wasn't supposed to be listening, but I did hear the words "Nazareth's Home." Nazareth's was an orphanage. Now I hadn't read *Oliver Twist* at that time, but the visions of an orphanage were pretty awful."[5] While Harry's fears about Nazareth's Home did not materialize, the outcome of this family meeting was perhaps even more heartbreaking than he had imagined it would be, for the eight young children—Johnny, Charlie, Mary, Lily, Harry, Teresa, Paddy, and Louis—were split up among family, never again to spend time together under the same roof.

Arrangements were made to send Charlie and Mary to America to live with relatives there. The day after Mary arrived in Detroit in 1926, her Aunt Margaret O'Donnell Carpenter made sure that she started classes at St. Anthony's High School She graduated two years later and then attended nursing school. In my conversation with Mary, I began to see that the goal-oriented attitude towards education that she shared with her brother was one of the elusive traits that had prompted my investigation in the first place.[6]

The other two girls, Lily and Teresa, were sent to the parochial house in Glenties to stay with their uncle, Charles Canon Kennedy,[7] a priest, and his housekeeper, Maggie Keyes. When I asked Lily about her life at the parochial house, I was met with the same silence I had encountered when questioning my father about these years. Later in life, however, Teresa recalled this experience in notes she wrote about her early life for the benefit of her children:

> I heard Lily and I were to go to Glenties to live at the Parochial House. I saw Maggie in her big black coat and fawn felt hat when she and the Canon came for us. Thus began four very hard years. That was January 1924. First event in Glenties, we had to be dressed. I got a navy coat and pink felt hat with velvet lacing around it. Lily got a navy coat and red velvet hat with silver trimming. These were our first ready-made clothes.[8]

I never had a chance to talk with Teresa about these years or about Maggie Keyes since Teresa died before I started my inquiry. However, it is clear from her notes that Maggie Keyes ruled the girls with an iron hand and was particularly harsh with Teresa. This was not the first time I had heard about Maggie Keyes, as Harry had mentioned her name when he was describing the first automobile he remembered.

> The first automobile I remember belonged to our uncle, Canon Kennedy. He had a Chevy. That would be about 1926-27. Lily and Theresa were living with him at the time, at the Parochial house in Glenties which was about 14 miles away. He would drive up often of a Sunday afternoon and bring them up to reacquaint them with us. . . . That was the first car I ever rode in. Canon Kennedy did bring Paddy, Louie and myself down one summer. We spent the summer down at Glenties, at the Parochial house there, with Lily and Theresa. It was a change of scenery anyway. It wasn't any freer, because he had a real tyrant of a housekeeper, Maggie Keyes. She ruled him and she ruled us— and boy we had to toe the line there. Priests' housekeepers in Ireland in the old days were notorious for being so bossy. She certainly was as bossy as you could get.[9]

The family today in Ireland appears more inclined to favor the Kennedys over the O'Donnells. The "aunts" in the Post Office seem to have been less motherly than the Kennedy aunts. However, Louis was quick to brag about Lizzy's cooking. He said, "I'll tell you one thing. That Aunt Lizzy, I would say, was the greatest cook in Ireland. She could bring in a hen, an old hen, and cook it on a Sunday morning. It was delicious. And the cake, she'd cook it with coals."[10]

There was a room in the house known as the "men's room," for which there were a number of different explanations. My father remembers it as being to the left when one entered the house and so called because two men lived in that room while they were working on building the new Bruckless Church after the old church had burned down.[11] On the other hand, my father's sister Lily remembers the room being at the back of the house and says it was where everyone would go to Henry O'Donnell for advice on "writing letters and things like that."[12]

In my interviews with my father's siblings, I found that they remembered the years after their parents' death more than the years they had lived together with their parents. Aside from Grandmother Ellen's letter to my father at Saint Eunan's, I have no information to contradict my notion that life in Bruckless was the model of the perfect family. But that perfect model was shattered by the untimely deaths of both my father's parents, his arrest, and his need to emigrate to the United States.

Chapter Three

NEW FAMILY IN AMERICA

In spite of this concern for Ireland, my father did not have much time to keep up a correspondence with his siblings.

In 1935, his sister Teresa wrote that she thought he had forgotten that they existed. In this letter, my father learned that his brother Harry was going to the seminary at Dalgan to become a priest. He also was told that Lily was already teaching in Fintra, and that Teresa herself had almost finished her preparation to become a teacher.[13] Paddy and Louis (the little ones at the train station the morning my father left Donegal) were in St. Eunan's at that time. In 1936 Paddy wrote to his brother from St. Eunan's:

> I am half-way through my last year in my course here
> in St. Eunan's. I have emulated you in so far as I am a
> Pupil Teacher. I suppose you have forgotten that in days
> long gone by you played right fullback along with Packy

O'Donnell for Bruckless against Loughmult. Well I haven't, and I used to be very proud to hear fellows on the lines declare that you were the outstanding player on the field.[14]

My father's time was devoted to getting through law school and establishing himself in New York. When he began making the connections with Irish immigrants like himself who were going to make a major impact on the life of New York City, he joined the *Clan na Gael*.[15] At the same time, he was to meet at the *Clan na Gael* a woman who had the most impact on his life, Katherine Gwendolyn Genevieve Large, known to all as Gwynne.

At the time, Gwynne was living with her family on Walton Avenue in the Bronx, New York. Mary Regan Large, her mother, was raising a large family that included five marriageable girls, ranging in age from twenty-five to seventeen. Mary had urged her oldest daughter, Agnes, to get involved in New York City politics. This would be one way, insisted Mary, to meet fine young men and at the same time advance in the world of business. Mary Large was a forceful and perceptive thinker who was well aware of the *Clan na Gael* meetings.

At that time, proper young women did not travel alone, so twenty-five year old Agnes reluctantly accepted her nineteen year old sister Gwynne as a tag-along companion to a *Clan na Gael* meeting in the Bronx. On this particularly important night in my history, Gwynne, suffering from boredom, spent the evening absent-mindedly twisting the string of costume pearls she wore. By the end of the meeting, the weary string broke and the pearls rolled onto the floor. As she attempted to gather up the wayward pearls, she found herself assisted by a handsome gentleman. Gwynne Large and John Francis O'Donnell met for the first time.

As gentlemen were prone to do at that time, John told Gwynne and Agnes that he would give them a ride home. In 1933, however, he didn't own an automobile. He was relying on his buddy Charlie Connolly, the *Irish Echo* publisher, who did have a car, to help with the good deed. This is one of the few tales about the earlier years in my mother's life that she would readily share. One afternoon at the kitchen table in Katonah I recorded her account:

By the time Jack [as my mother referred to my father], Agnes, and I reached Connolly's car there were already four people in the car. Jack made the fifth person, so I had to sit on his lap. Agnes had to squeeze in between somebody and me at the window. After that, Jack called every once in a while. He was living and working at the Protectory at that time.[16]

Katherine Gwendolyn Genevieve Large was born on July 17, 1914, the sixth child and fourth daughter of Mary Regan Large and Arthur Large, in the family residence in Woodcliff, New Jersey.[17] "I guess I was born in the house," she told me. At that time, Gwynne explained, "most babies were born in a house. You didn't go to a hospital to have a baby. You had a midwife come in."[18] Around 1922, the Large family moved to Hull Avenue in the Bronx. Arthur Large was a tool and die maker by trade. During the depression, he was forced to find a job outside New York City. He lived and worked in Watervliet, New York, (near Troy) and sent money home to his family.

Mary Large was always buying and selling houses, Gwynne remembers. The only time they lived in an apartment was in between houses when the family lived on 145th Street:

> When my mother rented that apartment she had agreed to the conditions that she did not have any children. So she sneaked us all in at night. There was a band of us; there were five or six of us. Once when we were caught coming down the stairs, the superintendent complained. My mother told him that any damage we children did, she would reimburse him for. We stayed there for a couple of months.[19]

By early 1934, as the Great Depression was at its worst, John and Gwynne knew that they wanted to get married. At the time, John was working at the *Irish Echo* and doing his practicum[20] with James E. Smith. The decision to marry was not well received by Mary Regan Large. Gwynne was already engaged to a German named Hans, the owner of a bakery and an established member of the community.

Gwynne told me that her "mother liked Hans—she wasn't quite sure of Jack, who was very beguiling."[21] Charm, Mary Large asserted, would not support a wife. Because the couple was young, there was, of course, the problem of money, aggravated by the timing of the depression. John had some money saved. His big decision at the time was whether he should use the money he had saved to buy furniture or a suit in which to get married. He chose the suit.

Finally Mary Large agreed to the wedding, provided the couple waited until Gwynne's father's birthday on February 4. At this time, Arthur would be home from Watervliet for a birthday celebration and would be there to give Gwynne away in marriage. Thus, Gwynne and John O'Donnell were married on February 4, 1935 in St. Simon Stock Church in the Bronx. After the wedding, the couple moved into a two-room apartment on Sherman Avenue and 227th Street in the Bronx. Gwynne and John went to Gimbels and bought a bedroom set and living room furniture, taking on the responsibility of time payments. Since they did not have a table, they ate off the boxes that the furniture came in. In time, however, they were able to buy a bridge set.

Trouble came to the couple when John's ulcer acted up. It was imperative, the doctor said, that he stay in bed and remain quiet since his ulcer was bleeding. "He always said it was my cooking that had given him the ulcer," my mother later recalled, "when in fact it was because of the way he had lived prior to our marriage."[22] Confined to bed, my father continued to write editorials for the *Irish Echo* and to work on papers sent to his home by James Smith. In this way, he was able to finish his practicum.

Soon after Gwynne and John were married, he bought a "big, black, ugly looking second hand car."[23] His friend at the Protectory, Jim O'Rourke, would come around to the house to teach him how to drive. At that point in time, Jim O'Rourke was a New York City policeman. On one of the trial driving runs, my mother was in the car also and was about five months pregnant. With a smile on her face, my mother recalled:

> The joke of the matter was that a cop stopped us. Jim jumped out of the car and told the cop that they were rushing me to the hospital because my baby was due. The cop

came around and looked in the car at me. He let us go quickly.[24]

My brother Sean (really John F. Jr.) was soon followed by me and by the end of the depression, the O'Donnell family added the third child, my sister Cathleen. But the depression was also quickly followed by the war. At this time, we lived in Parkchester, a new housing development built and owned by the Metropolitan Insurance Company in the Bronx, a complex built partly on the grounds of the Protectory, where my father had worked earlier. My memories of my father during these years are vague, both because of my young age and because he was away from home a lot during the week.

Chapter Four

THE WAR YEARS

During World War II, my father was in his early thirties, was married and had three children, and therefore was not required to register. However, he did attempt to enlist in the United States Army. Because his earlier ulcer prevented him from being accepted in the regular army, he enlisted in the 69th Regiment of the New York Guard on March 30, 1942. In August of that year, he was made a Corporal, and on February 2, 1943 he was promoted to Sergeant. Three months later, he accepted a commission: "This is to certify, That John F. O'Donnell, a Sergeant of Company B of the Sixty-ninth Regiment New York Guard, is hereby honorable discharged from the New York Guard by reason of accepting commission in the New York Guard, S.O. #140, June 18, 1943. Adjutant General's Office, Albany, N.Y."[25]

His brother Harry, now an ordained Columban priest, was drafted into the British Army to serve as a chaplain. He saw active duty in the European theatre of operations, and faced the worst at the Battle of the Bulge. He wrote to my father, telling him of the war, but typical of the O'Donnell sense of humor, he could turn a horrible time into a story worth telling. This is his story as retold by my father:

> The Battle of the Bulge resulted from the German army break-through of the allied lands. The Germans spotted a weakness in the line where the British and American forces joined. The break-through was led by Germans wearing allied uniforms which, for a time, created a situation close to chaos.
>
> Father Harry was then assigned as chaplain to the British regiment adjoining the American forces. He strayed somehow into U.S.-held territory and was quickly picked up by an American platoon searching for mis-uniformed Germans. Father Harry's north of Ireland accent was so different from the others in the British unit that his captors were unusually suspicious of him. The Americans produced a lieutenant who had been in the Catholic seminary. He was ordered to find out if Father Harry was really a priest.
>
> After a few preliminary questions, he looked Father Harry in the eye and said: "Say the *Munda cor meum*."[26] Completely surprised, Father Harry's mind went blank. No way could he remember the words of the familiar prayer. The lieutenant was about to turn him in as a fraud when Father Harry noticed a truck a few feet away. He had an idea and asked the lieutenant if he could go to the back of the truck. As soon as he bent over the back of the truck—in the familiar posture of the priest saying the prayer during Mass—the words came back to him. They were his passwords to freedom.[27]

Their younger sister Teresa had a wonderful philosophy that she shared with my brother when he visited her in Ireland shortly before her death: "If nothing goes wrong, you have no stories to tell."[28] This had to be the motto of the family.

Chapter Five

CANDLEWOOD

By this time in 1948, my father, besides being "father of the union"[29] was the father of four children, as my sister Tricia had joined the family in 1946.

If you were to ask me what my fondest memories of my youth were, I would have to say Candlewood. After the war, my parents bought a small cottage on about a half acre of land with lots of trees near Candlewood Lake on the outskirts of Danbury, Connecticut. We were still living in the Bronx in New York City but on weekends my parents, Sean, Cathleen, Tricia, and I would all pile into the car for the long ride to the Lake. During the ride my Father would recite some of the poetry he had memorized as a child, or he would sing (way off key). On the way home on Sunday night, we would listen on the radio to the Fred Allen, Jack Benny, or Edgar Bergen and Charlie McCarthy shows.

Even though my father was still traveling frequently, he would always manage to join us for our weekends together in Candlewood. As children, we also spent the summers there, and my father would commute by train to Brewster, New York, where my mother would pick him up. While at Candlewood, my father would work in the yard. In fact that is how he gained a reputation for his tree removal abilities.

On one occasion my father and my Uncle Tom were working together clearing trees.[30] As my father told it:

> I remember it was this day, Memorial Day, many years ago. We were cutting trees down in the back lot. They were tall skinny ones. I had a rope on the tree, kind of high up to make sure it wouldn't fall on the house. I was the one on the saw. You know how you saw a tree? You cut a V in on one side, that's the way you want it to fall. Then on the other side, you cut straight in—usually no problem. I don't know what the hell happened—I probably didn't cut the thing right; but the tree started to fall. It was pulling Tom with it. Tom let go of the rope and he ran. It came down across the wires.
>
> This was the first time [that I did this.] I got down to the house you see, and of course there's no lights, no nothing and everybody's up for the Memorial Day weekend. It only affected people up beyond us. So in a minute or two I see Beerman [our not-too-fond-of-us next door neighbor] coming out. I got in the car and went down to the Trading Post to call the Utility Company. I told them they had a problem, so they came right around and cleared it up.
> Now on another occasion the same damn thing happened, but Jim O'Rourke did it. Jim was up there over the weekend with Margaret [his wife]. I wasn't there. He didn't know about the problem we had had before. So he helped out by dropping one or two of the trees and he dropped one of them on the wires.[31]

I remember one fourth of July at the lake when I had been invited up the street to have a nice roasted chicken dinner with

Betty Ott and her family. Mrs. Ott was just putting the finishing touches on the dinner and suddenly the lights went out. In the darkness somebody said, "O'Donnell must be cutting down trees again." Sure enough, my father had been at it again. When I confronted my father with this story, he commented, "Well it wasn't the cutting of the trees; it was the way the damn things fell."[32] I loved his logic.

Another Candlewood story concerned a skunk. For this tale, I have two different versions. First I will give my father's version, followed by Father Harry's version:

> I was digging out underneath the house at the Lake [Candlewood]. It was built on dirt and I was trying to dig out a basement. There was just one little piece of it where they had an oil burner. The rest of it was not dug out. I was digging out some of the rest of it.
>
> I didn't smell him [the skunk], I saw him. I was digging in there. I was just under the wall of the house. I remember I saw these eyes looking at me. I went out. I said, 'There's an animal in there.' So we [my father and his brother, Father Harry] started to dig down from the outside to get at it. We saw it down there but it didn't come out. We saw that it was a skunk. I went and I got Ceil Joyce because Ceil Joyce had no sense of smell. She came over. We got a long spade or something and she went over there. She went to get it out with the spade. It let go and she found she did have a sense of smell. She just screamed and ran—so did Father Harry.[33]

Father Harry's version of the same story:
> I think at that time you were all up in Candlewood. It was summer—which is beautiful there, of course. As usual, your father wasn't idle; he did all kind of improvements around the house. That's when I had the encounter with the skunk. He [Jack] was preparing some kind of chamber underneath the house. Perhaps it was a heating thing, I don't know. I was usually being more in the way than anything else, but I was trying to help anyway. We were digging

out earth and I thought what I saw was a piece of rope and I put in my hand and pulled it out. That's when I got the blast from the skunk—which I have never forgotten—never gotten it out of my system really.[34]

Somewhere in there is the true story.

As in any challenging situation, my father's attitude seemed to be the same. His credo was always face the problem head on, be it in a contract negotiation or a tree-removal crisis or a skunk, and deal with the resulting problems as they come; but, most importantly, never forget to look for the humor in life.

Chapter Six

FAMILY HOMES

From the Bronx, our family moved to a large house in Yonkers, near Bronxville, and after that to a house in Greenburgh. My brother Sean and I both left to start our own families before my parents moved to Katonah. I married first, in 1958. Cathleen's memory of my wedding includes a tale about Dad:

> Since Eileen's marriage was the first in the family, Dad was a little excited. He showed up at the church missing parts of his tuxedo but not his cigars. The reception was down in New York City and everyone had a really good time—including Dad. As we were leaving the reception, someone noticed that Dad was wearing a woman's hat. He was still wearing it in the limousine, but when asked he had no idea whose it was. We never did find out![35]

When the County of Westchester cut a large swath of land from the front of our Yonkers property, my father wanted to regain his green space, so we moved a little further north to Greenburgh. The Greenburgh house had a pool, and it was around this pool that we gathered for family parties and where my parents' rapidly increasing family spent many happy hours.

By this time, I had three of my five children, and my brother had his two. Grandfatherhood suited my father well, and he enjoyed being with the next generation. No matter where he was in his travels, he remembered birthdays and a variety of other events from first communions to graduations. He reveled in a house full of dogs, cats, and grandchildren. With a scotch in one hand and a cigar in the other, he presided as paterfamilias.

Perhaps because his forebears in Ireland had only been able to lease, not own land, owning land was important to my father, and this led to his buying a large plot in Katonah, in the town of Bedford in northern Westchester County. There he took great pains working with the architect to make sure his final house was exactly the way he wanted it. He took pride in doing all the land work himself. Some of my sister Cathleen's favorite memories of our father were from this time:

> [I remember] sitting at the kitchen table waiting for Dad to come home from work. He would walk in the door, smoking his cigar, and give Mom a big hug. After hanging up his coat and putting away his briefcase, Mom would give him his drink, and dinner had officially started. To this day, I can still hear his voice as he greeted everyone.
>
> Dad did most of the yard work at the homes we lived in. He bought a lawn tractor to handle the large lawn areas. He loved it. On the weekend, you would find him outside sitting on his tractor and mowing the lawn with a big cigar sticking out of his mouth. Mom would often suggest that Sean [our brother] should be mowing the lawn but Dad wouldn't let anyone touch his tractor. We began calling it his tinker toy.

FAMILY HOMES

He commuted every day to his office in New York City by train, enjoying the company of a group of commuters who were avid bridge players. His passion for bridge was close to his passion for travel, fishing, Johnnie Walker Black scotch, and cigars. On the train, it was customary for the conductor to hold a four-seater for the players (there were several so-called "tables" per train) and to provide the cards. So each day, there were several lively sets of bridge going on any given southbound train out of Katonah or northbound train out of New York. One day, on his return from a long day at the office, the engine of his train derailed just above 125th Street. The passengers were ordered to leave the train. Ah, ah. Not so fast. He held a great hand. So his foursome did not abandon the smoldering train until the hand was played out and Jack and his partner had scored their triumph.[36]

He so loved that house in Katonah that most nights he and the dogs would walk the property lines.

Chapter Seven

VACATIONS—OR, WHAT NEXT CAN GO WRONG

Planning vacations was another of my father's obsession. He loved to plan for our trips. As Cathleen recalls:
He would get the maps out and plan every detail. He drove us nuts with the planning. Part of his planning was shortcuts – Dad loved shortcuts. I remember one trip to Florida. We stayed overnight at a motel and early in the morning, over breakfast, out came the maps. He explained he found a great shortcut around some construction. We started out and drove all day. That evening, when it was time to stop, we started looking for a motel. We found one—the same one we stayed in the night before. We had gone around in one large circle.[37]

The trips were all marked by some comic confusion. The first major trip we took was to California. My brother, Sean, and I were both in college and could not leave for Los Angeles until our spring break, a day or two after our parents and two sisters were able to leave. My brother had had been working at Idlewild (now Kennedy) airport and was sure he knew all there was to know about airports. On a lay-over in Chicago, he got off the plane to get us two box lunches. At Chicago, they did not announce departures in the food area, so when he returned to the gate, he found that the plane had taken off without him. On the plane, of course, I was inconsolable. I cried so hard that the pilot came out to talk with me. The other passengers thought my brother was my husband and that he had abandoned me. In Los Angeles, my folks met the plane. My mother was aghast when I was the last one off the plane—by myself, still crying, and with my brother's coat draped over one arm. Needless to say, we had another trip to the airport the next morning to meet my brother coming in on the red-eye from Chicago—with two uneaten box lunches under his arm.

On the same trip, we had a misadventure in a classy restaurant. Cathleen remembers that part of the trip to California quite well:

> At the end of the trip Dad took us to an expensive restaurant, Trader Vics. Because it was the last night of the vacation, Dad said we could order anything we liked—money was no object! So we did. It was a wonderful meal and we were all enjoying it. It was time to leave so Dad asked for the bill. He took out his Diners' Club card and handed it to the waiter. The waiter's face fell and he quietly informed Dad that they no longer took Diners' Club. We all had to empty purses, pockets, etc. to come up with the money. We were all laughing so hard that I'm surprised they didn't throw us out. We came up with enough for the meal but the tip was rather a measly one.[38]

What makes this story even funnier is a trip to Cape Cod two years later, in early September 1960. During a family dinner in a great fish restaurant on the Cape, my father retold the story to some guests at dinner with us. As he finished the story of having to empty wallets to pay for the meal in California, the waiter came to the table with the bill, and no, they did not take credit cards. All over again, the family reached into various pockets and wallets to ante up to pay yet another restaurant bill.

> Another trip Cathleen remembers was not a spring trip: Dad had the opportunity to go skiing in Vermont with the New York Athletic Club, and he asked me if I would like to go along. Neither one of us could ski, but at least I had been on skis before. When we got to the slopes, we rented our ski equipment and headed off to the ski lift by the bunny hill. This particular one was a J-bar. Dad was all excited and listened carefully as we were instructed on how to use the lift. We were told to gently lean back on the bar but definitely not to sit on it like a chair. When Dad was sure he knew what to do, he told me to go first so when I fell he would be there to help.
>
> Since this was my first time on any ski lift, I was very nervous and was sure I would make a fool of myself. I cautiously put my skis into the ruts to await my bar. I gently leaned back as instructed and started up the hill. Suddenly the lift stopped. I turned around as best I could without falling and look back. There was a man sprawled on the ground under one of the J-bars, and people were helping him up. It was Dad! He got his skis back on and again stood in the ruts awaiting the bar. Almost immediately the lift stopped again. There was Dad sitting on his bottom and looking quite embarrassed. He tried one more time and then gave up. He just couldn't get the hang of it—he wanted to sit down.[39]

Probably the favorite family story is about a trip to the Bahamas that my mother and father took with Cathleen and Tricia. As Tricia tells it:

> It's about 1964 and over the last few years, my father has taken us away at Easter time for a vacation. He asks his fishing friends for a suggestion and this year we are going

to a resort in the Bahamas. It's called Small Hope Bay Lodge and is found on the largest of all the islands of the Bahamas. The third-largest coral reef in the world is just 5 minutes off the beach and extends for 100 miles. This is going to be great! My brother and oldest sister have married; therefore, there will only be the four of us, my parents, my sister Cathleen and myself.

It has always been a family custom that we all get new outfits for Easter and we ask Dad if it would be appropriate to take these outfits or will it be more casual. Oh, most definitely! You should wear the outfits down there. He is sure it will be an elegant place and we will need to dress for dinner.

The day comes for us to leave and dressed to the nines, we all pile into the car for the trip to the airport. All the baggage is stuffed into the trunk along with my father's elusive fishing rods, a must for any trip. We fly from New York to Miami, Miami to Nassau, and then on a small plane for the final flight to Andros Island. We fly over brilliant turquoise shallow waters and secluded pink and white beaches. The pilot announces that we are about to land and I look out the window searching for a first glimpse of the airport.

I'm starting to get a feeling that things are not quite right. Although the pilot says he is circling the airport—there is no airport down there! However, the pilot perseveres and lands in a small grass-covered field—not a building in sight. He helps us disembark and piles our luggage off to the side. He assures us someone will be along shortly and off he goes.

So there we stand, decorating the countryside in our Easter finery, feeling totally abandoned. Suddenly out of the blue comes the local bus to take us to the hotel. After a short drive, we pull up in front of a fancy hotel. At last, we're here! Yes? No. Trepidation is growing and hits an all time high when I hear someone ask "Is this the O'Donnell party?" and turn to see 'Robinson Crusoe' in the flesh. A blond haired man with a shaggy beard, no shirt, no shoes and cut-off jeans introduces himself as Dick Birch, owner of the Small Hope Bay Lodge. He will be with us shortly; it's just a short ride across the inlet. Just wait down by the boat and he'll take care of the luggage. Boat? What boat? I walk down the pier looking for the closest thing to a boat. Sure enough, there it is down at the end of the pier. The reason we didn't see it is that it wasn't as high as the pier. Large rowboats generally are not! I notice that there seems to be an elderly local woman and a priest waiting as well. This should be interesting.

Dick Birch returns with our luggage and three crates, one each of lettuce, eggs, and chickens. The luggage and crates are loaded and we follow along—with Dick, the elderly lady, and the priest. There is now about an inch of play before the boat starts to sink. Across we chug. There we are—Dad in his suit and tie, my sister and I in our dresses and heels and the *pièce de resistance*, my mother regally enthroned in the center with her fur stole.

Once on the other side we disembark, say goodbye to the elderly lady and gaze at our next means of transportation. Standing by the shore is a new Volkswagen bus, recently rolled, which explains the lack of doors. This will be a tighter fit, but no problem—the priest can hold the lettuce, Dad the chickens, and Mom the eggs.

With a brief stop at the church to drop off the priest, we finally arrive at our destination. After our arrival, we never did get dressed up and actually went barefoot to church on Easter. Dick Birch was originally from Canada, and he and his family and brother built the central lodge and accompanying cabins. Although not exactly the vacation that we expected, we had a marvelous time fishing, swimming, and scuba diving.[40]

As Cathleen summed it up:
> The place was lovely but Mom wasn't thrilled when she found out that our traveling companions would be one of our meals. The incident with the chickens reminded Dad of the time when they lived in the Bronx. They were

renting a house and Mom raised two chickens in the back yard. It soon became necessary for them to go. Dad took them to the butcher's. Since Mom thought of them as pets, she told Dad to be sure they were not the ones he brought back. When he came home with the package from the butcher, he assured Mom they were not the same chickens. That afternoon Mom started to prepare dinner. She opened the package from the butcher and screamed. The butcher included the heads and she recognized her pets.[41]

Chapter Eight

THE NEED TO FISH

Almost every vacation also involved fishing. As Tricia put it: "Labor was Dad's passion, but fishing was his joy." Eventually it even saved his life.

On every trip, whether business or pleasure, if there was water of any sort nearby, his poles went with him." Of course, as Cathleen observed: "No matter where we went, Dad had to bring his fishing rods. The problem was, at the last minute, he would forget them. Back we would go for the rods." Tricia's image of him in pursuit of the best fishing spot really captures him:

> When we arrived at a lodge, the first thing that Dad would do was scout out the area for the best fishing. All you had to do was watch him and as soon as he found his fishing spot, he would get into his pointer stance: cigar in his

mouth, head jutted forward, nose pointed to the best spot. Too bad he didn't have a tail.[42]

It was never necessary that he catch anything; he just loved the sport. There is still a plaque hanging in a place of honor on his study wall that he won in 1963 for the largest bluefish caught at a New York Athletic Club fishing tournament—1 pound, 6 ounces. On a trip to the Grand Tetons, Tricia tells the story of Dad going off fishing and on his return, proudly bringing his catch to the chef. The kitchen would generally cook his catch and serve it to the family for dinner. This one time, after being served, Dad mentioned to the chef that the fish seemed bigger after cooking. The chef showed him his fish lying under the larger one. The chef didn't want them to starve.[43]

He did have successful trips where he caught large marlin, dolphin, tuna, and more. He had the pictures to prove it!

Even when the family were on a cruise where fishing was not considered one of the activities, Tricia recalls that

> Some of the crew would invariably fish off the stern during their off hours and there would be Dad; or they may even borrow a zodiac and Dad would tag along. More than once the ship would be waiting for his return before moving to our next port of call.[44]

One memorable visit was to the Bali Hai on Morea, in the heart of French Polynesia, where he and Mom had an overwater bungalow with a two-foot square Plexiglas panel in the middle of the floor. In Tricia's words:

> At night, with the light turned on under the bungalow, you could watch the tropical fish swimming. Now this was heaven! You guessed it. Dad would raise the Plexiglas and fish while lying in bed. You might wonder what he used for bait. Well, it was on this trip that he discovered the fish really enjoyed ham and cheese sandwiches. They also liked bacon and he would swipe some from breakfast.[45]

THE NEED TO FISH 243

And then there was his love of fishing in the reservoir behind the Katonah house and the fishing trip that saved his life. I turn to Tricia for this story:

> One fateful year he decided to try ice fishing. In cold winters, it is a favorite sport with fisherman in this area. One thing you should learn is never to go alone. Dad, however, took himself off this day and went to a spot where he had seen a father and son fishing earlier in the season on Titicus Reservoir. He left the jeep running while he explored the area to try and find the exact spot. The Titicus Reservoir has been made by underground springs. This causes the ice to be uneven and thicker in some areas than others. Dad was so intent of finding the right spot that he didn't realize he was on a thinner part of the ice and eventually fell through. He was in a heavy all-in-one from Sears as well as boots and a heavy jacket. As he tried to get out, the ice would break around him. When a car passed by, no one would hear him call because their windows were closed. Finally on one of his last attempts, he found a thicker piece of ice and rolled out and to shore. He managed to get into the Jeep and took off for home. Mom said he looked like a drowned rat. The doctor told her to put him to bed and when he stopped shivering to bring him in. According to the doctor the all-in-one saved his life. It insulated him from the cold water longer.
>
> It was through the full physical resulting from this accident that they discovered the early stages of colon cancer.[46]

He then underwent treatment that successfully destroyed the cancer at that time.

Chapter Nine

DAD AS ROLE MODEL

I found a copy of my father's speech nominating Mike Quill in the New York University Library in 1991 on one of my many research trips to New York City. My father and I would ride the train into the City together from Katonah; then he would go on to his office and I would go to the Tamiment Library at New York University. On the day I found this speech, I handed a copy of it to my father to read during the train ride back to Katonah. It did my heart good to see the proud smile on my father's face when he commented, "Pretty good, don't you think?"

While my father was reading, I was thinking back to a humiliating incident that took place around 1946 when I was a shy ten year old Catholic school student. During the course of the lesson, my teacher was expounding on the ravages wrought by the Communists and their people in power. People, she said, such as Michael Quill and (turning and pointing to me with an accusatory look) she exclaimed, "Your father, John O'Donnell!" True to my nature, I went home in tears to tell my father about the horrible accusation the nun had made. True to his nature, he chuckled.

He was undeterred by what others thought of him when he knew he was in the right. He cared for those who struggled to earn a living, to be treated justly. And he taught that to his children. He was always so sympathetic later on when I would complain about the unruly students I faced in my years teaching high school math in Charleston. I loved to hear his laughter over the telephone as I told of my latest classroom crisis. His consistent comment was "Ah, that should be your biggest problem." After some thought, I learned to agree with him.

He practiced toleration, and wanted his children to learn to accept all people. With three of my classmates from the College of New Rochelle, I went on a student association sponsored trip to Europe. At the last minute a side trip to Poland, sponsored by the Ford Foundation, was offered. My father insisted that I take the side trip even though it meant leaving my traveling classmates in Vienna, Austria, and going off with a new group. Although this was twelve years after World War II had ended, the visible signs of destruction were plentiful. The education that we received went far beyond the textbook and classroom variety. The group of twelve students and a student tour leader left Austria and traveled by train across Czechoslovakia. As planned, we visited the concentration camp at Auschwitz (Oswiecim). There were students traveling with us from other countries, including Germany. During the lecture/films preparing us for our visit to Auschwitz, not a sound was made anywhere in the audience. I think we were all in shock, and we had yet to visit the camp. We heard a lot of mind-boggling numbers—200,000 to 400,000 Jews had been killed during the war. On August 3, 1957, a day I will not forget, we twelve American students left our school bus and toured Auschwitz. The one Jewish girl in our group, sobbing and overcome with emotion, was never able to leave the bus. Slowly each one of us drifted back to her, unable to comprehend the enormity of it all: life size photos, a glass cabinet filled with women's and children's hair, another glass cabinet of gold teeth.

DAD AS ROLE MODEL

From there I made my first trip to Ireland where I met my father's family; but no amount of laughing or music could ever make me forget Auschwitz. When I returned home, my father made sure I related every thought and impression I had to the family and even brought me down to his office to describe my impressions to the law partners.

Up to that time in my life, I had been sheltered and reared in the world of my religion. It was important to my father that I know more of the world, its people, the different religions and cultures. When I shared my experiences with his friends, he was obviously pleased that I had learned.

While a man of peace and toleration, my father did have some limits that tested his mettle, yet, as usual, he knew how to handle a tough situation with wit and without compromising his principles. He and my mother were in Bermuda in March of 1964 when Queen Elizabeth II gave birth to her fourth child, Edward. The manager of the hotel they were staying at, beside himself with joy, broke out the champagne for a toast at dinner. All were asked to rise to drink to the Queen of England and the new Prince. That was a bit more than he could do—his Irish blood in sharp conflict with his civility and his gentlemanly instincts. He hesitated as all the other guests rose to celebrate. Then he stood and raised his glass and with his booming voice and Irish lilt, he announced that he would drink—to the health of the mother and the newborn.[47]

Chapter Ten

THE GRANDCHILDREN REMEMBER

John F. O'Donnell loomed large in the lives and memories of his eight grandchildren. Not only did they cherish their visits with him, he and my mother encouraged each one of them to get the best possible education. Thus, I asked each of them to provide a story for this section of the book.

My son Neil Sheehan recalls how wonderful Christmas gifts somehow just appeared.

> We were oblivious as to the source and would never have noticed the variation in Santa's handwriting. I know Grandpa didn't drive the gifts to our house. My mother used to drive us up to Katonah shortly after Christmas every year—always on her own. My father preferred a 75-mile buffer between him and the wrath of Grandma.

> But I do remember one gift exchange, probably around 1970. On a cold December night (obviously), both my parents piled the entire screaming clan into our Volkswagen bus. We headed north with no explanation. In the middle of nowhere we pulled into a closed gas station. Parked there in a yellow Toyota Land Cruiser was none other Grandpa. Still no explanation. Grandpa silently began transferring mysterious packages from the Toyota into our car. I'm sure snatches of wrapping paper were visible, but being intellectually non-inquisitive, none of us ever asked. Transfer completed, Grandpa bid us farewell without so much as the usual $20 bill squeezed into each palm.
>
> The next time I met Grandpa on neutral territory was in 1982. Carol and I had gotten engaged; both Grandma and Grandpa approved of her. But apparently . . . they thought it wise to interview Carol's parents. You can tell a lot about someone from her parents, I guess. More importantly, I think they wanted to demonstrate the diversity of my gene pool. The six of us had a very civilized dinner at a lovely restaurant halfway between Katonah and central Jersey. I've always suspected it was very close to that 1970 gas station, but never had the nerve to ask.

My daughter Mary Eileen Sheehan Layton's earliest memory of her grandfather occurred during one of her stays in Katonah while I was caring for her new sibling.

> I remember my visit with my grandparents (getting to spend the night with them). We went to pick up Aunt Tricia. It was late when we got home to Katonah. I must have started crying. Grandpa put me on top of the counter and tried to talk to me; calm me down I guess. This went on until Grandma told him that he should take me home. Grandpa then drove me home and never complained.

Mary Eileen viewed her grandfather as "a big important man." It was little things about him that stand out in her mind. She told me that she remembered:

At dinner he ate his salad in that big bowl…the drink he would drink…and how he went to church every Sunday. At my wedding, my friends kept telling me about how my grandfather came to their table and talked with each one of them.

I will never forget one time when we were in Florida and I was swimming. He swam with me for at least an hour.

The last thing I remember happened long after Grandpa died. I was looking through some old files of mine and I found a long letter he had written to a doctor about me. It was nice to see.

My brother's daughter, Cairenn (Kerry) O'Donnell Broderick has lasting memories to share:

When my husband Michael and I were closing on our house, Grandpa insisted on representing us. He drove up to the bank the morning of the closing in his Jeep, cigar in mouth, sporting his loudest Hawaiian shirt. We could see the bank representatives looking at one another wondering who this guy was. Until he gave them his card. Then they knew. He had already thrown them off base, but then came the best. The bank lawyer slid a paper across the table to us to sign. We had to attest that no money that we were using had come from illegal drug sales or other criminal activities. "Ah," he said with his wry smile, turning the paper immediately back to the bank lawyer, "And where is the bank's sworn statement that none of the money it is using has come from illegal drug sales or other criminal activities?" The paper was quickly withdrawn, and later we all had a good laugh.

In my early teaching career in Vermont, I ended up as vice-president of the teachers' union in a contract year. Needless to say, we spent a lot of time, he and I, on the phone, I, a devoted disciple, trying to learn as much as possible in the shortest possible time. We did cut a good contract, thanks to Grandpa. Today, I am the president of the teachers' union in White Plains, New York. I use every lesson I learned from him. And I carry a cigar in my brief case to every negotiation to keep him close.

Michael Broderick, Kerry's husband, a staunch union shop steward in CWA, cherishes the recollections of the golf outings with his grand-father-in-law. He recalls especially the fun that my father had just whacking the ball all over the course. But he especially remembers the respect accorded to my father by union and management alike on these outings.[48]

My son, John F. (Sean) O'Donnell Sheehan, took his first trip to Ireland with his grandfather, under some sad circumstances. In December 1977, my father learned that his sister Teresa McBrearty was dying. He decided to take my son Sean with him to visit her for the last time. Of course, Sean did not have a passport. Would that stop my father? As Sean wrote, his grandfather knew all the angles:

> It already being late winter, the normal wait period for a passport would not do. Knowing this, my grandfather had purchased plane tickets to Ireland to leave within the next two weeks (of course never intending to use them). When he presented that to the Passport office, it was reason enough to accelerate the processing of my passport such that it would be ready in days, not weeks. Mission accomplished.
>
> After checking in and sleeping off said jetlag, the next day [7 January 1978] was spent at Lily's house (grandpa's younger sister). It was a small house with lots of foliage in the front. Inside I encountered the entire clan for the first time.... I do not recall what her [Lily's] age was at that time in 1978 but she did not seem slowed in spirit or humor.
>
> The next day we went to Donegal to visit Teresa. It was a four-hour drive filled with stories and laughter from Lily and Grandpa. I heard recitations of Gaelic lessons of long ago and small talk about memories. I saw Grandpa's father's grave [in Donegal]. Also I saw the house Grandpa's father built. I also was at where Grandpa was born and

THE GRANDCHILDREN REMEMBER

where Grandpa's mother was born. We went to Killybegs again to visit Grandpa's sister Teresa. Grandpa told me about his life.

A few days later, I was told Teresa had slipped into a coma. She would not emerge. Maybe we had timed our visit precisely, or maybe our visit was the end for her. I do not know but we were there and we were all able to say goodbye.

These are my memories of my trip to Ireland in 1978. They are vague and I did not heed my mother's warning of writing it all down. But what I do remember is entrenched in me. I am forever grateful to my Grandfather for introducing me to Ireland and for being my tour guide. I cannot think of any better way it should have been done.

My brother's son, John F. (Sean) O'Donnell III, recalls a happy time from the early part of his career as an organ builder and restorer, the unveiling of the first major organ he worked on in Springfield, Massachusetts, in March 1990:

To celebrate the completion of a major project in the pipe organ shop I worked in and the acquisition of my new home in 1990, we had an open house at the workshop followed by a party at my house. There were a large number of guests coming to the house, mostly 20-something-year-old musicians and craftsmen and other bohemian types. I invited family too, of course, and was delighted that Grandpa and Father Harry came up. Not surprisingly, Grandpa wanted to know every detail of how the organ worked, and would not settle for the general answers I usually give people. He wanted details, and he asked lots of follow-up questions. But the real fun was at the house party afterwards.

The work-shop end of things turned out to be a real handful, and I ended up arriving at the house party quite late, fearful that Grandpa and Fr. Harry were going to be feeling neglected amidst this sea of characters. Silly me.

I will always remember the scene in my living room that afternoon: Grandpa and Fr. Harry sitting on the sofa telling stories to an enraptured room full of my friends, who were sitting packed together on the floor and standing along the walls. That *was* the party. For years afterwards, my friends would ask after Fr. Harry and Grandpa, and several that I lost touch with sought me out when they heard of Grandpa's death a few years later to remind me how great it was to have had him there that day.

My daughter Alison Sheehan Caruso added her memories:
> I've always been more than a little intimidated by my grandfather. After all, my upbringing in southern New Jersey was no comparison to his youth in Ireland. I grew up with my father, mother, and siblings. My grandfather lost his parents and was separated from his siblings so early. How could I talk to a man who had been through so much? What could I offer to any conversation? But he loved me. I knew that. I always knew that even when I didn't exactly know why. I felt so plain next to him but so lucky to have him in my life. He would start stories and I would pretend I understood the texture of the story but I didn't. I would pretend I knew the hardship he faced but I couldn't. But when his storied ended in laughter, I laughed as hard as anyone else. My grandfather could bring you along with him on a story and you wanted to be there with him.
>
> My memories of my grandfather aren't the memories of the great labor lawyer. They're the memories of a great man who held a cigar in one hand and a drink in the other and made a room full of people laugh. My memories are of a man who tucked a five dollar bill into my hand as I left each trip. My thoughts go back to seeing him in the driveway as we pulled away to drive back to New Jersey from his upstate New York home. I always cried. I missed him and my grandmother, that was for sure but I always felt a little more human; more ordinary when I was away from this great man. He loved me and I adored him.

THE GRANDCHILDREN REMEMBER

The memories of my son Rory Sheehan from around 1983 involve boats and rivers and Father Harry and a trip to Ireland to visit his cousins, the Henrys. Call it the "Incident on the Shannon." There are two versions of this story—one from my son Rory and one from my Dublin cousin, George Henry.

First I'll give you George's version since it also includes the background about what led up to the sting of the story.

> Given his ability to tell stories no doubt Johnny (Jack) made a great story out of what if truth be told, was not a major nautical catastrophe. "Never let the truth get in the way of a good story" springs to mind.
>
> The reason Jack got such a kick out of it [the whole incident] was the fact that I had made so much out of a similar incident one Easter when I was in college. In that case six of us rented a cruiser for a week, starting from Carrick-on-Shannon, doing a round trip to Athlone and back to Carrick. On the last day the engine of the cruiser "blew up" (my embellishment), but we were marooned in Lough Boderg, and had to be towed back to Carrick by the cruiser company. The end result was that the company reimbursed us the total cost of the boat hire, out of concern for our safety, whereas we had been terrified that we would have to pay them some compensation for having damaged their boat.
>
> So move on to Jack, Fr. Harry, Rory and I on our weekend on the self-same river, same cruiser company and starting point, Carrick. While Jack was steering the cruiser to a berth, he managed to run it aground on a rock. He actually put a hole in it so that technically we were sinking, although we were only in a couple of feet of water. So we were not in any mortal danger, and we were able to continue our trip in a replacement boat provided by the Cruiser company. Thankfully they did not make any connection to my previous escapade with them. He [Jack] of course was delighted that he had outdone me, as he

saw it, by sinking his boat and getting a replacement, whereas I had merely disabled mine. I, on the other hand, still reckon getting my money back won that particular contest.[49]

My son Rory's version is much more concise:
> This could make another entry in the travel stories or "what more can go wrong." In the 1980s, Grandpa, Father Harry, my Dublin cousin George Henry, and I rented a boat to cruise the Shannon River. George had done the same a few years before, and had ended up hitting a rock and sinking. So what did we do? Almost the same. With grandpa as helmsman, we ran aground, put a small hole in the boat, and started to take on water. He supervised our offloading in preparation for getting another boat sent by the rental company. He saved the Scotch and the cigars, while Father Harry, George, and I took care of everything else.[50]

My nephew Brian Paprocki reminded his mother, Cathleen, about his most notable memory of his Grandfather. As she tells it:
> When we were visiting from Chicago, Brian would sit next to Dad at the kitchen table. He loved it when Dad, doing the coin trick, would reach behind his ear and find a coin. He kept asking Dad how he did it but Dad would never show him.

Throughout all these stories runs the common theme of a man who loved life, who cherished family, who was not above a little mischievous fun, and who shared that love of life with all with whom he came in contact.

Chapter Eleven

THE LAST YEAR

In November of 1992, O'Donnell visited Ireland for the last time. In August his brother, Father Harry, had died, and my father was not able to be present for his funeral. Besides visiting Father Harry's grave, my father wanted to visit with his sister Lily and his brother Louis and Louis's wife Máire. My father's other surviving sister, Mary, was in Detroit.

My sister Tricia, my mother, and my Aunt "Sister" (Eve Houghton) accompanied my father to Dalgan Park, the home of the Columban Fathers, in Navan, County Meath where Father Harry was buried.

According to Tricia:

> We continued on to Donegal and the Central Hotel. We stayed in Donegal for two or three days and visited with Máire, Louis and several of the local pubs. We also visited Bruckless, the church and graveyard and drove all over the area while Dad reminisced.[51]

Included in this farewell trip of my father's were visits to his sister Lily and her family, and his nephew Ian and his family. Two weeks later, my father left Ireland for the last time.

Towards the end of November in 1992, he had a driving accident when his "toy" (as my mother referred to his Jeep) hit a patch of ice and he spun around hitting the curb. Thankfully, he suffered only a few bruises to the head—and still he worked.

On December 7, 1992, John O'Donnell celebrated his eighty-fifth birthday. Unbeknownst to him, the family was planning a big celebration to commemorate this occasion. The whole family gathered at the Kittle House in Chappaqua, New York, and we did succeed in surprising him. We all knew, including my father, that this was the last time we would all be sharing a meal together. While my father was in pain, however, his humor was, as always, still present.

About a week later, my brother and his family went for a Sunday afternoon visit in Katonah with his wife, their daughter Kerry, her husband Michael Broderick, and their firstborn, nineteen-month-old Brian O'Donnell Broderick. According to Kerry, my mother had told my father that the TV had to stay off. But it was a Sunday in December and the New York Giants were playing! Brian, even at that early age, was, like his great-grandfather, an avid football fan. As Brian ran into the room to hug his "great-papa," he turned abruptly to the blank TV set, pointed at it with a little pout and a stamp of his foot, and announced for all to hear: "Great-papa! Football game! Football game?" "Ah," said his happy great-grandfather as he swept Brian into one arm while turning on the TV deftly with the other hand, "We can't disappoint the lad now, can we?" And great-grandfather and great-grandson shared one last Sunday, Brian happily ensconced in "great-papa's" lap, watching the Giants try to win.

At the beginning of January, 1993, John O'Donnell was finally forced to go to the hospital. The pain was getting unbearable. There was a tumor pinching a nerve in his back, and this caused him to lose the use of one of his arms, and he was facing paralysis. On January 14, he was admonished for walking around the hospital, visiting patients when he was supposed to be bedridden. He did admit to me that he was not reading anymore; for him, of course, this was not a good sign. However, he was working diligently to get a bottle of Johnny Walker Black. Darryl Anderson, his law partner in Washington, brought him a couple of bottles from Washington, and these had been stashed in the closet while my father waited for the appropriate time to share them.

On January 17, my father told me his latest story about the man who went into the bar and asked the bartender for three shots of scotch, in separate glasses. He toasted his brother in Ireland, toasted his brother in Australia, and toasted himself. A week later the same man came in and repeated the process. The next week the man asked for two shots. He toasted his brother in Ireland and toasted his brother in Australia, then left. As he was leaving, the bartender asked him about the toast to himself. He answered, "No, I'm off the stuff". That was the last time I ever spoke to my father.

On January 28, the world lost a wonderful human being. It seemed so fitting that my last conversation with my father revolved around a joke. For a man whose capacity to see humor at all points in his life, this last conversation seemed really to encapsulate much of his personality.

Dad was buried with two of his favorite things—a bottle of Johnny Walker Black Scotch and, in his pocket, a cigar.

On the cold but bright February morning as we left St. Mary's Church in Katonah and headed for Gate of Heaven cemetery, the words of Phil Coulter's song "The Old Man" resonated:

>And I never will forget him
>For he made me what I am
>And tho' he may be gone
>Memories linger on.
>And I miss him,
>The old man.

The man with mischievous eyes and a beguiling voice is no longer with us, but that sparkle, that chuckle, the generous "ah—but," the resonance of the man who challenged us all to think on our feet, to share what we have, to value education, to act ethically—that resonance we have, that resonance we cherish.

ENDNOTES

1. John F. O'Donnell, Letter found among his papers in Katonah, New York. Louis and Paddy were John F. O'Donnell's youngest brothers. Charlie was the brother closest to John in age. Min was John's mother's sister.
2. Father Patrick Cunningham Personal interview, St. John's Point, Donegal, Ireland, April 3, 2000
3. Seamus MacShane, Personal Interview, MacShane's Pub, Dunkineely, Ireland, April 1, 2000.
4. He told this story to my brother, Sean, and his wife, who recounted it to me, July 23, 2008.
5. Harry O'Donnell, Personal interview, August 15, 1992.
6. Mary O'Donnell Loranger, Personal interview, November 1999.
7. A canon is a title given to priests who lived "within the precinct or close of a cathedral or collegiate church." (*Oxford English Dictionary* online s.v. "Canon.").
8. Teresa O'Donnell McBrearty, from notes dated 1 June 1970, which she gave to her daughter, Clare McBrearty Tully, who subsequently shared them with me in 2000. Copies in the papers of Eileen O'Donnell Sheehan, Charleston, South Carolina.
9. Harry O'Donnell, Personal interview, August 15, 1992.
10. Louis O'Donnell, Personal interview, Bruckless, Donegal, Ireland, April 2000.
11. John F. O'Donnell, Telephone interview June 14, 1992.
12. Lily O'Donnell Henry, Personal interview, April 11, 2000.
13. Teresa O'Donnell McBrearty, Letter to John F. O'Donnell. Original letter in the papers of Eileen O'Donnell Sheehan, Charleston, South Carolina.
14. Patrick O'Donnell, Letter from St. Eunan's, 1936. Copy in the papers of Eileen O'Donnell Sheehan, Charleston, South Carolina.
15. See Part 1 for more information on the *Clan na Gael*.
16. Gwynne O'Donnell, Personal interview, Katonah, New York, August 20, 1993.
17. The family would add another daughter and another son after Gwynne's birth.
18. Gwynne O'Donnell, Personal interview, Katonah, New York, August 20, 1993.
19. Gwynne O'Donnell, Personal interview, Katonah, New York, August 20, 1993.
20. Practicum is the part of a college or university course consisting of practical work in a particular field.
21. Gwynne O'Donnell, Personal interview, Katonah, New York, August 20, 1993.
22. Gwynne O'Donnell, Personal interview, Katonah, New York, August 20, 1993.
23. Gwynne O'Donnell, Personal interview, Katonah, New York, August 20, 1993.
24. Gwynne O'Donnell, Personal interview, Katonah, New York, August 20, 1993.
25. This is among the papers of John F. O'Donnell, a copy of which is in the possession of Eileen O'Donnell Sheehan, Charleston, South Carolina.
26. The *Munda cor meum* is Latin for "Cleanse my heart." It is the prayer the priest said before reading the Gospel in the old Latin Mass.
27. This is among the papers of John F. O'Donnell, a copy of which is in the possession of Eileen O'Donnell Sheehan, Charleston, South Carolina.
28. John F. (Sean) O'Donnell, Jr., Personal interview, 21 July 2008.
29. As Scoogie Ryers termed him in a personal interview, January 19, 1999.
30. Thomas Berry was married to my mother's sister Grace.
31. John F. O'Donnell, Telephone interview, May 26, 1991.
32. John F. O'Donnell, Telephone interview, June 14, 1992.
33. John F. O'Donnell, Telephone interview, June 14, 1992.

34. Harry O'Donnell, Personal interview, April 15, 1992.
35. Cathleen O'Donnell Paprocki, Letter to Eileen Sheehan, December 2005.
36. John F. O'Donnell, Jr., Personal interview, 21 July 2008.
37. Cathleen O'Donnell Paprocki, Letter to Eileen Sheehan, December 2005.
38. Cathleen O'Donnell Paprocki, Letter to Eileen Sheehan, December 2005.
39. Cathleen O'Donnell Paprocki, Letter to Eileen Sheehan, December 2005.
40. Patricia Ann O'Donnell, Personal interview, November, 2000.
41. Cathleen O'Donnell Paprocki, Letter to Eileen Sheehan, December 2005.
42. Patricia Ann O'Donnell, Personal interview, November, 2000.
43. Patricia Ann O'Donnell, Personal interview, November, 2000.
44. Patricia Ann O'Donnell, Personal interview, November, 2000.
45. Patricia Ann O'Donnell, Personal interview, November, 2000.
46. Patricia Ann O'Donnell, Personal interview, November, 2000.
47. John F. (Sean) O'Donnell, Jr. Personal interview, May 2009.
48. Michael P. Broderick, as told to John F. (Sean) O'Donnell, Jr., July 22, 2008.
49. George Henry, Letter to Eileen Sheehan, October 8, 2007.
50. Rory Sheehan, as told to Mary Ann O'Donnell, July 23, 2008.
51. Patricia Ann O'Donnell, Personal interview, July 2006.

Sisters Teresa O'Donnell McBreaty and Lily O'Donnell Henry in Katonah in the later 1980s

Louis O'Donnell and Maire McMullin O'Donnell

Brothers and Sisters: On top row Paddy, John, Louis. Seated are Teresa and Lily

Father and Son: John Francis O'Donnell Sr. and Jr. fishing

THE LAST YEAR

Cathleen and Tricia O'Donnell with Santa around 1948

John O'Donnell with Great-grandson John Francis O'Donnell Sheehan in the Dallas airport in 1991

John O'Donnell with Great-grandson John Francis O'Donnell III in Katonah, NY

John O'Donnell with Sheehan Grandchildren: Rory, Eileen, O'Donnell, Sean, Alison, Carol Schmidt Sheehan, Neil in the early 1980s

A MAN FROM BRUCKLESS

Gwynne and John O'Donnell celebrate their 50th wedding anniversary in 1985

My father and I in *The Kiddle House* in December 1992

Our family home on Candlewood Isle in Danbury, Connecticut

The family home on Worthington Road in Greenburg NY

THE LAST YEAR

The family home in Katonah, NY

The view from the deck of the Katonah House

WORKS CITED

Published and On-Line Sources

AFL-CIO 7 Web site. <http://www.aflcio.org>.

"B. C. Vladeck Dies: City Councilman." *The New York Times*, October 31, 1938, p. 1.

Bain, Brian. "The NLRB: The Wagner Act of 1935." University of St. Francis, 2002. <http://www.stfrancis.edu/ba/ghkickul/stu-webs/btopics/works/wagner.htm>.

Bayor, Ronald H., and Timothy J. Meagher, eds. *The New York Irish*. Baltimore: Johns Hopkins University Press, 1996.

"Beset 5th Av. Lines Again Turn to Court." *The New York Post*, March 28, 1962, p. 5.

Biller Moe. *The American Postal Worker*. February 1993, p. 5.

Bornstein, Jerry. *Unions in Transition*. New York: Messner, 1981.

Brief History of the American Labor Movement. 5th ed. Washington, D.C.: U.S. Department of Labor, Bureau of Labor Statistics, 1976.

"British Liner Athenia Torpedoed, Sunk," *The New York Times*, September 4, 1939, p. 1.

Catholic Church. Parish of Killybegs (Donegal). *Parochial Registers of Killybegs (Donegal), 1850-1914*. 1 reel. Salt Lake City: Filmed by the Genealogical Society of Utah, 1984. FHL#1279234. Microfilm of original at Letterkenny, Co. Donegal.

"Catholic Emancipation." *Encyclopædia Britannica*. 2007. Encyclopædia Britannica Online. <http://search.eb.com/eb/article-9021825>.

Comerford, James J. *My Kilkenny I.R.A. Days, 1916-22*. Leggettsrath, Kilkenny, Ireland: Dinan Publishing Co., 1978.

"Company Upheld in Phone Dispute." *The New York Times*, February 1, 1971, p. 28.

Coogan, Tim Pat. *The IRA*. Rev. ed. New York: Palgrave, 2000.

"Court Decision Voids $37m Suit against TWU." *TWU Express*, July 1962.

Cowley, Robert, and Geoffrey Parker, eds. *The Reader's Companion to Military History* New York: Houghton Mifflin, 1996.

Dales, Douglas. "Senate Puts Off Action on Buses." *The New York Times*, March 16, 1962, p. 1.

Derry People's Press, May 2, 1959.

Donovan, Ronald. *Administering the Taylor Law: Public Employee Relations in New York*. Ithaca: ILR Press, School of Industrial and Labor Relations, Cornell University, 1990.

Edmonds, Richard. "Transit Workers OK New Contract." *[New York] Daily News*, May 13, 1980, p. 1.

"8-Cents Boost Ends Tieup in Philadelphia." [Rochester, NY] *Times-Union*, February 21, 1949.

"End of the Line in Transit." *The New York Times*, November 6, 1965, p. 28.

"Facts in Transit." *The New York Times*, December 8, 1965, p. 46.

Feinberg, Alexander. "TWU Executive Board Urges Removal of 2 Leftist Chiefs." *The New York Times*, September 5, 1948, p.1.

[Flood, Andrew]. "The 1798 Rebellion," *Red and Black Revolution* no. 4 (1998): 18-25. PDF version, Nov 2000. <http://struggle.ws/pdfs/RBR4.pdf>.

Freeman, Joshua B. *In Transit: The Transport Workers Union in New York City, 1933-1966*. New York: Oxford University Press, 1989.

Galbraith, John Kenneth. *The Great Crash 1929*. Boston: Houghton Mifflin, 1988.

Goldfield, Michael. *The Decline of Organized Labor in the United States*. Chicago: University of Chicago Press, 1987.

"The Great Irish Famine," New Jersey Commission on Holocaust Education. <http://www.nde.state.ne.us/ss/irish/irish_pf.html>.

Great Britain. Office of the General Valuation of Ireland. *General Valuation of Rateable Property in Ireland, 1847-1864*. 170 vols. Dublin: A. Thom, 1848-1861. Vol. 38. Donegal: Glenties Union: 1858.

Great Britain. Office of the General Valuation of Ireland. *General Valuation Revision Lists, Donegal Union 1858-1943*. 12 reels. Salt Lake City: Filmed by the Genealogical Society of Utah, 1970. #FHL 0832511. Microfilm of original records at the Ireland Valuation Office, Dublin.

WORKS CITED

Hammer, Alexander R. "Control of Fifth Avenue Coach Sold to B.S.F. for $3 Million." *The New York Times,* January 30, 1964, p. 37.

Hammer, Alexander R. "Pact Due in Fight at 5th Ave. Coach." *The New York Times,* February 15, 1962, p. 39.

Heckscher, August, with Phyllis Robinson. *When LaGuardia Was Mayor: New York's Legendary Years.* New York: Norton, 1978.

Ingalls, Leonard. "Bus Award Reduce Hours, Raises Pay on Private Lines." *The New York Times,* November 19, 1953, p. 23.

Ireland. General Register Office. *Marriage Record, 1845-1870, with Indexes to Marriages, 1845-1921, in the General Registry Office of Ireland.* 334 reels. Salt Lake City: Filmed by the Genealogical Society of Utah, 1953), microfilm #FHL 0101505. Microfilm of original records in Custom House, Dublin.

The Irish Democrat. <http://www.irishdemocrat.co.uk/about/ca-history/>.

"Irish Republican Army," *The Blackwell Companion to Modern Irish Culture.* Oxford: Blackwell, 1999. 306.

"Jersey Mail Facility Disrupted in Dispute Over New Hours." *The New York Times,* January 22, 1974, p. 1.

Katz, Ralph. "5th Ave. Bus Line Sues Quill Union for $37,305,000." *The New York Times,* March 10, 1962, p. 1.

Katz, Ralph. "Governor Plans Own Legislation on Bus Take-Over." *The New York Times,* March 11, 1962, p. 1.

Kee, Robert. *Ireland: A History.* London: Abacus, 1995.

Kempton, Murray. "The Big Wheel." *The New York Post,* December 14, 1961, p. 57.

Kheel Center for Labor Management Documentation and Archives at Cornell University Web Site. <http://www.ilr.cornell.edu/library/kheel/about/history/theodorekheel.html>.

"Labor Party Is Key." *The New York Times,* November 3, 1937, p. 1.

Lambert, Bruce. "John F. O'Donnell, 85, A Lawyer and Advocate for Union Workers [Obituary]." *The New York Times,* January 29, 1993, p. A17.

Lefkowitz, Bernard. "Non-Union Bus Drivers." *The New York Post,* March 26, 1962, p. 4.

Levey, Stanley. "City Units Accused by Bus Arbitrator," *The New York Times*, April 29, 1953, p. 18.

Levey, Stanley. "Estimate Board Denies Permits to 5th Ave. Line." *The New York Times*, March 9, 1962, p. 1.

Levin, Alan. "First Buses Set to Roll on Saturday." *The New York Post*, March 22, 1962, p. 5.

"Lewis Will Speak in Garden Tonight." *The New York Times*, October 4, 1937, p. 6.

Lissner, Will. "Phone Union Votes to Continue Strike; Upstate Offices Hit." *The New York Times*, January 15, 1971, p. 1.

Lukas, Paul, and Maggie Overfelt. "UPS: United Parcel Service." *FSB: Fortune Small Business*, April 2003, p. 24.

"Macy Uses United Parcel." *The New York Times*, June 27, 1946, p. 36.

Malcolm, Elizabeth. "Black and Tans." *The Oxford Companion to Irish History*. Ed. S. J. Connolly. Oxford: Oxford University Press, 2007.

Marmo, Michael. *More Profile than Courage.* Albany: State University of New York Press, 1990.

McCaffrey, James P. "$1,100,000 Back Pay Won by 3rd Ave. Men; Line Asks 10¢ Fare." *The New York Times*, February 8, 1950, p. 1.

McGinley. James J. *Labor Relations in the New York Rapid Transit Systems 1904-1944.* New York: King's Crown Press, 1949.

McKivigan, John R. and Thomas J. Robertson. "The Irish American Worker in Transition, 1877-1914: New York City as a Test Case." *The New York Irish*. Ed. Ronald H. Bayor and Timothy J. Meagher. Baltimore: Johns Hopkins University Press, 1996.

McNickle Chris. "When New York Was Irish, and After." *The New York Irish*. Ed. Ronald H. Bayor and Timothy J. Meagher. Baltimore: Johns Hopkins University Press, 1996.

Montgomery, Paul L. "Phone Workers to Return Today." *The New York Times*, January 25, 1971, p. 17.

New York Irish Center. Web site. <http://www.newyorkirishcenter.org>.

New York University. Tamiment Library. <http://www.nyu.edu/library/bobst/research/ tam/>

"$9 Million Listed For Bus Pensions." *The New York Times*, May 10, 1965, p. 28.

WORKS CITED

Norwood, Stephen H. *Strikebreaking and Intimidation: Mercenaries and Masculinity in Twentieth-Century America.* Chapel Hill: University of North Carolina Press, 2002.

O'Donnell John F. Letter to the Editor, *The Evening Bulletin,* Philadelphia, January 10, 1950.

O'Donnell, John F. "TWU Fights for Oldsters' Pensions." *TWU Express,* December 1962, p. 2.

O'Donnell, John F. *Irish Echo,* December 7, 1938.

Oreskes, Michael. *[New York] Sunday News Magazine,* March 16, 1980, p. 23.

Oreskes, Michael. "TWU: MTA Is April Foolish." *[New York] Daily News,* March 7, 1980.

Oreskes, Michael. "The Inside Story of Transit Strike." *[New York] Daily News,* April 13, 1980, p. 3.

Oxford English Dictionary on-line.

Patterson, Edward. *The County Donegal Railways.* London: Pan Books, 1962.

"Panel to Decide Telephone Issue." *The New York Times,* January 26, 1971, p. 37.

"Penal Laws." *Encyclopædia Britannica* 2007. *Encyclopædia Britannica Online.* <http://search.eb.com/eb/article-9059041>.

Perlmutter, Emanuel. "Judge Orders End to Phone Strike." *The New York Times,* January 12, 1971, p. 28.

"Philadelphia Pact Reached in Strike." *The New York Times,* February 20, 1949, pp. 1, 47.

"A Pledge of Transit Peace" [Editorial]. *The New York Times,* June 28, 1950, p. 28.

Porter, Russell. "'Bonanza' Is Seen in Bus Take-Over." *The New York Times,* March 4, 1962, p. 48.

"Postal Workers' Contract Talks Break Down." *The New York Times,* November 22, 1990, p. B14.

"Quill Quits ALP; One of Founders." *The New York Times,* April 21, 1948, p. 22.

Quindlen Anna. "About New York: A Behind-the-Scenes Life in the Labor Movement," *The New York Times,* September 5, 1981, p. 23.

Raskin, A. H. "Illinois CIO Chiefs Shun TWU Session." *The New York Times,* December 4, 1948, p. 28.

Raskin, A. H. "Quill Re-Elected as TWU Ousts Left From 14-year Rule." *The New York Times*, December 7, 1948, p. 1.

Raskin A. H. "4-Week Bus Strike Is Ended; Third Ave. Service Resumed; Other Lines to Roll Today." *New York Times*, January 29, 1953, p. 1.

Raskin, A. H. "Bus Men to Ballot on Formula Today." *The New York Times*, January 28, 1953, pp. 1, 21.

Raskin, A. H. "Bus Economy Plan Advanced for City." *The New York Times*, March 6, 1953, p. 19.

Resner, Lawrence. "2 Hurt as Violence Marks Macy Strike." *The New York Times*, July 13, 1946, p. 3.

Serrin, William. "Grandfatherly Power behind Transport Workers' Bargaining." *The New York Times*, April 1, 1980, p. 1.

Serrin, William. "Lindsay Led Talks in '66, But Koch Remains Aloof." *The New York Times* 2 April 1980, B3.

Serrin, William. "The 1980 New York City Transit Negotiations: Public Battles and Private Deals." *The New York Times*, May 7, 1980, p A1.

Stark, Louis. "Labor Groups Firm on Terms of Peace." *The New York Times*, October 29, 1937, p. 6.

Stetson, Damon. "Transit Workers Shout Approval of Tuesday Strike." *The New York Times* 28 March 1980, A1.

"Strike Threatens to Close Macy's." *The New York Times*, July 11, 1946, p. 13.

"Support Pledged for Blanket Code," *The New York Times*, July 22, 1933, p. 5.

"A Tale of Two Cities; Dublin-New York." *TWU Express*, September 1962.

"Tammany Hall," *Encyclopædia Britannica*, 2006. Encyclopædia Britannica Online. 15 July 2006 <http://search.eb.com/eb/article-9071120>.

6 Transport Workers Union. "The President's Report." *Report of Proceedings, Sixth Biennial Convention*, Chicago, IL, December 6-10, 1948 [New York: Transport Worker's Union, 1949].

7 Transport Workers Union. *Report of Proceedings, Seventh Biennial Convention*, December 6-10, 1950 [New York: Transport Workers Union, 1951].

WORKS CITED

8 Transport Workers Union. *Report of Proceedings, Eighth Biennial Convention*, Philadelphia, PA, December 9-13, 1952 [New York: Transport Workers Union, 1953].

10 Transport Workers Union. "The President's Report." *Report of Proceedings, Tenth Biennial Convention*, New York, NY October 21-25, 1957. [New York: Transport Workers Union, 1958.

12 Transport Workers Union. "The President's Report." *Report of Proceedings, Twelfth Biennial Convention*, New York, NY October 11-15, 1965. [New York: Transport Workers Union, 1966.

13 Transport Workers Union. "The President's Report." *Report of Proceedings, Thirteenth Biennial Convention*, Bal Harbor, FL September 8-12, 1969. [New York: Transport Workers Union, 1970.

16 Transport Workers Union. "The President's Report." Sixteenth Constitutional Convention Transport Workers Union of America, Legal Section, San Francisco, CA, September 28, 1981. [New York: Transport Workers Union, 1982.

18 Transport Workers Union. "The President's Report." Eighteenth Constitutional Convention Transport Workers Union of America, Miami, FL, October 2-6 1989. New York: Transport Workers Union, 1989.

"TWU Aide Sentenced, Counsel Gets 10-Month Term Suspended, Fine in Tax Case." *The New York Times*, September 24, 1955, p. 16.

"TWU Completes Fact-Board Plea." *The New York Times*, February 8, 1950, p. 16.

"TWU Counsel Denies Income Tax Cheating." *The New York Times*, January 1, 1955, p. 26.

TWU Express, February 1962.

"Union Aides Back Telephone Strike." *The New York Times*, January 18, 1971, p. 19.

United Parcel Service. "Company History: Timeline, 1930-1980." 1994-2006. <http://www.ups.com/content/corp/about/history/1980.html>.

United States Court of Appeals, For the Second Circuit, Nos. 856, 857, 858—September Term, 1970, Argued April 2, 1971,

Decided June 22, 1971, Docket Nos. 71-1140, 71-1141, 71-1142, p. 3783. Copy in the papers of Eileen O'Donnell Sheehan.

Walsh, John and Garth Mangum. *Labor Struggle in the Post Office*. Armonk, NY: M. E. Sharpe, 1992.

Weiss, Robert P. "Private Detective Agencies and Labour Discipline in the United States, 1855-1946." *The Historical Journal* 29.1 (March 1986): 87-107.

Wiert, William G. "Transit Men Back in Philadelphia." *The New York Times*, 21 February 1949, pp. 25, 40.

Zipser, Alfred R. "5th Avenue Coach Management Assailed by Critics of Policies." *The New York Times*, May 9, 1961, p. 53.

Interviews conducted by Eileen O'Donnell Sheehan

Anderson, Darryl, Personal interview, April 8, 1997.
Biller, Moe, Telephone interview, September 5, 1993.
Biller, Moe, Telephone interview, April 7, 1997.
Cunningham, Father Patrick, Personal interview, St. Johns Point, Donegal, Ireland, April 2000.
Donoghue, Joseph, Telephone interview, March 1, 1999.
Henry, Lily O'Donnell, Personal interview, April 11, 2000.
Kovenetsky, Sam, Telephone interview, August 11, 1991.
Loranger, Mary O'Donnell, Personal interview, Grosse Point Farms, Michigan, November 1999.
O'Donnell, Gwynne, Personal interview, August 20, 1993.
O'Donnell, Harry, Personal interview, August 15, 1992.
O'Donnell, Louis, Personal interview, Bruckless, Donegal, Ireland, April 2000.
O'Donnell, John F., Personal interview, June 15, 1988.
O'Donnell, John F., Personal interview, December 28, 1989.
O'Donnell, John F., Personal interview, July 12, 1990.
O'Donnell, John F., Telephone interview, July 18, 1990.
O'Donnell, John F., Telephone interview, July 19, 1990.
O'Donnell, John F., Telephone interview, February 10, 1991.
O'Donnell, John F., Telephone interview, February 24, 1991.
O'Donnell, John F., Telephone interview, March 3, 1991.
O'Donnell, John F., Telephone interview, March 10, 1991.

WORKS CITED 275

O'Donnell, John F., Telephone interview, March 17, 1991.
O'Donnell, John F., Telephone interview, March 24, 1991.
O'Donnell, John F., Telephone interview, April 14, 1991.
O'Donnell, John F., Telephone interview, April 21, 1991.
O'Donnell, John F., Telephone interview, May 19, 1991.
O'Donnell, John F., Telephone interview, May 26, 1991.
O'Donnell, John F., Personal interview, July 15, 1991.
O'Donnell, John F., Telephone interview, July 17, 1991.
O'Donnell, John F., Telephone interview, August 4, 1991.
O'Donnell, John F., Telephone interview, August 11, 1991.
O'Donnell, John F., Telephone interview, August 25, 1991.
O'Donnell, John F., Telephone interview, December 1, 1991.
O'Donnell, John F., Telephone interview, December 8, 1991.
O'Donnell, John F., Telephone interview, February 4, 1992
O'Donnell, John F., Telephone interview, January 6, 1992.
O'Donnell, John F., Telephone interview, June 14, 1992.
O'Donnell, John F. Jr., Personal interview, 21 July 2008.
O'Donnell, Patricia Ann, Personal interview, November, 2000.
O'Donnell, Patricia Ann, Personal interview, July 2006.
Ravitch, Richard, Personal interview, New York City, February 3, 2006.
Rosen, David B., Personal interview, March 25, 2002.
Ryers, Scoogie, Personal interview, January 19, 1999.
Schwartz, Asher, Personal interview, July 11, 1991.
Sheehan, Neil, Telephone interview, March 24, 1991.

Personal Papers in the Possession of the O'Donnell Family

Fields, Horace L. to John F. O'Donnell, 16 February 1928. O'Donnell papers, Katonah, New York.
Gallagher, Francis. Letter to the Committee of Character and Fitness, First Judicial Department of the Appellate Division of the Supreme Court of the State of New York, November 26, 1935. Papers of Eileen O'Donnell Sheehan, Charleston, South Carolina.
Gallagher, Francis. Letter to the Committee on Character of Fitness, First Judicial Department of the Appellate Division of

the Supreme Court of the State of New York, 26 November 1935. Papers of Eileen O'Donnell Sheehan, Charleston, South Carolina.

Garuso, Hyman W. Appellate Division of the Supreme Court of the State of New York, First Judicial Department, October 18, 1937. Papers of Eileen O'Donnell Sheehan, Charleston, South Carolina.

McBrearty, Teresa O'Donnell. Notes shared by her daughter, Clare McBrearty Tully. Copy. Papers of Eileen O'Donnell Sheehan, Charleston, South Carolina.

MacMenamin William T. Letter to the Committee of Character and Fitness, First Judicial Department of the Appellate Division of the Supreme Court of the State of New York, November 19, 1935. O'Donnell papers, Katonah, New York.

O'Donnell John F. Diary. O'Donnell papers, Katonah, New York.

O'Donnell John F. Letter to Hon. B. Charney Vladeck, January 20, 1938. Copy. Papers of Eileen O'Donnell Sheehan, Charleston, South Carolina.

O'Donnell John F. Papers submitted to the Appellate Division of the Supreme Court, May 29, 1937. O'Donnell papers, Katonah, New York.

O'Donnell John F. Papers submitted to the Appellate Division of the Supreme Court, First Judicial Department, New York NY, May 29, 1937.

O'Donnell, John F. "1966 New York Transit Strike," Speech at the Labor Management Luncheon, New School for Social Research, May 4, 1966. Copy of notes taken by Michael Marmo of O'Donnell's speech. Copy. Papers of Eileen O'Donnell Sheehan, Charleston, South Carolina.

O'Donnell, John F. "His Homecoming." English 1.D. paper submitted to College of the City of New York, summer 1929. Copy. Papers of Eileen O'Donnell Sheehan, Charleston, South Carolina.

O'Donnell, John F. Columbia University Seminar on Labor, April 19, 1967. O'Donnell papers, Katonah, New York.

O'Donnell, John F. Address before the House Committee on Labor, April, 1953. Typescript. Papers of Eileen O'Donnell Sheehan, Charleston, South Carolina.

WORKS CITED

O'Donnell, John F. Letter to Councilman B. Charney Vladeck, January 20, 1938. Copy. Papers of Eileen O'Donnell Sheehan, Charleston, South Carolina.

O'Donnell, John F. Letter to Miss Helen Dennison, January 15, 1976. Papers of Eileen O'Donnell Sheehan, Charleston, South Carolina.

O'Donnell, John F. Script from radio broadcast in 1935. Copy. Papers of Eileen O'Donnell Sheehan, Charleston, South Carolina.

O'Donnell, John F. "Brief for Defendants-Appellants Local 1101 and Howard Banker," March 10, 1971. Copy. Papers of Eileen O'Donnell Sheehan.

O'Donnell John F. Personal notes. Copies. Papers of Eileen O'Donnell Sheehan, Charleston, South Carolina.

O'Donnell, John F. (Sean) III. Written statement. Papers of Eileen O'Donnell Sheehan, Charleston, South Carolina.

O'Donnell, Patrick. Letter from St. Eunan's, 1936. Copy. Papers of Eileen O'Donnell Sheehan, Charleston, South Carolina.

O'Shenrahan, Sean. Letter to the Committee of Character and Fitness, First Judicial Department of the Appellate Division of the Supreme Court of the State of New York, December 7, 1935. Copy. Papers of Eileen O'Donnell Sheehan, Charleston, South Carolina.

Paprocki, Cathleen O'Donnell. Letter to Eileen O'Donnell Sheehan, December 2005. Papers of Eileen O'Donnell Sheehan, Charleston, South Carolina.

Materials from the Tamiment Library, New York University. Quoted with permission.

Note: After I used most of the papers, the staff of the Tamiment has organized and classified most of what I used. I give the collection numbers now used, where possible.

O'Donnell, John F. Papers. Tamiment Library, New York University. WAG 170.

O'Reilly, Gerald. *The Birth and Growth of the Transport Workers Union.* N.p.: n.p., 1988. Copy in the Papers of Gerald O'Reilly. Tamiment Library, New York University. WAG 105.

Transport Workers Union. Papers. Tamiment Library, New York University. WAG 234.

Banker, Harold. Personal interview with Gail Malmgreen, Tamiment Library, New York University, September 15, 1994. Courtesy of the Tamiment Library, New York University.
United Parcel Files. Tamiment Library, New York University.
Hearing before a Fact-Finding Committee in the City of Houston, Texas, 1950 Copy in the Tamiment Library, New York University. Courtesy of the Tamiment Library, New York University.
John J. Ryan, Hearing before a Fact-Finding Committee in the City of Houston, Texas. Copy in the Tamiment Library, New York University. Courtesy of the Tamiment Library, New York University.
"Report of the Mayor's Advisory Transit Committee to Honorable William O'Dwyer, Mayor of the City of New York," September 9, 1946.
"Report of the New York City Transit Fact-Finding Board to Honorable William O'Dwyer, Mayor of the City of New York," May 31, 1950.
"Memorandum of Understanding between Board of Transportation and Various Labor Organizations Representing Its Employees," June 27, 1950.
"Amendment to Memorandum of Understanding between Board of Transportation and Various Labor Organizations Representing Its Employees," June 27, 1951.
Transcript of 1984 Postal Arbitration Proceedings, December 11, 1984, p. 32. Copy in the papers of Eileen O'Donnell Sheehan.

INDEX

1948 Convention, 80
1974 Bulk Strike, 179
69th Regiment of the New York Guard, 225
Amalgamated Association of Street and Electric Railway Employees of America, 52, 67, 68, 69, 75, 81, 85, 86
Amalgamated Clothing and Textile Workers, 177, 178
Amalgamated Transit Union (ATU), 145
American Federation of Labor, 42, 53, 67, 68, 73, 74, 75, 86, 162
American Labor Party, xvi, 37, 46, 47, 48, 49, 50, 52, 79
American Postal Workers Union, 60, 61, 173, 176, 177, 180, 181, 182, 184, 185, 186, 188, 191
American Telephone & Telegraph Company, 168
Amter, Israel, 72
Ancient Order of Hibernians, 71, 72
Anderson, Darryl, 181, 182, 183, 184, 185, 186, 188, 192, 198, 199, 205, 259
Anticipatory contempt, 99
Antonini, Luigi, 47
Associate Counsel for the National Association for the Protection of the Foreign Born, 52

Avenue B and East Broadway Transit Company, 122, 128
Bakke. E. Wight, 153
Banker, Howard, 165, 166, 167, 168, 169, 170
Barr, Morty, 168
Barton, Hugh W., 3
Beakies, 72
Berry, Tom, 228
Biller, Moe, x, 60, 173, 174, 175, 176, 177, 178, 179, 180, 181, 182, 183, 184, 185, 188, 189, 191, 192, 198
Birch, Dick, 239
Blount, Winton M., 187
Blue Eagle, 38, 39
Board of Aldermen, 45, 46
Board of Estimate, 78, 125, 128, 131
Board of Transportation, 116, 117, 118, 119, 120, 137
Boland, Dr. John P., 40
Bolger, William F., 182, 187
Bradley, Roland, 35
Broderick, Brian O'Donnell, 258
Broderick, Cairenn O'Donnell, 251, 252, 258
Broderick, Michael, 251, 252, 258, 259
Brooklyn Manhattan Transit, 73, 116, 119, 129
Brophy, John, 39

Brotherhood of Consolidated Edison Employees, Independent, 53
Brotherhood of IRT Company Employees, 32, 40, 42, 53, 69, 70
Brotherhood of Locomotive Engineers, 120
Browder, Earl, 72, 76
Brown, William R., 109
BSF Company, 133, 134
Candlewood Lake, xi, 227, 228, 229
Cannella, Judge John M., 168
Carpenter Margaret O'Donnell, 16, 20, 216
Carson, Edward, 32
Caruso, Alison Sheehan, 254
Casey, James, 38
Catholic Emancipation Act in 1829, 3
Catler, Susan L., 181
Ceannt, Eamonn, 33
Checkoff, 81
City College of New York, 24
City Council, 45, 46, 47, 49, 52, 57, 58, 155
Civil Service Forum, 120, 138
Clan na Gael, 28, 30, 35, 220, 223
Clan Na Gael and IRA Club. See Clan Na Gael
Clark Sr., Joseph F., 100
Cloone, Michael, 72
Cohn, Roy M., 129, 130, 132, 133, 138
Cole, David L, viii, 117, 153
Comerford, James J., 27, 35, 36
Committee of Character and Fitness, 27, 30, 37
Communications Workers of America, 165, 168, 169, 252
Communist Party, 44, 47, 48, 49, 50, 51, 63, 71, 72, 73, 77, 79, 80, 81, 83, 84, 90, 94, 107, 245
Condon-Wadlin Law, 116, 152, 153
Cone, Justice John E., 120
Congress of Industrial Organizations, 41, 42, 43, 45, 53, 61, 68, 74, 75, 79, 81, 82, 102, 103, 107, 124, 126
Connolly, Charles, viii, 26, 28, 29, 31, 32, 33, 34, 70, 83, 87, 220, 221
Connolly, James, 33
Connolly, Paddy, 70
Connors, Hamm, 95, 97, 98
Courtenay, William J., 39
Cullman, Howard S., 129, 130, 134, 138
Cunningham, Father, 212, 213
Curtin, John F., 124
Cushing, Charles C., 169
Dallas Transit Company, 133, 138
Darcy, Tom, 41
Delivery and Allied Workers Independent Union, 39
Dewey, Thomas E., 46
Donoghue, Joseph, 84, 87, 115, 137

INDEX 281

Donoghue, Tom, 181
Donovan, Ronald, 151, 152, 162
Duane, William F., 39
Dubinsky, David, 47, 48, 49, 52, 162
Dunlop, John T., 153
Dwyer, Lou, 99
Earle, Genevieve B., 57
Ebert, Charlie, 95, 96, 97, 100
Eisenberg, Irving, 41
Executive Order 10988, 174
Farah Manufacturing Company, 177
Farley, James J., 47
Feeney, Jack, 35
Feinsinger, Nathan P., 144, 150
Fennell, Thomas F., 78
Fields, Horace L., 25, 36
Fifth Avenue Coach, 53, 54, 55, 56, 77, 122, 128, 129, 130, 131, 132, 133, 134, 136, 138, 139, 261
Filbey, Francis, 176, 177, 178
Fine, Justice Sidney A., 137
Fordham University School of Law, Evening Division, 26
Forge, Maurice, 72, 73
Foster, William, 76
Francis, Leslie T., 41
Frank, Anthony M., 144, 189, 190
Franklin, Robert, 82
Froelke, D. Richard, 186
Ganzglass, Martin R., 181
Garrett, Sylvester, 144, 150
Garuso, Hyman W., 31, 37
Gellhorn, Walter, 157

General Post Office, 33
Gilhooley, John J., 144
Gilmartin, Daniel, 144, 150
Goldberg, Arthur, viii, 81, 86
Goldfield, Michael, 154, 162
Goldstein, Malcolm, 201, 205
Goodman, Rhoda, 41
Gottlieb, Sol, 41
Greenfield, Albert M., 100
Guinan, Matthew, viii, 30, 58, 127, 138, 144, 150, 202
Gwynne, 30, 36, 62, 220, 221, 222, 223
Hajjar, Anton, 181, 182
Harbison, Frederick H., 153
Harding, Richard H., 186
Harten, Carl K., 56, 57, 58
Hayes, James F., 39
Hayes, Major General Philip, 91
Hecht Jr., Justice William C., 136
Hendricks, M. D., 111
Henry, George, 255, 256, 259
Henry, Lily O'Donnell, 2, 6, 8, 216, 217, 219, 252, 257, 258
Henry, Scotty, 203, 205
High, Robert, 23, 93, 101
Hillman, Sidney, 42, 47, 75, 81, 86, 87
Hoffenstein, Phil, 41
Hogan, Austin, 73, 77, 82, 84
Home Relief Agencies, 29
Horst, Jim, 144
Houghton, Everitas Large, 257
Houston Transit Company, 108, 109
Houston, Dr. W. V., 108, 113

Huffines, Robert L., 133, 134
Impellitteri, Vincent R., 124, 138
Interborough Rapid Transit, 69, 70, 71, 72, 73, 116, 119, 129
Interest Arbitration, 173, 185,186, 188, 200
International Brotherhood of Teamsters. See Teamsters
International Executive Board, 81
International Ladies Garment Workers Union, 49, 162
Irish American Independent Political Units (IAIPU), 29
Irish Echo, 26, 28, 29, 31, 35, 36, 39, 40, 46, 48, 62, 220, 221, 222
Jamaica Buses, 122, 128
Johnson, Hugh, 38
Joint Bargaining Committee, 182, 186, 187, 188, 190
Joyce, Ceil, 229
Judge Kun, 97, 98, 99
Kaden, Lewis B., 160
Kaelin, Andrew, 93, 94, 101
Kaufman, Judge Samuel H., 121
Kaufman, Steve, 156
Kavanagh, Mark, 144, 150
Kelber, Harry, xvi
Kempton, Murray, 127, 138
Kennedy, Charles, 3, 4
Kennedy, Charles Canon, 2, 4, 6, 16, 31, 216, 217
Kennedy, Ellen, 2, 4, 6, 22
Kennedy, Francis, 4, 20
Kennedy, Min, 12

Kerr, Clark, 185, 186, 188, 192
Keyes, Maggie, 2, 216, 217
Kheel, Theodore W., 83, 87, 116, 117, 124, 127, 133, 135, 136, 137, 139, 144, 150, 151, 173, 186, 188, 191, 200, 204, 205, 262
Klees, Frank, 144
Koch, Edward, 155, 156, 161, 162, 265
Kovenetsky, Sam, 40, 41, 42, 43, 44, 45, 62
Kresky, Edward, 157
Krock, Edward, 133, 134, 148
LaGuardia, Fiorello, 47, 48
Large, Agnes, 220, 221
Large, Arthur, 221
Large, Mary Regan, 220, 221, 222
Larkin, Leo A., 131, 134, 139
Lawe, John E., 155, 156, 157, 158, 159, 160, 202, 203, 204
Lawton, E. B., 41
Layton, Mary Eileen Sheehan, 250
Lazarus, Ruben, 46
Levey, Stanley, 125, 138, 139
Levy, Abraham N., 57
Levy, Matthew M., 52
Lindner, William, 155, 156, 157
Lindsay, John V., 144, 145, 146, 147, 148, 149, 151, 162
Local 100, 52, 53, 57, 58, 76, 79, 80, 81, 82, 87, 116, 119, 127, 129, 138, 144, 155, 156, 160, 197
Local 1101, 165, 166, 170

INDEX

Local 1-S, Macy's Department Store Workers, 40
Local 234, 89, 90, 94, 99, 102
Local 260, 107, 109, 111, 113
Local 3 (Div N.) Electrical Workers Union, 53
Local 56 Firemen and Oilers Union, 53
Local Executive Board, 158
Loranger, Mary O'Donnell, 2, 6, 8, 14, 20, 216, 257
Luby, Arthur, 181, 200, 205
Lynch, Walter A., 122, 123, 124, 125
Lyons, Tommy, 39, 40
MacDermott, Sean, 33
MacDonagh, Thomas, 33
MacDonald, John M., 78
MacMahon, Douglas L., 73, 82, 83, 90, 112, 144, 149, 150
MacMenamin, William T., 31, 37
MacShane, Seamus, 213, 214, 223
Macy, 40, 41, 42, 43, 62, 263
Macy's Herald Square Department Store. See Macy
Mahon, Joseph, 186, 188
Mail Handlers Union, 189
Maintenance Employees, 176
Malmgreen, Gail, 168, 170
Mangus, William, 144
Manhattan and Bronx Surface Transit Operating Authority, 131, 135, 136, 150
Manhattan Bronx Postal Union, 173, 174, 175, 176, 177, 179
Marmo, Michael, 146, 162
McBrearty, Teresa O'Donnell, 2, 6, 216, 217, 219, 226, 252, 253
McCarthy, John E., 54, 55, 78, 138
McCoer, Tom, 41
McCormick Scholarship, 8
McCormick, William J., 78
McGeever, Mary, 4
McGinley, James J., 68, 85
McLean, Robert, 41
McManus, Seamus, 13
McNelis, Annie Kennedy, 16
McNelis, Patrick John, 23
McReynolds, William J., 95, 100
Memorandum of Understanding, 118, 119, 137
Merchandise Delivery Drivers and Employees, Local 804, 40
Metro Area Postal Union, x, 179
Metropolitan Transportation Authority, 156, 157, 159, 163
Meyer, Arthur S., 92, 112, 116
Mittenthal, Richard, 188
Moe Biller, Moe, 60, 173, 174, 179, 182, 184, 191, 192, 198
Morgan, Thomas A., 117
Morrow, John, 213
Motor Vehicle Operators, 176
Motormen's Benevolent Association, 144
Mulrooney, Edward P., 116, 117
Murray, Phil, 41, 45, 81
Murrins, 213

Muscat group, 133, 135
Muscat, Victor, 133, 134, 135
Nash, Peter, 186, 188
National Association of Letter Carriers, 173, 182, 184, 186, 188
National Association of Postmasters, 187
National Industrial Recovery Act (NIRA), 38
National Labor Relations Act. See Wagner Act
National Labor Relations Board, 40, 45, 90
National Postal Workers Union, 174, 176
National Recovery Administration (NRA), 38
New Directions, 197
New York City Omnibus, 77, 122, 128, 129
New York Telephone Company, 165, 166, 167, 168, 169
Nixon, Richard, 175
Norris-LaGuardia Act, 70, 167
O'Donnell & Schwartz, iv, 58, 63, 181
O'Donnell III, John F., 160, 163, 253
O'Donnell Jr., John F., 63, 223, 227, 231, 232, 236
O'Donnell Patrick, 2, 212, 216, 219
O'Donnell, Charlie, 2, 6, 8, 20, 22, 25, 26, 212, 216

O'Donnell, Harry, 2, 6, 216, 219, 226, 229, 253, 254, 255, 256, 257
O'Donnell, Henry, 2, 4, 5, 6, 217
O'Donnell, Louis, 2, 6, 212, 216, 217, 257
O'Donnell, Máire McMullin, 257
O'Donnell, Owen, 5, 6, 213
O'Donnell, Tricia, x, 227, 237, 241, 242, 243, 250, 257
O'Dwyer, William F., 34, 52, 53, 77, 78, 79, 81, 83, 116, 118, 121
O'Gara, John E., 41, 43
O'Grady, Joseph E., 144, 146, 147, 149, 151
O'Reilly, Gerald, 30, 70, 71, 72, 76, 82, 83, 86, 87
O'Rourke, James, 24, 222, 228
O'Shea, Tom, 72
O'Donnell, Elizabeth, 6, 11, 21, 217
O'Donnell, Ellen Kennedy, 2, 4, 5, 6, 8, 10, 15, 22, 212, 218
Oreskes, Michael, 155, 156, 158, 162, 163
Ott, Betty, 229
Pan American, 80
Paprocki, Brian, 256
Paprocki, Cathleen O'Donnell, 223, 227, 231, 232, 235, 236, 237, 238, 239, 241, 256
Patterson, Charles, 127
Pearse, Padraig, 33
Penal Laws, 3, 19, 20

INDEX 285

Philadelphia Transportation Company, 89, 90, 91, 92, 93, 94, 98, 100, 104, 105
Pilzer, Penny A., 181
Pinkerton, 69, 71, 85
Plunkett, Joseph Mary, 33
Popkin, Joel, 184, 187
Postal Reorganization Act of 1970, 175, 176
Potofsky, Jacob, 177, 178
Queensborough Bridge Railway Company, 122
Queens-Nassau Transit Corporation, 122, 128
Quill, Michael J., 34, 40, 43, 44, 46, 47, 48, 49, 50, 51, 52, 53, 57, 58, 59, 60, 67, 70, 71, 72, 73, 74, 75, 76, 77, 78, 79, 81, 82, 83, 84, 85, 90, 91, 92, 93, 94, 95, 96, 97, 98, 99, 100, 101, 108, 109, 122, 123, 124, 127, 132, 144, 145, 146, 149, 151, 152, 202, 245
Quindlen, Anna, xv, xvii
Quinn, Justice Peter A., 132
Railway Labor Act, 118
Rank, John, 169
Raskin, A. H., 86, 87, 122, 123, 124, 138, 148
Ravitch, Richard, 156, 157, 158, 159, 160, 161, 163
Retail, Wholesale and Department Store Union [RWDSU],, 42, 44, 45
Rockefeller, Nelson A., 131, 144, 153
Roosevelt, Franklin D., 47, 91

Rose, Alex, 47, 162
Rosen, David, 58, 59, 197
Rosenberg, Anna M., 42, 43, 116
Rowland, John, 144
Ruml, Beardsley, 43
Ryan, Claude, 38
Ryan, John, 107, 108, 109, 113
Ryers, Scoogie, 85, 87, 151, 152, 162, 233
Sacher, Harry, 58, 63, 73, 79, 90, 117
Samuels, Barney, 92, 100
Santo, John, 72, 73, 82
Scannell, Daniel T., 144, 156, 157, 159, 160
Schwartz, Asher W., 57, 58, 59, 63, 126, 181, 203
Secular, Keith, 186
Serrin, William, 143, 159, 161, 162, 163
Sheehan, Carol Schmidt, 250
Sheehan, Frank, 144, 150
Sheehan, John F. O'Donnell, 252
Sheehan, Neil, 178, 191, 249
Sheehan, Rory, 255
Shipman, Mitchell M., 169
Shultz, George, 175, 176
Silvergleid, David, 176
Simon, Bruce, 186, 188
Smith, Al, 46
Smith, James E., 27, 28, 30, 221, 222
Smolikoff, Charlie, 107
Sombrotto, Vincent, 182, 183, 184, 185, 186, 188, 189

South Bronx Civic Association, 47
Sovereignty, 121
Special Delivery Messengers, 176
St. Eunan's College, 4, 8
Stein, Emanuel, 121
Steinrich, Kenneth P., 133, 134
Steinway Omnibus Corporation, 122
Stone, Clay, 109
Straus, Jack I., 41, 42, 43
Straus, Robert K., 57
Surface Transit, Inc, 133, 134
Sweeny, Mary, 5, 6, 23, 213
Taft-Hartley Act, 86, 102, 105, 106
Tamiment Library, 37, 62, 63, 86, 112, 113, 138, 139, 170, 245, 264
Taylor Law, 151, 153, 154, 155, 160, 162
Taylor, George W., 153
Teamsters, 40, 42, 47, 53, 68
The Athenia, 18, 19
The Dubliner, 180, 181
The New York Catholic Protectory, 23
The Ulster Volunteers, 32
The United States Postal Service, 175, 183, 184, 201
Third Assembly District Bronx County, 49
Third Avenue Transit System, 77, 78, 89, 121, 123, 124, 125, 128, 129, 204
Tichy, George J., 186
Tom Clarke, Tom, 33
Transit Authority, 77, 78, 119, 120, 127, 128, 131, 138, 144, 145, 146, 147, 150, 156, 157, 160, 196, 201
Transport Workers Union, 30, 44, 48, 52, 53, 58, 61, 63, 67, 68, 69, 70, 71, 73, 74, 75, 76, 77, 78, 79, 80, 82, 83, 84, 85, 86, 87, 89, 90, 92, 93, 94, 98, 99, 100, 107, 108, 109, 111, 112, 113, 115, 117, 118, 119, 120, 122, 124, 125, 126, 127, 128, 129, 130, 131, 132, 133, 134, 137, 138, 139, 144, 145, 148, 150, 152, 153, 154, 155, 156, 157, 160, 162, 163, 195, 196, 205, 261
Triboro Coach Corporation, 122
Tripp, Joseph F., xvi
Troy, Matthew J., 35
Truman, Harry S., 102
TWU Express, 130
Uncle Francy, 15, 17
United Federation of Postal Clerks, 176
United Irish Brotherhood, 71
United Parcel Service, 37, 38, 39, 40, 42, 43, 61, 62
United States Postal Service, 179, 180, 181, 182, 184, 185, 186, 187, 188, 189, 190, 201
Usery, William, 175, 176
Van Riper, Ellis, 144, 150
Victor, Eugene, 175

INDEX

Vladeck, B. Charney, 36, 46, 47, 48, 61, 62
Wachter, Michael, 187
Wagner Act, 38, 39, 61, 112, 196, See NLRA
Wagner Jr., Robert F., 38, 39, 61, 63, 70, 86, 112, 129, 131, 138, 144, 146
Waldman, Louis, 144
Walsh and Mangum, 179, 191, 192
Weinberg group, 129, 133, 134, 135
Weinberg, Harry, 129, 130, 131, 133, 134, 135, 138, 139
Weisman, Lawrence I., 129, 130, 132, 133, 134, 138
Werner, Sally, 101
Western Electric, 168
When Ireland Speaks!, 35
Whipple, Judge Lawrence A., 179, 180
Wolchok, Samuel, 41, 42, 43, 44, 45
Worters, Rose, 72

Made in the USA
Monee, IL
12 December 2020

In 1980 William Serrin of The New York Times wrote that John F. O'Donnell was not widely known as a public figure. *"Yet if power is what power does, he is a man of power."*

"A sentimental portrait of John F. O'Donnell, the sage, skillful New York labor lawyer who helped score victories for workers during transit and postal strikes.

...the book contributes to the body of literature on the rise of organized labor. O'Donnell is presented as a behind-the-scenes champion for worker's rights who understood the power of united effort, but also that power is only good if it can be used to find solutions.

A flattering yet engaging biography of a legal swordsman who dueled on behalf of the worker." - **KIRKUS**

ISBN 9781452844855